A Duke's Daughter

by

Kathleen Buckley

A Duke's Daughter

Cover Art by *Abigail Owen*

The Wild Rose Press, Inc.
PO Box 708
Adams Basin, NY 14410-0708
Visit us at www.thewildrosepress.com

Publishing History
First Tea Rose Edition, 2020
Print ISBN 978-1-5092-3091-4
Digital ISBN 978-1-5092-3092-1

Published in the United States of America

"Emily…you have not reconsidered marrying Hawkins, have you?"

"How could I?" Lud, the announcement had appeared, which would mean jilting him, and how could she change her mind anyway? She could not permit the head of the family to be tossed into debtors' prison, even if she had not rather liked him, now that they were better acquainted. She must marry for her own sake, as well. All her life she had done her duty, or as she was told. To stop now, when she was one step from joining her cousin in debtor's prison or being out on the street, would be ridiculous. "Why would I? His manner is pleasant, and he is"—she intended to say, *attractive*, but instead ended—"not ugly or old or fat."

"I only wondered because of something I heard from friends. Brewer saw the announcement and mentioned something he'd been told. I hope it's not true, and if you're willing to go ahead with the marriage, I won't try to dissuade you. Our position— my position, I should say, as none of it's your fault—is hopeless without the kind of marriage settlement Hawkins is willing to make."

"What was it you heard?" The feeling of relief, even pleasure, she had enjoyed since agreeing to the marriage turned to dread.

"They say he was a pirate."

She contemplated His Grace, the Duke of Normande. It went against all her training to question the head of her family, whose dependent she was. On the other hand, she remembered first meeting him when his face was still spotty.

Dedication

To absent friends: E.K.S., W.D.B.,
and too many others

Chapter 1

Late January, 1741

Ambrose Hawkins sauntered into the upstairs salon of the Fortunate Gentleman's Coffee House at the Sign of the Money-Bag, wherein met a group of men who called themselves the Lucky Bastards. The first-floor salon was reserved for their use, at a very reasonable rent. When the house first opened, the buxom proprietress had been the mistress of one of the founding members. Her enterprise being in need of some support, an arrangement was entered into giving her lover's circle of friends and associates exclusive use of the large room upstairs. It brought in some revenue, both in rent and in purchases, gave the men a place to meet privately, and the well-dressed men who entered its door attracted more business to the coffee house proper.

Mistress Hardraw had no objection to "gentlemen *being* gentlemen" as she put it, meaning that she tolerated gambling, profane language, drunkenness, and noise. She drew the line at doxies and at the Lucky Bastards taking unwanted liberties with her female staff. But she usually made sure waiters served them. She preferred they not fight on the premises; if they did, she reproached them only for broken furniture and dishes, or if serious injury was inflicted. "For the arrival of a doctor is no very good advertisement," as she pointed out. As a result of her shrewd management, she had prospered and now owned a house let out in lodgings, presided over by her hapless brother and his sensible wife.

"Ha! Hawkins!" Ogilvy called out. "You've not shown your phiz in months. Come, take a seat and tell us what you've been doing."

"Been a month and a half. I've been busy."

"Licking his wounds, most like." Marston raised his hand to signal for more coffee. "He was after the Cantarell woman, and Easterday got her."

"Mistress Cantarell to you. Or Mistress Easterday, now." He did not care for Captain Marston, and not because they were often competitors and Marston envied him his success.

"Ay, of course. No offense meant."

Hawkins acknowledged this curtly. The fact was, the loss of Olivia Cantarell had stung badly. He had not loved her, not at first, anyway, but he had wanted her in a perfectly respectable way for her family connections: a baron grandfather. He needed to marry a lady of good family. Initially attracted by her vulnerability as the heiress of a shipping company—impossible for a woman to run—gentility and a pedigree were all the dowry he asked. By the time he realized she would never marry him, he lusted for her calm manner and her appreciation of beauty. Olivia's knowledge of Chinese art and surprisingly extensive holdings had been a bonus.

The conversation veered into other channels. When they exhausted the topic of horseflesh, Durward said, "I heard an amusing rumor the other day. My nephew

Willis is looking for a well-born wife and says de Toledo—Solomon the moneylender, you know—is looking for a husband for a duke's daughter. She's for sale to the highest bidder. Not that he put it in those words, I'm sure, but that's what it comes down to, ain't it?"

"Who's the chit?" someone inquired.

"Willis didn't know. He wants a girl with money as well as birth."

"Has she any attractions besides birth?"

"I haven't seen her. Solomon said he could arrange a discreet viewing for the right prospect."

"Not a bad fellow, for a moneylender."

"According to Willis, she has no dowry, but still, a duke's daughter is worth something in the right market."

"To a rich cit, mayhap, or a high stickler who don't need an heiress and can't attract one on his own."

His friends began to speculate on which duke was willing to trade his offspring for gelt.

Oswald, whose brother was a baron, interrupted. "What I want to know is, why's Solomon involved? Does the duke owe him that much?—for you know the girl won't go cheap. When my brother had to raise the rhino by marrying a cit's daughter, he found one easy enough."

It was a good question, but no one had any persuasive answer. Hawkins took his leave then, giving an appointment as his excuse.

Chapter 2

Even Peg Woffington's popular breeches role as Harry Wildair in *The Constant Couple* could not hold Emily Saintonge's attention. Her cousin, Henry, eighth duke of Normande, was engrossed in it. She herself might have found it diverting (although she could not like the idea of a female wearing male attire, even on the stage) except for her fear that something was terribly amiss. Why had he brought her to Covent Garden? Henry largely ignored her, not as a slight but because they had never met until her father, Ralph Saintonge, the sixth Duke of Normande, died without a living son and Henry's father succeeded to the title. Claude Saintonge enjoyed his elevation only five years. In the year since his father had died, Henry had never escorted her to any entertainment, ball, play, or opera, and not because of the period of mourning. He did not attend respectable social events. He went to the theater with his friends, but they watched from the pit. Still, she was grateful to have a home in her cousin's family's townhouse in London, the mansion at Normande and the ducal townhouse both having been leased to wealthy cits.

Papa should have married again as quickly as possible after Mama's death. Mourning for a wife could not be allowed to take precedence over securing the succession. Even if he had mourned for a full year, getting a new wife would have required only the most minimal effort. Certainly he should have bestirred himself after her brother's death. Dozens of aristocratic families had girls they would be happy to see wed to a duke. Better yet would have been a young widow of proven fertility, youthful enough to provide Papa with sons but old enough not to be an embarrassment as a stepmama.

She suspected her father had ignored his friends' and acquaintances' letters suggesting this lady or that among their female connections. Who would not promote a relation's elevation to duchess, given the chance? Her father either had not replied or had declined all offers. Had he shown the slightest interest, a wedding would have resulted. The prospective bride's family would have mounted a determined assault and might have overwhelmed his passivity. Papa had not responded to her own delicate hints that she would like a stepmama.

Instead, his cousin Claude had inherited.

While the situation was not ideal, it had some advantages. Claude had two daughters, fourteen and sixteen years of age, and as he had inherited the ailing ducal finances as well as the ill-managed estate and Saintonge House in London, Claude was able to economize by replacing the girls' governess with Emily and by leasing out the duchy's London residence. As he was more concerned with the girls learning the deportment and skills expected of a duke's daughters, she had been able to fill the position with no difficulty. Her knowledge of history, geography, and literature were superficial, but she could play the harpsichord, dance, and curtsy prettily, speak French fluently, and embroider sufficiently well to produce a monogrammed handkerchief. She understood the social hierarchy with its daunting rules of precedence, consequence, and condescension.

Claude's duchess, never strong, died. When it came time for the older girl to have a season in London, Emily served as her companion; the duke had by then made enough aristocratic acquaintances that a fashionable and well-connected countess offered to bring the girl out. This saw Lavinia married within the year to a viscount. While not the marriage a duke's daughter could have expected, she might have done a great deal worse. In addition to being titled, the viscount was not purse-pinched and seemed amiable. The countess, a widow, may have believed her favor to a widowed duke would lead to an offer of marriage. If so, she was mistaken.

Emily, invisible as Lavinia's companion, returned to Petty Normande and carried on with the duties ordinarily performed by a wife. She had, after all, been trained to manage a duke's household. Marriage seemed out of the question. How could she marry without a dowry and with no one to make a push to find her a husband? When Cecily, the younger girl, was of an age to make her own appearance in society, Lavinia took her in charge. Emily was not needed even as a chaperon. She was then four and twenty herself, and quite without prospects.

However, she was in her old home with congenial activities to occupy her. Living with little money was no new thing, and as her social life was limited, wearing gowns two or three years old did not trouble her...much. Cousin Claude had no fault to find with the arrangement. A certain lack of attention to matters which were not pressing seemed to be a family characteristic.

The next few months explained a great deal. Even Emily could not be unaware that some bills were now delinquent. The wine merchant's respectful but firm letter declining to fill her order for claret, port, and brandy until his account was brought current was only the first of several similar communications.

Cousin Claude demanded of his bailiff/steward why the bills had not been paid. Crofton timidly explained that things had got all tangled in the months after his predecessor had resigned and before he had been hired by the late duke. When pressed for a reason why the problems persisted, he stammered, "The sixth duke had...ummm...very economical ways, being a gentleman of retiring habits."

A recluse, Crofton meant.

"The late Lord Houghton, his son, enjoyed country sports and seldom went to London, which was a great saving, too." It was a pity, Emily thought, that her brother had not taken the estate's affairs in hand as their father slackened his hold. If she had been male, she might have done so. As a mere female, however, she had done no more with such matters than monitoring the housekeeper's and butler's ledgers. Perhaps she should have pressed him to take charge. Probably he would not have listened: ladies were not expected to put forward their opinions on such matters.

This led to a diatribe by the seventh duke concerning Crofton's failure to improve the estate's revenue. The bailiff confessed he could do nothing about the deficient revenues without making a significant outlay in improvements to the land, which would require securing a loan, and even then, it would be some time before those improvements bore fruit. Or hops or wool, as the case might be. And of course the loan would have to be repaid out of the increased revenue. Raising the tenants' rents would not provide a significant augmentation of income.

Cousin Claude then railed about the expenses incurred by young lords (he meant Henry) who spent their time in town, the unreasonably low prices for wool and hops, and the ridiculous cost of candles, wine, tea, sugar, and all the other provisions a gentleman required.

Emily left these sordid financial affairs in the hands of those responsible. Cousin Claude was not sunk in despondency as her father had been, and Crofton seemed competent. No doubt they would manage, being men. Her conviction that it would somehow be sorted out received a rude check when Cousin Claude suffered a heart seizure during the last of his meetings with Crofton. He lingered long enough for Henry to be sent for. He arrived on a lathered mount, flung himself off, pale and appearing younger than his years, and hastened to his father's bed.

By the next day, Henry was the eighth Duke of Normande. Emily most sincerely pitied him.

The duchy's business agent, the Saintonge attorney, and Crofton, attended by their respective clerks, had all met with Henry the day following the funeral. The new duke had emerged from the meeting white as milk, with haunted eyes. His first official action was to dismiss most of the servants, leaving a staff barely adequate to maintain the house and grounds. He could, he pointed out, have temporary servants recruited from the nearby village if he chose to rusticate for a few weeks in the summer. Soon thereafter Petty Normande was leased to a cit who had made a fortune in the East India trade.

Emily perforce moved to town with him to keep the modest house his branch of the Saintonges owned. The ducal mansion, Saintonge House, was leased to a mushroom, a mere tradesman who had scrambled together a fortune. The worst of their troubles must be past, as Henry resumed what Emily guessed had been his previous habits: going out every evening with his rackety friends. Then he took to inviting them to the house. She was not afraid of Henry, who was careless but generally good-natured. His acquaintances did worry her: some of them were worse than merely high-spirited, judging from one or two meetings when they had come to dine with him, though she had naturally retired to her bedchamber almost immediately. Of late, she had locked the door, and she was considering locking it from the outside, then concealing herself in an unused room or perhaps in the attic room where trunks and old furniture were stored.

Yesterday morning, Henry had been in a pother over the loss of his valet, but by supper, after an afternoon out of the house, he appeared to have cast off not only that blow but all of his cares. His sudden change of mood was yet another cause for worry.

This morning after the arrival of the mail, Henry had announced he would take her to a play at Covent Garden. When she inquired delicately who else was to be of the party, he replied with obvious surprise that it would only be the two of them. She might have understood it if one of his rakish friends had invited him; that he would rent a box and escort his older, spinster cousin to the theater was inexplicable. It was all out of character, as was his newfound good spirits. The insouciance she recalled from his occasional visits before his father's death had failed him after the funeral.

She kept her eyes fixed upon the stage. Did everyone know their desperate straits? The sensation of being stared at was unmistakable. The boisterous men in the pit always did stare at ladies in the boxes, but at least one gentleman in a box across the theater was gazing at them, too, and had been doing so almost since they took their seats. Emily made an effort to ignore him. The box held only the staring gentleman and another, who sat farther back and did not stare. She made little pleats in the silk of her four-year-old mantua and tried to keep her mind on the stage.

Her mind wandered from the play, unable to resist stealing glances at the rude gentleman. It took her by surprise to discover her cousin's attention was also drawn to the man. Perhaps Henry had noticed that he was watching her. At least she need not worry that the fellow's lack of manners would cause Henry to challenge him. Her cousin was no more of a physically quarrelsome disposition than he was prone to verbal confrontation. Also she could not suppose he cared enough about her to take umbrage.

What will become of me?

Emily put the peculiar incident from her mind; she had worries enough. The staring gentleman must have mistaken her for someone he knew, or assumed she was Henry's mistress, which was a humiliating thought. He could not be of her cousin's circle, as he was clearly years older, and those years harsh.

At the interval, Henry suggested remaining in their box rather than contending with the theatergoers who had left their own boxes to visit those of friends or to seek refreshment, as he had arranged to bring their footman with a basket containing wine, biscuits, and fruit. There had been no expenditure for the drink, at least, the cellar still being well-stocked. Henry had sensibly brought the remaining contents of the wine cellar from Petty Normande to town when the house had been leased out.

Bringing refreshments from home was less expensive than purchasing them, even with the added cost for the footman to attend them. Not spending the money at all would have been preferable to either, given their many economies at home. Henry's orders to the footmen, maids, and cook were to be sparing in the use of coal, to light candles only when he or Emily were using a room, and to employ nothing but tallow dips in the kitchen and servants' areas. If she had failed to draw a conclusion from her cousin's instructions, the fact they were using a most inferior quality of tea told her all she needed to know.

"How do you find the play?" her cousin inquired after they had been served. "Are you enjoying it?"

"Very much, thank you." She could hardly admit she was eaten up by worry over the evening's cost. Before she could think of something else to say, or Henry could attempt to make more conversation, the footman opened the door in response to a brisk knock.

"Your Grace." The voice was deep and rougher than a gentleman's voice should be.

Henry sprang up. "Hawkins. Good to see you.

Mmmm, Emily, may I present Mr. Ambrose Hawkins. Hawkins, this is my cousin, Lady Emily Saintonge." Having taken her assent for granted, he added, "I met Hawkins recently."

Emily rose and dropped a very slight curtsy. The visitor had wheat gold hair and his complexion was not fashionably pale. Men spent more time out of doors than ladies, but cosmetics could remedy the sun's evil effects, if a gentleman cared for his appearance. Worse, his handsome coat and breeches could not disguise more muscles than the most ardent sportsman should show. However had Henry met this man? Quite apart from Mr. Hawkins not appearing to be the sort to be found in Henry's circle, the man was twelve or fifteen years older. What could he have in common with her cousin? She was certain he was not a sycophant currying favor with a nobleman.

He bowed to her, without the extreme flourishes a fop might have employed. When he straightened, he smiled at her, an amused, frankly admiring, secret-sharing kind of smile. Almost a grin. Lud! Had she been staring at him? The warmth in her cheeks must be the result of the stuffiness of the theater. No matter, as the powder on her face and bosom should conceal any rush of color.

Ambrose Hawkins said something. She responded appropriately. Afterward, she could not recall the subject of the exchange, beyond its having been something of no importance whatsoever: Are you enjoying the performance? Or: I find myself rather overheated. Do you also? Perhaps her blush came from the thought of this man ogling Peg Woffington's legs. Her thighs, too. It was a good thing she was able to carry on a conversation with half her mind distracted.

The interval drawing to an end, Mr. Hawkins departed and the audience settled down to watch the next act. Hawkins, on returning to his own box, did not immediately turn his attention to the stage. He paused by the other occupant of the box and bent to speak to him briefly, before taking his seat again.

Chapter 3

Their butler gave notice, followed by her own maid. The senior footman was long gone. The coachman had been let go when the town coach was sold.

At least her maid, hired when the last duchess's dresser took another position, was apologetic. "Jem Riggins, the greengrocer, made me an offer, and I mean to take it. He has a good business and two young children who need a mother. And I'm sorry, but my wages are more than three months late, so it's like I'm working for room and board. Not very good board, either, no disrespect meant to Cook."

What was there to do but to wish Rose well and give her a pretty little bag in the shape of a frog, given Emily by an elderly great-aunt. She thought it had belonged to her own grandmother and had contained sweet-smelling herbs. It held sentimental value, but it was not the sort of thing ladies carried now, and it could just as well hold a few coins for Rose.

The girl was visibly affected by the little gift, and even better, it brought a return.

"My lady...you'll need a maid, no matter what. Martha, the scullery maid, is wonderful good at sewing. She should by rights be a seamstress, only her face is scarred and she was no beauty even before, I'd say, and mantua-makers only hire girls who are pretty. She could probably do whatever's needful for you, for only a penny or two more in wages, as well as her kitchen duties."

"Thank you, Rose." It might be the first time she had ever thanked a servant, but she was truly grateful. The news of Rose's departure had raised the question of how she could dress herself and care for her clothes. Tightening one's corset laces, pinning on the stomacher evenly and invisibly, adjusting the panniers, even putting on a close-fitting gown would be all but impossible. "Ask her to come to my boudoir sometime today when Cook can spare her."

Henry had been out again since the morning, returning in a serious mood only in time for an early supper. News of the defections made no noticeable impression on him, though she judged he had not been drinking, or not enough to be affected by it. When she would have left the table, he said, "Stay a bit, Emily." To the footman he added, "William, pour us the rest of the wine. No need to store it, is there."

She sat down again, bracing for bad news. That many of the household accounts went unpaid for several months at a time gave her no qualms. Gentlemen paid at their own convenience. However, the coal merchant's coming to speak with Henry a week since had troubled her. Soon after, Henry's best linked sleeve buttons and a ruby ring disappeared. A middle-aged gentleman, perhaps an attorney, had called upon Henry, too, though her cousin did not introduce him.

If Henry were sent to debtor's prison or fled to the Continent, what would become of her? She could not support herself. Her only skills were in running an aristocratic household and the usual ladylike accomplishments. How would she find a position? Would anyone hire a governess with no academic knowledge? Or she might be a chaperon or companion. For a duke's daughter, any of those occupations would be almost as unsuitable as being a kitchen maid or a courtesan. She had been reared to be the wife of a nobleman. She had done everything she was told and done exactly as she ought and everything had gone wrong anyway!

When William had divided the claret between them, half a glass apiece, her cousin signaled him to leave the dining room.

"I wish my father hadn't died, Emily."

"I know. I'm sorry."

"Yes, well, apart from missing him, I wasn't ready to take over his responsibilities. He wasn't ready for them, either. Between us, we've let things go, Father because he wasn't accustomed to dealing with such a large, complicated estate and me because I thought we had plenty of money. A duchy, after all—you expect a duchy to be plump in the pocket. Then when I found out we were in the suds, I didn't know how to fix things. Wilcox, m'father's man of business, wasn't much help, either."

"You did lease out Petty Normande and Saintonge House. That was a saving, I'm sure."

He smiled lopsidedly. "Ay, the rents pay for the upkeep. But it isn't enough. I wasn't brought up to be thrifty. Father tried, but he wasn't prepared for how difficult it was."

"Neither my papa nor my mama were accustomed to counting pence." But that was before Mama died and the sixth duke ceased to take any interest in the duchy's affairs, impoverishing it. She might as well not have existed, for all the thought her father had spared for her and her future.

"The fact is, we're done for, Emily. Our creditors—sorry, I should say 'my creditors'—are after me. I don't know if they'd actually put a duke in debtor's prison, and I was ashamed to ask Wilcox or old Keeble, the attorney. That's how I came to make a decision that may be the saving of us." He drank his wine down at one swallow. "We may perhaps have a stroke of luck."

"Oh?"

"I went to a moneylender. A friend mentioned borrowing from him once when he lost his entire quarter's allowance by wagering on a sure thing. He thought the man would simply give him the money and he'd have to figure out how to repay the debt and interest on his own and he could see he was like to get in deeper and deeper, and he didn't know what to do. Calvert's a good fellow and wasn't a spendthrift, but he believed Thompson when he said St. Tawdrey couldn't lose the race, and he was too new to town to know that Thompson is an idiot about horses. No one takes his advice about racing. Cal's father was thought to be dying so he couldn't go to him when he lost, and his mother was beside herself with worry, so…" He sank into moody silence, staring at the glass he was turning in his fingers.

She permitted him time for reflection before taking it upon herself to prompt him. "You were explaining how it happened that Cal met this moneylender. Have I met Cal?"

"No, after that scare he went back to Dorset. The

thing is, he said the moneylender helped him work out how much money he really needed until next quarter-day if he went home to the country and explained how much interest he'd be paying on that amount. Cal didn't need as much as he'd thought, only to pay a few bills and travel to Dorset. When he got his next quarter's allowance, he paid Solomon and was able to start fresh, and he'd decided he liked the country and talking about crops and cows and such things. Doesn't come to town much now. Earnest fellow."

She waited, keeping an agreeable expression firmly in place. Gentlemen did not enjoy reproach. Henry had gone to a usurer and thought their troubles were solved?

"I thought Solomon was worth a try. Sounded as if he'd be fair." He must have read her thought in her face, because he hurried on. "I didn't borrow from him. He had a better notion."

Emily revised her previous opinion of Henry. He must be more observant than she'd thought. The idea of a moneylender having a better notion of how to deal with their debt was a little worrisome, however.

"Cal claimed you wouldn't know the fellow from a gentleman, and he was right. He came up with a prime idea, one I'd never thought of."

"And you spent the money to take me to the theater, which cannot have been cheap, which was kind of you, Henry."

He blushed, reminding her that he was only two and twenty, and less mature than a female of the same age. "Solomon paid for the box and the hackney. That's how badly we're fixed. I couldn't afford the price of the box. Devil take it, the hackney fare would have been a stretch. Anyhow, I wanted to explain things to prepare you for tomorrow."

"Really? Why did this Solomon do such a thing? And what's tomorrow?"

"It's what I'm trying to explain. A fellow who's not well fixed can repair his fortunes by marrying some rich cit's daughter. It's worth it to a merchant to catch a man with a title for his girl. For the gentleman, it's worth it for the dowry." He sighed. "Solomon found someone who wants an alliance with a noble family. He's calling in the morning, which is one reason I'm not going out tonight. The other being, there's not much entertainment to be had when you can scarce afford even to visit a coffee house."

"What a good idea," Emily said slowly. "It might not be what my father would have liked, but under the circumstances it would do very well. You would be relieved of the duchy's debt—for I suppose you would not marry some girl of that class for anything less—and would have time to learn how to manage better than my father did." One must be tactful with gentlemen.

"Or my father, come to that. I'm glad you take it so well, Emily. I know it must be an unexpected shock, yet it's for the best all around."

"I agree, Henry. It will be pleasant not to have to wonder if the chandler will refuse to let us have more candles. Do you know anything about the chit? Will she drop her h's? If she's merely ignorant of deportment, I can teach her how to conduct herself."

Henry stopped playing with his empty glass and stared at her, reminding Emily of the man at the theater. "Chit?" he echoed.

"The cit's daughter your moneylender has found." Surely less than a bottle of wine could not have robbed

Henry of his wits. He'd been rational enough till now.

"Ahhh...Emily. It's not only impoverished gentlemen who marry into merchant families. There's men with plenty of money who'll pay to marry a lady from a noble family."

Emily, sitting ramrod straight as she had been taught, hands clasped in her lap, suddenly understood why low-bred girls fidgeted. But she would not show her discomfiture. "Someone is willing to wed me because I am the daughter of a duke?"

Not having to worry about being dunned by the grocer would be a great relief. But what sort of man would be willing to pay the duchy's debts for the honor of marrying her? Buying her. She would be a sacrificial lamb. Would wealth compensate for having to endure a husband who came from trade, behaved and dressed vulgarly, and spoke as if he'd grown up in the gutter? Fury flooded through her, in spite of the wine she had drunk, at the thought of marriage—and marital intimacy—with a common tradesman.

Henry expelled a breath he must have been holding. Did he really think she would fly into a rage or swoon or treat him to a fit of the vapors? "He's coming to meet you. He saw you in the theater—that's why we went—and if he's taken with you, I think he will make you an offer. You're very pretty and well bred, and with money, you can move in the highest levels of the beau monde. In our class, marriages are arranged every day with fewer advantages on either side. I'm sure your mother told you how it is. Or your governess."

She did not miss the desperation in his voice. Everything he said was true. She would certainly have married any man her papa had found for her. Bitterly: *If he had troubled himself to do so.* Would the moneylender's candidate be any worse than a nobleman who was old and ugly, or violent in his cups, or…or other things she did not care to think about?

"Do you know anything about him? The man at Covent Garden who came to our box, was he the one?"

"Ay, he was there with Solomon. He's rich. He comes of the gentry but made his money in shipping, among other things, I understand. Solomon vouches for his not gambling to excess. He's five and thirty or thereabouts. He may be a bit unpolished, but it's not as if he'd grown up in the rookeries and made his fortune in some truly disgusting trade." He ran a thumb over a darned spot in the tablecloth, to Emily's annoyance. Could he not pretend not to notice it?

"And you'll be free of debt." *By selling me.* She felt like a mare at auction.

"I know it sounds like a sacrifice. Well, it is a sacrifice, I admit. Girls always want to marry for love, and in any case, you should be marrying a man with a title. But you'll gain, too. You'll be comfortably established in your own home, I dare say with a good deal of pin money. You'll like that, won't you? In our situation, you haven't had any chance of marrying at all."

When she was a girl, she had dreamed of a grand romance, followed by marriage. By the time she was fifteen, she had accepted that her duty was to marry to oblige her family. According to her mama and her governess, an arranged marriage was to her benefit: her family would select a man of suitable rank and fortune and prevent her marrying improvidently. Mama pointed out that love was quite unnecessary, as long as she had a position in society and the wealth to maintain it. Her governess told her bracingly that she could come to appreciate her husband and perhaps even grow fond of him. What Henry proposed was not a whit different from what her family had intended for her, if everything had not fallen apart at her mother's death.

He watched her anxiously, knuckles white on the stem of his glass. He was very young to shoulder the responsibilities of a duke.

"I can see it's the only way. I confess I've been worried," Emily admitted. "I will do my duty." Hawkins was presentable in appearance, at least, and his smile was attractive. Alarmingly so. He could have been much worse. Of course, she would not know the worst about him until too late.

"If it's any balm for your heart, I'm in the same position. Solomon's looking about for a bride for me. Even with all the debts paid off, there's not enough income to live comfortably until Crofton and Wilcox have funds to improve the estate and the investments. He says he doesn't apprehend any difficulty in finding me a suitable girl." He sighed again.

"Some of the bankers and merchants are said to be quite gentlemanly. Surely they have their daughters brought up like ladies." A banker had called upon her father at Petty Normande. Emily met him by chance as His Grace had been bidding him a cool farewell in the entry hall when she returned from calling on a neighbor. She had not been informed of his profession, of course. That information had come by way of her maid. While Emily would not ordinarily encourage a servant's gossip, she had been curious. The man was unknown to her and neither dressed nor spoke like either country gentry or an aristocrat, but his clothing and bearing were too fine for the middling sort, like a doctor or lawyer. "If the girl is pretty and of a pleasing disposition, it will be no worse than if Uncle had arranged a marriage for you." She smiled encouragingly and nibbled at a cheese cake. The cakes were left over from the day before but still good.

He gave a short hoot of laughter. "Especially if my mother had had her way and persuaded him to marry me to her little squab of a goddaughter."

"She was a little deficient in composure. Less liveliness would have been more dignified," Emily said primly. "But if His Grace had decided you should marry her, he would of course have been correct. No doubt she would have outgrown her childish lack of restraint." *Probably. I would have instructed her.*

The duke frowned. The expression sat oddly on his usually cheerful face. He began stroking the darn once more. "Unless I found a lady equally acceptable? Or more so?"

He had not been trained to be a duke, or anything more than a country gentleman. Few noblemen's heirs would fail to do as the head of their family bade. Poor Henry; he had probably assumed he could follow his own inclination. The idea of an arranged marriage must be more difficult for him to accept than for her.

Chapter 4

Ambrose Hawkins had faced a variety of taxing situations, some involving cannon fire, cutlasses, and blood on the deck, others mere financial loss. Stepping into the shabby drawing room fell somewhere between the two. The chief difference was that this was uncharted territory for him. What if the girl were stupid or annoying in some other way? Their meeting at the theater had been too brief for him to form any opinion as to her intelligence and character. All he knew was that her face, figure, and voice were pleasing.

What did it matter anyway? He need not spend much time with her. The beau monde did not expect a couple to cling to each other. This was business, nothing more. A merger. He had done business with men he did not like and with whom he would not willingly associate. If she were so dreadful he could not bear to live in the same house, he need not make an offer. What were the odds? She was well-connected and presentable in appearance. How bad could she be? If he could not have the woman he loved, Emily Saintonge would do as well as any, and better than most. A duke's daughter, after all.

Had his valet chosen rightly? "Rich but sober, sir," was Pirtle's advice, hence the plum-colored velvet with no embroidery at all on the coat, with buttons covered in silk thread to match the velvet. The waistcoat's front was embroidered in soft, harmonizing colors, but not ostentatiously, with little use of gold thread. The suit was meant to convey good taste and respectability. "Nothing popinjay about it," Pirtle had said, with massive understatement. Not that Hawkins ever dressed like a fop, though he did like rich colors. Pirtle did not care for the orange velvet coat and breeches, especially with the leaf-green waistcoat. Some question had arisen about whether Hawkins should wear a smallsword. Pirtle felt it inappropriate. Hawkins conceded the point, but he never went unarmed. London was a dangerous place. Hell, the world was dangerous. They compromised on his sword stick with the piqué ivory knob.

In an older man, the Duke of Normande's effusive greeting would have been an objectionable display. His youth and desperate financial straits rendered it understandable. Hawkins supposed he would have to take the graceless pup in hand, God help him.

He did not notice her until she rose from a chair in a dim corner and came forward to make her curtsy.

"Lady Emily." He bowed.

Unlike the Saxon-fair duke, she possessed brown hair and brown eyes. He had not noticed that at Covent Garden. He rather liked brown-eyed women. In the light of day, her features were perfectly regular and her complexion flawless. These attributes should have made her beautiful even if her hair was an undistinguished color. What was lacking was animation. Hawkins was willing to overlook this fault, as too much liveliness in a wife might be tiresome. Very likely she was nervous and trying to conceal it. The situation must be awkward for a lady bred in the highest level of the nobility—if one overlooked the royal family, which was easy to do.

A footman brought in refreshments: claret and biscuits. Lady Emily seated herself. The duke gestured Hawkins to a chair near where she sat and became mute. Perhaps he also found it difficult. The conversational void became impossible to ignore after the glasses of wine had been handed around.

Had this negotiation resembled his usual business, Hawkins would have known what to say. "I understand one or both of you must marry money. I'm in the market for a wife. Lady Emily is available, and if her qualifications are satisfactory, I see no reason we should not come to an agreement." Or if he were already even a little acquainted with a lady and wanted her, he would have known how to proceed. "You must be aware of my admiration and deepest respect. May I hope that my feelings are reciprocated, if only to the slightest degree?" It would not be one of his best efforts. Courting Olivia Cantarell had been easy because he knew the important things about her, or most of them: she was intelligent, courageous, and had exquisite taste.

He knew nothing about Emily Saintonge except that her cousin needed to marry her to a rich man, and she needed to marry someone who could support her. He had come almost certain he meant to offer for her. Now that it came to the sticking place, he wasn't sure. He wanted more: some warmth, perhaps, or some sign of a passionate nature. Depth of feeling about anything would do: the breeding of lap dogs, opera, gardening. His fine linen shirt clung damply to his skin, despite the coolness of the day. He took a metaphorical deep breath.

"Lady Emily, there is a degree of commercialism about this matter which must offend you. We do not know each other. All three of us understand the necessity of your marrying. However, I do not expect you to make a decision until we have had a chance to get to know each other. I am not your only possibility."

"No, indeed," Henry Saintonge agreed. "There is an earl who might suit."

Emily Saintonge did not seem pleased to be reminded, although Hawkins saw only the faintest change of expression on her face. According to Sol, the earl was only a distant possibility. Emily Saintonge spoke for the first time since bidding him welcome.

"This is really no different than what the duke, my father, would have arranged." She colored slightly. "I mean, he would have chosen a gentleman, and I would have agreed to him. I know my duty."

"I would not want your duty to be unpleasant, my lady." In for a penny, in for a pound. "Before I make a formal offer, I would like to know more about you, and you should know more about me. You might find you prefer the earl. He must be of your world, after all."

He watched her eyes widen in surprise or alarm. At what? Being asked her opinion? Or at the possibility he was shearing off?

"Let us take a little time at least to become acquainted before making any decision. I know there are arranged marriages in which the couple have hardly met, or not met at all, before they wed. Few would be foolish enough to buy a horse or property without first inspecting it."

He had meant to lighten the tone of the moment.

The stiffening of Lady Emily's and the duke's faces suggested he had erred. Damn, he had implied he was buying Lady Emily. He would be, of course, if he offered for her, but they would understandably prefer not to be reminded of the fact. Apologizing would only make it worse.

"Duke, before Lady Emily agrees to accept a pig in a poke, we must have an opportunity to become acquainted." He hoped likening himself to a pig, in a poke or otherwise, would take the sting out of his gaffe. "I am sure Lady Emily would prefer to have something like a normal courtship."

Lady Emily's lips quirked. The minute reaction was encouraging. She might have a sense of humor. He raised his eyebrows pointedly at Henry, Duke of Normande.

"Certainly, Hawkins. I assume you mean you would court my cousin at entertainments?"

"I believe that is how it is usually accomplished."

Lady Emily colored. "We have not been attending many events." After a significant pause, she added, "With His Grace still new to his position, he has not had the heart to go about much in society, and it would not be right to attend events without his escort. I am not sure, either, how easy it is to become acquainted at a large gathering."

Her last point was a good one. One needed some privacy to converse or steal a kiss, and it would not be found at a ball, where some curst nuisance would always be interrupting, wanting to dance with the lady. Other reasons for her demurral occurred to him: reluctance to be seen with a man like him or shame because her gowns were all several years old. Solomon had minced no words regarding the duchy's finances. A female would dress in her best to receive a wealthy potential suitor. Emily's mantua, expensive when new, was several years out of date, as even he could tell.

"We might stroll in the Mall or a park at some unfashionable time of day. Or attend the opera? We could converse uninterrupted." Unheard, too, even by her cousin and chaperon: few opera-goers felt it necessary to listen in silence to the music. "Perhaps a carriage ride to Chelsea? Have you visited the Bun House?" He had taken Olivia and her aunt there, and they had enjoyed the excursion.

The duke and Lady Emily traded glances, the young duke's blank. "Any of those things would be pleasant," she said.

"St. James's Park tomorrow morning? The sunny weather is likely to hold." The coach ride to and from the park would provide an opportunity for talk, too.

Chapter 5

Emily was warmly dressed, from her sensible shoes and wool stockings, quilted petticoat, and matching jacket of blue wool, to her hooded red cape. She would have liked to wear her most fashionable *robe à l'anglaise*, but she would also like to survive to marry Ambrose Hawkins. Living at Petty Normande had taught her to value warmth over elegance, at least when no one of the beau monde was in sight. None were present, this chilly morning. Many would not yet have left their beds. Others were still at breakfast. They might come out later in the day to walk, but perhaps not, given the cold. The sun was welcome, even as heavily clad as she was.

Hawkins made a prodigious elegant figure. He also radiated heat; the warmth of his arm was perceptible even through his coat and her glove.

"Mayhap a true gentleman would not refer to your reasons for being willing to consider my suit," Hawkins said, "yet it seems foolish to pretend, when you would not otherwise think of marrying someone like me."

"The highest levels of society tend to be quite practical about marriage and inheritance. We have to be. You are practical about your commercial interests, are you not?"

"Exceedingly so. Will you tell me a little about your family? I have not heard how it is you come to be in the position of…"

Conversation between a lady and a suitor of Emily's class would be as formal as the minuet and without any exchange of information. Talking with Ambrose Hawkins would be like purchasing a length of silk: firmly based in reality. Perhaps it was for the best.

"Of allowing you the honor of rescuing my remaining family from ruin? I beg your pardon, Mr. Hawkins. I did not mean to sound bitter. After all, these things happen."

"And they are seldom the fault of the ladies of the family. I trust you have no love for playing deep?"

"None at all, sir. 'Twas not gaming that brought my family to this pass. Nor lavish spending, neither."

"No?" The single word and his raised brows clearly requested an explanation.

"Nor foolish investments. I am surprised the duke's moneylender who arranged our meeting did not tell you."

"Solomon did not know, beyond having heard Petty Normande's lands lacked good management."

She would have to expose their family secrets. They were approaching Rosamond's Pond, a desolate sight with the trees leafless and no one leaning on the railing which enclosed it. On a pleasant spring or summer day (assuming it were not wet), the shaded walks would be delightful. Across the park to the east, framed by trees, the towers of Westminster Abbey rose.

The words stuck in her throat.

"I was too young to know if the estate was well managed before my mother's death. I do know her loss deeply affected my father. Our bailiff gave notice about two years later when he found employment closer to his family's home. He had served us for as long as I can remember. I wondered at his preferring to work for a baron rather than a duke, even if it was within a few hours' ride of his relatives. He had been gone several months before my father could find a man to replace him."

Before Father began to look for a new bailiff. She hurried on, hoping to avoid any questions. "Then my brother broke his neck on a skittish horse."

"It must have been a severe blow to both of you, Lady Emily, after your mother was taken from you."

"It was, Mr. Hawkins." Why mention that Geoffrey's accident took place four years after their mother's death? Their father should have recovered from her death by then. His heir's death only hastened his downward spiral.

"I believe it can be awkward for the dependents when someone not in the direct line inherits, as in your case."

Tactfully phrased. Claude Saintonge, her father's cousin, became the seventh Duke of Normande. Emily met Claude for the first time at her father's funeral, some quarrel having resulted in so complete an estrangement between her grandfather and his only brother that their heirs had never mended it.

A breeze raised ripples in the pond. Pausing to admire the scene gave her the opportunity to frame a reply. Claude Saintonge had inherited responsibility for Emily as if she were some unwanted heirloom which could not be thrown away. Emily, nearly nineteen when Claude inherited the title, had not a single surviving maternal relative who might have made a push to see she was married, in spite of her father's neglect of his duty.

Still, had all gone as it should, Claude's duchess should have introduced Emily to the beau monde, to find her a husband. Alas, Susan was sadly lacking in the fortitude expected of a duchess. Unequal to the task, she was out of her depth—she was only a country gentleman's daughter, after all—and in poor health besides. The duke could have seen to it that Emily was brought out by some other lady, but Claude was no better suited to his new position than his wife. One must be fair: they had never moved in more than merely genteel society and could not be expected to introduce Emily into circles they had never navigated. As the daughter of a duke, Emily was expected to marry, if not a duke, at least someone of the upper nobility. A marquess or an earl would be unexceptionable. A viscount would not be impossible...might, indeed, be the best to be had, considering that after her father's death, she had gradually come to understand she had no dowry worth mentioning. However, Petty Normande, ancestral home of the Saintonges since soon after Raoul de Saintonge arrived in England in William the Bastard's retinue, was rather isolated. Her father having foregone social life in his bereavement, Emily had not met even a marriageable baronet.

"Being my uncle's dependent was not unpleasant."

Hawkins turned from watching the breeze ruffle the water to look down at her. "Judiciously put, my lady."

She met his gaze reluctantly. "It might have been a great deal more uncomfortable, sir. Cousin Claude did not begrudge the need to support me." In a similar situation, the new heir might have made an unwanted dependent uncomfortable enough to leave. She had feared she might be placed in the position of having to support herself as a companion or some such thing, as she knew nothing about the man until his arrival at Petty Normande.

It was too bad Papa initiated no contact when Claude became the heir presumptive, only reluctantly directing his attorney to write informing Claude of the fact. If her father himself had written—as he certainly should have done—she knew nothing of it. Nor had Claude been invited to visit the Saintonge estate. By then, all hope that her papa would marry and beget another son was gone. Far be it from Emily to criticize his actions, but even she knew one does not step into a duke's shoes without years of preparation.

She could not be unaware of her old cape and her scuffed shoes and knew Ambrose Hawkins had observed them. She still had not explained how the duchy had fallen into penury. A member of the beau monde would have known. Word would have spread from nearby bailiffs and landowners to their friends and rippled outward until everyone who counted was aware of the facts. Hawkins and Henry's moneylender were outside that exclusive circle.

"My father never recovered from my mother's death. He simply stopped attending to estate affairs and left matters undone." Papa had not begun to look for another bailiff until the post had been vacant for months, and only then because the tenants' rent fell due, and they came to him to pay it. He had declined to see tenants with questions or grievances, but he could not refuse to receive their rent. The work of taking in the money and entering the names and sums fell to the butler, while the duke glowered behind his desk and wrote to his man of business to hire someone. Crofton was probably a competent steward, but he had not been able to persuade the duke to take the necessary actions, judging by comments overhead after church and the increasing decrepitude of the tenant farms.

"Grief and melancholia," their doctor said when the sixth duke was gathered to his ancestors. *Too little backbone and too much drink.* Uncharitable of her, perhaps, but the truth.

"You must not be thinking Cousin Claude bore any blame, or not much, for our problems, sir. My father should have asked him to come to Petty Normande to become familiar with it. But considering the depth of his grief, I do not think he could have made the effort to train Cousin Claude." As for Claude, he had been a second son and only inherited a modest manor on his elder brother's demise. He had never been brought up to land ownership. Still, after owning that manor for a decade, he should have had some idea how to go on, even if Petty Normande were on a far larger scale.

Hawkins nodded. "I know his son inherited before he was ready for the responsibility and fell into the hands of a pack of hangers-on. De Toledo has given him good advice. If the duke follows it, the estate should be in good heart eventually."

"I do not quite understand how a moneylender could know anything about managing the finances of a dukedom."

"You might be surprised at some of Solomon's clients. Nor are the financial affairs of titled gentlemen much different in essence from those of merchants or tradesmen. 'Tis mostly common sense: keep a sharp eye on your accounts, put money into improving your business—or lands and livestock—keep some back, and be moderate in your personal expenditures."

Emily stifled a laugh at the idea of comparing the circumstances of noblemen and tradesmen. On reflection, however, her escort was correct. A modicum of common sense and self-discipline would have prevented most of her family's problems.

"Do you wish to ask me any questions, Lady Emily?"

One hardly liked to ask personal questions, despite the avowed reason for this "courtship" being to give them both a chance to know each other. She would not ask if he had a mistress or mistresses, because what man did not? She knew he was rich, or he would not be able to settle the duchy's debts. Henry said Solomon de Toledo told him the man had no outstanding vices. It might be true or not, but marriage never came with guarantees for a female; she might as well believe the assertion.

"From what part of the country did you come originally?" It was not an overly intrusive question. One might ask the same of any person if one knew nothing of their history.

"Hampshire."

She thought for a moment he had taken offense, until he continued rather reluctantly, "My family had a manor. Has a manor, I suppose."

From the brevity of his reply, she concluded it was not a topic he cared to discuss.

"But you chose to go to sea?" She shivered in the chill, thinking how much colder it must be on a ship.

"I did. We should start back to the coach. Those

clouds off to the west are coming in." He placed himself between Emily and the wind and took her left arm. "Ay, I made my way to Portsmouth and found a ship. I was tall and strong for my age."

He entertained her all the way home with stories about his travels before the mast and as a second officer before he left the sea to found his own company. Some were thrilling, some so droll she could not help laughing in a most ungenteel manner. When he handed her out of his coach and escorted her to the door, she knew no more of his family circumstances than she had learned from Henry. Instead she had felt the heavy heat and smelled the spices in foreign marketplaces and the fragrance of vivid blooms she would never see.

****

Cousin Henry became restive. "He's taken us to the play, Vauxhall Gardens, and the opera, Emily. How much better do you need to know him?"

"I have no doubts about the marriage. I told you I would do my duty. I am only waiting for him to ask me." Emily poured herself another cup of inferior tea. It was weak. She hoped the housekeeper wasn't buying used tea leaves, as poor people did. There was a lively trade in them, an acquaintance having confided her servants took the household's used tea leaves, dried them, and sold them to those who could not afford even the cheapest grade of tea.

"He's not having second thoughts, is he? Or having trouble raising the money? No, Solomon would know whether he was good for it. Shall I have a word with him?"

Her cousin was pacing. The last post had brought several more dunning letters. Apparently the hint of a marriage between Emily and a rich cit was not enough to reassure the Saintonge creditors. Once the announcement appeared, all would be well.

"No. I'm sure he would not still be inviting me to walk or drive with him or taking us to the theater if he had changed his mind. I expect him to call tomorrow, and I will bring the matter to a head then."

Chapter 6

The footman made no pretense of ascertaining whether Lady Emily was at home, though Hawkins had arrived an hour earlier than he might have been expected. Discourteous of him, but it was useful to take the other party by surprise in commercial negotiations. Sometimes he gained an advantage. He need not have employed the trick here; the terms of the settlement were already agreed. Nothing remained but to offer and be accepted.

Ushered directly into the drawing room, Hawkins stood by the fireplace. The room was chilly: no fire in the hearth. The duke and Lady Emily probably used some more easily warmed small parlor. A servant would have lit the fire here shortly before a guest's anticipated arrival. In theory, at least. The servants still with the family were those who would have difficulty obtaining other positions by reason of age or lack of polish. He supposed he would have to offer them all pensions or a place in his as-yet-unpurchased townhouse if young Henry replaced them.

The door opened abruptly. Normande entered with more haste than dignity.

"Mr. Hawkins, good day. Ah...Lady Emily will join us shortly. May I offer you a glass of brandy? It's quite good. Left over from..." He shrugged.

"Perhaps a little later, Duke." This form of address

would be a shocking familiarity, considering the difference in their social standing, but Hawkins was not much impressed by rank. He would soon be a connection of Normande's.

"Of course, of course."

This time the door was opened sedately, and Lady Emily swept in. She must not have changed her mantua. Lady Emily had likely done no more than smooth her hair and adjust her fichu. Did she have a better gown? He had never seen her in anything unmistakably new. The best seamstress could not wholly disguise alterations to bring a garment into the current mode. Nor could a change of trimmings conceal all signs of wear.

She made him a curtsey. "Mr. Hawkins. Will you be seated?" She sank onto a chair.

Before she could offer refreshments or tedious civilities, he said, "My lady, all I require is your time." Too curt; both she and Normande tensed, Lady Emily almost invisibly—but Hawkins was used to watching men's reactions, no matter how slight—and the duke noticeably. They thought he was going to withdraw his tentative offer.

Hawkins smiled. He hoped it was reassuring. "Duke, if I might speak with Lady Emily?"

The boy took his meaning.

"Emily, I have a letter which requires a brief answer. If you and Mr. Hawkins will excuse me for a few minutes?"

"Certainly, Cousin."

He went out, drawing the door only partly closed. The footman must be lingering in the hall as a chaperon.

The lady's expression was politely inquiring. Hawkins took the chair nearest hers. It creaked, from loosened joints rather than his weight. He trusted it would not collapse and turn the interview into farce.

"You have lived mostly in the country, my lady. Would you be averse to living in town much of the year?"

She gave an almost undetectable sigh, a release of tension. "I like the country, but I do not dislike London. There is a great deal to do here, and I believe I would enjoy more society. Petty Normande, the family seat, you know, is rather isolated."

Excellent. Willing to live in London and to entertain. She sounded sincere, but in her situation, she might have agreed to live in Hades. "I do not yet own a suitable house in London. I have been living mostly in lodgings." No need to mention the house off Old Gravel Road where he sometimes kept a mistress. Though when they married, they would probably live there until he found a more suitable property. "I do own a good many works of art which I would want to display. Should you dislike sharing a house with them?"

"Classical statues?" she inquired cautiously.

"No, smaller pieces, mostly from China, in porcelain, jade, and ivory. There are scroll paintings, too. One or two items of furniture."

"I have seen Chinese porcelain dishes, of course. Oh, and silk painted in the Chinese style. There would be no…mmmm…undraped classical statues?" She bit her full lower lip. It was a kissable mouth. If she were not as stunningly lovely as his last mistress, Emily Saintonge was at least extremely pretty, in addition to being well bred and well connected.

41

"None at all."

"Then I am sure I would like your collection."

This colorless response was what one would expect from a young lady reluctant to discourage a suitor. Was she passionate about anything? She was unlikely to volunteer an opinion, making it necessary to tease out her true feelings. He asked the first question to pop into his mind.

"How would you choose to name your children?"

She blushed, which he might have anticipated, and stared down at her clasped hands. "I am not in favor of peculiar names, Mr. Hawkins, by which I mean the sort sometimes used by Puritans, like Praise-God or Humility or the odder names from the Old Testament, like Abishag."

"Excellent. You are not of the Puritan persuasion, I perceive."

"Nor do I care for foreign names, unless the person is foreign. It is perfectly reasonable then to call a child Casimir or Ludwig."

She had some views, at least. She might be shy of revealing more of herself lest she offend him. The duchy really was in very serious trouble. She would be anxious to make a good impression, as her marriage would secure her a comfortable life. Though she must care that it extricated her cousin from the worst of his financial problems also, or she could have managed to marry a titled man with less wealth. This argued she possessed a strong sense of duty to her family, as any baron with a modest fortune would be a less humiliating choice than himself.

"I agree. I would prefer my children to have ordinary names, like John or Edward or Ann or

Elizabeth. Depending on the child's sex, you understand."

She responded gravely, "I fear a boy called Elizabeth would face difficulty at school."

"Or anywhere else," he agreed with a grin. A sense of humor was something to build on. He would never have guessed she owned one, though she had laughed at some of his tales. "Tell me, what do you enjoy doing?"

She was slow to answer. "It's ridiculous, sir, but I find your question surprisingly hard to answer."

"How so, Lady Emily?" How could it be difficult to say what one enjoyed? He found it pleasant to look at and handle his Chinese treasures, to watch one of his ships set sail or make port with a valuable cargo, to sip the best quality of tea, to negotiate a profitable bargain. With a little thought, he could list as many as half a hundred lesser things, too: a hot bath, fine linen sheets, a naked woman, a good meal.

"I never thought about it before." She paused, and her eyes narrowed. "My father, mother, and governess trained me to be an appropriate wife for a duke, marquess, or earl. To possess the usual accomplishments, to oversee a nobleman's houses, to move easily in the highest society, to do my duty, whatever it was, and never to show discomposure. I can do those things. I do not recall anyone ever asking me what I liked to do."

"Or what you wanted to be when you grew up?"

"Oh, there was never a question about that, Mr. Hawkins."

No. She had been reared to be a nobleman's wife. Thank God he'd come of the minor gentry. Being born to a noble family sounded devilish hard.

Her head tilted to one side. "I have seen two or three plays and the opera since we moved to town. I liked them."

"*The Constant Couple*?"

"I confess I can hardly remember it. A gentleman in another box kept staring at me."

"You were well worth staring at."

She blushed again, delightfully. Her aristocratic upbringing had not been able to keep the blood from rushing to her cheeks.

"Thank you," she mumbled.

"Can you think of anything else you have liked to do? Most ladies delight in shopping, I know."

"One cannot really enjoy shopping when one cannot afford to buy. I rather like dancing, but one's pleasure in balls is dimmed when one's gowns are remade from one's mother's bride clothes or show where the trim has been changed several times. I need not scruple to mention this, as you are all too aware of the Normande duchy's finances."

"Or lack of them. Do you play cards?"

She stiffened. "I know the games and play socially when I must. I once heard a lady say she loved the thrill of playing deep. I do not see the enjoyment in such wagers." She toyed with her fan. "In the schoolroom, I liked some of the books about history and foreign lands. I might want to read a novel. My mother and my governess considered the reading of such things likely to give girls romantical notions. I think I am past the age of being influenced by them. Oh, and wild flowers! When I walked in Petty Normande's park, I loved the wild flowers that grew without being planted or tended. Dog roses, columbine, kingcup, cornflower, and scarlet pimpernel. I preferred them to our formal garden. The roses had a lovely scent, but the flowers growing in the meadows and groves were so free and exuberant, like the silks that are painted with Chinese patterns. If I had a garden, I believe I would have the gardener plant at least a part of it with those flowers. I beg your pardon! I should not have prattled on, when you cannot be interested in such things."

"On the contrary. I wanted to know more about you, Lady Emily. Is there anything you wish to ask me?"

She fixed her gaze on her hands. "I do not believe I have any questions, sir."

She would not think it right to question him. Having been trained to do her duty, she thought she knew the important thing about him: he was wealthy and in a position to settle the estate's debts.

She would do. The next part would be awkward. He was seated some distance from her; whether by bad luck or design, no chair was nearer. If she were on the settee, all would be easy. He rose, picked up the rickety chair, and placed it at right angles to hers, close enough that their knees almost touched when he sat. He would be damned if he'd go down on one knee. "Lady Emily, your position is difficult. Even if your cousin married well tomorrow and was freed of his debts, your situation would continue to be awkward. His bride may come of the commercial class, without the connections to sponsor you in society so you could meet eligible men. If he is fortunate enough to marry a lady of good family with enough money to, ah…"

"Make the marriage worthwhile?"

"Ay. No matter who His Grace marries, you will

no longer be the mistress of his house. You need to marry a man who can support you as befits your station."

"I know it, sir." She sat motionless, as he had seen nuns sit in Catholic countries.

"You are not obligated to accept my proposal, but I would be honored if you would marry me, Lady Emily."

She swallowed. "Are you proposing, Mr. Hawkins?"

"I am. You have been brought up to expect a marriage with no more than mutual respect, and I require a lady of social standing. We might both benefit. Do you need time to consider?"

"No, Mr. Hawkins. I accept your proposal. Thank you."

"Will you give me your hand?"

She appeared surprised. "I have just said so, sir."

"I mean, your actual hand. I would like to kiss it."

"Oh!" She tendered her right hand hesitantly.

Surely she must have had it kissed previously at some point. He had intended a merely formal brushing of his lips against her knuckles. On impulse, he pressed his lips against the back of her hand. The veins showed blue through the alabaster-pale skin, and her fingers were long and slender, faintly scented with some delicate floral perfume. They trembled.

He had not meant to turn that pretty hand palm up. But she was not ready for a kiss upon the lips, which he might reasonably have claimed, given that they were now betrothed. He felt her startle and heard her catch her breath at his ardent kiss upon her palm. He straightened and would have gazed into her eyes, but she was blushing and staring down at her other hand, clenching a delicate handkerchief.

Damn his eyes, she was maidenly shy as a girl entering society for the first time. How could she have lived to be five- or six-and-twenty and still be disconcerted by such mild flirtation? Comparatively mild. He'd never encountered the like. But then, she was likely raised sheltered. Lived mostly in the country, too, hadn't she?

"May I now take your left hand?"

She tendered it, releasing the crumpled handkerchief. Hawkins pulled the ring out of his pocket and slipped it onto her finger. He waited for her reaction.

She glanced down at the emerald in its dainty enameled setting and gasped. "Mr. Hawkins, it's lovely. Is it a family treasure?"

"Hardly. There is a story to it, which I will tell you some other time. May I kiss you?"

She assented shyly, closing her eyes and raising her face. Her breathing was fast, from nerves rather than desire, but that would come. She tasted faintly of honey, perhaps from lip salve. Her lips did not part, and he made no effort to penetrate them or to embrace her closely. One hand at the back of her waist, the other stroking the nape of her neck would do for the present. Lady Emily was not ready for passion. Not like Olivia Cantarell, who had ignited at their first kiss. She was untutored in the art. He would enjoy the challenge of teaching her.

"My dear Emily, I will take my leave of you and have a few words with your cousin if he is free to see me." If! The fellow was probably wearing the carpet out with his pacing.

"I am sure he will make the time to speak with you, sir." She had regained her composure. But her slight smile was a little warmer than formal courtesy required.

Ay, the marriage would do. He would send a notice to the paper today, which would pacify the duke's creditors, and they would marry as soon as possible. The settlements would not take long to arrange: Solomon de Toledo had drafted a memorandum of the terms to which Normande and he had already agreed. Hawkins's attorney need only add the legal rigmarole.

Chapter 7

Emily and Martha, freed from her work in the scullery for the entire day in spite of the cook's objections, were furbishing up her six-year-old *robe volante*. They had already completed slightly more complex renovations to her favorite mantua. She liked the soft rose and plain style which was easily trimmed with old lace her mama had kept, and some small silk flowers made from scraps left over after Martha had remodeled another gown.

Her cousin had suggested she order a new gown to wear on her wedding day, but Emily declined. The wedding was to be small, and she could not in good conscience let Henry incur the expense. Besides, the *robe volante* was Spitalfields silk, woven with silver blossoms on the green of spring leaves, the last garment bought before her father's death. Thank God for Martha. Without her skills, Emily must have been the veriest dowdy.

A tap at the door and Henry's voice: "Emily? May I enter?"

"Come in. There's nothing to alarm you."

Rather than entering, he opened the door and peered in. "Ah. May I have a word with you, Cousin?"

"Certainly. Shall I come to your study, so Martha may continue sewing?"

"Ay, ay, that will do very well."

Once they had retired to Henry's study, which was no more than a room with some bookshelves, a pair of chairs, and a desk which saw very little use, Normande appeared to have difficulty coming to the point. He stirred the handful of coals in the fireplace without rekindling the fire, then fidgeted with the poker.

"Emily...you have not reconsidered marrying Hawkins, have you?"

"How could I?" Lud, the announcement had appeared, which would mean jilting him, and how could she change her mind anyway? She could not permit the head of the family to be tossed into debtors' prison, even if she had not rather liked him, now that they were better acquainted. She must marry for her own sake, as well. All her life she had done her duty, or as she was told. To stop now, when she was one step from joining her cousin in debtor's prison or being out on the street, would be ridiculous. "Why would I? His manner is pleasant, and he is"—she intended to say, *attractive*, but instead ended—"not ugly or old or fat."

"I only wondered because of something I heard from friends. Brewer saw the announcement and mentioned something he'd been told. I hope it's not true, and if you're willing to go ahead with the marriage, I won't try to dissuade you. Our position— my position, I should say, as none of it's your fault—is hopeless without the kind of marriage settlement Hawkins is willing to make."

"What was it you heard?" The feeling of relief, even pleasure, she had enjoyed since agreeing to the marriage turned to dread.

"They say he was a pirate."

She contemplated His Grace, the Duke of

Normande. It went against all her training to question the head of her family, whose dependent she was. On the other hand, she remembered first meeting him when his face was still spotty.

"Then why was he not hanged? Isn't piracy a capital crime?"

He shrugged. "Not enough evidence? Bribes in the right places?"

"On what evidence is this rumor based?"

"Well…there can't be any proof or he'd have been tried, Emily. It's just what everyone says."

"Did the story come from anyone who had sailed with him as a pirate?"

" 'Pon my soul, Emily! No one would admit to being a pirate himself. But it's well known he sailed in the West Indies and Spanish Main. He has a reputation for ruthlessness. And his whole demeanor—" Henry shrugged again. "It's not too late to end the betrothal. The settlement documents have not been signed, and no one would wonder at your changing your mind, given the rumors."

Ambrose Hawkins did look dangerous. His features were regular, except his nose which was decidedly aquiline, but they gave an impression of harshness. He might look menacing if he were angry. An even temper might not be habitual with him, but he had been good-humored at their meetings and he had laugh lines around his eyes.

Her right thumb rubbed over the stone set in the betrothal ring Ambrose Hawkins had slipped onto her finger the day she accepted his suit. It had not been, as she expected, a rather ostentatious ring from one of London's leading jewelers.

"It was given to a lady of Charles the Second's court by her affianced husband," he had told her later. "The jeweler said only that the family had fallen on hard times and wished to sell the ring. He refused to tell me their names, which is understandable, though it might make a better story. 'Tis a pretty tale, at least. The style of the piece is right for the period."

The square table-cut emerald was as wide as the nail of her little finger, the sides of the gold mounting covered in scrollwork enclosing green, blue, and white enameled designs. Green for new love, blue for true love, and white for purity, she supposed. A pretty conceit, which she appreciated whether it was sentiment or merely exquisite taste on Hawkins's part.

"Henry, there is always talk about someone in the beau monde. Quite often, shocking or amusing as it may be, it is either grossly exaggerated or actually untrue." Emily had spent enough time in society to know how gossip worked, even if no ill will were involved. *Mistress Caroline dresses like a slattern*, becomes *Mistress Caroline looks like a doxy*, which becomes *Mistress Caroline is no better than a whore*. She did not suppose men's loose talk was any better. "I would base my judgment on something more substantial than idle chatter."

"Well…I did go to Solomon, the moneylender, you know, to ask him. He arranged the introduction to Hawkins, and it was my understanding Hawkins was not an undesirable match. Apart from being in trade, that is."

"I do not think you can compare an owner of ships to a greengrocer. What did this Solomon have to say?"

"He claimed Hawkins had been a sailor on a

merchantman taken by pirates, and they, er, pressed him and several others, having lost some of their own crew in the fight. According to him, Hawkins and the other men who'd been abducted waited until they'd made landfall on some island in the West Indies, then damaged the ship and made off for the nearest town to bring back enough men to capture the pirates. Solomon made some inquiries and said he was convinced."

"Then why are you worried about it now, Henry, if you already knew about it?"

"I didn't realize it was known and talked of, until I mentioned Hawkins in passing to friends at a coffee house."

"But if it isn't true—"

"What does it matter if it's true or not, Emily? It's an embarrassment. Besides, I have only Solomon's word for it, and although he's given me some good advice, he'll make a commission if the marriage takes place."

"A large one?"

"No. That is, it's a pittance by our standards, except since we've been in such difficulties. But it might seem a great deal to him."

"As the marriage means a great deal to us."

"That's very true." Henry sighed. "I suppose Solomon could find another prospect for you. Hawkins was simply the best available choice."

The talk about Hawkins having been a pirate was troubling. On the other hand, it was only rumor. She could do far worse than marry him. That kiss he had pressed upon her palm had thrilled her. The kiss on her lips had been pleasant, too. Emily pointed out, "His behavior in all our meetings has been gentlemanly. It speaks well for him that he understood the awkwardness of our situation. I found his manner reassuring. If you have reservations about the wisdom of the marriage, we might postpone it for a bit. Perhaps your moneylender can find you a bride with a rich father first, and then if Mr. Hawkins shows signs of evil tendencies, I might break off our engagement."

"I asked Solomon if it wouldn't do as well for me to marry first. It's his opinion that I would stand little chance of securing a bride with a sufficiently large dowry and who is also a suitable duchess—I can't marry just any cit's daughter—when my debts are so large and pressing. Once they're paid, I'll be a far more attractive match for a girl of decent family who has a good dowry."

"Then I will marry Mr. Hawkins. Things will work out." She could not, no, absolutely could not, face the consequences of the duke's financial ruin. Who would take her in? The life of a companion, the only paid position for which she was qualified, was insecure. At best, it would be miserable, judging from the companions she had observed. They were treated like servants, present at their employers' entertainments but ignored by the guests, and expected to look cheerful even when berated. Emily found herself heartily sorry that she had spared few words for the impoverished gentlewomen reduced to companion status whom she had encountered over the years.

The moneylender might be able to find her another match, but common sense told her another man might be far worse than a rumored pirate. She could endure a few rumors, whereas a husband who was unattractive or ill-natured (if he was no worse!) would be a trial their entire married life.

Chapter 8

The man's old-fashioned full-bottomed wig and stockings rolled up over the bottom of his breeches legs proved only that he had no interest in the latest mode, as the cloth and tailoring were good. His features were coarse but dignified. From his pursed lips, it appeared he disapproved of Hawkins & Company's Cinnamon Street premises. He looked to be a moderately successful tradesman or artisan risen from humble beginnings. The signs were all there: brisk manner, weathered face, callused hands.

He had no cause to sneer at Hawkins & Company: the building and its sign were kept painted, and Hawkins's office was comfortably furnished. Hawkins had leased it when he first set up as a ship owner. Now he could afford better than the ramshackle wooden structure in Wapping. Premises like Marcus Easterday's sedate office on Leadenhall Street, near the East India House, would make it clear that Hawkins & Company was one of the most prosperous firms in London. He had not moved partly because packing up the records, furniture, and clerks and setting them up elsewhere with no disruption to his business was not an appealing prospect. Besides, it was convenient to the Thames. He would miss seeing the ships at anchor, the barges, tilt-boats, and the wherries darting between them like dragonflies.

Studying the fellow, he noticed one inconsistent detail: he wore a signet ring of jade set in heavy gold rather than the cheaper metal sort a plain man who needed a signet would use. Unusual, for one who dressed simply.

"Mr. Salem Cole," his junior clerk announced and backed out the door, closing it softly behind him.

"Please be seated, Mr. Cole. You wanted to speak to me?"

"Ay. Captain Joel Marston gave me your name as one who could speak for his character." Cole sat, leaning forward slightly, hands on knees.

"A character for...?" Marston could not mean to take a position with the fellow. Did he mean to sell one of his ships? If he did—

"In a manner of speaking. He's asked for my daughter in marriage. I want to be sure he's all he claims, not that I haven't made some inquiries of my own."

"I see." Damn Marston. He must have chosen the acquaintances who were most successful and thus most likely to impress Cole.

"You do know him?" His hesitation had not escaped his visitor's notice.

"I do. He is not a close friend of mine, but I have known him for years. We are both members of a little group that meets at a coffee house. Most of us with business in the Pool of London know each other or of each other, at least."

Cole nodded. "What can you tell me about the man?"

"He was a very skilled captain, and now he's ashore, he's chosen good men to captain the *Marigold* and the *Belle*. I wouldn't hesitate to ship cargo on either." *If I didn't have ships of my own.*

"I've heard as much from others. Doing well, too, they say—and so do the City men who know banking and investment. Is he honest?" He fired the question off as if it were a musket ball.

"As far as I know. His customers would complain and it would be common knowledge in the Pool if he wasn't."

"Is he a decent man?" Cole's eyes, hard as musket balls themselves, skewered him from under bushy gray brows. Pierced him, Hawkins supposed. A pistol or musket ball pierces, a cutlass hacks. A smallsword skewers. Which was what Hawkins would like to do to Marston.

"He is respected in the Pool of London." Treated warily, too. *I am what he would like to be.*

Cole snorted. "Does he drink to excess? Does he frequent brothels or keep a woman? Does he gamble? Does he attend church regular of a Sunday?"

"I'm sure he always read the Sunday service at sea for the crew's benefit. That's standard." It was a relief to say something that might draw off the prospective papa-in-law. "I can't speak to his churchgoing habits now. He lives in a different parish." Not that he himself was regular in attending.

"The other things?"

"He drinks no more than most of us do, and he holds it well. As for women…" Hawkins shrugged. "I don't think I know a man who doesn't have some dealings with females."

"I don't, since my wife died." Cole's mouth turned down. "And I seldom drink anything stronger than small beer."

Strike me blind. Marston's courting a Methodist's chit. "I'm sure he is discreet and avoids any woman who might be poxed." Hard to imagine where Marston could have met Cole's girl, or how he had been smitten by love for her. Still, he knew from his own experience that love ran by few rules. He could not have imagined being attracted by Olivia Cantarell until he came to know her. The girl might be less of a religious enthusiast than her father, might be glad to live a more worldly life. "He's not known for gambling, except as all sailors do. Every voyage is a game of hazard." Best to be clear about the matter.

Cole grunted. "What sort is Marston as a man?"

The question posed a quandary. Hawkins mulled over the problem. It would be like trying to explain a wolf to a horse. "If he gives his word, he keeps it," was certainly true, and implied honesty. The man was reasonably honest in dealing with his customers. How would a rigidly honest man judge Marston? His own reputation was worse than Marston's because of that damned talk about his career as a pirate. If the rumors about Marston were true, he was less squeamish than Hawkins about some things. "If he's set on something, there's not much will stop him. If he doesn't drown"— *or hang*—"he'll likely be rich someday instead of only prosperous. He's not a skinflint, but he's no spendthrift, either. A careful man. He knows how to sail close to the wind to make good speed." *Without coming to grief.*

"I believe I have no more questions for you. Thank you, Mr. Hawkins." With a short nod, Cole stumped out.

Cole was even more lacking in social graces than

Hawkins himself. At least he was able to feign a gentleman's behavior when he remembered. He put Cole out of his mind.

Ordinary business, meeting with his attorney about the marriage settlements and his will, arranging more staff for the Old Gravel Lane house, and buying a wedding ring and wedding gift for his bride, filled his days. He visited Doctors' Commons in Knightrider Street to apply for the marriage license.

Normande had suggested a common license, as being cheaper (though it was doubtful the duke would have been able to come up even with its very moderate cost). The price of a special license was immaterial to Hawkins. The chief difference lay in the requirement of the ordinary license to marry in the parish church, while with a special license, one could marry anywhere: one's own home, a barge on the Thames, a park. A church wedding would attract the curious, eager to marvel at the marriage of a lady of high rank to the next thing to a cit. The allegation he gave for needing the special license had required some thought as neither he nor the young duke was familiar with the application procedure. After some indecision, he pled the issue of differing social status, which was certainly true. The most common reasons for a special license, the bride being pregnant, the couple's religions differing, and family opposition, certainly did not apply.

Lady Emily's hesitantly stated preference for the ceremony was the duke's home. While not actually Normande House, now leased to a rich merchant, it suited Hawkins well enough. It did come complete with a duke, after all. He persuaded Normande to let him bring in his own people to decorate, prepare, and serve the wedding breakfast. Henry, Duke of Normande, young, unsure of himself, and with hardly a penny to his name, allowed Hawkins to convince him that Hawkins's servants had too little to keep them busy, and that in the absence of a female relative of the bride, it could not matter who took over the arrangements.

Chapter 9

The day passed without significant mortification. Although the ceremony befitted a family in financial straits, the wedding breakfast was superb. Emily did wish she possessed a gown equal to the magnificence of the orange velvet suit and cream brocade waistcoat Hawkins wore, while knowing that no one would be deceived. Normande was all but penniless, as everyone was aware. Too, it would have been pleasant to have more family present. Apart from Henry, only Cecily and her husband attended, Lavinia having pled that distance and a delicate constitution prevented her making the journey. She probably meant she was breeding.

Emily liked Cecily, who had always treated her as if she were a young aunt. A few of the seventh duke's friends came, but she did not know them well, and none of Henry's carousing companions had been invited. Even the optimistic Henry could not claim they would behave, and in any case, he had distanced himself from them. Someone had advised him his friends had led him into debt and excess in the first place, and that as a duke, he had a responsibility to act with more dignity than a pack of undisciplined younger sons. In an unguarded moment, Henry confided, "De Toledo—my moneylender—told me to grow up. Said it would make a better impression on gentlemen of substance looking for titled husbands for their girls." She thought he must be quoting verbatim. He would have been more likely to say "rich cits" than "gentlemen of substance." Ladies did not speak of moneylenders, or to them, but if the man gave Henry such advice, she was happy for the association, if glad he had not been invited.

A number of her bridegroom's friends attended. They were quite different from what she expected, genteel or even aristocratic, rather than merchants. Marcus and Olivia Easterday both came of decent families in spite of their commercial interests, and several of their friends or relations were present. Emily was happy for their presence, which increased the size and festivity of the gathering, however tenuous their connection to Hawkins. The most illustrious of these were the Duke and Duchess of Guysbridge. The duke was a friend of Easterday's, though how they had become acquainted Emily could not imagine, and Hawkins had imported some curiosity for Guysbridge. Also present were Alderman Richard Saltstall, another of Captain Easterday's friends, and Mr. and Mrs. Giles Nevis. Rachel Nevis was Mistress Easterday's aunt, and Nevis was Hawkins's old friend and mentor. Saltstall added consequence to her wedding, and she immediately liked Mistress Nevis, whose father had been a baron.

After the breakfast, Cecily, the duchess, Mistress Easterday, and Mistress Nevis withdrew to a quiet corner where they engaged in brief, earnest conversation. What could they be discussing? She was destined to discover the subject later in the festivities, when guests began to depart.

"My dear, may I have a few words with you in the

library?" Hawkins drew her out of the room.

"Certainly, sir."

He opened the door to the library and said in her ear, "Mistress Easterday wishes for a short talk with you in private." And her husband left her with Olivia Easterday, who rose from the chair in which she had been sitting and came forward.

"May I call you Emily? And will you call me Olivia?"

As her social superior, Emily should insist on being called by her courtesy title. Under the circumstances, she hardly liked to do so. "Please do," she said, hoping she had not paused too long.

"I won't keep you long. I think you have no female relatives or friends who are older than you, none at least who are here. Or who have already spoken with you about your wedding night?"

Blushing fiercely, Emily mumbled, "No."

"We thought not. Well, then, I am appointed your temporary mother."

As Olivia was not much older than she, Emily gave a gasp of laughter.

Olivia laughed, too. "Your cousin Cecily felt she could not do it because she is several years younger. Easily embarrassed, too, I vow. The Duchess of Guysbridge is also younger, but while she was willing, her mind is of a, er, too medical bent to be quite suitable. My aunt, Mistress Nevis, instructed me before my own marriage, which is why I offered to be a volunteer instructress. Here it is, then, the lecture that the bride should receive about the part of marriage she has not been trained for…"

Some hours later, Emily was very glad of the

instruction and advice, horrifyingly embarrassing as it was at the time.

Chapter 10

"I hope we are now on first-name terms, Emily, for I wish you will call me Ambrose," her husband told her at breakfast the following morning.

Her husband. The heat in her cheeks told her she had colored up. Thank God Olivia Easterday had explained matters to her. Seeing livestock mate would have been poor preparation for the night's events.

"Very well, Ambrose."

Ambrose's cook was excellent, and Emily found herself able to do full justice to poached eggs, a morsel of ham, hot bread, marmalade of quinces, and tea. Her husband, devouring cold sirloin of beef, accompanied by ale, smiled at her between bites. Really, she must think of something to say to him.

"This is a pleasant house." No larger than one a successful professional man might occupy but luxuriously furnished, it was oddly situated among market gardens rather than on a square or in a genteel street.

"It's not what you are accustomed to, but I have been living in lodgings. I did not want to buy a suitable house without your advice. This is merely a property I purchased for an investment. I have sometimes spent a day or two here when I wanted quiet and a country atmosphere."

She heard something evasive in his voice. She

might be a duke's daughter and sheltered, but she was not a miss in the schoolroom. He had kept a mistress here or used the house for assignations with married women, perhaps. She did not hold it against him. One expected men to have amorous connections—here she was blushing again—and indeed, their wedding night might have been somewhat awkward, had he not been in such good practice.

His wishing to consult her opinion over choosing a house boded well for their marriage. "Will we look at houses soon?"

"Today, if you like. I have a list of available properties. It's cold, so you must dress warmly, and I'll have the kitchen heat some bricks to keep your feet warm. Will an hour give you time enough to dress?"

"Of course."

The sky was clear, and a sharp wind was blowing away some of London's haze of soot. It might not be an ideal day for a prolonged carriage ride, but it would give them something to do. Emily did not quite know how they could get through the day at home. On their arrival the previous evening, she had suggested she speak with the housekeeper about menus for the next several days. It would fill the interval until supper, for what was she to do alone with her husband? A young lady was never alone with a man except her father or brother. But Hawkins had assured her it was unnecessary to give any directions to the servants unless she had a fancy for some particular dish.

Perhaps the question of how to become accustomed to living intimately with a man did not often arise. A number of her own family connections and friends had begun marriage by travelling to the bridegroom's family seat. It gave the couple an opportunity to become comfortable together while not leaving them entirely on their own if they did not already know each other well.

No wedding trip had been mentioned, possibly because Hawkins was in business and could not leave it, or because neither of them had any family to visit. He had implied that he might have family living; if so, they must be estranged or surely they would have been at the wedding. Unless they lived too far away to attend? Being confined in the coach today might offer a chance to learn more about him.

"Going upriver by my shallop would have been faster and pleasant on a warm day," he said, tucking a thick blanket over her lap. "However, the wind on the river would be fierce and the hired coach we would need when we landed upriver would not have a lap robe or hot bricks."

Emily was content. It would be harder to have a private conversation with her new husband in a boat, and he was certainly correct about the coach being more comfortable on a winter's day. Before she could frame her first question, he spoke again.

"I must beg your pardon for not noticing yesterday that you had no maid with you and had to make do with the upstairs maid last night and this morning. I have already sent a message to my head clerk to have a selection of lady's maids available for interview within the next two or three days. He will arrange for the interviews to take place in a private parlor at a good inn. My office would be unsuitable, and the Gravel Lane house would be inconvenient for the applicants. I will let you know when they will be available for you to interview. He will also advertise for a butler and a cook. Some of the Gravel Lane staff will come to our new house but not the cook. She is excellent for good, plain food but has no experience with large or fashionable dinners and no desire to attempt them. You need not interview the cook or butler applicants yourself. I will interview the applicants for the butler's position, and once I have hired one, he will choose the cook."

The last several sentences made little impression upon her, as something he had said earlier caught her attention. Inconvenient for the applicants? One did not consider the convenience of servants. But then, the house was some considerable distance from the fashionable neighborhoods. It might be rather a long walk for some, especially as many London maids were not fond of walking. How surprising he would think of such a thing. No wonder Ambrose Hawkins's servants appeared to be pleased with him.

"Thank you. I did not notice any deficiency. I have not had a real personal maid for some time. The last was merely a maid who was clever at sewing and arranging hair. It will be pleasant to have the services of a proper lady's maid again."

Conversation lapsed. A lady was supposed to be able to set others at ease in a social exchange (except servants and the lower orders, who did not matter) and take part in light discourse without effort. This was a little different: Hawkins did not belong to her world, but he was not a vulgar cit, either. If she had found herself with some country gentleman, she would have asked how he liked London, if his family had also come up from the country, and how his children did. On the other hand, idle chitchat would not acquaint her with her husband. She knew Hawkins owned ships and where they sailed and with what cargo. To assist him in entering into good society, however, she needed to know more about him than his business.

"I suppose there was not time for any of your people to make the journey to attend our wedding," she ventured. "Though of course travel is difficult and often family don't come from long distances unless they mean to stay for a while." She began to feel nervous about probing, as this might be a sore point if he and his relations were on bad terms. She did not even know whether he had invited any family members. His clerk had sent the invitations, working from a list she had provided and whatever instructions Hawkins had given him.

Ambrose Hawkins turned his head from contemplating Montagu House as they passed and stared at her.

"I beg your pardon," she began, now afraid she had given offense, "I did not mean to pry…"

"I didn't invite them. I don't know whether any of my family still live." He rubbed his chin as he had done once or twice on their wedding day. It seemed to betoken perplexity or mayhap nervousness.

"Oh!"

"I haven't seen them since I was twelve and ran away from home."

"They must have treated you very badly."

"They didn't. Not even my stepfather, though I loathed him for being lazy and spendthrift. My mother doted on the fellow. Do you know, Emily, I can't say now why I decided to leave, unless it was the sum of a great many little things. The way a man may die of a dozen small wounds that weaken him until he dies of infection."

"I see."

"Would that I might. I resented the way my stepfather wasted the money my father would have put back into improving the land. He said there was not enough money to keep my brother at a good school and to pay my tutor. 'Tis the last feather breaks the horse's back. For me, it may have been that he intended to send me to a boarding grammar school for two years to complete my education. Do you know the sort? Some needy parson willing to house several boys and teach them something. After, my stepfather would find me a position with some genteel tradesman."

"How appalling." What else was there to say? Gentlemen of some means sent their sons to boarding schools or had them tutored at home. Their heirs and even younger sons sometimes went to university. The younger sons then went into the Church, the law, or perhaps some other profession. Banking would not be objectionable, or public service such as in the government or with the East India Company. Gentlemen of less fortune might find positions through a relation or family friend. The Lords Mayor of London were drawn from the livery companies, like the Worshipful Companies of mercers, goldsmiths, skinners, merchant tailors, grocers, and the like, and they would hardly be chosen if they were men of no education or manners. But still, a young boy of genteel family might well view apprenticeship with loathing.

"Instead, I decided to go to sea. I could not see myself as a haberdasher's assistant." His rakish, go-to-hell smile invited her to laugh at the notion, and how could she resist? The idea of Hawkins behind a counter, selling caps, ribbons, and other small wares was irresistibly comical.

The memory lightened her mood during their excursion, which took them to several squares and half a dozen streets. Fully half of the houses they viewed could be dismissed out of hand, some without descending from the coach, though every dwelling on the list had been passed as acceptable by one of Hawkins's clerks. Hawkins suggested they stop for a meal after the next house, as he knew of a good inn nearby.

"I am not sure it is right to bring you here, even with a private parlor," Hawkins said. "The food is good and the other patrons decent, but it's not a place for a lady. We could continue our inspection another day. Still, it would be a long journey back to my house."

"I see nothing to dislike here. You say the food is good, and the inn appears prosperous. I confess I am hungry. I've never climbed so many steps in so short a period." She added, "I liked that last house."

The waiter poured out glasses of claret. When the man had gone, promising that their meal would arrive "in a trice, sir, I assure you," Hawkins said, "I do, as well. It's not a grand house for a duke's daughter—"

"Our family did not move much in society after my mother's death. The house is large enough for entertaining, even for a small ball. Five floors! There are rooms enough for as many servants as we might need." She checked. This was surely the first time she had used "we" in connection with Hawkins and herself. *My husband.* "The lower floor is well laid out for the servants." Having overseen the household management at Petty Normande, she took a lively interest in the subject. The ducal seat's kitchen could not have changed much since its construction.

"The house is not above five or ten years old. St. James's Square is near, and York Street is a handsome thoroughfare. I had hoped for a more imposing residence for you, though it is of good size. The fourth story would do for the nursery and schoolroom, Emily."

Emily chose not to contemplate the latter topic. The activity which might lead to needing an extensive nursery and children's floor, while enjoyable, still caused some embarrassment. Instead she said, "It's a pretty house. It is also more appropriate than a mansion."

Their food arrived and was served forth with as much ceremony as a dinner in any gentleman's home. Roast chicken, cold ham, pickles, a dish of mushrooms, and one of broccoli, with almond cheesecakes to complete the meal.

"How so?" Hawkins asked as he served her several slices of chicken.

How could she answer in an inoffensive way? "You wed me to gain access to the beau monde. A residence such as Marlborough House or Montagu House, both built for dukes, would be thought...excessive."

A long, thoughtful silence ensued, only partly explained by her husband's steady mastication of ham. "Excessive as in 'ostentatious' or 'vulgar'?"

"A little thrusting, perhaps."

"Then if you are pleased with York Street, I will make an offer this afternoon."

"That would be excellent, Ambrose." The house

possessed a simple elegance she found restful, and she would be humiliated neither by too humble a house nor by a jumped-up merchant's demi-palace. This marriage might be no sacrifice.

Chapter 11

Today Emily had asked whether he would mind if she ordered some new gowns. He gave permission, feeling guilty. He should have encouraged her to do so, as it had been clear even to him that her wardrobe was both limited and out of date. Consequently, she was spending the afternoon at a mantua-maker's establishment, supported by Olivia's aunt Rachel. He might spend an hour or two at the Fortunate Gentleman's Coffee House for the first time in two or three weeks.

Company was thin in their private room, no more than six or eight men. He was subjected to some good-humored banter over his marriage and long absence from their club.

"Domesticated, Hawk?" Pruitt slapped him on the back.

"Better things to do than idling here, listening to you complain about your latest mistress. I suppose you've been through two at least since I saw you last."

Pruitt guffawed. "Three!"

Harrison praised a new brothel; Andrews contemplated investing in a Portuguese vineyard. Several others called for a fresh pack of cards and commenced playing loo—the cutthroat sort, not the ladies' well-mannered version. He was invited to join in and declined. He preferred maritime risks to games of chance.

He was deep in conversation with old Wilson, whose son had been sent down from Oxford ("And no loss. He's no scholar," his papa remarked) and wanted his opinion on what to do with the pup.

"Get him out of London," was Hawkins's terse advice. "Get him a post with the East India Company, or send him to sea or to the American colonies. Not much vice there!"

"My brother owns a plantation in Jamaica. It might do."

"The climate is enervating, and the men I've met who have spent time there seem generally lazy and self-indulgent. They leave all the work to their overseers."

"Surely India's heat is more enervating yet, Hawkins."

"It is—but the boy's superiors will keep his nose to the grindstone—" Wilson's gaze shifted to Hawkins's left shoulder. His obvious surprise was the only warning Hawkins had before he was spun around by a hard hand.

"Damn you, Hawkins, you slandered me to Cole! I'd've sworn you'd be honest enough to give me a good character. Instead you vilified me," Marston snarled.

At times in the past, Hawkins would have reacted by knocking the fellow down. Lately, he'd decided he too often acted more violently than the occasion required. His years at sea were to blame. "To hell with you. I said nothing to your detriment."

"Then why did he refuse me his chit? My banker gave him a fair notion of my means."

"I told him you were respected, kept your word, didn't gamble or drink to excess, and were discreet about your relations with women. How could he take any of that amiss?"

"Rot me if I know. Somehow he took the notion you were half-hearted in giving me a reference."

"I'm sorry if he thought it. Did the other witnesses to your character not convince him?"

"I was sure he'd listen to you and my banker."

"Bad luck. You might ask Cole how you can convince him of your worthiness."

"I tried. He wouldn't listen."

Oh, hell. "Marston, mayhap he inquired about me as well. My reputation is none too good. I don't cheat in business, like you I'm no sot or gamester, but you know many believe I was a pirate. Some think me violent in temper." Olivia Cantarell had made it clear by expression alone that she was angry he had cuffed her messenger. "Could be Cole thought the recommendation of a suspected buccaneer did you no credit."

Marston swore viciously, attracting some attention, although the other men had sheared off when Marston first accosted Hawkins.

"It's little consolation if you are attached to the girl, but Cole would be the devil of a father-in-law."

"The wench is plain as a penny loaf and virtuous as bedamned, but her dowry is pretty indeed and she's his heir."

"Then find other men to try to change Cole's mind." *If you can.*

Marston scowled.

"Or find some other chit with a dowry and a less particular papa."

"It's none so easy."

"Is the girl attracted to you? If she slips away to a clandestine meeting with you, her father would insist on the marriage."

This suggestion struck Marston forcibly, judging by his poleaxed expression. He nodded absently, muttered, "My thanks," and stalked out of the room before Hawkins could reconsider his flippant advice. Not that it had been advice. Not exactly. In any event, it would only work if the wench were willing to agree to a secret, unchaperoned meeting with Marston, which, judging from his description of her, she would not. He dismissed the slight unease he felt at Marston's peculiar reaction to his half-joking comment.

Chapter 12

Her maid gave a last tweak to her fichu. Hawkins's clerk had done an excellent job of finding potentially suitable lady's maids for her. A week after the wedding, Emily had spent two hours interviewing sixteen applicants. Some she dismissed after only a few minutes: too young, too loquacious, too friendly, too inexperienced. She told half a dozen who might do to wait. All were women who had been employed for years as dressers to titled ladies.

One was rather stout; would she be sufficiently brisk about her duties? Another was too old. A third peered in a way which might mean poor eyesight. Another spoke in the grating Yorkshire dialect. Agnes Putnam, bone thin, grizzled, and stern, reminded Emily of her mother's dresser. Putnam was now seeking employment only because the marchioness she had served for twenty years had recently died. Emily rather wondered that she would lower herself to work for the wife of a commoner. However, perhaps the woman considered that a duke's daughter was some compensation. Emily engaged her on the spot. Now she could settle into the gracious life of a married lady, as soon as they moved into the York Street house.

"Very good, Putnam. Did you order the coach?"

"Certainly, my lady. And instructed the kitchen to have hot bricks ready, and I will tell the kitchen staff at

Guysbridge House to heat them again while you pay your call. 'Tis a duke's household; no doubt they can manage to do it. Though my late mistress, the marchioness, had no high opinion of the Anascotes, and by all accounts, the new duchess is a very odd female."

"It was kind of them to come to my wedding."

In some respects, not taking a wedding journey was a good thing. Though visiting one's connections after marrying was common, Hawkins had not been in contact with his family in decades, and she really had no one, apart from Cousin Henry and his sisters. Cousin Cecily was living in Buckinghamshire with her husband, a mere squire, whose household, to judge by her letters, was somewhat chaotic. They might not even have bedchambers enough for visitors. Emily did not count Cousin Lavinia as family in any real sense, as Lavinia had treated her like a poor relation. She had been, of course, but her rank entitled her to some respect. Lavinia's behavior was what one would expect from a chit whose father had had no hope of inheriting the title until so many disasters had befallen Emily's family. How had Cecily grown up to be a pleasant young lady, while Lavinia might have been a cit's daughter, always concerned about her own consequence?

Then, too, if they had taken a wedding journey, who would have seen to the furnishing of their new home? She was enjoyably occupied with studying drapery and upholstery fabric samples and shopping for silverware and dishes, though Captain Easterday had given them a set of Meissen porcelain for twelve, and Mistress Easterday had made them a gift of a Chinese tea set.

It was perhaps strange that a husband and wife had given separate gifts, but then, there had been odd currents at the wedding. Captain Easterday was her husband's friend, she understood, while Olivia Easterday's manner had seemed somewhat constrained. Did she not approve of Hawkins? She had shown no discomfort with Emily.

Both the Easterdays were gentry, though the captain's business, like Hawkins's, meant his and Olivia's acquaintance would not be of social assistance to Hawkins. Nor was Olivia likely to be a real friend: her speech and manners were those of a lady, but she was interested in the strangest things. She cared little for fashion (though her gown was modish and the color perfect for her), but she was able to explain the difference between the hand of Chinese silk and that woven by Huguenot weavers in England. She claimed the Chinese rolled a weighted cylinder over the silk to increase its luster and smoothness.

Ambrose had told her nothing of Mistress Easterday beyond the fact she had but recently married the captain. She must have been virtually an old maid, being several years older than Emily, who had been at her own last prayers. From something Captain Easterday had mentioned, his wife actually operated a shipping business inherited from her father, even after her marriage.

The Duchess of Guysbridge was a better choice for entrée into the fashionable world, in spite of having been raised in merely genteel circumstances by a country doctor. Guysbridge was a duke, after all, with enough hauteur for both of them, rendering almost moot his wife's upbringing. As she met the duchess's friends, she and Hawkins would begin to receive invitations from other members of the beau monde.

The York Street house must be prepared to receive company as soon as possible. Furniture posed no difficulty. Hawkins had some pieces in his bachelor lodgings, which would do for his study and some of the other rooms. The furniture in the Old Gravel Lane house was his, too, and of excellent quality. She could take her time furnishing the nursery. The dining room needed almost everything, as neither Ambrose's rooms nor the Old Gravel Lane house had a large enough table. Gravel Lane's furniture was good but insufficient for the new house's larger drawing room. Hawkins had told her to buy whatever she wanted, and certainly she would have to purchase a quantity of things. But she meant to ask Henry if she might have some of the furniture in Petty Normande's attics. To be able to say "That coffer belonged to the Normande who died at Bosworth Field," or "That bed came with Lady Jane Angwin, who was one of Queen Elizabeth's ladies until her marriage" would be very satisfying.

She would ask Hawkins to accompany her to the furniture warehouses to choose the necessary new items. Not to consult one who would be using the furniture would be a mistake. She would enjoy having his company for those excursions, too.

Then there was the kitchen. It had a work table, perhaps because it was too large to be removed without being taken apart. The previous owner had taken everything else. Emily had no difficulty listing what was needed for the dining room, but the kitchen was terra incognita. She could plan a menu for any occasion; she could not cook so much as a boiled egg herself. During Emily's infrequent visits to the Petty Normande kitchen, she had not paid much attention to how it was furnished. One had a cook (or sometimes two), kitchen maids, scullery maids, a kitchen porter, and for all she knew, other kitchen staff as well. She would ask the cook here at the Old Gravel Lane house for advice, and Anne Guysbridge, too. They would be holding dinner parties which would require more servants and possibly different utensils. They would need a turnspit dog or two. Asking about kitchen wares would make a good excuse for calling upon the Duchess of Guysbridge.

Chapter 13

Married life was unexpectedly satisfying. Hawkins had been prepared for the cool courtesy one found in many arranged marriages, no more than a business partnership. Certainly Emily was ladylike, composed, and more than capable of organizing their home and social life. He had wed her for those qualities. She was not Olivia Cantarell, yet she possessed other attractive features, though he could not quite define them, apart from her enthusiasm for bed sport. No need to keep a mistress now! Apart from that delightful discovery, she was grateful, less for the material advantages he offered than for his attention. After two weeks of marriage, she still displayed surprise when he asked her opinion or set her cape around her shoulders. *Damn my eyes, has no one ever paid her any notice?*

He was still smiling as he strolled into the Lucky Bastards' club room.

"Ho, the honeymoon is not over yet," Andrews called out, and several others greeted him with similar remarks.

Marston surged up from a table a few feet away, his face set and suffused with angry blood. "You son of a bitch," Marston snarled and struck him a clout on the jaw so unexpected it knocked him down.

It had been years since he'd been in a brawl, but earlier experience had given him quick reactions. He rolled aside as the others grabbed Marston by the arms before he could kick Hawkins senseless. Those intervening would have risked their own injury in a real fight, but fortunately for all concerned, no weapons were involved. He scrambled to his feet, gingerly feeling his jaw. No teeth loosened, as best he could tell. "Damn you, Marston. What's this about?"

Before Marston could reply, all were frozen by the brisk tap of footsteps and Mistress Hardraw's demand, "What's this, then? I'll not have the furniture broke, as well you know." The captain stopped trying to shake off the hands restraining him, though his fists were still clenched and his eyes narrowed.

Someone offered, " 'Tisn't furniture, Joan, only Hawkins."

"He's lost me the wench I meant to marry," Marston snapped, cutting across this quip.

"Well, if you mean to fight, you must leave my premises. I don't mind smashed dishes or furniture once in a while, but I won't tolerate blood on the floor. It's too hard to clean up. Out, now. Shoo!"

Grissom, one of Marston's friends who had often invested in his voyages, suggested they should repair to the Anchor for flip or hot punch, with fewer women and rules.

"Best let them go ahead," Pruitt muttered in his ear. "What was that about?"

"I'm damned if I know."

****

The painting and minor renovations done, they moved to York Street. The main rooms were habitable, and a few of her acquaintances had already called upon Emily. For the most part, they were the ones of lesser consequence, who might see an advantage in currying favor with the wife of a wealthy man, and of course, the inveterate gossips could not stay away. However, the duchess had visited her also. The sight of the coach with the Guysbridge arms on the doors would do them no harm with their neighbors.

Ambrose Hawkins continued to surprise her. He had commissioned glass-doored cabinets for his Chinese collection after consulting with her as to where they should be located in the new house, a courtesy she had not expected. Now she had seen his porcelain and jade, it was obvious his selection of her betrothal ring had not been an accident. He had excellent taste. His liking for brilliant colors in suits and waistcoats was not precisely a fault, as many a popinjay dressed as richly and far more garishly. 'Twas only his height and muscular body made his dress sometimes startling. His occasional lapses of taste or manners all seemed to result from trying too hard to fit in among men of higher rank and greater sophistication. Fortunately, he was amenable to tactful hints.

And the servants liked him, not a minor consideration. Her husband seldom complained about small matters, and he was often thoughtful. Knowing the cook at Old Gravel Lane had family living nearby, he intended to recommend her to the new tenants. Although the thought of marrying a cit, even with roots in the lower gentry, had appalled her at first, the marriage was turning out better than she could have dreamed.

And that judgment was without taking into account their private dealings, which she could not contemplate without wanting to wriggle in an unladylike, even indecent, manner. The thought led to blushing and wishing the day were more advanced. To the later evening, in fact. Ambrose could be almost poetic at such moments. Whatever had those married women been thinking of, when she overheard them imply the marriage bed was merely the tedious price one paid for security, one's own home, and children? The physical pleasures of the wedded state had figured largely in Olivia Easterday's explanation of marital intimacy.

Having no social engagement this evening, they supped at an unfashionably early hour, for a man in business often kept country hours. Ambrose went to his office in Wapping in the mornings and sometimes did not return until late afternoon. Emily did not mind. She was still adapting to married life with an extremely rich man who was happy to let her shop for furnishings and a new wardrobe for herself.

She smiled as she stitched at a petit point cushion cover for a chair in her husband's bookroom. After studying his collection of Chinese objects, she had copied a scene from a lacquered cabinet showing odd, awkward-looking ships in an exotic harbor. She hoped he would like it, as it embodied both maritime and Chinese themes.

He was occupied with putting pieces of his collection into the new glass-fronted cabinets. She looked up to find him pondering a cylindrical vase.

"It's very plain," she remarked. "However, I am beginning to see the attraction of the Chinese style."

"It's a scholar's brush pot. They write with brushes, rather than quills. Olivia Easterday told me what it was, and that the design of pine, plum, and bamboo signified long life. I think I would like to display it with other desk accessories. A brush-washing pot, brush rest, and inkstone. I will have to ask her if there are other things which would be found on a Chinese desk. She is amazingly knowledgeable."

"I thought Mistress Easterday was somewhat cool to you at our wedding," Emily remarked.

Hawkins laughed. "I'm sorry to say she had reason to be. I courted her before Easterday did, and she took offense at my methods."

"Surely it is unreasonable to expect all gentlemen to solicit a lady's affections in precisely the same way."

He smiled ruefully. "I started out well, I think, but then I made a mistake. I was impatient."

"And stole a kiss or two? Embraced her?" Why Ambrose would have courted Olivia Easterday, who was not a great beauty and possessed no remarkable charm, was a mystery. But gentlemen were odd.

"I beg you will not mention this to anyone else, but I abducted her with the intent of…er, encouraging her to marry me."

"Lud! And yet she would not?" Or had Captain Easterday thwarted the attempt? He appeared to be a man of resolve. Had there been a duel?

"She produced a pistol. I had no doubt she would shoot me if I did not desist."

"Lud!" Emily repeated. "What shocking conduct. How could she?" Thank goodness Olivia had succeeded in discouraging Hawkins, thus saving him for Emily.

"Quite easily. It was very bad of me."

"But for a lady to threaten a gentleman with a pistol is all but inconceivable. Yet Captain Easterday was willing to have her."

"I believe he would have admired her for it, as I

did, though it was not her courage which first charmed me. I was drawn to her knowledge of Chinese art. Lord, I've met East India Company supercargoes less expert than she. The incident has caused some restraint between us. I'm hopeful she will forgive me in time, given that she was willing to attend our wedding."

"I wonder you should have courted me, given that I lack familiarity both with pistols and with Chinese goods." To be second choice to a female who engaged in commerce, was plain, and lacking in charm, was not flattering.

Her husband's expression suggested he had only then realized that to praise another woman to his wife was tactless. "It was after she refused me I realized that we would not have dealt well together. She was unwilling to let me control her company and disliked the idea of cultivating the beau monde. I wanted a lady who would be my hostess. Easterday seems not to object to a wife who tends her own business interests. She has compromised with him by doing it from their home. For the most part."

"Remarkable," she allowed. But she could not easily give up her annoyance, in spite of reflecting that she had Hawkins and a life which was almost exactly what any well-bred lady would dream of. Feeling unable to conceal her pique, she pleaded a sick headache and retired to her beautifully appointed bedchamber. It was ridiculous to be hurt by her husband's admiration for another woman; such heart-burnings were for love matches, not marriages of convenience, however comfortable.

Chapter 14

From *The Evening Post*: *Yesterday evening about nine o'clock, Captain Joel Marston, owner of the brigantines* Marigold *and* Belle, *was taken ill at a ridotto held at the Haymarket Theater and died soon thereafter. Captain Marston having been a man of no more than thirty years of age and in good health, an inquest is to be held tomorrow.*

From the inquest:

Q. Dr. Willard, Captain Marston was brought to you after his collapse, I think?

A. He was, though there was nothing I could do for him.

Q. Did you form any opinion as to the cause of death? That is, was it most probably disease or an apoplexy or some other cause?

A. I cannot state with any certainty the precise cause of death.

Q. Sir, the phrasing of your reply suggests you have a theory, at least. Please share it with us.

A. When I examined the body, I found a slit of several inches in the decedent's left calf. The cut was not deep enough to cause death, and there was little blood loss.

Q. Would you say this wound occurred shortly before death?

A. It must certainly have occurred between the

time Captain Marston put on his domino and his fainting at the Haymarket Opera House, as his domino displayed the same cut as his stocking and body.

Q. Is it possible that this injury, while not fatal of itself, led to an apoplexy or heart seizure?

A. Sir, in medicine many things are possible. However, I would not expect a man of the captain's age, habitus, and occupation to die of so minor a wound when, by the scars I found on his body, he had survived far worse. I should add that on the domino and stocking and on the skin surrounding the wound, I found a dark paste or pitchy material which I could not identify.

This statement caused a stir.

Q. Silence, please. Doctor, do you imply that this substance may have caused the death?

A. I can state that it almost certainly did, as I could not otherwise account for the death or for the presence of this paste. I therefore obtained a rat from a ratcatcher, applied a bit of the substance to a knife, and made a shallow incision on the rat's side. The creature ceased its struggles within moments, and within a few minutes, it was dead.

Q. Good God! I beg your pardon. This is very startling. We owe you a debt of gratitude for your investigation. May we take it that 'tis your opinion the death was caused by poison introduced by the cut?

A. So I suspect.

Q. Can you tell us what poison it was?

A. No, sir. Poisons are usually given in food or drink. I am unaware of any which would be administered as this one was. However, I am not an expert on the subject of poisoning.

Q. Can you tell us what sort of weapon was used?

A. Not with any particularity, though I can state that it must have been exceedingly sharp to make so clean a cut in the domino and stocking. It might perhaps be a very finely honed razor or even a surgical knife. Which is not to imply the owner was either a barber or a surgeon.

This was said with faint, dry humor.

Another witness:

Q. Mr. Jessup, how long had you been with Captain Marston when he fell to the floor?

A. I met him as he entered the Opera House, and we proceeded toward the Long Room. No more than a few minutes.

Q. Was there no warning of his impending death?

A. He complained when I first encountered him that someone had brushed past behind him in the crowd as he approached the entrance. "Some fool who can't wear a sword without its lifting a female's skirt or tripping someone gave me a blow on the leg as he passed," he said. We spoke to a fellow we both knew in the entry and began to climb the stair. I noticed then Marston rubbed his eyes once, and he seemed somewhat unsteady on his feet. I would have thought him in his cups except that I'd seen no sign of it at first. At the top of the stairs, he dropped as if he'd been shot.

From *The Evening Post*: *The death three nights ago of Captain Joel Marston at the Haymarket ridotto has been ruled at the inquest as homicide by a person or persons unknown, by means of poison. Anyone having knowledge relating to Captain Marston's death is requested to inform the Bow Street Magistrate of the same.*

Chapter 15

At first when the constables came for Hawkins, he was simply numb with surprise. Thank God the officers had made no attempt to lay hands upon him: he would have fought. He had not lost the ingrained reflexes of his earlier years. The men were not discourteous, merely requesting that he accompany two of them to Bow Street to be questioned by the magistrate, while the other two searched his office.

They allowed him time to issue a string of instructions to his head clerk regarding the day's business while his clerks sat frozen in shock. He was a very rich man and therefore entitled to more consideration than a laborer or common tradesman.

Timothy had come out of his closet of an office in one corner of the clerks' room and stood by, waiting to receive orders of a different sort.

"Tell Captain Easterday. Let Lady Emily know I may be late getting home."

Timothy gave a nod. "You may need money," he said.

Hawkins considered the handful of crowns, shillings, and smaller coins in his pocket, amounting to something over a guinea, and made a detour to his cashbox.

The numbness turned to bewilderment during the questioning as he understood he was suspected of

Marston's murder. Why would he kill Marston? It made no sense. It was not until afterwards, when they reached Newgate Prison—in a hackney he paid for—that he realized the seriousness of his situation. Then he was simply furious, as he had not been since before he left home as a boy. Many times in the intervening years he had been angry: as a seaman when he'd been flogged, later when he lost a cargo or a ship, when he lost Olivia Cantarell. The only thing he could compare to his current white-hot rage was when he'd been forced to sail with pirates.

Thinking about why the one ate into his very soul when the other merely impelled him to swear bitterly and perhaps throw something had at least the benefit of occupying his mind. Those first hours in Newgate, he had no commercial venture to plan and nothing to read, no worry of sufficient weight to offset his present trouble.

At least he was not as miserable as most of the poor devils here. God help the prisoners who had no money nor any means of getting some. Everything in Newgate came at a price: decent food, bedding, gin, removal of chains. By means of a bribe to the keepers, he had been able to get into a private cell immediately, sparing him a wretched night in the damp, filthy holding cell. His accommodations would cost him more than any inn in England would dare charge and would still be grim, but at least he had a bed with a flock mattress and blankets, provided for another fee.

By the time the keeper showed Marcus Easterday to his cell, Hawkins had managed to regain an appearance of nonchalance.

"Thank God I made my will," Hawkins said. He

hoped he sounded amused rather than despairing. "Take the chair, Easterday. I'll sit on the bed." Luckily he had been able to pay for a roomy cell in Newgate's "Castle" section, and luxuries such as bedding, a chair, and a table. Mayhap he should pay for a second chair or a stool.

"We'll try to make sure it is not necessary for some years yet."

"Do you claim no innocent man has ever hanged?" Hawkins smiled crookedly.

"No. But most of them are poor, some are stupid, and few have friends capable of assisting in their defense. You have at least three advantages over them."

"I am innocent, Easterday."

"That is your fourth advantage."

"Even so, there's no guarantee I'll get off. Emily will be worried. See that she knows she is my heir and need not worry about money. If I hang, help her sell the company and manage the rest. Emily isn't like O— Mistress Easterday."

"We'll see to it she's not cheated or the prey of a fortune hunter. Though I don't despair of your coming through this."

"How? I can't prove I didn't murder the fellow. My reputation is against me."

"Who's your attorney? He must engage a barrister. I will try to find out who else had cause to kill Marston."

"Wadsworth, Chancery Lane, by Cursitors Alley. I have heard no talk about anyone having a killing grievance against Marston." A snort. "My friends at the Fortunate Gentleman's Coffee House were quick enough to talk about our encounter."

"You've had other things to do than gossip. You had a fistfight at the coffee house, I know. Was that why you were thought a suspect?"

"Hardly a fistfight. He took me by surprise and knocked me down. The others stopped it going further. Or the proprietress did. A scuffle doesn't lead to a killing unless it happens by mischance during the fight."

"He took you by surprise and knocked you down?" Easterday repeated.

"I was speaking with several of the Lucky Bastards—that's our informal club, all men who have prospered in spite of disadvantages—and Marston came up and gave me a clout on the jaw. If I'd seen it coming, 'twouldn't have stretched me on my back."

"Why did he hit you?"

"I don't know."

Easterday stared at Hawkins. "Did he say nothing?"

"If he did, I can't recall it. His friends rushed him out. Mistress Hardraw doesn't like a brawl, even if we pay for the breakage." Behavior in some coffee houses might occasionally be disorderly, but at Mistress Hardraw's Fortunate Gentleman, her customers were seldom worse than boisterous and profane.

"There was no dispute between you? Over a cargo or a wench, mayhap?"

"No, I can't—I'm wrong. Three weeks or a month ago, we had words. He claimed I'd slandered him to the papa of some girl he wanted to marry. But we parted on civil terms. Or so I believed."

"Had you?"

"Slandered him? No. I gave the fellow as good an

account of Marston as I could. You know Marston; he's no saint. Was no saint. I praised what I could without lying."

"I've heard rumors about Marston."

Hawkins was no saint himself. He wondered what Easterday would have said of him if asked. "I think after he hit me, he claimed I'd lost him the wench."

"Marston killing you over a supposed slander might be understandable. For you to kill Marston because of a blow seems unlikely. Who was the girl? Or her father? He might consider he had reason to kill Marston if he felt his daughter had been insulted or her prospects affected by Marston's courtship."

"Some grocer named Cole. A Puritan sort of fellow. I can't think how Marston crossed paths with him. I gathered from something Marston said the girl was no beauty but well-dowered."

"A grocer seems an unlikely murderer. What of this poison you are accused of using?"

Hawkins shrugged. "I know nothing more about it than was published in the *Evening Post*."

"How went your interview with de Veil?"

Hawkins barked a laugh. "Interview? Inquisition, more like. Three hours if 'twere a minute. He asked the same questions again and again, creeping up on them from different sides. I couldn't make out what he was about, except that he suspected me."

"Did you tell him everything you've told me?"

"He didn't ask why Marston hit me, so the subject of Cole didn't arise."

"It seems strange he would not inquire about the cause of Marston's anger."

"As to that, he had clearly spoken with some of the

Lucky Bastards and knew about our earlier dispute. He must have heard that we're not noted for being a Methodist meeting house," he added with a faint smile. "He was interested in where I'd sailed in the Carib sea. Damned if I know why."

"I had best learn something of Cole. Who was present when Marston assaulted you? One of them may remember something useful."

"I was talking with Pruitt. Grissom took Marston away; perhaps Marston said something to him which would make sense of it. The others...I can't think of them all, but speak to the proprietress, Joan Hardraw. She's like to remember."

"I will. Now, I know little of law beyond that relating to commerce, but it seems to me that the best way of proving you innocent is to show you were in company at the time Marston was murdered. Where were you that evening?"

Hawkins exclaimed, "How the devil do I know? It was weeks ago."

"Less than a week."

Strike him dead, Easterday was correct. The stress of facing trial and the gallows was making him stupid. It was common in boys and young men new to shipboard life. Until they were accustomed, they tended to lose their heads in a crisis. At sea, Hawkins would be steady as any stone. Here he was as untried as a youth on his first voyage.

"Did you read of his death in the paper?" Easterday inquired.

"Damme, yes! I was surprised and not surprised, both at the same time."

"The news was published the day after his death.

Where were you when you read of it?"

"I must have been at the Fortunate Gentleman's Coffee House. Barnes brought it to my attention. Edward Barnes. He's made a fortune importing furs. Asked if I knew of Marston's death."

"What time of day was it?"

"The afternoon. Three or four of the clock, I suppose. Barnes was eating something. A mutton chop, I think, brought in from the chop house next door. I wasn't hungry. I'd eaten at an ordinary at noon, and I'd have to go home to supper soon."

"Married life does bring changes," Easterday remarked.

Hawkins closed his eyes. "I'd have started for home sooner because I hadn't seen her at breakfast. I usually do, unless we've been out late the night before. I was putting off going home, or I wouldn't have stopped at the coffee house. Something I said the evening before offended her, and she went to bed with a megrim." He scowled. "Then the night before must have been the night Marston died."

"Her testimony wouldn't do much good, as the court would assume that she would lie for you, but your servants can testify you were at home. Or if you went out by yourself, who would know? Your coachman? Friends or acquaintances at your destination? It's a good thing the period in which Marston's wounding must have taken place is quite limited."

Hawkins's heart sank. "I don't think anyone knows. After Emily went up to her chamber, I went out to walk."

"Your butler or footman would know when you left."

"Damn my eyes, Easterday, I know that much! It was an hour or an hour and a half, maybe, after we'd eaten. We hadn't been in the withdrawing room long before I said something that hurt Emily's feelings. So it must have been eight or earlier when I went out." Which would have been plenty of time to reach the Haymarket, he realized.

"Did you know Marston would be attending the ridotto?"

"No. I hadn't seen him since he knocked me down. Or heard from anyone that he would attend, either, if you were going to ask."

The remarkable thing was that being accused of the crime made him feel guilty, as if he had actually committed it or done something to cause it.

"I wasn't going to ask. If you had killed him, you'd lie. I don't think you did. You'd have come at him straight on."

"Easterday, is there any real chance? How can you or anyone clear me?"

"As you did not kill him and had no apparent reason to do it, I am hopeful. I wish we could use the, ah, late John Barlicorn's sources. Alack, the new Earl of Barlyon has no connections in Wapping and Shadwell, even if he were not rusticating in Kent. It might be worthwhile trying Solomon to see if a financial motive existed."

"Ay, that's a thought. Here's another: ask my head clerk for Timothy. Have you a pencil and a scrap of paper?"

Easterday produced both pencil and a sheet of paper from a small notebook. Hawkins scrawled, *Timothy—Follow Capt. Easterday's orders and report progress to him. Hawk.*

"Just Timothy, with no last name?"

"His name's Zaccheus Timothy. He prefers Timothy. He's good at ferreting out secrets, following, all sorts of things, and he'll be less conspicuous doing it than you or anyone you could employ. He can loiter in the same place for several days and never be noticed. He'll be a beggar one day, a peddler the next, a clodhopper up from the country gawking at the sights the day after that. You'll find him useful. If you will deal with my man of business, attorney, de Veil, and any who need handling by a man of status, he'll deal with the rest. Pass on anything you learn to Timothy; he can report to me."

"Good. I plan to talk to Roger Markham. He may know something of the parties." Easterday smiled. "I'll hope the cold air carries the prison reek from my clothes before I reach his house."

It was probably a vain hope. Those who passed by Newgate covered their faces with their handkerchiefs. Few if any physicians would enter Newgate at any season, lest they take a contagion from the mephitic air.

"Is there anything you'd like sent in?"

"Writing materials. A book or two. I've already sent Timothy to ask for changes of clothing."

"Towels, bowl, and pitcher? I don't think they'll allow you a razor."

"I can pay to be shaved, but towels and utensils for my wash stand"—he gestured ironically at the table—"would be welcome."

"I'll see to it."

Chapter 16

Emily was gazing at a wall in the morning room, wondering what sort of painting would best suit it. A landscape would not clamor for attention as a classical or military subject would. Yes, a landscape, definitely: pleasant and undemanding. And she should suggest that Ambrose have his portrait painted. While not precisely handsome, he possessed strong features and a good form. Heavy jowls or straining waistcoats detracted from a portrait. One should not judge a man's character by his appearance, but still—

The under-footman, Thomas, entered and cleared his throat nervously. He needed more polish, being yet new to his position. The butler would supply it in time, no doubt.

"Lady Emily, ma'am, there's a fellow asking to speak to you. He says he's a clerk, come from Mr. Hawkins."

How peculiar. "I will see him here, but mind you stay in the passage and do not close the door." She rose and stood by her chair to assert her position as mistress of the house.

The man bore no resemblance to the duchy's clerk and those she had observed in the law office serving the Saintonge family, all of whom were bland, self-effacing, and respectful. She did not quite like the sharpness of his gray eyes, which met hers as if he were her equal. He might do well enough for a shipping company, where he was unlikely to meet anyone who would be offended by his demeanor.

"Your ladyship, my name is Timothy. I take care of things outside the office for Mr. Hawkins. He sent me to ask you to have a valise packed for him. I can take it with me if you'll have his valet see to it at once. And it will give me time to explain."

"A valise? Why? Is he going on a journey?" The fellow's voice, while not obviously educated, indicated some polish. He was utterly unremarkable in appearance and clothing. Timothy might be anything at all, depending on how he was dressed. Only his voice would give him away. A thought occurred to Emily: perhaps he could change his voice as easily as his clothing.

"I'm sorry to bring this news, my lady. Some constables came to take Mr. Hawkins to the magistrate. He told his head clerk to send to Captain Easterday and for me to let you know he'd be late getting home. But I had a quiet word with the constables who stayed to search, and I don't reckon the magistrate will turn him loose. It's Lombard Street to an eggshell he'll be committed to prison to wait for the quarter sessions."

"Why? What is the charge?" Something to do with the rumor of piracy Cousin Henry had mentioned?

"There's no charge yet, I don't think, but the magistrate wants to question Mr. Hawkins about Captain Marston's death at the Haymarket ridotto."

The world stopped around Emily. She simply stood, like a rustic gaping at a calf with two heads. Then she stretched out a hand to rest on the chair back.

"Do they think he killed this man?" How could this

be happening?

"It's likely he'll be bound over for trial. The magistrate wouldn't send four constables otherwise. Two to go back with Mr. Hawkins and two to stay and search the office."

Entwhistle, the butler, came to the door. He must somehow have divined the existence of a problem, in the way good servants sometimes could. "Lady Emily, shall I send for your maid? And tell Pirtle to pack for the master?"

He had heard part of Timothy's disclosure, then. A lady should maintain an unruffled calm, particularly before servants and the lower classes. The need to give instructions to the servants freed her from her paralysis. "I do not require my maid. Entwhistle, do you know anything of this?"

Entwhistle murmured hesitantly, " 'Tis talked of in the coffee houses and everywhere, ma'am. Captain Joel Marston dropping down dead at the ridotto about a week ago, I mean."

She had heard nothing of the matter. But why be surprised? While the gentlemen might well hear of it in the coffee houses and newssheets, they would not mention it to their ladies. The only news and gossip a decent lady heard concerned the closed circle of society and the court. Why, anything could happen outside that safe preserve, and one might be utterly ignorant of it.

"Men and women do sometimes die suddenly. What is startling in such a death?"

Timothy spoke up before the butler could draw breath. "The captain was in the prime of life and in good health, my lady, which meant an inquest. They found he'd been stabbed with a poisoned blade. That means murder."

"Good God!" An inappropriate exclamation but really, there was no suitable response to news that might have come from the court of the Borgias. "But why would my husband be accused?"

Entwhistle's eyes slid toward the clerk, or whatever he was, who finally said, "Mr. Hawkins and the captain were acquainted."

"I am acquainted with hundreds of people. Would I be suspected of murdering one of them?"

"No, my lady, it's this way: since the inquest, friends of them both say they came to blows in a coffee house, and Marston knocked Mr. Hawkins down."

"Oh, men. Even a sheltered lady knows men will be fighting, usually over nothing."

"There's talk about Mr. Hawkins being a pirate years ago, which isn't strictly true, as I understand, though I didn't know him then," Timothy added. "It's true he's a hard man, but no one who works for him believes he'd murder in that skulking way. He'd do it to the fellow's face, fair and square."

No doubt Hawkins's loyal clerk thought this reassuring; it struck Emily as unsettling. "Mr. Hawkins is a gentleman. Gentlemen do not murder."

Entwhistle and Timothy traded glances as if she had uttered an absurdity.

Entwhistle cleared his throat. "I expect the magistrate's been misled, and there's nothing to it, my lady."

"I'm sure you are correct. However, it will do no harm to be prepared. Have Pirtle pack a valise for Mr. Hawkins for…well, for all contingencies. Where should it be delivered, Timothy?"

"Newgate Prison, ma'am."

She must have failed to conceal her horror at realizing the need for a valise was because Ambrose might be detained by the magistrate, which meant prison. Of course it would be Newgate.

Entwhistle drew nearer, close enough to catch her if she swooned. "Perhaps you should sit down, Lady Emily?"

Emily took this well-intentioned advice in spite of feeling that a lady, a duke's daughter, should stand firm in every disaster, be it riot in the servants' quarters or a husband in prison. Her knees had inexplicably lost their strength. All her life she had avoided scandal. Now, through no fault of her own—Never mind that now; Hawkins could not possibly be guilty. Or at least, surely he could not be hanged or transported. She gathered her straying wits, while Entwhistle went soft-footed to the drawing room door and spoke to Thomas.

"What must I do, apart from providing Mr. Hawkins changes of clothing? When will he be tried? Who will see to his business?"

Having given Thomas instructions, Entwhistle returned to stand near Emily.

Timothy said, "As to that, my lady, the rest's taken care of. Mr. Jenkins, our head clerk, can manage Hawkins & Company. Mr. Hawkins has enough gelt for garnish-money and to pay for a private room and have his meals sent in from a tavern, so all's well."

It did not sound well to Emily. However, she could do nothing now but bear herself with dignity and be loyal to her husband. After the trial…she would not think of that until it came to pass.

She sent the clerk to the kitchen for refreshment

and to wait until Pirtle had packed a bag, Entwhistle having suggested that Thomas, inexperienced as he was, might not be a good choice to send to Newgate. Then she was left alone to contemplate the disaster her marriage had become. Despite her resolve not to think so far ahead, she could not stop thinking of it. Surely the authorities seldom took an innocent person into custody?

Fortunately, as she was sitting with her embroidery, setting a stitch but intermittently between the scenarios playing out in her brain, Entwhistle announced Olivia Easterday. He had failed to confirm that "Lady Emily is at home," a breach of protocol for which she found it easy to forgive him. She needed the distraction.

"I insisted on seeing you" were Mistress Easterday's first words on entering, cutting across Emily's greeting. "You must by now have heard about your husband's arrest."

"Yes." She waved toward a chair. "Please, sit. Entwhistle, send up a tea tray."

"We thought, as you have no female relatives nearby, you might need a woman's companionship."

"Thank you for thinking of it." Sympathy was useless, but to have a caller to take her mind off the future was welcome. After Hawkins had stated his admiration for Mistress Easterday, the memory of her kindness at the wedding breakfast had dimmed. Mayhap Olivia Easterday's peculiarly unfeminine support would prove more helpful than the sighs, wrung handkerchiefs, and pitying eyes of more genteel ladies.

"Marcus—Captain Easterday—has gone to see Thomas de Veil, the magistrate, and will also see your husband's attorney to arrange for a barrister. Be prepared to have your house searched by constables; I believe they are already searching the offices of Hawkins & Company."

Constables searching here? What would the neighbors think?

"If we are lucky, they will arrive while I am here. And if you wish, I will stay with you for a few days, until this is straightened out."

"Is the trial to be held so soon?" she managed to ask.

"I believe it is a month until the sessions. We hope Hawkins will not come to trial." She added after a brief but significant pause, "We hope to find a more likely suspect. Hawkins will probably not succumb to gaol fever in a private cell. I strongly suspect gaol fever is most likely to befall the prisoners who cannot afford an adequate diet and are packed in filthy cells. That is what Anne Guysbridge claims, at all events."

"Oh." Emily swallowed bile. Entwhistle arrived with the tea tray then, and she was able to concentrate on measuring out the tea from the locked canister and offering her guest Shrewsbury cakes while the tea brewed.

The door had barely closed behind Entwhistle when Mistress Easterday said, "My husband will have witnesses searched for and try to discover other suspects. Marston was a man who might well have made enemies."

"How do you take your tea, Mistress Easterday?"

"A little cream, please. No sugar. Do call me Olivia. I believe we got past formal usages at your wedding."

Emily passed the cup to her, thinking "no sugar" suited the woman very well. "I beg your pardon, the news has scattered my wits. We are friends." It was no fault of Olivia's that Hawkins admired her.

"Thank you, Emily. I fear this is not a situation which calls for conventional manners. Now, what can I do to help?"

"I don't know. What can anyone do? If there were witnesses, would they not have come forward already?"

"Not necessarily. Some people are reluctant to become involved. Some don't realize they have seen anything significant until they are asked."

"But is there any point?"

Olivia's pale brows rose. "Do you think he's guilty?"

"I don't know."

Her guest frowned a little, apparently unconcerned about causing wrinkles. "I suppose you didn't know Hawkins well before your marriage. Have you formed no opinion of his character since?"

That question was harder to answer. "He's generous. He has been very considerate." This seemed a grudging, tepid description of her husband. He displayed a sense of humor. He was often charming. But were any of those characteristics proof he would not murder?

"I know he has a hot temper and can be impetuous," Olivia said. "But I cannot imagine him murdering by stealth."

Which was what his clerk had maintained. She could not forebear to ask, "Do you know Hawkins well?" She must, if Ambrose had tried to abduct her.

"Quite well, as we are both in the shipping trade."

Her visitor's dry tone reminded Emily of the restraint she had sensed between Hawkins and Mistress Easterday at the wedding breakfast.

A pair of constables from the magistrate's court came and went, leaving Emily white and shaking. Only rigid self-control and Olivia Easterday's presence had carried her through the ordeal. Olivia insisted they watch the search "to keep them honest." By then, it was late afternoon.

The constables had taken away several knives and a spear which had hung in the bookroom. Olivia wrote out two copies of a detailed description of each, with the location from which it had been taken. The constables, thoroughly cowed, signed each sheet.

"We will keep one, and you have one for the magistrate. Come, Emily." Olivia escorted the men to the door and watched as the butler bolted it behind them.

Entwhistle addressed Emily, who would have been sitting paralyzed in her boudoir if not for Mistress Easterday's bracing presence. "I fear Cook has done little about supper, ma'am, the staff having been somewhat unsettled by events. There is soup, bread, fruit, cheese, and custard, and two places set in the dining room."

Emily had never felt less like eating, but she had a guest, and now that she considered it, they had not eaten or drunk anything since the morning's tea and cakes. "I think that will be adequate, Entwhistle." She turned to Olivia. "You will stay to supper? I will have our coach take you home, after." She would miss her calm and her brisk good sense. She herself would never have thought of getting a receipt for the weapons.

Olivia smiled at her. "I am afraid I did not wait for an invitation to stay with you but sent my footman home to fetch a portmanteau. As you have no companion or female friend who has come to bear you company, I thought it wrong to leave you alone tonight. Tomorrow you may wish to send for some friend or else, if you wish, I will stay."

"How kind you are, Olivia." Her relief must show in her face, and she could not even care. Her mother and governess could never have contemplated this situation and thus had never trained her to deal with it. "If Captain Easterday permits, I would be grateful for your company. The sad fact is, I don't think any of my friends will wish to stay with me under the circumstances. And if one did agree, she would be perfectly useless." If she were truthful, she must admit she had no friends in town, only acquaintances.

"The ability to make light conversation, flirt with one's fan, and embroider is not of much assistance in some situations," Olivia agreed as they took their places in the dining room. "I am going to commit another breach of convention. There are things we must discuss."

The footman served their soup.

"You may go, Gregory. We will serve ourselves now."

"They will all know the worst soon enough, Emily. However, it will be best if you address them after supper to tell them what to expect. Assuming they do not already know."

"The worst?" She froze, the spoon suspended halfway to her lips.

"If you must go out, you should leave by the

kitchen entrance and meet your coach in the alley."

"I think I must visit Hawkins where…where he is kept."

"By no means. Emily, even I would not visit Newgate, unless I had no one else to go on my behalf. Marcus will go, indeed, has likely done so already, and clerks from Hawkins & Company can deliver fresh clothing and carry messages."

"But my vows to be loyal in sickness and in health presumably include being in prison."

"My dear, do you really think Ambrose Hawkins would want to see you in such a place?"

He treated her as if she were made of the finest porcelain. "Perhaps not. I should write to him at least."

"That would be best."

"But whatever will I do, Olivia?" she burst out.

"First we will finish our supper. Then you can write your letter while I make a list of things to do next."

"I mean when he's hanged." There! It was spoken.

"It is by no means certain he will be found guilty. None of the knives or weapons they took away today are likely to have been the one used to wound Marston. Wield a spear outside the Haymarket? Hardly. If a knife was used, the attacker must have stooped to reach Marston's lower leg and that should have been noticed. We will try if we can find anyone who saw the incident. By 'we,' I mean Marcus will have inquiries made. Hawkins has other friends as well who may be able to help."

"But how?"

"By finding other men who might have wished to kill Marston, and who could have had access to some exotic poison. Which should provide a number of suspects, as many of Marston's enemies would likely be sailors or others associated with the shipping trade."

"Then there is a chance?"

"Yes, and we are fortunate that the murder was in Westminster, for say what you may about magistrates in general, de Veil is hardworking. If presented with other possibilities, he will pursue them."

Chapter 17

Easterday was gone. Had Hawkins betrayed his fear? He thought not. As a sailor, earlier in his life, he had faced death by disease, shipwreck, attack, and simple shipboard accident, without the thought worrying him much. He'd been younger then, and boys thought themselves immortal, unless proof to the contrary was all around. Now he had more to lose, he could not be so careless of his life. Somehow, too, the prospect of hanging was worse than those other possible deaths. Hangings were a popular public spectacle. The prisoner usually died slowly with all the attendant bodily reactions of strangulation before a crowd of hundreds. He regretted ever having attended one.

He did not expect life to be fair. Still, the parsons' contention that the righteous got their reward in Heaven and the wicked went to Hell was little consolation here and now. And what of ordinarily virtuous people whose circumstances led them to commit crime rather than starve? Small comfort for them! Not that he was an innocent, except of Marston's murder. He had prospered, not always by strictly fair means, because the odds ran against the poor and those who lacked powerful friends. In his own defense, he had never taken advantage of anyone who hadn't deserved it.

The churning of his brain, when he finally lay

down to sleep, kept him wakeful. He lay under two blankets (because the cross-barred window which admitted fresh air also let in the cold and damp), grappling with corrosive bitterness. It reminded him of the fury he had experienced when he had been dragooned into a pirate crew through no fault of his own. Yes, and as a boy when he and his brother had been the victims of his stepfather's carelessness and bad decisions.

Facing trial and execution for a crime he had not committed, Hawkins found that his own helplessness added an extra depth of anguish. A memory from his youth surfaced with startling clarity: a summer Sunday, the windows open to let in hot, sweet-scented air, and the vicar talking about Job's afflictions. Hawkins had paid some attention as the sermon was more interesting than usual and brought to mind his own personal misfortune, his mother's new husband. He didn't recall the lesson they were supposed to draw from Job's misery.

Later misfortunes left him less angry than merely annoyed. He had been flogged for speaking his mind at a volume the captain could not ignore, and he had only himself to blame for losing his chance with Olivia. Even the loss of one of his ships in bad weather had resulted from his decision to entrust it to a captain he knew took risks. The man had never previously lost a ship, and if his decision to leave port in spite of incoming bad weather had not led to shipwreck, Hawkins would have made a tidy profit. They had both gambled and lost. He had brought those problems on himself. He could live with that. Or in this case, die.

And there was nothing he could do to save himself.

He would have to rely on the assistance of Easterday and Timothy, and whoever they recruited to assist them. He wished John Barlicorn were in town. Barlicorn's connections in the criminal world would have been able to find out who else might want to kill Marston. But Barlicorn had departed several months ago, on hearing he was the late Earl of Barlyon's heir. He had not yet returned. When he did, he could never resume his position as an archrogue, with sources of information all over town. Timothy could be trusted to hear any rumors about Marston's enemies in the Pool of London, while Easterday meant to search out motives and witnesses. That would have to do. It was only a month or a little more until the next quarter sessions opened, when the matter would come to trial.

****

Emily held a collection of sermons, which seemed more appropriate than reading a novel under the circumstances, though she would not have been able to concentrate on a novel either. The sermons might have been some consolation if they had related in any way to a man like her husband. He had apparently not been a dutiful son, he was sometimes profane, and while he made no graven images, he was not regular in attending divine services. On the other hand, he gave to two charities that she knew of, he was fair to the servants, and kind—more than kind—to her. But he might have been a pirate, he had admitted to abducting Olivia, and as for turning the other cheek? Very likely not. How did the virtues weigh against the sins? And could he have killed Marston? She would have questioned Olivia, discreetly, about Hawkins, but Olivia was writing letters at the little desk. Business correspondence, probably.

They were both startled when the butler announced Captain Easterday. When he took a seat on the divan, Olivia put aside her quill and joined him. Emily had seen no indication of sentiment in either Olivia or the captain, yet they seemed fond of each other. Even extremely fond, judging from how close Olivia was sitting to her husband. Could they be in love? If they were, they displayed none of the signs she associated with such an unregulated emotion as observed in ballrooms: the sighs, coy glances, smoldering gazes, obsession with the object of one's devotion. Only permissively reared girls newly out of the schoolroom and callow young men behaved thus, of course. They soon learned that one married for practical reasons, a far better basis for marriage. Yet her marriage had been made for sound financial reasons, and once again she had been abandoned by a man who should have protected her.

"Lady Emily, I've visited your husband. He is as comfortable as one can be in Newgate. I've spoken with his attorney about the possibility of bail, but it won't be granted, as the charge is murder. His attorney will hire a barrister for trial. Before then, we hope to find someone with a reason to kill Marston and thereby clear Hawkins."

"Thank you," she whispered. "But what if you cannot exonerate him? What am I to do if Hawkins is convicted?"

"His friends do not believe he is guilty, and we will do everything we can to prove him innocent."

"How many of those brought to trial are found innocent?" A lady did not follow news of criminal proceedings; her knowledge of such matters might come only from the prints of infamous crimes and criminals displayed in the windows of printers' shops, and from broadside ballads about executions.

"A good many are brought in innocent of minor crimes," Easterday replied. "Juries do not like to hang anyone for some small offense or one with which they sympathize. Those who are convicted likely have a history of crimes. Too, a defendant often has no resources to counter the charge against him: someone who is poor and uneducated cannot easily seek out witnesses who might clear him and is seldom eloquent when called upon to counter the charge. I will talk to your husband's friends and Marston's associates. One of them may know something to suggest a reason for the murder. Or at least to cast enough doubt upon his guilt that the jury will not convict him."

"Do you mean to advertise for witnesses, Marcus? Someone must have seen something."

"I will advertise, but many people are remarkably unobservant unless it's their duty to observe, and even then, if you have three witnesses, you may get three different accounts. A good many will have drunk deep before arriving at the Haymarket, and unless the killer was wielding a spear, the wounding may have passed unobserved. I've already met with a man Hawkins employs who can search for witnesses who may have seen something outside the theater. Tomorrow I hope to find out whether Marston made a will or had any relative who would be his heir and needs money."

"Then I suppose everything that can be done is being done, Captain. Thank you."

"I would like to find out more about a fellow

named Cole, a tradesman, as both of Marston's confrontations with Hawkins involved this Cole or his daughter. I'll speak with the men who saw the second confrontation. One might remember something helpful. Hawkins is unsure why Marston hit him. It may be that while his wits were scrambled, he missed the explanation. I hope to have better news to report in a day or two, Lady Emily."

Olivia patted his hand. "I have little doubt you will discover the truth." To Emily she said, "When I inherited my father's company, I encountered some difficulties, which Marcus set right."

"A good deal of the credit is due to you, my dear. Now, there are one or two other matters to discuss. Do you have some female relative who can stay with you, Lady Emily?"

Olivia answered. "As it happens, Lady Emily is deficient in female relatives who could come to support her. I will remain here for the foreseeable future."

She was not asking her husband's permission, but Easterday accepted her statement as though she had a right to make the decision. What a peculiar relationship.

"Ay, Lady Emily will need a friend while this business is in progress."

Emily swallowed. "But if all that fails?"

"Hawkins asked me to assure you that in the worst event, you will be well provided for. He made a new will on your wedding day. If he dies, you will inherit everything, apart from a few bequests to employees and charities. I am named as your trustee."

Emily sat speechless; it was so unexpected. Her family was not skilled at managing money. She would have expected her cousin to be made her trustee. Cousin

Henry might be making progress in learning economy and handling money, but she would have feared to be penniless again, with her inheritance under his control. Captain Easterday would be prudent, which relieved her of her fear of being cast once again on someone's charity.

"He made a will?"

"Certainly. His circumstances had changed. It was essential he provide for you."

"I cannot tell you how that relieves my mind." There remained the fear of being left alone. Duke's daughter or not, the wife of an executed murderer could do little but retire from society.

Captain Easterday rose with a barely perceptible sigh. "Now I really must drag myself away home." He and Olivia exchanged a long look.

Lud, they were in love. Who would have thought it?

Olivia sat bolt upright. "Marcus, what was that name?"

"What name?"

"You wanted to find out something about someone Marston and Hawkins argued about. What was his name?"

Captain Easterday appeared to gather his wits with difficulty. "Simon...no, Salem Cole. Why? Have you heard of him?"

"Salem Cole! We import raisins, currants, figs, coffee, pistachio nuts, and a few other items for his shop."

"Do you, indeed? Hawkins did say he was a grocer. But I understood the girl had a good dowry."

"She would. Cole's quite successful. He owns

Hodgeson's Fine Provisioners. He was a friend of my father's."

"Really? Do you know anyone who can find out..." Captain Easterday stopped abruptly. "I've forgotten what I meant to say."

Emily had been staring down at the book in her lap, to let them converse, as they seemed to have forgotten her presence. She should have withdrawn from the room earlier, but it would have been rude to leave guests alone. Though if Olivia was to be a house guest, it might be thought permissible. A moment of silence caused her to look up in time to catch an exchange of glances between the Easterdays.

Olivia bit her lower lip. "I will feel my way."

"You, Olivia?"

"Why not? I have not seen him since he came to my father's funeral. We need Naples biscuits and preserved fruits, and I am rather partial to pistachios. Where should I buy them if not from a Cantarell Shipping customer?"

"My dear," he protested.

How did shopping for imported foods follow the captain's uncompleted question, "Do you know anyone who can find out...""? Evidently Olivia had understood his meaning, however.

"I will take a footman with me to carry my parcels. Nothing can happen to a lady at a shop near St. James's Square."

"Will you promise to be careful?"

"I am always careful, Marcus." She must have noted Emily's puzzled expression, for she explained, "My husband worries, unnecessarily I must say, as we may be expecting a happy event some months from now."

This forthright mention of an intimate subject silenced Emily. As an unmarried lady she had hardly ever heard such a thing hinted at, certainly not in a man's presence. She would not be so forthright about an impending event of that sort, if such a condition ever befell her, which now seemed unlikely any time in the near future. She sighed. If Captain Easterday could not prove her husband's innocence, there would be a year of mourning, then who knew how long to attract the interest of some gentleman, before there could be any chance of finding herself in That Condition.

"In any event," Olivia added prosaically, "I cannot believe Salem Cole had anything to do with Marston's murder."

Easterday took his leave, pressing a kiss upon his wife's hand, clearly reluctant to leave.

"Captain, would you not care to stay for something to eat? The kitchen can supply at least a simple meal. I should have asked sooner, but my wits have been wandering, since—" She could not bear to end the sentence with "—my husband was charged with murder."

"Thank you, Lady Emily, but I have some business to attend to before I go home."

"Marcus, would it not be best if Lady Emily came to stay with us?" Olivia asked. She turned to Emily. "You have not lived here long, so I suppose it does not yet feel like home."

"I should not leave my husband's house. I should also not keep you from your home, Olivia."

"Removing as a temporary measure might be wise," Easterday said. "Once news of the arrest has spread, a mob may collect outside, staring and perhaps throwing rocks and other things. It happens sometimes. While the militia would turn out to disperse them, it would be unpleasant for you. More unpleasant than the situation already is."

"But how could I abandon our home?"

"You have a garrison of servants to defend the keep. If necessary, Hawkins's head clerk can send some of his less clerkly men to act as guards."

"Whatever you decide, I will not leave you alone, Emily. It would be more convenient for Marcus to report to you at our home, but your wishes must govern."

Undoubtedly it would be inconvenient for Captain Easterday to have to detour to York Street regularly. Worse, the Easterdays would miss each other's company. Emily could howl like a child with loneliness and terror and longing, but no well-bred lady made a display of her emotions.

"If it would not be too much of an imposition, I would be glad to stay with you. It's true this house does not yet feel like home, and at least you would not be separated from your husband."

"That's settled, then. Marcus, I'll stay here with Emily tonight, to give her maid an opportunity to pack."

Easterday departed, looking much more cheerful.

Wrung out by the day's events, Emily sent for Putnam and went upstairs soon after, leaving Olivia writing instructions to her shipping office clerks. Sitting at the dressing table while Putnam took the pins out of her hair, she said, "Pack what I will need for a stay of..." How long? Had Easterday said the quarter sessions would start in about a month? She could hardly impose on the Easterdays so long. "Two or three weeks, I suppose."

"Where will you go, my lady? So that I know what sort of garments will be necessary."

"Mistress Easterday has invited me to stay with them. I am told we may expect a vulgar mob outside this house, which would be very disagreeable."

"It would, indeed, your ladyship. Hmmph!" Putnam removed the last hairpins, letting Emily's hair fall down over her shoulders. She enjoyed the neatness of hair well pinned up, but by the end of the day, it was sometimes uncomfortable.

"As to what to pack, I shall need nothing elaborate as I will not be attending entertainments."

Putnam nodded, beginning to comb out her hair. "Your ladyship would not wish to be an object of curiosity or pity. As well to distance ourselves from Mr. Hawkins, though it would be better to return to His Grace, your cousin's, house. The Easterday connection will do you no good."

"My presence would not aid His Grace in finding a suitable bride, which he must do soon to secure the succession." Her maid might not be aware of Normande's financial straits, and why enlighten her? Not that the succession was less important, when as far as Emily knew, there was no one left to inherit the title if Cousin Henry died without a son. The Duchy of Normande would end.

Putnam's expression, seen in the mirror, revealed consternation; perhaps she had supposed he was older, his place in society already established.

"I confess I had not considered the effect of the

problem of Mr. Hawkins on the duke, my lady." She began to braid Emily's hair for the night, a little more tightly than Emily would have preferred, but Putnam did not approve of tendrils escaping. Neither did Emily, but in her husband's absence, she would have settled for more comfort at the price of less neatness.

"It's a pity you are deprived of His Grace's support. However, as Captain Easterday and Mistress Easterday—" She sniffed. "—do not move in the best society, you will be out of sight and out of mind, which may be the best we can hope for at the moment."

Chapter 18

Soon after breakfast, Hawkins's coach bore Emily, Olivia, Putnam, and Thomas, the under-footman, to the Easterdays' home in Queen's Square. Olivia had encouraged her to bring a footman as well as her maid, assuring her the servants would be no imposition and would add greatly to Emily's comfort, as the Easterdays did not keep a large staff. On arrival, Olivia showed her to a pretty bedchamber with old but handsome furnishings, reminding her of Petty Normande. She immediately felt at home. Perhaps her visit would not be an ordeal.

Putnam clucked irritably as she set about unpacking. She had let Emily know without saying a word that she disapproved of Olivia and was in two minds about their remove to Queen's Square. The bedchamber had no dressing room; her lips pinched with censure at the clothes press. Putnam took out a gown of black crape: mourning attire from the death of Cousin Claude. She gave it a brisk shake before refolding it to put away. Putnam was prepared for Hawkins's execution.

"While you settle in, I thought I would go out for a short while," Olivia murmured, eying the black crape reproachfully. She must think it premature.

"Out?" With all her training, she could not suppress the longing in her voice. She had not been out of the house, except to travel from York Street to Queen's Square, in two or three days. More important, she wanted distraction from her maid's belief she would soon be a widow, and Putnam's unvoiced opinion that it would be for the best.

"Only to make some purchases, Emily. I won't be long. I assume you will not wish to risk being recognized."

"Olivia," she began and stopped. It would be embarrassing to beg not to be left alone with her thoughts and Putnam, and she yearned for open air and exercise. "As you have seen, my maid packed mourning from the last Duke of Normande's death. She thought it advisable to have it at hand." No need to explain why. "If I went in mourning, with a veil, could I not accompany you?"

Olivia's brow furrowed. "It might be thought unusual for a lady in deepest mourning to go out. However, I am no advocate for strictly conventional behavior. But I hope to learn something useful during my errand. If introductions are necessary, your own name might be recognized, which would be awkward. Should you object to a slight ruse?"

"Using another name is hardly any worse than concealing my face with a mourning veil. What do you suggest?"

"It might be enough to refer to you by your former name. May I introduce you simply as Emily Saintonge, without your title?"

"I don't mind." Imagine being so anonymous. No stranger, however, than her husband being in danger of hanging. Nor could she contemplate staying in alone as if she were also in prison.

"You will have to guard what you say and your reactions to anything you hear. Can you do that?"

She drew herself up. "I was reared to be the wife of a duke, or at least of a marquess. There is very little I don't know about keeping my countenance in trying circumstances."

"I beg your pardon. Being unfamiliar with life in the upper reaches of the aristocracy, I failed to take that into account. Very well, then, we will go as soon as you have changed your clothing."

They went by hackney as Easterday did not keep a coach. As they jarred over the cobbles, Olivia told her about their errand. "Salem Cole owns Hodgeson's Fine Provisioners and does very well out of it. He inherited from a maternal uncle and chose not to change the name because Hodgeson's was already well established with most of its customers being of the beau monde. He carries a very fine selection of dried, candied, and preserved fruits, marzipan, Naples biscuits, and spices, among other things. He sells raw ingredients to affluent households and ready-made delicacies to households in which it is impractical for the cook to make them and to unmarried gentlemen in lodgings. He ships to country houses. If one has the money, buying from Hodgeson's is often a convenience, especially for large entertainments."

"And Marston had an argument with Hawkins about Cole?"

"Yes, that was what Hawkins told Marcus. Your husband mentioned it concerned Cole's daughter."

Emily had heard of Hodgeson's Fine Provisioners. The ducal household had ordered from Hodgeson's before their finances had reached the critical stage, though she herself had never set foot in the shop or even known where it was. She was surprised when the hired coach halted just off St. James's Street before Hodgeson's elegant premises. Olivia's footman clambered down from his place by the coachman to help them to descend. Emily admired the display in the bow window as she followed Olivia into the shop: pots of marmalade, pickles, and preserved meat; thin, crisp biscuits; candied flowers, fruits, and nuts. The fragrance of spices inside was as heavy as incense. Olivia presented her list to one of the neat, well-spoken clerks and said, "Is Mr. Cole in? He's an old acquaintance of my father, Jonas Cantarell of Cantarell Shipping. I haven't seen him recently and would like to call upon him."

"I will inquire, ma'am." The clerk snapped his fingers and another, more junior, clerk was sent upstairs.

Five minutes later, she and Olivia were shown into Cole's comfortable office. Cole greeted Olivia warmly and glanced inquiringly toward Emily, swathed in black.

"Emily, may I present Mr. Salem Cole, owner of Hodgeson's? Mr. Cole, Mistress Emily Saintonge. She is staying with me as she feels she can no longer remain in her former home. I thought to make her aware of your firm."

Both her mourning and her stay with Olivia were thus explained. Anyone would understand that her former home was now in the possession of a male heir, and she had removed herself, either because she did not like the new owner and his family or because she had been made to feel unwelcome. It was a common tale.

"Mistress Saintonge, I'll hope to count you among my customers. Please be seated, ma'am, Olivia—or should I call you Mistress Easterday now?—and tell me how I can serve you."

"Sir, you have called me by my given name since I was a gangling girl. I would miss it if you changed now. As I had no chance to speak with you at my father's funeral, I wished to thank you for coming to it. He counted you among his few friends." Her smile animated her face, making a most amazing difference in her looks.

The grocer plied them with ratafia and a honey-and-sesame-seed candy from Greece on which he wanted their opinion.

"It's good. The tin-lined chests work as well for it as they do for tea."

With a fractional smile, he said, "You're still involved in the shipping business, Olivia? I'd have thought marriage would put a stop to it."

Emily, who had little to say beyond responding to questions or remarks directed to her, was able to study their surroundings and their host. Did a tradesman count as a host if he entertained them in his office with refreshments? She had never previously pondered the point. On the other hand, he was evidently a family friend of Olivia's. She took a dainty sip of her liqueur. She had contrived to hitch up her mourning veil to nose level, enabling her to drink. She would not be identifiable from her chin and mouth.

"Captain Easterday understands I need to be busy, and not as many ladies are, with nothing but social calls and shopping. I don't usually go to Thames Street now. I work from home, and my excellent head clerk manages things in the shipping office."

"Ay, your new clerk is an improvement. Munns was as useless as a ship without masts."

"And he would not work for a female. But how are you, sir? I should have called sooner, but it's taken me time to settle into marriage and a new house."

He stared into his glass of small beer. "My family is not as well as I would like." He sighed heavily. "Olivia, you are almost like a niece to me. If my sisters lived in London, I could talk to them, but they don't, and this is not something I care to put in a letter. Also, though my sisters have common sense about servants and household matters, I am not sure I trust their instincts about society. You are sensible and have some familiarity with the beau monde as 'tis called. Easterday is a lucky man."

"I'm lucky he appreciates sense in a female."

"I need a woman's advice, and I've been at a stand to think of another I could ask. Will you hear me out?"

Salem Cole seemed to have forgotten Emily's presence. She sat perfectly still, to make no rustle which might remind him. She should not witness such a personal conversation. Yet Olivia had told her she hoped to learn something from Cole, and if Emily interrupted this exchange, she might lose the chance.

"I'll be glad to help if I can."

" 'Tis plaguey hard being a father to a girl with no mother. I might have done well enough with a boy, but we had no more children after Sarah."

Olivia nodded sympathetically.

"A fellow approached me to ask for Sarah in marriage. He was acceptable in some ways. In others, I wasn't sure. I investigated him." He slumped in his chair, his thick eyebrows drawing almost together over his nose. "Have you noticed that a man will seldom speak ill of someone in his own line of work? I never criticize those fellows who have a shop over on Piccadilly, and I don't recall Cantarell talking against other shippers."

"One wouldn't want to appear to promote one's own business by disparaging another's."

"No. The man gave me a character reference as well as the name of his banker. The banker gave me a good report of his finances. His friend was…" He made an indeterminate movement with one hand.

"Lukewarm? Reserved?"

"Ay. I know when men are dancing around a subject. I did not quite trust the reference's character, either. I was left with doubts about the suitor, so I refused my permission."

"Was Sarah heartbroken?"

"She had seen him only once or twice, not enough to feel a partiality for him, except that like most girls she was flattered by his attention. Of course she dreams of marrying. After I sent him away, he enticed her into a foolish meeting with him."

"Oh, dear. So you feel you must give your permission for the man to marry her?"

"No. I would not permit her to marry him, come what may. A bad marriage can be worse than none."

"I see," Olivia murmured doubtfully. "Then the problem…?"

How embarrassing this was. Yet now that this extremely delicate subject had been broached, Emily hoped Cole would not remember she was there, which would be humiliating for him rather than merely uncomfortable for her.

Cole cleared his throat and took a long swallow of beer before replying. "One of Sarah's cousins would marry her. You might think that an ideal solution," he continued with a sour smile. "However, I don't care for cousins marrying, and besides, he and Sarah are like brother and sister. I'd send Sarah off to visit in the country if I knew anyone to send her to. Anyone I could trust, anyway."

"Surely something might be managed to keep her out of the unsuitable suitor's way."

Both Emily's governess and her mother had warned her from an early age that slipping off to meet a gentleman could have profound consequences for a young lady's future, none of them good. Girls not carefully chaperoned would fall prey to the most inappropriate men. Evidently the same difficulties arose in the mercantile class as well.

"I'm not worried about him now, but I'd like her out of her cousin's way for a while. I can't forbid him the house when he's run tame in our home since he was two or three. He's a hard worker and not a drunkard or given to gambling or, er, wenches. Though he does take notions sometimes."

"Young men often do. They grow out of it, but it would be unwise to marry someone who was not yet settled into maturity."

Salem Cole did not trust his daughter's companion or maid to keep the suitor or the cousin away from her.

"Sir, how would it be if Sarah came to stay at our house for a time? A change of surroundings might be good for her. The presence of a young lady in our house might cheer Mistress Saintonge, as well."

Emily inclined her head and mumbled, "Oh, yes, indeed," feeling awkward and wrong-footed as she had not done even when newly released from the schoolroom.

Cole flushed a little, reminded of Emily's presence. "If you are truly willing to take charge of my chit, I will be deeply in your debt. Are you and Mistress Saintonge sure you wish to have her underfoot, however?"

"I do not have an active social life, both because I spend part of the day on business and also because Easterday and I expect an addition to our family some months from now. However, in the afternoons, I either call upon friends or receive them. It may do your daughter good to meet the Duchess of Guysbridge and a few other friends of ours."

"You are moving in high circles," Cole remarked.

"The duke is Easterday's friend, and thus I have become well acquainted with the duchess."

" 'Twould be the very thing to take Sarah's mind off her predicament. May I bring her to you this afternoon?"

Chapter 19

It was a wonder he had not worn a groove in the stone floor. Hawkins was not used to being inactive, and pacing was no substitute for striding from office to warehouse to coffee house to quay, up rope ladders to the decks of his ships, and down their companionways into their holds. Neither was the schoolwork Easterday had assigned him: to list anyone who might know anything of Marston's private life, anyone who might have a grudge against Marston over a cargo or a business matter, and anything at all that might be relevant.

How was he to remember such stuff? But the shadow of the gallows concentrated the mind amazingly, particularly with few other distractions. When he began, with separate headings on one sheet, details floated to the surface as he worked, filling all the remaining space. For his second attempt, he assigned each question its own sheet.

By the time he finished, while he had begun to suspect Easterday's purpose had been to take his mind off his situation, it was clear he actually knew more than he had realized. Mayhap some point would repay investigation and free him.

The freedom of even the worst parts of London seemed to him as desirable as the prospect of Heaven to a religious man. Not that his imprisonment compared to that of the prisoners in the common cells. He was lodged in comparative comfort. He had furniture, a portmanteau of clothing, writing materials, a supply of candles, and several books. His meals were brought in from a tavern. They might be cool by the time they arrived, but they were edible. He had lived in worse conditions as a sailor. Those who could not afford to pay lived on bread and water and slept on filthy straw.

The memory of his wife was the worst affliction. He had rushed into marriage with Emily Saintonge because she had seemed suitable and was certain to accept his proposal. To think he had once stated his intention not to allow some spendthrift nobleman to bleed him in return for a bride! Still, he had got a duke's daughter for his money, and she was pretty and a pleasant companion. Moreover, she showed signs of enjoying the pleasures of the bed. He'd done well to marry her, although as it turned out, she would suffer for it.

Reputation and social position mattered to her. Being known as the widow of an executed murderer would shame her. He wrenched his thoughts away from the idea of Emily being widowed in such a way, without anyone to care for or protect her, as she had been for years before they married. In the sole care of a father who drank himself to death, who had left her first a dependent of his cousin, then of the cousin's son, no one had guarded her interests until she had become his wife. Now he would fail her as well, which he bitterly regretted. They had not been married long, but his life had already been the better for having her as his wife. He had a home, rather than lodgings, and she was awakening long-buried memories of his father and mother's marriage.

Soon after their wedding, she had asked about his family. He could not recall how the matter had arisen; it made little impression upon him at the time. Now he found himself remembering how he had answered.

He had not had contact with any member of his family since he ran away. They would not have known how to contact him. He had never written his mother, sister, or brother, or even sought word of them. Once he'd made a success of himself, he could have sent someone to find out how they fared. Were they even still alive? He should have made inquiries years ago. He need not have gone himself. Timothy could have done it. Mayhap if he had known his mother lived, he might have written. Or his brother. Now it was too late.

Would they hear of his execution? Damnation, they might already know he was to be tried for murder. Even the provincial newspapers would surely report the bizarre manner of Marston's death.

Yet running away to sea had not been a bad idea. His stepfather's indolence and spendthrift ways angered him beyond endurance. His mother's agreement to every cozening word the fellow spoke chafed him. On reflection, his mother would have had little choice if she wished a peaceful household. She was her husband's property. As a child, Hawkins had written to his father's cousin, who had been like an uncle to him and his brother. He had felt betrayed when no answer came. Looking back, he conceded there might be several reasons for his almost-uncle's apparent neglect. Nehemiah might have viewed it as no more than a boy's grumbling. He lived at some distance; the letter might have been lost—or not been sent by his stepfather's order.

He could have stayed home and been of assistance to his mother and brother, except that he had begun to think about doing harm to his mother's scoundrel of a husband. Too, the fellow was talking about apprenticing him. No, running away had been the better choice. But he should have written his mother and brother, or (because that wheedle-cutting slippery fellow might have intercepted his letters) written the vicar for news of his people.

His brother would have inherited the manor, though by the time he was of age it might have been in poor condition. At fourteen, Allen had already been a cheerful, responsible boy. Unless he'd died or changed, he would have set matters right and taken care of their mother. Their sister had married a squire with a good property; the chances were that she was not in want. Still, he didn't know. His brother might have died or be struggling to right their stepfather's years of neglect of the land. His sister might be a widow treated badly by her late husband's kin.

If he had known, he could have done something. Even now he could make arrangements. He could ask Emily to do something. Would she? He wished he knew her better. She was every inch a lady, and she knew what it was to be purse-pinched and dependent. She was also supremely practical. She had hesitated not at all to marry a man like him for the sake of his money or for an easy, secure life. All he really knew of her was that she was well bred, showed no signs of extravagance, and made him comfortable. Her character was uncharted territory. Was she honest and loyal? He would have had no doubt of the answer if she were

Olivia Cantarell. Olivia Easterday.

At Easterday's next visit, he could ask that a man be sent to find out how his family fared. If they were in need, he could arrange annuities. If they were in easy circumstances, he still had one obligation to fulfill. He ceased his pacing and sat down at the deal table that served him for dining room furniture, wash stand, and desk.

****

On their return from Hodgeson's, Olivia, claiming she had a few matters to attend in her office, suggested Emily go to her chamber and rest for a while.

"When you have rested, come down to the drawing room, and I'll show you the rest of the house. We sup at six as a rule. You will have guessed we are not fashionable. The business day begins earlier than that of the beau monde."

"Thank you, Olivia. I do not know how I could have remained in the York Street house, even with your company. It felt empty without Mr. Hawkins."

"He does fill any space he occupies." Her hostess smiled wryly. "I promise to keep you busy enough that you will not have time to worry. I will need help with Sarah. Your example would be most useful: Sarah Cole's dowry might well attract a titled gentleman. In that event, she would need to understand the workings of good society. I'm certainly not able to teach her," she ended with devastating honesty.

"Perhaps I can take her mind off her troubles and give her a little polish."

"I'm sure you will do her good and help her to a more proper frame of mind. I've never met her myself," Olivia admitted. "You won't forget we must call you

Mistress Saintonge? I've warned the servants and sent a note to Marcus."

Emily was glad of the chance to rest. Between her worries for Hawkins and for herself and terrifying dreams which woke her several times, her night's sleep had been broken. The unaccustomed nap refreshed her somewhat.

All the same, she felt a trifle awkward as she made her way downstairs. It was her first experience of staying with someone not of her class, apart from her marriage to Hawkins, of course. Now Emily crept toward the drawing room, having taken longer to compose herself than she meant to do. The other guest must have arrived already—how embarrassing that she had been hiding upstairs!—for she heard voices even before the footman opened the door for her. She swept in as Olivia, Mr. Cole, and a short, rather plump girl rose to greet her.

"Emily, this is Sarah Cole. Sarah, this is Mistress Emily Saintonge."

Sarah Cole curtsied, her face turning pink. Her smile was fixed, but her eyes were desperately shy. Poor child; Emily recognized the expression from a dozen girls of her own class, making their first appearance at a ball without adequate training and confidence.

"Ma'am," the girl almost whispered.

Her diction was acceptable, and she was decently clad in a pale yellow round gown appropriate to her age, and in good taste. If she were able to carry on a conversation, there would be nothing at which to cavil. Experience and training would root out the excessive shyness. She smiled kindly at the chit.

Sarah's papa greeted Emily by saying, "I hope my girl's presence is not a burden in your, er, bereavement."

Of course he was puzzled to see her no longer wearing mourning; she had changed out of her black crape on returning. Emily gave silent thanks to her old governess for preparing her to meet any awkward social moment.

"You are surprised to see me out of black, sir. I have only one set of mourning garments." She swallowed a sudden lump in her throat, thinking of Ambrose Hawkins, who was not dead yet. "There were reasons I felt I must leave my former home in some haste. And my—my husband did not care to see ladies in black. He said mourning should be in one's heart instead of being advertised by one's clothing." She had once heard someone take this stand. Mayhap a lady fond of bright colors, who felt black did not become her. "Because the world is censorious, I wear black in public and honor his wishes in private." For some inexplicable reason, tears stung her eyes, thinking of Hawkins.

"I'm sorry for your loss, mistress. I hope time will heal your grief."

She liked him for the sentiment despite his being a tradesman, and something of a rough diamond.

Sarah hardly spoke at first, except to answer questions, subdued either from her own plight or intimidated at finding herself in more elevated company than the mercantile set. Emily forced herself to draw the girl out, as Olivia, for all her kindness, was not skilled at chit-chat. She was as like as not to speak of how a ship had escaped a Spanish privateer. Or mayhap a

French privateer. In any case, Captain Easterday's shipment of port wine was safe and would keep London's gentlemen afloat in one of their favorite beverages.

"Do you have brothers and sisters, Sarah?"

"No, ma'am. Though I have a cousin who's as good as a brother."

"I've often wished I'd had another brother. One closer to me in age than my elder brother." She had never given it a thought, until Geoffrey's death.

Her slightly mendacious remark touched some responsive chord in Sarah. "No one could wish for a better foster brother than Will. Once the kitchen cat died leaving a litter of young kittens, and Will fed them every few hours all day and night. Everyone said they could not be saved because they were too young to lap milk. But my cousin used a scent funnel bought from a pawnbroker and tied a linen scrap around the narrow end. Then he dribbled warm milk in, and the kittens sucked it from the linen. His tutor gave him a caning for being so tired during lessons and insisting on taking time to feed the poor little things, but Papa told the tutor to let be, as the kittens were important to Will and me. All but one of the kittens lived."

"How kind of him, and how clever. He had a tutor, rather than being sent to school?" She would not have expected that the merchant class would educate a boy at home.

"Papa did send Will away to school for a term. I missed him prodigiously. Then Papa brought him home, which was good, because Will liked the school as little as I liked him being gone."

Olivia Easterday, who had been deep in

conversation with Cole about raisins—could they really be talking about raisins?—must have been following Emily and Sarah's exchange with half her attention. Her expression suggested she would like to change the subject but had no idea how to do it. Of course, Mr. Cole wished to separate his daughter from the cousin, though he apparently liked him. Some did not approve of marriage between cousins, though there were perfectly sound reasons for such unions. They kept land and money in the family, and the cousin would be of similar background and rank. On the other hand, she would not have wanted to marry Henry and was sure he would have felt the same.

Sarah, prattling on, disclosed that Will's papa having died when he was young, Cole had been like a father to him and had hoped Will would work in the grocery business.

"He would do anything to oblige Papa or me, but he has always been good at making things. Will built the dearest set of furniture for my doll when I was a child. He wanted to be apprenticed to a cabinetmaker. Now he's finished his apprenticeship, he makes the most beautiful things."

Ah, that was it! Sarah's father was a successful grocer and scorned a more menial trade, in spite of the success of the fashionable furniture makers.

"My papa arranged for him to sell them through a furniture warehouse, so Will does not have to maintain a shop of his own."

Emily took pity on Olivia's desire to move the subject away from Sarah's cousin, and asked Olivia about the side table in the hall. "Who made it? I have never seen one like it."

Kathleen Buckley

" 'Tis Chinese. Would you enjoy visiting the shop that sold it? I have a Chinese bed also, and an armoire."

It seemed wrong to contemplate shopping while her husband languished in Newgate. Nevertheless, they must take Sarah Cole's mind off whatever troubled her, for she was troubled, Emily could see, and for that matter, off her own worry for Hawkins. She had not expected to have to go out again disguised, but—

Olivia put the awkward meeting to an end.

"I should show Sarah to her chamber. My maid unpacked for her, and she may wish to change for supper. Mr. Cole, will you stay?"

"Nay, ma'am. I've things to see to yet this evening, though I will remain to say a few words to you when you come down, if you've no objection."

"Very well. Emily, would you mind entertaining Mr. Cole for a few minutes? Sarah?"

"Not at all." Inspiration struck. "I was fascinated to visit Hodgeson's and have many questions to ask about the grocer's trade."

Olivia and Sarah left the room.

"I'll swear you leave such matters to your butler or housekeeper, ma'am."

"I do," she conceded. She recalled she was supposed to be dispossessed from her home. "At least, I would if I had either at the moment. I really wanted to ask you about your daughter. I understand your concern about Mistress Sarah, I think. Should we expect the unwelcome suitor to turn up here?"

Cole shook his head. "I've no fear of it. No, I'm more concerned about her cousin. I'd rather he not have an opportunity to persuade her, if that's what he has in mind. Will was always a good lad, but there's one of

144

my clerks I might consider for Sarah eventually. He'd be able to manage Hodgeson's, and he's well-liked and good-humored. His looks wouldn't displease a girl, I think. I'd rather Will took it over, but it won't do. Will's needle-witted in things that interest him, like mathematics and natural philosophy, but he's not good with people, or with subjects he sees no use for, like Latin. If he were, I'd make him my heir." He rumbled a laugh. "The Latin don't matter, in the grocer's trade, but you must be able to deal at least with those you employ and those you buy from. I don't do much with my customers, now I've got well-spoken young sprigs of the gentry working for me. I'm a bit too rough-hewn.

"It's only to keep them apart for a while. I'll tell Will she's gone to visit friends for a month; he'll nod, most likely, and not ask again until a month's passed."

"He is easily discouraged, then, Mr. Cole."

"Will's hard to explain. I'd trust him with her as if he was her true brother. He's never spoken to me about courting her, and I see no sign she thinks of him as a beau." He paused. "I spoke pretty free when Mistress Easterday and you visited Hodgeson's. I reckon you'll understand my fear that if my girl finds herself with child, she and her cousin will decide marrying is the only answer. They're young."

How fortunate she had learned to govern her expression. Otherwise Emily would have gaped like a zany. Cole had certainly mentioned Sarah had been compromised, but Emily had not realized—never imagined!—he meant…well, the sort of thing that might lead to a baby. In her circle, an embrace, if witnessed, or a clandestine meeting, however chaste, would compromise an unmarried girl. No one among the Saintonges' friends would confide a daughter's loss of virtue to a mere family friend, let alone a stranger.

He went on, "Mayhap in some circumstances there would be no other way to make things right. But money can smooth over many problems. I can't help but wonder if I should have given my permission for the man to court Sarah. I maybe set my standards unreasonable high. I was no pattern of virtue as a young man, and yet I improved."

"His compromising your daughter after you refused him suggests a serious lack of character."

"Or wildness. I was wild myself," Cole said. "I came of decent folk. My father was a printer, and my mother's family had a grocer's shop. Neither trade appealed to me, though I worked for my uncle until I was fifteen, making deliveries and unloading crates. I don't think I was worse than other boys, but like most, I wanted excitement and change. My father finally let me go to sea.

"With the seaman's trade I learned to drink spirits, blaspheme, and practice other vices as well. Slackness in religion, gambling, wenching. Thank God I was never poxed. I beg pardon, ma'am. Thinking back, I forgot I was talking to a lady."

"Forgiven, Mr. Cole. Even ladies are not unaware of such risks."

He acknowledged this with a dip of his head and a wry smile. "Then after one voyage, I went on the randan and missed my sailing. Well, I'd spent all my pay, and the press gangs were on the prowl. I signed on to the first ship I could find. It didn't matter to me where it was bound." He shook his head at the memory.

"When I heard we were sailing for Africa, I never

gave it a thought. Wasn't until our goods were unloaded and we were ready to take on cargo that I really understood I was aboard a slave ship. By the time we finished loading, I was spilling my guts over the side. Said I must have eaten something that had gone off." He swallowed hard. "That was the true end of my life at sea, though I finished the voyage. We made landfall in the West Indies, and I've never been more glad of anything in my life, not my marriage, not Sarah's birth. I got a place on a ship that was bound for Portsmouth, for by then I hated the sight of my shipmates. I gave up drinking spirits, went home, begged my parents' pardon for being a foolish boy, and went to work again for my Uncle Hodgeson. My cousin had died, so he was willing to have me back. That's why I wonder if all would have been well, had I agreed to let the fellow marry my girl. A deal of pain and worry might have been averted."

"I think the difference is you reformed your way of life before you married," she said slowly. "Evidently, he has not yet given up his wildness. I don't believe I would place any reliance upon his reforming in the future."

Cole barked a laugh, startling her. "Nay, 'tis not likely he'll reform now. Thank you, Mistress Saintonge. I've no doubt your common sense will be good for my Sarah."

Olivia returned, ending the grocer's confidences, if he had more to share, and Emily excused herself. She suspected Cole wished to speak with Olivia privately, possibly on the same subjects she and Cole had discussed.

Chapter 20

Timothy labored almost an hour over his letter. At his recent meeting with Captain Easterday, he had learned that Easterday had not discovered the names of Marston's family and heirs by asking Marston's man of business. No surprise there! The captain had a reputation for fairness and honesty, which was a fine thing. Generally. Easterday would now inquire of Marston's friends for the information. They would be unlikely to know, if Marston had been as secretive as Hawkins.

This was why Ambrose Hawkins paid him at a rate above what even the most experienced clerks earned. This was what he could do better than anyone else: pass unnoticed, seem to be something he was not, observe, and ask questions. Timothy would never be rich like Hawk or even well-to-do, like Easterday, but neither of them could gather the threads to make a case against someone other than Hawkins. Hawk, even if he had not been imprisoned, was too memorable. In the plainest suit, he still stood out in any company. His height, for one thing, and something else: his energy, perhaps. He lacked subtlety of perception, too. His business practices might be devious on occasion, but his mind worked in uncomplicated ways. Timothy did not know Captain Easterday well, but it required no depth of acquaintance to realize he could not or would not lie.

His own methods were a little less forthright. Finally satisfied with the composition, he copied it out as fair as he could and set it aside for the ink to dry. 'Twould be faster to write in pencil, but who would take a penciled letter seriously, except it were a ransom demand?

Sir,

It being my Understanding you attend to the late Captain Joel Marston's business, I write to you to inquire as to a small but valuable cargo I Meant to buy from him. Our negotiations not being Complete at his death, I suppose I must take the matter up with his executor or Heir. If you are not his executor, I beg you will supply me with his Name. I receive my correspondence at The Cup in Hand Coffee House when I am in London.

Y'r Most Humble,

Thos. Zachary

Having addressed it and let that ink dry, he folded it neatly and sealed it with a blue wafer. Then he checked that task off his additions to the list Captain Easterday had given him. Some urgency attended his next task.

Captain Easterday was advertising for anyone who had been outside the Haymarket Opera House on the fatal night, in the hope someone might have seen the man who had wounded Marston. Likely he would receive no responses. Timothy would talk to the beggars, street sellers, and whores who could be found there in the evening. They would be unlikely to see the notice, assuming they could read. He wanted to question them before their memories faded.

Chapter 21

Emily would have liked to wake later in the morning to leave less of the day to endure. Her sleep had been uneasy again, broken by half a dozen wakings, when she lay in the dark missing Ambrose's warm presence beside her. He did not usually leave her bed after…well, after. If he could not be proven innocent, he would never lie beside her again. Her eyes stung with tears. There was nothing she could do to save him. Captain Easterday would do his best, but would it be enough? If it were not, what would become of her when she was left the widow of a notorious murderer? She could move back to her cousin's house, if her presence would not be too great an embarrassment. But she would be alone again, as she had been alone for years, in spite of living with her father and then with Cousin Claude's family. By contrast, Ambrose's pride in her, his care for her, made her previous life appear the more desolate. She could not bear the thought of losing him.

She could not lie abed any longer. If she kept busy enough, she would not have time to miss her husband. She washed her face and hands in the water left over from the night before. How fortunate she was used to a house with few servants. She scrambled into petticoats, front-laced jumps, and a *robe volante* without help, and drifted downstairs. It was early for breakfast and she was not really hungry, but she recalled seeing several magazines and books in the drawing room. She could read for a while, until the rest of the house rose.

On reaching the ground floor, however, she realized her error when she encountered Sarah Cole, depositing a letter in the box on the hall table. "Good morning, Mistress Saintonge. Do you know this box is for any correspondence you wish to send? I asked Captain Easterday, who told me a messenger would take it to the penny post later. I am going in to breakfast now. Will you join me? The captain has already gone out."

Of course it was not surprising to the daughter of a merchant that the captain, also in business, had already left. It was pleasing to find the girl able to converse sensibly. She must have been overwhelmed yesterday by her abrupt translation to the home of strangers. "Some tea would be welcome. Did you sleep well?" Judging by the dark smudges under her eyes, Sarah had rested no better than herself.

"Oh...I woke several times. It was being in an unfamiliar bed, I suppose. Does Mistress Easterday breakfast later?" the girl asked.

Sarah would not know Olivia was *enceinte*. Such news was not something one would share with an unmarried female, not one who might be considered almost a lady.

"I believe she prefers to take something light in her chamber." Or perhaps in her office, as Emily understood she conducted business related to her shipping company from her home in the morning. That fact was no more suitable for an impressionable girl than the news she was breeding. "We are unlikely to see her before noon. What would you like to do this morning? We might go out to shop or to walk, or both." Emily was not eager to be seen in public disguised, but she had a duty to her hostess. Besides, the poor girl's spirits needed to be raised somehow, as did Emily's own.

"I do enjoy those things, but I think this morning I would like to stay in to finish sewing a shirt for Will. He wears them out, working as he does."

"What a good foster sister you are, Sarah."

The girl smiled sadly. "I miss Will, since he moved to his new workshop. I can't remember when he wasn't with us. He used to take me out, sometimes to visit the shops, but sometimes to visit furniture warehouses or places that sell fine woods. Once we went to a cabinet founder, a man who makes furniture hardware, because Will wanted a set made from his own design."

"Do you have no female cousins with whom to look for fripperies?"

"No, there's not much of our family at all. I have cousins on my father's side, but they and my aunts and uncles live in Bristol."

"It's good that you have a cousin with whom you are close to take the place of a sibling."

"And such a good one! He always had time to mend my toys or sit playing games with me, when I was ill. I was not healthy as a child," she added. "I don't see him as often now. After he finished his apprenticeship, Papa found a shed in a yard not far from our house, where Will could build his furniture. But it was too small for the commissions he was receiving, and now he lives out of town and has plenty of room. Papa and I visited when Will first moved there. I wanted to help him furnish the house nicely, but he said there was no need. I suppose he is right, as he does not entertain. He's always in the barn, working."

"He must return to the house in the evening, surely?"

"Yes, that is when he draws plans and works out how much wood he needs and thinks about designs for more furniture. He has a big table and a chair in the kitchen, and a candle stand with half a dozen arms to give him light. He says those things and a bed are all he needs."

"Good heavens. Still, I suppose a man, if he lives alone, finds it easier to live simply."

"He has an old woman servant who cooks for him, though only the simplest things. Eggs and bacon for breakfast, and a meat pie or soup for supper. She buys the food and sees to the laundry. I wouldn't want her in the house, myself. She looks like a witch and hardly speaks. But Will says she doesn't bother him, and anyhow she needed a place to live. She'd been living in a hut on someone's land, but he died and the farm was sold and she was turned out."

Sarah was fortunate to have such an unusually kind man for a cousin. It was perhaps a pity her father did not wish them to form an attachment that might lead to marriage.

****

Cousin Henry called upon her the next day. While Emily appreciated his visit, she wished he had not been so visibly appalled by the situation. Hawkins's friends might believe in his innocence; the Duke of Normande clearly had grave doubts.

"I would have come sooner, but I was out of town

for a few days. Solomon, the moneylender, you know, arranged for me to meet a merchant's chit."

"Oh, dear."

"It's not as bad as all that. She's been carefully reared and manages her papa's country house to perfection. She's accepted by the local gentry. You wouldn't guess at her origins to meet her. Never mind: nothing's settled or even spoken of, yet. We merely met by accident, as it were, at the local assembly. My point was, I didn't hear about this difficulty until I returned to town. As soon as I heard, I visited York Street and was concerned when I found you not in residence. It's as well you are staying with friends rather than alone. But if you should wish to return to my home…"

She filled in the phrase for herself: after the execution. She sympathized with his feelings. As her only remaining relative (apart from Hawkins), he felt he owed her his support, while realizing that the presence of a murderer's widow in his home would have a discouraging effect upon any suitable family which might want to marry their daughter to a duke.

"That is good of you, Henry. However, I have every expectation that my husband will be cleared of that ridiculous charge." Would that she were really as confident as her statement. "In the worst case, I believe I would lease a house in the country for a year or two. I've always enjoyed the country, and lack of society would present no difficulty." Out of sight, out of mind, improving Henry's chance for marriage to a well-dowered young lady and leaving her free to mourn her loss in private.

He took her meaning and was plainly relieved. "The gaiety of town life might form a melancholy contrast to one's sorrow."

"I am not ordering my widow's weeds yet. His friends and even employees"—or at least, one employee—"are certain he is innocent," because whatever Hawkins's other failings, they refused to believe he would kill furtively.

"Then I will assure anyone who mentions the matter to me that we have every expectation of his being cleared."

Not that it was likely anyone would speak of it to Henry, who was becoming almost ducal.

****

Olivia suggested they call upon the Duchess of Guysbridge that afternoon. If not for the nagging worry about Hawkins, Emily would have been pleased by the prospect. As it was, she was merely reassured that she had not really fallen from the level of society to which she had been born, as happened when a lady married a man of lower estate. The duchess herself was only some collateral relation of an earl. Sarah Cole was almost speechless with awe at the prospect, being unaccustomed to the aristocracy.

Sarah was not quite ready; it took longer to dress to call upon a duchess, she confided artlessly. Emily joined Olivia in the drawing room to wait for her.

"This is the first chance I have had to speak with you since receiving a most disturbing note from Anne Guysbridge this morning," Olivia said upon Emily's entrance. "The reason Hawkins was charged—"

The drawing room door opened and Sarah entered. "Entered" perhaps did not quite describe her arrival. "Popped in" or "erupted" might be closer to the mark. A governess should have corrected such hoydenish ways. Emily would have a word with her later about seemly behavior. She did wonder what Olivia had been about to tell her, but apparently Sarah must not hear it, whatever it was.

"If you are ready, let us go." Olivia stood, set her hat upon her head, tied the strings briskly, and marched out. The hackney was already waiting.

The duchess welcomed them warmly to her private parlor, declaring she was pleased to meet their new friend. Anne Guysbridge at home was rather different from Anne Guysbridge on her best behavior at Emily's wedding. During her own previous call upon Her Grace, Emily had been shown to the drawing room, which was reassuringly ordinary, and the talk had been of how to equip a modern kitchen. The duchess had advised a spit jack rather than turnspit dogs.

The room was Emily's first clue to how very different the Duchess of Guysbridge was from the stately duchesses and marchionesses of Emily's acquaintance. One expected that an aristocratic lady's boudoir would contain dainty furniture and pretty ornaments: china, a sewing box, elegant desk accessories. One did not expect a terrestrial globe, a businesslike desk, and many bookcases containing bones and odd bits of scientific apparatus in addition to books.

Emily had been prepared for light conversation about entertainments and a bit of gossip about members of the beau monde. Instead, after the initial greetings, the duchess asked Olivia about the precise difference between amber and copal, and the best sources of amber. Sarah, who should have been sitting silent, like a well-behaved girl in the presence of her betters, was interested, too, and soon all of them were gathered around the globe, learning about Baltic amber, which the duchess was considering for what she called "a little experiment." Then she displayed a hoard of coins and jewelry and peculiar metal objects which had been dug out of a mound on the Guysbridge property. Sarah was fascinated. While she turned the pieces over, Olivia drew Anne aside, as if inquiring about something on one of the shelves. Emily, who found the dirty, rusty collection uninteresting (except for the bits which were obviously gold), observed their soft-voiced exchange and wondered what it could be about.

Over tea and ratafia puffs, they fell to speaking of the amazing things to be found in foreign parts: the rhinoceros and crocodile in Africa, the luxuries from China and the East Indies, the enormous quantities of gold, silver, and emeralds Spain had brought out of New Spain and the Viceroyalty of Peru.

"The West Indies and Spanish Main must be fascinating to visit, if one could," Anne Guysbridge remarked. "Only recently John—the duke, that is—"

Emily's own mother had always called Emily's father, "Your Grace," or "my lord duke," and referred to him as "His Grace." Though perhaps when they were private—?

Anne Guysbridge continued, "—told me of an inquest a friend of his attended. He went because he chanced to be within a few feet of someone who appeared to swoon but in fact was found to be dead."

"How dreadful!" Sarah's eyes were as big as saucers.

"Yes, it's no wonder he was interested, though I suppose it might quite have taken the pleasure out of the evening for some. I do wish I'd been there. Or at the inquest," Anne said regretfully. "The duke claimed I would have wanted to anatomize the poor fellow on the spot. Which was ridiculous, of course. The lighting and accommodation at the Opera House would have been inadequate."

Olivia gave a little choke, probably a suppressed laugh. "I assume the inquest revealed points of significance?"

"It did, and fortunately the duke's friend was full of them. The doctor who examined the body found a cut on the back of the victim's lower leg, made through his domino. It must have been shortly before he entered the Opera House, as he complained to a companion of someone's sword having brushed his calf—"

What disgusting conversation for the tea table! The thought struck Emily like a thunderbolt: the duchess was talking about the murder of which Hawkins stood accused. Her hand unsteady, she set her tea bowl down on its saucer so abruptly it rattled.

The faint clatter of her cup on its saucer was covered by Sarah's question: "Someone was carrying an unsheathed sword? Surely that must have been noticed."

"How it was accomplished is part of the mystery." Anne Guysbridge frowned. "If it were concealed under a domino, it would have been hidden until he had to unsheathe it to make the wound. Drawing his sword should have been noticed. He might have carried it unsheathed under his domino. It would have been awkward, however, given the length of the blade, as the cut was about halfway between ankle and knee."

"You are thinking of a gentleman's sword, Anne.

A cutlass would be a better choice. Not as difficult to wield in close quarters, as it is shorter," Olivia contributed.

"Really? I hadn't thought of that. How much shorter? And how thick is the blade?"

"I'll lend you my father's cutlass."

"Thank you! I could conduct a series of experiments to see how inconspicuously it could be maneuvered under a domino." Anne heaved a sigh. "The medical testimony was apparently quite thorough. How I wish I had been present. There is no way of knowing what details Mr. Bridges omitted, assuming more came out at the inquest. I attended two with my grandfather, and sometimes the testimony was not as revealing as one would wish. I do not suppose anyone spoke of how the sword must have been wielded, or Bridges would have reported it. That is the sort of detail even a man with no scientific inclination would find interesting."

"If it was only a cut, however did it cause his death?" Sarah asked shyly.

"That is the most mysterious thing, Sarah. The physician found traces of a tarry material on the stocking, which he concluded was some sort of poison, though not one known to him. It was a mystery until I recalled something I read in Sir Walter Raleigh's *Discovery of the Large, Rich and Beautiful Empire of Guiana*. The natives in that part of the world used poisoned arrows or darts. I suppose they still do. While there is a good deal of nonsense in travelers' accounts written so long before our rational age, Raleigh claimed they hunted with poisoned darts and killed a number of the Spanish conquerors, too. After I read the passage again, I thought we should speak to the magistrate."

"Oh," Emily uttered faintly. This horrible conversation was the most she had heard of Marston's death. If Easterday or Hawkins's clerk had mentioned any of this, it had failed to penetrate her dismay.

"My husband was dubious. He pointed out that I was suggesting the cause of death was an exotic poison virtually unknown to natural philosophy, based on a hundred-and-fifty-year-old account which I admitted was likely full of errors. I pointed out that nothing else had been proposed to explain the death. It was a thread to follow to possible suspects, for how many could both know of the poison and have access to it? I take an interest in such matters and have never encountered any reference to such a substance except in the Raleigh book. John finally agreed we should give Thomas de Veil an idea of the, er, pool in which to fish for suspects. It never occurred to me he would settle upon—" Her gaze fixed abstractedly on the wall opposite, as distant as if she had been in Scotland rather than London, before her guilty glance slid toward Emily.

"The first suspect to come to hand," Olivia concluded.

Emily forced herself to give Anne Guysbridge a little smile, hoping to convey that she understood the duchess was apologizing for inadvertently casting suspicion on Hawkins. When she could command her voice, she asked, "But many men have sailed in that part of the world."

"Very true." Olivia's voice revealed nothing of her thoughts.

"I imagine there might be a naturalist or two with a

sample, as well," Anne added. "It is a pity the magistrate was satisfied with the, er, most convenient suspect."

"He must have had sound reasons for charging that man. And if he is not guilty, he must be able to prove it." Sarah reddened, seeing three pairs of eyes fixed upon her.

Once Emily would have agreed with Sarah. She would have said a magistrate was unlikely to make a mistake, and that the most obvious suspect must be guilty. Even now, she could not banish the fear that Hawkins actually was guilty. People were not to be relied upon. She would never have anticipated her own father would give himself up to despondency and drink after her mother's death. There were those rumors of piracy, as well.

"He must have believed he did. However, I am sure the friends of the accused are trying to find proof of his innocence." Olivia gave a little nod in Emily's direction.

It was the most reassurance Emily could expect with Sarah present.

Chapter 22

Captain Easterday had not been home since the previous morning. Emily's understanding of men suggested a prolonged session of hazard or piquet and very likely a visit to a woman. Olivia had received a note last evening which she read with her usual calm demeanor. It left her neither worried nor annoyed; perhaps men of the commercial class were different.

Olivia's eyes lit when he arrived only minutes before supper. How pleasant to see such affection between husband and wife, no matter how startling. One did not expect love in arranged marriages. Would she and Ambrose have come to be as fond of each other? She already missed him. Perhaps in time they might have grown as close as Olivia and Easterday.

The captain apologized for his failure to return home and briefly explained the problem that had kept him. Olivia understood it. What difference did it make where cargo was stowed in the ship's hold? For whatever reason, it had been necessary to unload some things, rearrange others, and then reload.

"These things happen in the shipping trade. Then I had to attend to other business and needed to be back in my office early, so sleeping at my office last night was a saving of time," he said.

To everyone's relief, Sarah went to her bedchamber soon after supper, worn out by the excitement of having visited a duchess and not merely for a brief courtesy call. Emily should withdraw, too. Easterday and his wife must hope to enjoy each other's company in private, although they were too polite to show it. But she wanted to discuss what they had learned from the Duchess of Guysbridge, and something Salem Cole had told her.

"I mean to retire soon, Olivia, but I wished to ask if you and Captain Easterday know—" Had Olivia understood what Cole meant when he spoke of Sarah being compromised? Training warred against the conviction she must speak, and before a gentleman at that. "I don't like to mention it, but I think you should know. From something Mr. Cole said during our tête-à-tête, I suspect that Sarah could be *enceinte*. That is, that the possibility exists." Her cheeks burned.

"I wondered if it might be the case. Given Sarah's likely dowry, a simple indiscretion would not ruin her chances of marriage or require her to marry any man who offered." Olivia passed her a cup of tea and poured one out for her husband without a sign of embarrassment.

Something Olivia and Easterday had spoken of before she and Olivia went to Hodgeson's, once meaningless to Emily, mated like a key turned in a lock.

"Why did you want to see Cole, Olivia? You said there was something you wanted to learn."

"You had had a difficult day. I am not surprised you did not follow our thinking when Marcus and I were discussing Cole. Marston confronted Hawkins regarding Sarah. We hoped to discover what caused the fight. I think we now have an idea, though not exactly why Marston attacked Hawkins."

"Marston had sent Cole to Hawkins for a character reference, as Marston was courting Mistress Sarah," Easterday interpolated.

"So Captain Marston is the man who compromised Sarah?" That explained why Cole was not worried about Sarah's unsuitable suitor.

"I think we can assume as much," Easterday said, "as he was courting her and was refused by Cole."

Emily bit her lip. "But if he compromised Sarah, Mr. Cole would have a good reason to kill Marston."

"Ay. But he's a respectable grocer with Dissenter tendencies, no more likely to murder than a curate. Though it's possible, I suppose."

Olivia opened her mouth, then closed it again. When she did speak, she said, "I don't like to think he would do it. My father thought well of him, and we've imported for Salem Cole since before I began to assist Father."

"I don't like to think of Hawkins hanging for a crime he didn't commit."

Emily agreed wholeheartedly with Easterday.

"No, indeed. And no one has suggested a motive for Hawkins to murder him."

Easterday nodded. "It's all supposition based on Hawkins's hot temper and the nonsense about his having been a pirate. We might supply the magistrate with Cole as a suspect. Mayhap doing so would increase Hawkins's chances of being acquitted. It would not guarantee it, given his and Cole's respective reputations. That poor girl would be ruined in truth. Many scandals never come to light, if they are known only to a few people, and those close-mouthed, but once she becomes the subject of newssheet articles and broadside ballads, she will have little chance of a decent marriage."

"But the source of the poison," Emily began.

Olivia said, "Marcus, we paid a call upon Anne Guysbridge and learned something which explains why Hawkins was charged on what seemed like flimsy evidence. You know what an enthusiast she is for natural philosophy. Anne heard about the doctor's testimony at the inquest and remembered a description of a poison used on arrows in parts of the Spanish Main. She says it's all but unknown outside those regions. She and the duke informed de Veil. It's well known Hawkins sailed in those waters. Given his encounter with Marston at the coffee house and his reputation, it's not surprising he was charged."

"But he had no reason to kill Marston. No obvious reason, such as Cole had," Emily amended.

"True," Easterday agreed. "On the other hand, Hawkins might have had the means. To make an accusation against Cole credible, we would have to show how he could have acquired the arrow poison."

"Anyone who had visited the West Indies might know of it, Marcus."

"Most would probably not have had access to it, given how little known it is, and fewer still would have a sample. Although sailors do bring back some unusual things," he admitted. "Cole is a grocer, not an old tar. It would be difficult to prove or even argue convincingly that he got some of the stuff, whatever it is, from a sailor." Easterday shrugged apologetically and addressed Emily. " 'Tis only wise to point out the weaknesses in our defense of your husband."

"But Mr. Cole did sail in the West Indies, I think

when he was quite young," Emily said, glad to be able finally to get a word in. "From what he told me, he made one voyage there on a slave ship and left the sea on returning to England."

"Did he? Then we can argue he had as much chance of acquiring it as Hawkins did. I would never have guessed he had been a sailor. He bears none of the signs."

Olivia looked up from the lap desk on which she had been making notes. "Neither do you, my love."

She had never heard her mother use such language to her father. They were both very formal; any show of affection would have taken place in private. From her father's reaction to the duchess's death, it had been generally supposed he was inconsolable. Had it really been grief or had she possessed the stronger character of the two, and without her guidance, the duke had been cast adrift?

Olivia was saying, "Now I think on it, my father once said Cole had sailed for a few years. It was only a passing remark, I forget in what connection. I'm sure I never heard where because that would have stuck in my mind. If he'd been to the East Indies or in the Mediterranean, you know."

"Because Cantarell Shipping operates in those areas," the captain translated.

Olivia frowned slightly. "I find it hard to believe he would do such a terrible thing when he still expected to be able to find a suitable husband for the girl."

"What if Marston threatened to make his seduction public when Cole refused to permit him to marry the girl?"

Cole was only a casual acquaintance to Emily,

rather than an old family friend. Having met and rather liked him, she hated to think of his being a murderer. Olivia must feel it more deeply.

"What gentleman would do such a dreadful thing? Every notion of decency would be offended, and it would almost certainly lead to a challenge."

Both Olivia and Easterday gazed at her as if she were some exhibit in a cabinet of curiosities.

"Emily, Marston was not a gentleman."

"Only gentlemen duel," Easterday added. "A gentleman offended by a tradesman or sailor might have him soundly thrashed. He wouldn't challenge him. And Cole isn't a gentleman either."

"I suppose I had forgotten." She was dealing with the social equivalent of a foreign country.

Olivia returned to the main issue. "I can believe Marston would do it, and that Cole might kill him to keep his daughter from falling into Marston's hands. However, I do not find it easy to believe he would use an exotic poison. It is more likely some flashy mountebank—an Italian, perhaps—would employ such a scheme, especially when arsenic is so readily available."

"We cannot overlook the possibility."

"No." This was murmured on a falling tone. "I do wish we might find some evidence that it truly was Cole before we do anything."

"I agree. I'll tell Hawkins's fellow, Timothy, to poke around for something to support our theory. Nevertheless, whether we find anything or not, we'll have to come forward before the trial."

Olivia nodded decisively. "Of course."

Emily could hardly wish for better friends to bend

their efforts to freeing Hawkins. She only wished they might be successful.

****

Timothy's arrival interrupted his grim reflections.

"I've some reports for you from the office, Hawk. Nothing you have to make a decision on, merely Jenkins being thorough."

Hawkins choked back a retort that he did not give a damn about how Hawkins & Company went on. Such an unthinkable sentiment would disclose far too much about his state of mind. He would care, if he survived. At the moment he could not convince himself he would not hang. How had his life taken this turn?

"Jenkins could have sent them by one of the junior clerks. No need to waste your time."

"I came to pass on news from Easterday. He learned something from Mistress Easterday and your lady. Cole's daughter is now staying with them to keep her away from some suitor her papa doesn't like."

"I'm surprised the girl's with the Easterdays. Marston was the suitor, but he's dead and she's safe from him. Unless there was someone else who thought he'd have a better chance if Marston was dead."

"I won't wager on it until I see some proof of a second swain. The captain wasn't quite clear about it and starched up when I pressed for details. He most likely wasn't sure himself, as the ladies only passed on to him what they'd heard. Cole is a better suspect than some moonshine admirer of the girl."

"That fellow? Why would he kill Marston?" Hawkins snorted derision.

"Marston compromised the girl when Cole turned him down. Seems a fine reason for vengeance, as according to Easterday, Cole was set against his daughter marrying Marston. I can't say I'd disagree with him."

"Ay. That's assuming Cole could kill him. I don't believe it."

"He's a grocer now, Hawk, but he made a few voyages first. One was to the West Indies, where he could have got the poison."

"De Veil asked me about the West Indies, I thought because of my brief career as a pirate. What's this about the poison?"

"Whatever the stuff was, it only comes from Guiana and around there. You may find this amusing: the ladies heard of it from the Duchess of Guysbridge, who's well read in these matters."

"I'd heard she was eccentric. So Cole is as much a suspect as I and with more reason. Good news."

"Ay. I'll be on that scent now."

They spent a few minutes bantering, or Timothy did, perhaps meaning to keep Hawkins's spirits up. It almost worked, given the possibility of another candidate for the role of murderer. Cole might be guilty, with both cause and as much access to the means of death as himself. Hawkins would have been convinced if he could imagine the middle-aged, austere Salem Cole behaving in such a sneaking way. Slice Marston's leg with a poisoned blade? Ha!

Sitting in the dark late that night, he tried to persuade himself of Cole's guilt. Men—and women, too—were full of surprises. Outside the grilled window, thin clouds scudded past, illuminated by a scrap of moon. London, like him, was wakeful. A watchman called the hour—"One o' the clock, mostly clear, and all's well." Night-soil carts rattled past, men stumbled home from ale houses and the hundreds of unlicensed sellers of gin. In some parts of town, coaches jolted over the cobbles, sedan chairmen's shoes thudded, gentlemen walking home conversed with each other or with the linkboy lighting their way.

The thief, Jack Sheppard, had escaped twice from Newgate. He'd had the assistance of his wife and a friend for his most famous escape, and it must have helped that he was slight of frame. Still, he'd hanged in the end. Hawkins would have to depend on his friends either to prove him innocent or secure a pardon by influence or a substantial bribe, which he could well afford. But even to know who to bribe, he needed Guysbridge and Barlyon. The former John Barlicorn would know, even if Guysbridge did not. And a duke's consequence was not to be overlooked. Few people were willing to disoblige a duke and even an earl had great influence. Even an earl! He laughed softly at the thought. Any man of title had power the richest merchant could only dream of. If he were convicted, he would have to count on Barlyon, with Guysbridge's backing. Emily's feckless cousin, the Duke of Normande, would likely add the weight of his title. They'd get him off, one way or another. Probably. In the morning, he would know the situation was less dire than his imaginings painted it. It was only night worries besetting him.

Chapter 23

The butler found Emily in the back parlor, trying to concentrate on her embroidery. "Madam, the mistress is, ah, not available, and there is a...gentleman...to see Mistress Sarah Cole. Mr. William Kimber."

Emily sighed. The man's tactful statement meant Olivia was laid upon her bed, trying to control her nausea. Kimber was the suitor-cousin. She knew the girl had written several letters. One of them might well have been to the young man. A careful chaperon would have monitored her correspondence. But she could not have expected her hostess to act the strict duenna, considering Olivia's history. Except that now the fellow was here—if indeed it was he and not a messenger from Cole—and she could hardly refuse to let him see Sarah, however much Cole wished to keep them apart. "Have Mistress Sarah told he's here, and show him into the front drawing room in a few minutes."

When Givens announced, "Mr. William Kimber, ma'am," Sarah had not yet come down, which was hardly surprising. If Kimber were her beau, she would take a few minutes to tidy her hair and straighten her fichu at least, if not to change her gown. Emily was glad of it. She wanted a chance to study him.

The young man stopped just inside the door when he realized Emily was present, or perhaps seeing that Sarah was absent. He surprised Emily. Kimber was of average height, and wiry, with hair the same light brown as his eyes. His face was thin, his nose long, his eyes a bit too close together, which faults might have been redeemed by charm or liveliness. He possessed neither, and though her presence had startled him, judging by his abrupt halt, his expression did not change. He seemed quite unlikely to be a young girl's dream.

"I am Emily Saintonge, Mr. Kimber. Mistress Sarah is being informed of your visit."

He made a graceful bow, better than she would have expected from his clothing. While clean and tidy, it proclaimed the tradesman. Then Sarah came in, exclaiming, "Will! Oh, Will, it's good to see you!" and hurried forward to take his hands. "I'm sorry for forgetting my manners, Emily, but this is my cousin Will. This is Emily Saintonge, who is also staying with Mistress Easterday."

Kimber nodded.

"Please be seated, Mr. Kimber. I take it you have come to see how Mistress Sarah goes on?" She sat on one of the wing-backed armchairs. Sarah and her cousin sat together on a settee, angled toward each other, both hands clasped. Instinct told her they often did so, improper as it was.

Will Kimber glanced at Olivia as if he could not understand why she was still present. "Ay, ma'am. Are you well, Sarey?"

"Yes, Will." She smiled with an edge of sadness.

"I wondered because at home you were like Rufus before he died."

Rufus?

"Poor Rufus! I still miss the way he slept on my

pillow at night. I would like another cat someday. Not right now, because I'm staying here for a while. Later."

"When you feel right again. When Uncle is right again, too."

"Papa? Is something wrong with him?"

"He's quiet, like you."

"I'm not…"

"Yes, you are. Uncle's like he was when you had lung fever and the doctor thought you would die."

"I suppose he's still angry."

"No. He's not stamping around or speaking quick and hard, like he was for a while."

Sarah's eyes went to Emily before she spoke. "He was very angry, Will." Emily thought she heard a sniffle.

"I know."

"Will…is Papa going to make me…? After all? If I'm…"

"No, Sarey. You're safe."

Emily sat stock-still, hardly breathing, not to draw attention to herself. She should speak or fidget, for this bid fair to become an extremely personal conversation, yet she did not wish to interrupt it or remind them she was here.

Sarah's cousin continued after long moments, "Why did he make you come here?"

"He didn't. He said it would do me good to get away from home and be with another lady, who could give my thoughts a more cheerful turn." She turned her head and smiled at Emily. "And it does help, for Mistress Saintonge and Mistress Easterday and I are busy much of the day. Imagine, we have called upon the Duchess of Guysbridge. They are in town because

173

work is being done on their country estate. Her Grace is not at all what you'd expect in a duchess."

Ah, Sarah had remembered Emily's presence.

"I would not have any expectations of a duchess. You like her?"

"Yes, because she is interested in such odd things, like foreign lands, and disease, and breeding animals. But what are you working on now?"

"The furniture warehouse sent me a man who wants an old chest repaired. Lord Somebody. He's an earl, I think. It was damaged when the servants dropped it on the stairs. He brought the pieces to me. I told him he should buy a new one, but he insisted I fix it as like it as I could."

"Perhaps it has sentimental associations for him and reminds him of his parents or his childhood, you know."

"He said it was made in 1589 and was used to store the armor his ancestor wore in 1588. I suppose he meant that thing with the Spaniards and their fleet. It's ugly."

"I suppose it would be, if it was damaged."

"It was ugly before." Emily almost thought she heard a faint smile in his voice, but it was hard to tell. "A deal of carving, though the workmanship is fine. I can mend it. People want the strangest things."

"It's good of you to oblige the earl or whatever he is."

"Andrews from the furniture warehouse asked me to do it. He leaves me alone, so I was willing to do it for him. That table in the hall, now, that's a fine piece. When I've done with the chest, I'll make a table like that one."

A Duke's Daughter

Kimber had good taste. He had noticed Olivia's Chinese altar table, which was a fine piece of work, if quite different from European furniture. What a strange blend of traits in one man.

"The Easterdays have several pieces of furniture from China. Emily, do you think Olivia would let my cousin see the other Chinese furnishings?"

"I'm sure she would, Sarah, but she is indisposed at the moment."

"Perhaps Will could come some other time to see them? I know Olivia is, ummm, busy in the mornings."

She should not let Sarah linger in Kimber's company when the girl's father wanted them kept apart. She should also not set a bad example by explaining why Olivia was "indisposed"; her own mother and governess would never mention a female complaint in a man's presence. But as she did not feel comfortable simply telling Kimber he must leave, Emily stated baldly, "Mistress Easterday is breeding." Such an announcement would scare off most men of three- or four-and-twenty. It did not have quite the result she expected.

"Mistress Easterday works on her business in the mornings, too, when she's not…ummm. She owns her own shipping company, Will! And her husband doesn't mind. Isn't that monstrous strange?" It was a valiant attempt to divert the conversation from Emily's shocking announcement. If Sarah had not quite left behind the gaucherie of extreme youth, the same was true of most girls her age.

"If she enjoys it, why not? Are you?"

"Am I what?"

"Breeding."

The girl blushed scarlet. Emily felt her own cheeks doing the same. Did Kimber have no notion of decent conversation?

"I don't know if you know..." Sarah could not meet her eyes. Her voice trailed away.

"Your papa told me a gentleman had taken advantage of your trusting nature. He did not go into detail," Emily replied.

"I will understand if you and Mistress Easterday do not wish to have any more to do with me."

"Pray do not be foolish. It is at such times a girl most needs friends to support her. And it is all too easy for a cunning man to lead a female into a mistake. We are taught never to be alone with a gentleman and yet to trust gentlemen, but the training to trust them is stronger, inasmuch as we must marry and rely upon them to make wise decisions, support us, and treat us well." This in spite of the undeniable fact that many men could not be trusted to do those things. 'Pon rep, where had that cynical thought sprung from? Still, it was the truth. All the men she had relied upon had disappointed her. Her father, cousins, Hawkins—if he were guilty. "We will get you through this somehow. Since the subject has arisen, are you with child?" Everyone else having cast decency to the winds, why should she not do the same?

Sarah made a sound like a sob. "I don't know. My old nurse says many women are very predictable, but some aren't. I'm not. Regular, you understand. I hope not, because if I am, I'll have to marry Captain Marston."

"No, you won't," Will Kimber said.

"Or whoever Papa can get to take me."

"You needn't worry about it. I'll marry you if Uncle thinks you must wed and there's no one you want to marry. Anyway, why he would insist?"

"A female who is with child and not married must marry or be called terrible names, and if she does not marry, the child is a bastard."

"I know it's what everyone says. But you aren't any different now than you were before except for not being happy."

The cousins had once again forgotten her existence. From their unguarded conversation, it was clear Sarah viewed Kimber as a brother and he was not courting the girl, though willing to marry her if necessary. Kimber's next words interrupted her train of thought.

"I should go, Sarey. I mean to look at some oak. A fellow is tearing down an old shed and will sell me the timbers and planks."

"You are welcome to come again to see the Chinese furniture," Emily made herself say. "I'm sure Mistress Easterday would be pleased to show you the pieces."

"I would like to see it. Do you think she would let me measure them?"

He would also see Sarah again. Emily ought to discourage it, perhaps, but to be weighed against her duty as a conscientious chaperon was the fact that Cole had a reason to kill Marston. If Kimber continued to visit, he might reveal some incriminating fact about Sarah's father. He had seemed no more than a respectable, successful grocer, not at all hot-headed. Still, a man might well kill to avenge his daughter.

177

Chapter 24

An opera by Handel was the entertainment tonight rather than an assembly or ridotto, but Timothy calculated the same street sellers would be present and the same pickpockets, beggars, and whores, too. He questioned a dozen or more without result. Disappointing, but perhaps to be expected, when the crowd outside the theater was smaller than it would have been the night of the masquerade ball. Of those he questioned, a pie man and a woman selling gingerbread, busy tending to buyers, had seen nothing. Nor had the beggars. A seller of nosegays had seen many things but nothing to the point. She was willing to flirt, however.

Enough for today. He would have a pint and supper in the nearest alehouse. Tomorrow he would return during the day to look for peddlers who had been present for the ridotto but not bothered to work the Haymarket tonight.

He almost missed the female standing on the edge of the throng. She was young, pretty but too thin, dressed in a gown that had been good and still was not dirty or frayed. In spite of her fixed, welcoming smile, despair was in her eyes. Probably she had seen nothing, if she had been present the night of Marston's death. He approached her anyway. Best to be thorough.

"Were you here the night of the recent ridotto?"

"Yes, sir." Her shoulders slumped when she

178

realized he was not a customer.

"Were you here all evening?"

"Ay."

"What can you tell me about it?"

"Are my memories worth anything to you?" The question was dispirited, hardly even an attempt to solicit a coin. She was well spoken, her diction not quite matching the quality of her mantua, but good enough, almost as good as his own when he wasn't passing as a laboring man or criminal.

"Yes." He held up a penny.

"There were more people going in than tonight. Some in costumes, some only in dominos. Laughing and talking and spending their money, but not on me. Some gentleman fainted away—if he didn't fall down drunk—or had an apoplexy. Someone said he was carried to the nearest doctor."

She remembered the ridotto, then. "Apart from that, did you see anything of interest?"

She shook her head. "I couldn't even see the ladies' gowns because of the dominos. Oh! There was one dressed like Queen Elizabeth. Terrible old-fashioned, but very well done. It might have been her great-grandmama's for it wasn't thrown together out of bits and pieces, and it was embroidered all over. Not like the man she was with. His costume looked like it'd come from a theater company. One man was dressed like a Turk."

"You have an eye for dress. Nothing else stands out in your mind? No scuffles or fights? Nothing odd?"

"There's nothing odd about fights where there are men." Then she frowned a little. "I recall one fellow. He didn't have a domino or costume either. 'Twas as if he was passing by on his way to someplace else, but he lingered a while. I watched him for a bit, then he cut through a group near the entrance and strode off. There was something about him. I can't think what."

"Was he a popinjay?"

"N-n-n-no. I'd remember if he was dressed fine or looked ridiculous."

"Was he tall or short? Wearing a bob wig? A tie-wig or a bag-wig?

She shook her head. "I don't think he was, but I can't say particular."

"Old or young?"

"If he'd been handsome or looked rich, I'd have noticed. If he'd moved like a gouty old fellow I might recall that. Didn't seem like he needed a cane."

A cane?

"That's the thing as made me notice him," she said slowly. "He had a cane but didn't seem to need it, and it was the wrong kind." She sketched a right angle in the air. "Old men who need the support use one they can grip. I've seen countrymen use the same kind for walking on rough ground. Gentlemen's walking sticks have a small top, like a ball of ivory, mayhap, that you can't really lean on."

He knew as much, himself, now she mentioned it.

She went on, " 'Twasn't the kind you'd carry in the city, if you didn't need it to walk. It was uncommon thick, too, even for the country. He might be taking it to some relative or friend who needed it, as he wasn't using it himself. He held it odd, not the way gentlemen carry their sticks. Down at his side, somehow."

"You've a noticing eye." It was probably nothing to do with Marston, but it was the most response he'd had so far.

"I was an upstairs maid, but I always took an interest in how people dressed. I thought I might be a lady's maid someday."

"Seduced and turned off?"

She exhaled sharply. "Ay, if you call it seduction. Luckier than some, for I wasn't with child, and the housekeeper and the mistress knew the master's son forced me. The mistress couldn't give me a character because the master forbade it, but she did give me money to live on until I got a position. I haven't found one, and…"

"And you can't, without a character, and your money's all spent." Foolish to hate London for its cruelty when the countryside was often as bad. At least in the country, you could creep away into a thicket and die quiet. In London, you'd lie in a filthy alley and likely be raped or murdered for your rags.

"I can't even get work as a scullery maid."

He heard the quaver in her voice. "What's your name?"

"Margaret Ash, sir."

"I'm no gentry-cove. My name's Timothy. I'll buy you supper, Margaret, and maybe I can help you find better work."

"I won't go into a brothel."

"I'm no cock-bawd, either. I know someone who may need a maid, mayhap even a lady's maid. What have you to lose?"

It was a pleasure to see how neatly but heartily Margaret ate. When he asked what she wanted to drink, she timidly asked if she might have tea, a wish he was glad to grant. The evening was chill, and she was wearing no cape.

"Was there anything else you can call to mind about the fellow with the cane?" he asked when she poured herself another cup of tea and sat back with a sigh.

"No. My mind was mostly on my troubles. I'd help you more if I could."

"You've done well. Have you a place to stay?"

"For another two nights or maybe three."

If the poor mort did not eat, he guessed. "Here's a shilling. I'll see you to your lodgings. Don't go out again, and by tomorrow or the day after, I'll have work for you. Decent work." One way or another.

She smiled sadly, not believing.

"Maggie, you've no reason to trust me, but the shilling will keep you for another few days, so if you wait for me until tomorrow afternoon, you're not out anything, are you?"

"It seems a great deal for you to pay for my few memories. It was my first night, standing out, waiting for a man to…you know."

Timothy overcame his reluctance to part with information. "What you've told me could be important to the man I work for. He'll see you safe." *Or I will.*

He walked Maggie to her lodging house. He was inclined to think the man she had seen was the murderer. A cane would be easier to wield inconspicuously than a sword. How better to inflict a cut on the leg than with a cane? It would have to be tipped with a blade, but at night, that might not be noticed. Rather than return to the Haymarket, he would report to Captain Easterday. It was late but not quite too late to seek him out at home.

Evidently the butler was accustomed to the arrival of messengers. He led Timothy up to the captain's library with no pretense about seeing if the captain was "at home." It came as a surprise—and not a happy one—that Mistress Easterday was present.

"News?"

"Ay, Captain." He glanced toward the lady.

"This is Timothy, my dear."

"I've seen you before," she said, studying his face. "Where was it?"

He cleared his throat. "Ah…mayhap outside Cantarell Shipping?"

"Timothy works for Hawkins."

"You were selling something. Pamphlets?"

"Ay, once or twice. I was there with a performing dog one day, and other times as a beggar or something else. Begging your pardon, ma'am, Hawkins was concerned for your safety and had several of us keep watch."

"Hmmpf!"

"What have you learned?" Easterday asked.

Timothy assumed Olivia Easterday, who had been standing, was about to leave the room. Instead, she seated herself in one of the chairs before the desk. Captain Easterday gave no sign of expecting her to go. He waved Timothy to another seat.

"I've found someone who was outside the theater the night of the ridotto. She saw a man who waited but never went into the theater, and he was carrying an old man's or a countryman's cane but not using it to walk. He went through the crowd entering the Haymarket and kept going."

"Do you think she's truthful? Saw what she says

she did?"

"I believe her, Captain. I didn't ask her outright if she'd seen the murder."

"It's not enough to free Hawkins unless she saw the man wound Marston," Easterday mused.

Olivia Easterday observed, "The cane explains how it was done, however. Using a knife or a spear—a spear, I ask you!—would have been noticed. Drawing and maneuvering a smallsword would have been awkward. I suggested a cutlass, but there would still have been the difficulty of drawing it."

"I agree, my dear. She did not by any chance recognize the man?"

"Alack, no. Nor can she describe him except as being of average height, not fat, and plainly clad. Maggie was a maidservant with an ambition to be a lady's maid, so she pays attention to clothing and such things." No need to explain why she was loitering outside the theater.

"I see. It's helpful, even if it's only one small piece. Will she be willing to testify to what she saw? Will you be able to find her again if necessary?"

"I think she would. And I know where she's living." At the moment.

"Good. Now, if you've nothing else—"

"I do. Tomorrow I'm going to sniff around Cole's home to find out what I can about the family."

Easterday raised his eyebrows. "I thought you would do that first of all."

"I had a man make discreet inquiries in the neighborhood first. I wanted to find out as much as possible about Cole before approaching his household directly."

"Do you think to get work there?" Olivia's question was a good one. Captain Easterday would never think of putting a spy in the house.

"I mean to see if I can get Maggie work. I could offer myself as a footman, but a servant's time is not his own, and I have other matters to look into. A maid is more likely to be needed, as maids leave to marry or are let go. Eyes and ears in that house may turn up something."

"Is she willing to pass on information?" Timothy heard disapproval in Easterday's voice.

"The girl is desperate. Anything, almost, is better than starving in the street. Or—"

"Just so," Easterday interrupted.

Timothy suppressed a grin. He might not be a gentleman any longer, despite his father having been one, but he had not intended to finish the sentence anyway. Captain Easterday would have been annoyed, and Hawkins, if he ever heard of it, would have knocked him down. One did not speak of a woman of the town before a lady, no matter how unconventional.

****

He found the letter waiting at the Cup in Hand the next morning.

Mr. Zachary,

Regarding the late Captain Marston's heir or heirs, if any, I can tell you nothing. I have begun inquiries among his acquaintances and sent a notice to the Gazette *in an effort to locate any family. To the best of my knowledge, he had made no Will.*

Edmund Wilkinson

It would have been far more satisfactory to know that there was a will and a known heir who could then be investigated. An unknown heir who had been tempted to hurry his inheritance along made it far more difficult. It might take Wilkinson months to locate Marston's next of kin, which would be far too late to do any good to Hawkins, except perhaps to exonerate his name. A posthumous clearing of his conviction would be scant consolation to his wife and friends.

He could have called for paper and ink and quill to write Easterday with his latest discovery. Instead he would wait until he had crossed another item off his list.

He timed his arrival at Cole's kitchen door carefully. The master would have breakfasted, then gone to his shop. By now, the dishes, pots, and pans would have been cleared away and the cook would be taking a rest, and no worry about preparing a midday meal for the chit, who was staying with the Easterdays, as well as the servants' dinner. He presented himself, hat in hand, explaining bashfully that he had heard about the master's son, was it, or nephew, that was a cabinetmaker, and maybe would advise him about how his own boy could learn the craft.

"He's a mite young yet, but no use waiting, is there? In a year or two, he'll be old enough to start. Or should he be older? I've done my best with him, but his mother's dead." He shrugged helplessly. The mythical ten-year-old Alfred took shape in Timothy's mind until he might have been real. He shouldn't have called the imaginary boy Alfred. He would have christened a son Alfred, after his own father. The child might have had Molly's green eyes. Might have...He never thought of Molly now without remembering the lines inscribed on a window in Harrison's Assembly Rooms in Bath. *I* *kiss'd her standing/Kiss'd her lying/Kiss'd her in health/And kiss'd her dying...*No. Forget that. He needed his wits about him.

That question brought out Cook's store of tales about the young Will Kimber. She showed Timothy the hanging cabinet he'd made for her to store the smaller kitchen tools: the little mortar and pestle, the graters, the sugar nippers, and chocolate mill. By then Timothy was sitting at the table and she'd given him a tankard of small beer and an aniseed bun, and the kitchen maid was eying him while grinding almonds in a big mortar.

"Still a lad when 'e built it and knew to the inch what I needed to store in it, too. Young Will would come to the kitchen and stay quiet as a mouse, when 'e come 'ere first. I think it was part because it's always warm and part because 'e'd often been 'ungry before the master took 'im in, even before 'is father died of the drink. The slabs of bread and butter I fed the boy! And cups of milk, and buns, and anything else that was 'andy. Be it as it may, 'e'd come to my kitchen."

"He must be right fond of you, Mistress Ellis."

"Now that's the odd thing, master. You'd think 'e might be, but 'e showed more affection for the kitchen cat than me or anyone else, until Sarah was born. With 'er, 'e was like a cat with one kitling. I 'spose she seemed like a pet to 'im. 'E's always liked the animals, leastwise the useful kind, like cats, dogs, and horses. 'E didn't favor rats or mice, thank the Lord, or 'e'd never 'ave tolerated old Lightning slaying them. Will never showed much fondness for people before Sarah, and 'e still don't, but 'e made me the cabinet, which showed 'e'd warmed to some of us anyhow." She laughed tolerantly. "Like enough 'e could tell you about apprenticing your little one, but don't expect 'im to take the boy on 'imself. 'Cept for those 'e likes, 'e 'asn't much use for people. 'E always comes down to see me when 'e visits Mistress Sarah or the master, even since he moved away. 'Cept for recent-like. Reckon 'e's busy making 'is furniture."

"I thank you for your advice, mistress. If I might impose on you for a little more…"

"More beer? Another bun?"

"No, no, mistress, though both were mortal good. Do you know anyone who needs a maid? My sister-in-law needs a situation, the family she was with having decided to move to Cumberland, and Maggie not wishing to go so far from her own people. She's been an upstairs maid but can turn her hand to anything, or learn it fast." Maggie Ash had her wits about her.

"As it 'appens, we do need a maid. It's terrible 'ard keeping good servants. She'd 'ave to pass muster with the 'ousekeeper, but if she's decent and willing and 'as a character from 'er last place, she should 'ave no difficulty. And the master's a good employer. Fair and not one to bother the female servants nor let anyone else bother them, neither."

"Thank you, Mistress Ellis. I'll send her around tomorrow, then."

He strode away from the door smiling. Two birds with one stone! He would make a detour, as the French called it, and visit Maggie on his way to Captain Easterday. It was not much out of the way, and she would be anxious for her future. Tonight he would write out a character for her. Lucky he had paid attention to his lessons and worked hard at them, until his father's school failed, leaving him bankrupt.

Maids having less freedom than male servants—and God knew, they often had little enough, as Timothy knew from personal experience—he would tell Maggie to write to him at the Cup in Hand when she had anything to report. As he was supposed to be her brother-in-law, there was nothing improper about it. She had best not commit her observations to writing but instead ask him to tell her sister what her half-day was so he could meet with her. Cole's household did not strike him as the kind to have a very strict housekeeper. It should be easy to obtain permission to speak with her outside at least briefly.

By the time he had spoken with Maggie and promised to return in the morning with a letter of reference ostensibly from a former employer, stopped at a stationer's to buy a better quality of paper than he ordinarily used, and reached Easterday's office near the East India House, he found the captain already gone home.

"He's been married no more than half a year," the clerk still on duty told him. "Likes to go home to his wife. They live in Queen's Square. You can leave a message there, if it's urgent, but you won't find him. They're to dine with the Duke of Guysbridge."

Nothing he had to say justified interrupting a duke's evening. He would go home, write out Maggie's letter of reference, and get a good night's sleep for once.

Chapter 25

When the butler came to the parlor, as Olivia quaintly termed it, to inform Emily that Mr. Kimber had called to see Mistress Sarah again, she was of two minds. She could instruct Givens to say the ladies were not at home. Will Kimber might not recognize it for a polite evasion. On the other hand, Sarah missed his company, as he had apparently visited the Cole house two or three times a week, even after he had moved his workshop out of town. Olivia Easterday might make an unsentimental decision; Emily, having often wished for closer family connections than she had ever had, could not. She bade Givens show Will Kimber into the parlor.

"I know Sarah would not want to miss your visit, Mr. Kimber. She and Mistress Easterday have gone out for a walk, but they should return soon. Will you wait?"

"Ay." He seemed to search for something else to say. "Thank you."

They sat, and Emily tried to think of some topic of conversation. Either Will Kimber was also wracking his brain or he simply did not see the need for talk.

The sound of Sarah and Olivia's voices came as a welcome relief. The butler murmured, and then Sarah burst into the salon, followed more slowly by Olivia.

"Will! I hope you haven't had to wait long."

He rose and took her hands before releasing them and turning to make his bow to Olivia.

"Ma'am, may I show Will the garden? I know you wish to take a little rest now. I have so much to tell him, and it would only bore you and Mistress Emily."

Emily saw her hostess hesitate, Olivia's glance darting to her.

"I will be here, embroidering, Olivia, so you can have a nap in good conscience." Meaning, *The garden is small, and I will keep an eye upon them.*

"I am somewhat weary," Olivia admitted. "Very well, Sarah, you may entertain your guest. Good day, Mr. Kimber."

Sarah burbled cheerfully as she led her cousin through the hall to the glazed double doors into the walled garden. Emily moved to the northwest corner of the informal drawing room. She could see most of the garden by shifting her chair only a few inches. Bending her head over her embroidery—a monogrammed handkerchief for Ambrose—she kept her eyes on Sarah and Will. She would make no progress on the initial, but really, what was the point of giving her husband a handkerchief she had made with her own hands when he was facing trial and execution? If they loved each other, it might be a cherished memento. As it was, she might as well buy him one. The thought that he might carry one she had embroidered as he mounted the gallows made her feel ill.

Rather to her surprise, the pair showed no sign of wishing to slip away to the other end of the garden. Instead, they sat on a garden bench well within Emily's field of vision. The girl was in full spate of words, smiling and once laughing. Eventually, she must have run out of anecdotes about the kitchen cat, the joke Mr. Nevis had told them when he and Mistress Easterday's aunt had come for dinner, and all the other small incidents that had interested or amused her. But when her flow of chat ended, her vivacity faded with it. Shoulders drooping, she spoke briefly.

Mr. Kimber's expression had not altered the entire time Sarah had been speaking. Now he looked grave. Frowning a little, he replied. Whatever his remark, it struck the girl speechless. Emily did not need to overhear to interpret her brief response as "No! It can't be," or "I don't believe it," or mayhap "Are you certain?"

Will nodded somberly, and Sarah's whole body sagged. She uttered a few distressed words, and her cousin shook his head. Kimber put his arm around her shoulders and said something. Her head came up, and she stared at him. Pulling a handkerchief out of the pocket concealed under the side seam of her petticoat, Sarah blotted her eyes.

Emily's own eyes were growing strained from peering at them while pretending to study her embroidery. Fortunately, the two sat without speaking for a few minutes longer, then returned to the house. The door to the parlor was ajar, but they passed it, continuing through the front hall. Emily heard the butler's voice bidding the visitor good day, and light steps pattering up the stair at a pace more quick than dignified. The street door closed behind Sarah's cousin, leaving Emily to wonder what had distressed her.

****

Olivia's discomfort in the morning had grown worse, making it necessary for her to do some work on her business in the afternoons, thereby throwing Emily and Sarah together a good deal. While pitying her hostess's malaise, Emily did not mind taking responsibility for Sarah's entertainment. The girl had far more in common with Emily than either of them had with Olivia and enjoyed shopping and paying visits.

While Sarah had been somewhat shy on first coming to stay in Queen's Square, her essential liveliness had emerged, like the sun coming out from behind clouds. But in the last few days, she seemed unable to settle to any amusement and had lost interest in admiring the goods in the shops. On one excursion, when Emily suggested a fan with its ivory sticks carved and pierced as fine as lace would be the perfect accessory for Sarah's cream brocade gown, she had burst out, "What does it matter if my fan match my gown? I am the wretchedest creature to think of such frivolities."

The poor child, for she was still a child, must finally have realized her plight. Five or six years' difference in age and being thrown on the charity of distant relatives had matured Emily. If Sarah's ruin was not yet talked of, it would come out eventually. Mr. Cole should find a suitable man willing to take his daughter for her dowry and explain matters first, rather than having Sarah's disgrace discovered on their wedding night. Unless—

They were in the chamber Emily had been given, going through Emily's mother's collection of old lace. "Sarah, are you with child, do you think?"

"No, thank God!"

"You have been uncommon low in spirits. That is why I asked."

"I wrote to my papa, asking him to call upon me. I miss him and—and would like to see him. But he is going out of town on business and said he would visit me on his return. I fear he is angry with me and I cannot blame him, but oh, I wish he weren't."

"Would it not help to talk to someone else? Either Mistress Easterday or I can be discreet and could perhaps advise you. She is very practical, and I am familiar with society. Or your cousin, perhaps? I know you are very close."

Sarah burst into tears. It occurred to Emily that Sarah's melancholy dated to Will Kimber's last visit. After supplying her with a second handkerchief, Emily asked, "Did Mr. Kimber say something to overset you?"

She mopped her eyes, blew her nose, and took in a deep breath. "He talked about that murder the Duchess of Guysbridge told us of."

"A most distressing subject, yet you did not dissolve in tears then. I suppose he dwelt upon the details and fantastical nature of the crime?"

"No…" She took another breath. "I did not know it was Captain Marston who died."

"Did you know him, then?"

Sarah mumbled, "He was the one who…"

"I'm sorry. He cannot have been a good man. If you had married him, he was unlikely to be a kind husband, no matter how charming or handsome he was."

"I didn't want to marry him. Not after what he did. I feared my papa would decide I must marry the captain, because that's what happens when…" She made a helpless gesture. "Will did not understand I didn't know Captain Marston was dead. Will saying he'd been murdered came as such a relief, I was glad.

194

It's horrible of me, I know."

"I expect he had hurt or angered others as well as you. It is shocking, of course, but it must have been God's will or it would not have happened."

"Do you really think so, Emily?"

"How often have we heard sermons on accepting God's will, however puzzling to us?" When one asked a clergyman how some terrible fate befalling an innocent person could be God's will, one never received a convincing answer. Sheep-like acceptance might be suitable for sheep or the lower classes. Though it had never satisfied Emily, she felt no guilt about falling back on the conventional explanation if it would salve Sarah's conscience. This time, at least, the Almighty's will had produced a result all to the good, except for Hawkins being blamed for it. "Do you feel better now, Sarah, dear?"

The girl stared down at her clasped hands dolefully and sniffed. "Someone said your husband is accused of Captain Marston's murder. Are you not a widow? Or perhaps I misunderstood. I have been so distraught, I hardly know if I am on my head or heels."

"I must apologize, Sarah. We did not set out to deceive you"—which was true, as she and Olivia initially only meant to deceive Mr. Cole—"but I did not want to embarrass my friends by letting it be known they were harboring the wife of a suspected murderer." Now, that was an untruth: Olivia and Captain Easterday had not hesitated for a moment to take her in. Mayhap for people whose world was the Pool of London's shipping trade rather than the beau monde, scandal was of little concern. Or no concern at all, judging by some of Olivia's revelations.

"It is I who owe you an apology. I am so sorry: I have been pitying myself when you are far more deserving of sympathy, and I did not know. Please say you forgive me."

Emily's voice did not betray her. "Of course I forgive you; how could you know of it? Ladies do not read newspapers. And men do not mention such matters to us. Generally. I suppose Mr. Kimber told you."

"Will? No, I overheard something."

Emily's raised eyebrows usually served to make a maid confess to breaking a dish or failing to finish the dusting.

"I would rather not say where or who spoke of it," Sarah said with surprising dignity.

Ah. She had heard the servants talking. They knew of her husband's arrest and her real name. It would be too much to expect they would not discuss it among themselves. The girl did not want to bring trouble down upon the gossipers.

" 'Tis no secret, my husband's situation."

"You have been all that is kind to me, when you must be heartsick with worry for your husband. Please let me try to support your spirits, Emily."

"Thank you, Sarah. I must rely upon my faith that all will be made right." This response felt somewhat dishonest, hypocritical even. She ached for Ambrose's plight, though Easterday had assured her he was in no great discomfort, being supplied with clean linen regularly, and with money for privileges in Newgate. "There is no need to take on about my circumstances. I fear your heart is too tender."

"But you must be worried to distraction, and if—" Sarah sobbed and burst into tears again.

196

If Hawkins were hanged. How fortunate their marriage was not deeply rooted. If she had fallen in love with him, how would she bear it? As things were, she was fond of him and would be grieved, although knowing she would not be penniless was some consolation. "I am worried. But you must not worry for me."

Sarah's incipient smile froze. The girl's face revealed too much: her inward gaze told Emily more clearly than words that some disquieting thought had occurred to her.

"What is it, Sarah? What else is troubling you?"

She swallowed. "Nothing." Seeing that Emily was unconvinced, she burst out, "It's terrible for you, and nothing can make it anything else. I thought I understood, but I didn't, really. I don't know how you can be strong, or calm, or not in tears, when I want to weep an ocean of them. Please don't mind about me. I'm a silly goose and shall be better presently."

"It's only that you're young." As Emily no longer was. Though she could not remember ever being so volatile.

Chapter 26

On his morning visit to the Cup in Hand, Timothy found a letter directed to him from Maggie.

Thomas,

Please tell Ellen My Half-day free is Wednesday afternoon. I mean to visit her and the baby, after I have visited J. Smith's Haberdasher to buy a little gift for Baby. I have so much to tell about my new situation.

Maggie

Ah. Clever girl. She meant him to meet her at the shop. She must have news, which was efficient on her part, and fortunate for him and his employer. Time was short, if Hawkins was to be saved from the noose. It would be difficult to find a position he liked as well as the niche he occupied at Hawkins & Co. He was tolerably sure Captain Easterday employed no one like him. And a new owner who did see the need for his services might not meet with Timothy's approval. Hawkins had his faults, but his notions of right and wrong marched with Timothy's for the most part.

****

For once, the weather was dry and sunny and almost warm. Timothy was idling along the pavement, looking in the shop windows, when Maggie came hurrying around the corner. He strode toward her, raising a hand in greeting.

"Oh, Timothy! I'm so looking forward to seeing

Ellen and my little nephew."

"Then let's be off."

"I must buy a little gift for Ellen and the baby first." She must be speaking for the benefit of a woman dressed like a servant who was passing by. Maggie Ash was a woman after his own heart.

She transacted her business in the haberdasher's briskly, rejecting their stock of infant caps, then purchasing a piece of white linen and white embroidery thread. "I'll make up a pretty cap for the baby. I'll deliver it my next half-day. Ellen will understand."

It would be another opportunity for them to meet.

"Thank you for coming to give me your escort, Timothy."

He grinned at her. "We'll walk to Leicester Fields, if you've no objection."

"I do like to walk," Maggie admitted. "I grew up in the country, where it was pleasant and safe."

In spite of the sun, it was still March. A wind had come up, and the temperature was beginning to drop. Sensibly, Maggie was wearing a warm cape, but the streets were emptying of those who had no urgent business.

When no one was close enough to overhear, Maggie said, "I don't know as I've much to report. Mr. Cole is said to be an easy master, if a bit gruff sometimes, though I haven't seen him yet, myself. The other servants don't talk much about him, not when I'm around, but a few things I have heard give me to think they're worried about him. According to Cook, he's fair lost his appetite. He's not at home much the last fortnight or so, which is not like him. Mr. Cole is always in the shop when it's open, but now his man says he goes to it early, and stays after it closes. Maybe his business isn't going well? Unless he's seeing a woman, though by all accounts he's not that kind."

"Interesting."

"The servants say he misses his daughter, who's staying with friends here in town. Why would she do that, when she's got a lovely home with a papa who dotes on her? The young lady's old nurse is terrible fretful, not having been taken with her on the visit, which I think is strange, as she doesn't have her own maid. Or not anymore, anyhow. I think the maid I replaced, who was turned off, took care of young Sarah, the girl not needing a real lady's maid. I can't but wonder if the girl's a rare handful and has been sent to someone who can do a better job of keeping her out of mischief. Nan Moore is as lame as a three-legged sheep, and can't have been going out of the house with her. Maybe the maid who's gone was the one to go shopping and visiting with the girl and connived at her pranks. Old Nan mumbles about Mr. Cole wanting his daughter to make a good marriage and sounds as if she thinks she won't." She drew breath.

Timothy wondered at her ability to go so long without seeming to breathe.

"I'm sorry to run on this way. I don't know what's important and what's not," she said apologetically, glancing up at him, "so I'm mentioning everything I've seen or heard or thought about it."

"That's just what I wanted, Maggie."

"I overheard Nan Moore saying Mr. Cole wanted to take Mistress Sarah's mind off her suitor that Mr. Cole had turned down, and a footman said, 'Ay, that Marston that was killed.' I didn't hear more than that, but it's peculiar, isn't it?"

"Is it?"

"I think so. You asked me about the night of the ridotto at the Opera House, when a man died, and you found me work in a house where a girl's suitor was killed, and asked me to tell you about the family. I'm grateful to you for helping me to a respectable job, but it does seem curious."

He laughed ruefully. "You're not wrong. It's connected. Telling you in advance might have made you weigh what you saw differently. Is there anything else you can tell me, Maggie, my girl?"

She blushed at "my girl" but did not comment on it. "Not about the master or the young mistress. I've heard some talk about Mr. Cole's nephew."

"The cabinetmaker? Will Kimber?"

"That's the one."

"What do they say of him?" Thoroughness and eating regularly competed for first place in Timothy's personal creed.

"It's the way they talk of anyone who's a bit odd or full of whimsies. The butler says he's eccentric. I suppose it means the same but is more genteel. Cook says the master's wife didn't take to poor Will and called him a changeling, but she was a countrywoman and believed such stuff, not like a London woman. Nurse Moore said she'd heard his birth was hard and Will's mother, the master's sister, couldn't nurse him or care for him. His father couldn't be bothered to hire a good nurse for the baby, poor little boy." She added, "Though I'm not from London, I wasn't brought up to believe in nonsense like witches and changelings." She stopped speaking; a pair of gentlemen were sauntering toward them, arguing over whether some horse was too short in the back.

"Are those men speaking the French language?" she asked. "They sound like the mantua-maker my old mistress visited. I went with her once, when her own maid was laid on her bed with a sprained ankle."

"Ay, there are a number of French people in this neighborhood. There's a French church near the Square," Timothy volunteered. When the men were well past them, he spoke again. "I don't see how any of that makes him odd."

"I was getting to that part. This is what I pieced together from a few words here and there, like a patchwork quilt, you know."

"A patchwork—?"

"Sewed together out of pieces of different fabric. My mother was a seamstress and always had scraps to use up."

"I understand. Go on, please."

"Will Kimber's polite, or as polite as he knows how to be, for I guess he's often short-spoken. He isn't much interested in people, Mistress Ellis said."

During his chat with the cook, she had told him something similar, though he hadn't made anything of it at the time. "Yet she likes him, doesn't she? I thought she did, when I talked with her."

"She does, maybe because she's known him since he first came to the house. It's hard not to be fond of a tiny child."

"How does he get along with his uncle?"

"Well enough. As a child, Will followed his uncle whenever he could and sat and listened to him talk. He'd slip into the bookroom in the evening, even if Mr.

Cole had a caller. They'd talk about the old days when the master was a sailor, if the visitor had been one, too. Cook reckoned Will liked tales of pirates and the Spanish Main and Africa as well as any little boy. You wouldn't know Mr. Cole had sailed anywhere, by his house. If I'd ever been to such places, I'd bring back things to remind me, if I could. He has a few things in a cabinet with glass doors in the bookroom, but they're not interesting or pretty. There's only a clay pot, and a piece of some kind of reed with a plug in it, and some bits of black glass. Anyway, the master's said to like Will, who's near as fond of his uncle as he is of his cousin Sarah. Once Sarah was born, little Will took to sitting in the nursery with her, like a dog that's been set to guard, or so Sarah's old nurse claims. Once she was toddling, you could hardly part the two of them. The housekeeper said the same."

When Maggie had finished answering the questions that occurred to him, he took her to a pastry cook's shop for a treat. After a brief tussle with his natural secretiveness, he wrote out two addresses for her before they started back to John Street. "If you need to reach me quickly, send to both places. If I'm not at one or the other, they'll have an idea where to find me and will send a messenger." He made sure she had a few pence for the penny post.

Easterday should still be in his office. Timothy made off toward the Thames at a brisk pace. Faster to take a wherry downriver from the nearest water stairs. At the other end, he could disembark either at the Old Swan Stairs or Billingsgate Stairs, depending on whether he cared to chance the wherryman's ability to shoot the seething waters under the arches of London

Bridge. The watermen were skillful; they had to be, in a river perpetually congested with ships, barges, shallops, and wherries. Still, accidents occurred, and he did not fancy his chances of surviving a wetting under the bridge. He'd risked it many times before, but now there was more at stake than his own life. Hawk's, for one. His other friends would work hard to save him, but they lacked Timothy's skills. Also he would like to get to know Maggie better. She did not resemble Molly in any way he could think of, and yet he was drawn to her, and it was not pity alone. But then, he was nothing like what he'd been ten years ago. Earnest, honest, and trusting did not thrive in London.

"Old Swan Stairs," he said.

****

He arrived at Easterday's offices just short of East India House to discover that the captain was in—and so was his wife. Good God, was the man never apart from her? They hadn't been married long, which might be some excuse, though both of them were old enough to be more temperate than to wish to sit in each other's pockets. Or mayhap not. He could almost imagine that kind of companionship with Maggie. He recounted what he had learned from her.

When he finished, Easterday sat frowning over Timothy's report.

"Then you did get that poor girl who was, mmmm, so observant at the Haymarket a place at Cole's house," the captain's wife remarked. "That position will do well enough at present, more than well enough for our purposes, in fact. However, it might not serve in the long run. If it proves necessary for the girl to give her testimony, I cannot think Cole would wish to keep her on."

It was a point which had given Timothy some concern, though it would not have prevented his trying to get Maggie work in the house as his intelligencer.

"I have written to several friends to ask if they needed a chambermaid or lady's maid or knew of someone who did," Mistress Easterday continued.

Timothy smiled at her. There might be one lady in a thousand who would take trouble for a servant who'd been ruined. " 'Tis good of you, ma'am. Thank you."

"And you, Mr. Timothy. If you ever wish—" She bit her lip. "—to change your employment, my company will hire you."

"You mean if Hawkins hangs, Mistress Easterday? I trust it will not come to that. If it does, I'll remember your offer."

Easterday, who had been showing some amusement while listening to the last exchange, finally spoke. "Ay, that's all very well, but I don't see we're much farther forward for your girl's information."

"Not yet, Captain. These things take time. We have learned that Cole is troubled in his mind—"

"Which any father likely would be if his daughter was ruined."

Timothy conceded the point.

"And the rest is merely confirmation of what we already knew, that Cole had visited the West Indies."

"That's true, as far as it goes," Timothy admitted. "But…" How to explain his feeling that something about the household seemed strange to him, relayed to him through Maggie though it was. He had worked in the houses of both the lower gentry and merchants as a footman soon after his father's bankruptcy and as a tutor. Some families were pleasant, some not; financial circumstances and domestic arrangements varied; the establishment might be troubled by some grief or disaster. Some were warm and supportive; others were not. From talking with both Maggie and the cook, he sensed Cole's family had been close. Cole missed his daughter, according to Maggie. Cole's household sounded uneasy in a way Timothy had not encountered before. He could not quite put a name to it.

In the midst of his brown study, he noticed that Easterday had taken his wife's hand and they were gazing at each other in their own fit of abstraction. He cleared his throat. "Mistress Easterday, does Cole visit Sarah?"

Easterday and his wife released each other's hands as if burned.

"Why, no. Not since he brought her to us."

Timothy contrived not to smile. The rosiness of her cheeks made Olivia Easterday's face less austere.

"Doesn't he?" Easterday asked. "I wonder why not?"

"It is puzzling, now that you mention it. Lady Emily says she misses her father and her cousin, too."

"The cousin and Cole are said to be fond of each other, yet Kimber has not come to see Cole since Maggie has been there. By what I've heard, he used to call upon Cole and Sarah frequently."

"Will Kimber has visited Sarah twice," Olivia offered.

"A falling-out in the family, then."

"Between Cole and both his daughter and nephew, Marcus? I know Cole wanted to keep Will Kimber away from Sarah, but why stay away himself?

Whatever could cause such a thing?"

Captain Easterday was held to be an expert sailor and businessman, if not as successful as Hawk, but clearly he was not perceptive about relationships. Likely that was why he had been jilted twice, according to rumor.

"Timothy?"

"There's something amiss in the family, Captain, and I think it dates to around the time of Marston's death."

"If there is something to find, I'm sure your Maggie will discover it," Olivia said. "She seems an observant young woman."

"Hmmm! I expect you are correct, my dear." Easterday commenced to give a summary of what he had learned from his sources, none of it of much use in proving Hawkins innocent.

Chapter 27

Emily's talk with Sarah had not allayed all the girl's concerns. In the days that followed, she continued to mope, though she attempted to conceal it beneath a stream of chatter—when she remembered to do so. Finally, Emily approached Olivia in her office and admitted her worry.

Olivia put aside her quill. "I had not noticed she was going into a decline. In the mornings, I concentrate on avoiding the scent of anything that gives my stomach a turn, and in the afternoons, I'm often busy. Ungenteel of me, I know, but I am often ungenteel."

"Kindness is more important than gentility, and you are kind." Once Emily had believed gentility was important above all else. Except perhaps religion? No, because one must be genteel even in matters of faith.

"What can we do to restore her spirits?"

"Nothing I have tried has worked. She has wished several times she might speak with her father, but he is out of town. I did wonder if a visit from her cousin would cheer her, but surely she would ask him to come if she wanted to see him?"

"She is a merchant's daughter, and Mr. Kimber has a business of his own. She may be reluctant to take him away from it."

"That is a point I had not considered. Would it be wrong of me to ask him to visit? For I think something he said brought on her megrims. He told her of Marston's death, and she somehow heard Hawkins was charged with the murder. However, she seems more strongly affected than can be accounted for by sympathy."

"She is very young, whereas you and I are mature and not easily cast into the Slough of Despond. Yes, do ask him to come."

"I think," said Emily, "that I should go in person rather than write. It would be difficult to explain the problem fully on paper. I must find out where his business is."

"I can tell you. We—Cantarell Shipping—are importing some exotic woods for him. I'll write out the direction. Send for your coach and a pair of the footmen from York Street. Best to be safe, though I don't suppose you will encounter a highwayman in broad daylight."

Coming from Olivia, the suggestion was alarming. Emily had never gone anywhere but by the ducal coach or without a maid and footman until the current duke's financial situation had grown critical. Shorter distances were accomplished in the late duchess's lacquered and gilded sedan chair, with two brawny footmen at the poles, and two more at the sides of the chair for safety. Cousin Henry had reluctantly given up the coach, horses, chair, and footmen on discovering how desperate was the duchy's financial situation.

"A hackney would be adequate, and it would not take as long to summon one, Olivia." In a hackney, a maid should be a sufficient chaperon: one heard of private coaches being stopped and their occupants robbed even in town, but it would hardly be worth a highwayman's effort to plunder someone traveling in a hired vehicle. By all accounts, Olivia had been accustomed to take a hackney without even a maid for escort.

"There is a desolate stretch of land on the way which has a bad reputation. Take the time to send for your own coach and order the footmen and coachman to be armed. You will at least travel in greater comfort than can be had in a hackney. Hawkins would insist upon it if he knew."

****

Olivia having told her the journey would be several miles or more, Emily resigned herself to a period of boredom. However, once they turned into Tottenham Court Road from Great Russell Street, they fairly rattled along. After passing the turnpike at the beginning of the road to Highgate, the footman riding beside the coachman called out that they would be watching for a lane on the left. "Not far now, my lady. Another mile, mayhap."

Gazing out at the empty landscape, she recalled that the fields behind Montagu House on Great Russell Street bore the reputation of being the haunt of depraved wretches who did not hesitate to rob and murder. Here, past the tidy fields by Tottenham Court, they were surrounded by waste ground. Small wonder Olivia Easterday, who until her marriage had spent her days in an office near Thames Street without either maid or footman, felt armed footmen necessary for this expedition.

William Kimber's workshop was located at the end of a rutted track lined with a straggle of old cottages. She saw a smithy and an alehouse, and at the end of the ragtag collection, a stone building that might almost be called a house by reason of being larger than the cottages. No smoke rose from its chimney.

"Are you sure this is the place?"

"Ay, your ladyship. Mistress Easterday told me the landmarks very careful. The workshop is the building behind. Could be he does not use the house, if it is a house," the man suggested doubtfully. It might have been standing since the Middle Ages, and no more welcoming now than it must have been at that time.

The coach drew up in the yard between the house and the other structure. The barn or byre or whatever it was, was also of stone, and a trickle of smoke issued from its chimney, which was reassuring.

The footman hopped down from his perch to open the door, set down the steps, and assist Emily and Putnam to alight. This was a business, not a genteel residence whose occupant might be at home to a caller or not. But the footman had to rap several times at the heavy door before it opened.

Will Kimber's face was no more welcoming than the house. He did not speak but only stared at the footman, then beyond, to Emily. His irritation faded, to be replaced by perplexity.

"Lady Emily Hawkins to see Mr. William Kimber," Samuel announced, and stood aside.

Fiddlesticks! She should have reminded the coachman and footmen she was using her maiden name, without her courtesy title. To her relief, Kimber seemed not to notice, or perhaps did not recall the name by which she had been introduced to him.

"Lady Emily?" He recognized her; the question really meant, "What are you doing here?"

"I must talk to you, Mr. Kimber. It would be more convenient in the house, I imagine." The room behind him, open to the rafters, was undoubtedly a workroom, with work benches and furniture in various stages of completion. The finished pieces stood near double doors, awaiting delivery, she supposed. A slab of wood rested on trestles, a dusting of sawdust on the floor beneath. The odor of beeswax hung heavy in the air.

"I don't use the house much, except to sleep." He gestured at a chair. "You can sit here. It's clean. Your servants can sit on the settle over there."

She nodded at them, and her maid and Samuel retreated to the high-backed seat near the fireplace. It was sufficiently distant that privacy would be possible if she kept her voice low. Kimber stood by the table while Emily seated herself.

"You will be wondering why I came to see you. It's about Sarah."

"Is she unwell? She often was, as a child."

"Physically she is well."

"She is not with you." The words were not accusatory, the statement no more than an observation, with perhaps a trace of surprise that she had not come.

"I asked her to walk in the park with Mistress Easterday while I went out on an errand. I needed to speak with you without her presence."

Kimber gazed at Emily, waiting for her to continue. The man had no conversation at all. Perhaps the lower classes didn't.

"She is melancholy. I think her unhappiness dates from your call upon her. Could you have said something to disturb her peace of mind?"

He ran his hand over the slab of wood as if it were

a horse or dog. It glowed like satin. Had it not been beyond her reach, she would have petted it, too. She noted Will Kimber's hands. They were not those of a gentleman, for though they were clean and the nails well-kept, they were not white and elegant. A few little scars and calluses marred them.

"She was worried. I told her something which should have reassured her. It surprised her." After a pause, he admitted, "It did upset her. Sarey does not like to know the kitchen cat catches rats and mice, but she gets over it in a few days."

"She is tenderhearted. And she is unhappy." Certainly Sarah had been agitated when her cousin had left her. She tried to recall when precisely she had noticed Sarah's alarming decline in mood. Had it really been from the date of Kimber's visit? Or did it begin later? The thing that seemed to distress her most was learning Emily's husband was awaiting trial for the crime. She had implied she had heard of it after her cousin called upon them. "It may be another matter that came to her attention after you saw her. She learned why I was staying with Mistress Easterday rather than with my husband."

"Is he travelling? Or…?"

Because Sarah's gauche cousin was unlikely to be embarrassed or shocked and she herself was tired to death of pretending unconcern, she said, "He is in Newgate, awaiting trial for murder."

This blunt declaration produced a mildly inquiring expression. "Is he?"

Emily could almost hear him wondering what to say. In a well-bred person, the question would never arise because Emily would never have mentioned such a scandalous thing, even though everyone would know about it.

"That is surprising. I suppose," he added.

"He is accused of killing an acquaintance, Captain Marston, by stabbing him with a poisoned blade. The man who dishonored Sarah. You must have read of the murder in the newssheets."

He stared at her, vertical lines between his brows. Eventually he responded, "I seldom read the papers. They're full of foolishness except for the news from abroad. I can do nothing to affect the progress of the war, so why read about it? I did not know about your husband."

"I can't talk about it even with friends." They would try to console her, and she did not deserve it, when so much of her concern was for her social standing, and because for all she knew of her husband, he might be guilty. "It's scandalous, as well, and makes one an object of pity or contempt. That is why I was staying with Mistress Easterday, and using my maiden name."

"Why was your husband charged?"

"He knew the man, and they came to blows over something at a coffee house."

Will Kimber's cold eyes widened slightly, and there was a perceptible pause before he repeated, "Your husband was charged with the murder because of a scuffle?"

He might well be astonished, though he hardly showed it. Men and gentlemen, too, indulged in fisticuffs all the time without it leading to murder, as she knew from the boys around Petty Normande bloodying each other's noses and blackening each other's eyes and from hearing of young gentlemen's disreputable exploits.

"It came out at the inquest that the poison, whatever it was, comes from the Spanish Main, and Mr. Hawkins had sailed in those waters. Those facts apparently were thought enough to suspect him. As it happened, he could not prove he was with others when the attack occurred. My husband's friends are trying to find proof of his innocence or at least witnesses to indicate some other is guilty, but it does not go well. I fear they will not succeed."

"Then he is in danger of hanging."

"Yes."

"What is your husband's name, ma'am?"

"Ambrose Hawkins."

"He's not a lord? Because you're Lady Emily?"

"No. I'm a lady by courtesy because my father was a duke. My husband is a commoner."

"Oh."

He traced a grainline in the wood with one forefinger, as if it were a map. "Would his death grieve you?"

Who would ask such a personal question? Even if a female were known to have hated her spouse, one would pretend to assume she would mourn. She liked Ambrose Hawkins for his kindness to her. But if he died, with Captain Easterday to administer the estate, she might eventually marry a suitable man. A widowed duke's daughter with a fortune might still expect a duke or marquess for her second husband, or at least an earl. Many titled gentlemen would find a rich widow tempting even with a scandal attached.

Everyone lost family members and friends to age,

sickness, accident, and war. One might weep at the death of one's parent, sibling, or child. An older lady had once told her the death of a husband could be considered comparable to the loss of one's favorite mount: one would miss the animal for its good appearance and paces and be inconvenienced until it were replaced.

She rubbed her thumb across the table-cut emerald in her betrothal ring. Stroking it had become a habit. How much thought had it taken Hawkins to choose an antique with a romantic history rather than a new ring?

He had asked her opinion of the houses they had inspected and which of his furnishings to keep for the York Street house. He had given her gifts: not only jewelry as one might expect, particularly as she had little of her own, but also other things, including a coffer inlaid with ivory, mother of pearl, and ebony, its many little compartments and drawers perfect for holding the trinkets she had inherited from her mother or been given in her youth. Gifts had been few in the years since her early girlhood.

He valued and protected her. It might not be love, but it was something, considering she had been nothing more than a burden or an obligation since her mother's death. She felt safe with him, too. He was not drowning in melancholy and wine like her father, or unable to learn and perform the duties of his position like her cousin, the late duke, or young and untested, like the current duke.

A gentleman did not think about making and keeping money or engage in trade, but it did give one a sense of security to know one's fortune would not all be spent foolishly or gambled away. She was comfortable with Hawkins. She would miss him bitterly when—if—he were hanged. She had not been merely secure and content since her marriage. She had been happy. Now it was likely she would lose everything except Ambrose's money. Once that would have been enough.

Humiliatingly, she sobbed and burst into tears with as little restraint as poor Sarah. She found her handkerchief and managed to summon her self-control as she wiped her eyes. Putnam had started up from the settle to come to her. Emily waved her back irritably. The footman had risen to his feet as well but stood looking uncertain.

"You would be sorry if he died." Kimber brought out a handkerchief, clean and much larger than her own, and passed it to her without another word. She was grateful both for the linen, her own being sodden, and for his not attempting to soothe her, which would have been even more hideously embarrassing than her public display of emotion. Having dried her face, she folded the now damp linen square tidily and started to set it down on the table.

Will Kimber whisked it away before it touched the surface and returned it to his pocket.

"I don't know what I will do without him. And—" How had she not thought of this? "I can't imagine how he must feel in a horrid cell, like an animal in a trap, knowing that he may die for a crime he did not commit."

"I had not thought of that." Will Kimber turned to the workbench and began to carve thin slivers off a block of beeswax.

"The Duke of Guysbridge has promised to seek a pardon for him, if 'tis necessary. It might not be granted; the duke is not of the court circle and possesses no court connections that I know of. My cousin, the Duke of Normande, is young and his branch of the family only recently succeeded to the title. Still, if two dukes petition, and I think there has been mention of an earl who might lend his influence—" She babbled to banish the vision of Hawkins on the gallows, a crowd come to watch him die.

"I don't know society," Kimber said, interrupting her thought. "I know wood and tools. I think you understand society as I know how to work different woods. Can you tell me, if a lady is ruined as they call it, how much difference it makes? I have heard it is a disaster, but I don't know why and people do say things that don't make sense."

Emily sighed. Mayhap among the lower commercial class, standards were different. "How bad it is depends upon how she is compromised and whether it is widely known. But if it is common knowledge, it can be fatal."

"Fatal?" His eyes widened.

"Not literally, Mr. Kimber. Figuratively. A minor error, like slipping away with a gentleman for one kiss, might be forgiven. Losing one's virtue will be painted as utter debauchery by the gossips. Some men would not marry a female with such a reputation. Some mothers will not let their daughters associate with her, and she will not receive invitations to select gatherings. Generally, if the man who compromised her marries her, all is well, even if a child results." There were factors which might mitigate the damage. Even a bastard could be overlooked if it were concealed and if the woman had a dowry or social connections for which some other man would ignore her lack of discretion. Explaining the exceptions to Kimber was quite beyond her.

"But why would it matter?"

How could she explain? She had never heard it spelled out herself, one simply grew up understanding it, or at least observing the convention, like so many foibles of good society. "It's like breeding horses or dogs. The breeder wants to control which horse or dog is bred to the mare or bitch, in order to achieve desired characteristics in the offspring. If you wish to breed for speed in horses, you would not want the mare covered by a carthorse. Gentlemen want their heirs to be of their own blood, which might not result if their wives were not chaste."

"Mmmm." He scooped the wax shavings into a small pot. "Sarey likes you. She would take it hard, if your husband died." When he turned toward her again, he gave a decisive nod. "You think I should visit Sarey?"

"If you would. She is very fond of you, and it may help."

"I'll do what I can. Not tomorrow or the next day, but the one after. I've got this table to finish."

Then he was ushering her out the door, followed by her servants, with only a curt "Good day, your ladyship."

Emily pondered this extraordinary conversation all the way back to Queen's Square. Still, Kimber had promised to visit Sarah; the rest was unimportant.

Chapter 28

The scratching at his cell's door interrupted Hawkins's attempt to write a letter. Rambling foolishness, mostly, that he would never send unless he could rewrite it in some less maudlin form. Timothy lounged in the doorway.

Hawkins slid the half-written epistle under the quire of blank paper as he jerked his head toward the second seat he'd procured. "News?"

Timothy sauntered in and made himself as comfortable as possible on a rickety stool in a drafty cell. "I met with Easterday. He talked to Roger Markham. Didn't get much. Markham didn't know anything about Marston that's not general knowledge. Owner of the *Marigold* and the *Belle*, accounted clever at making a penny—or a pound."

"Wasted effort, then."

"In accounting, if you're a ha'penny off in a sum of a hundred guineas, you can spare yourself the work to find it. Here—" He jerked a forefinger across his throat.

Hawkins nodded curtly. He didn't need the reminder.

"The captain wondered who inherits. It was worth pursuing. We agreed I'd find out."

"Planning to bribe the law clerk?"

Timothy grinned. "I was subtle and wrote a letter to Marston's man of business instead. But the fellow

220

doesn't know of any family, or whether Marston had made any, ah, testamentary dispositions. If he has a relative, I'd expect him to show up promptly to lay claim to his inheritance."

"Not in time to do me any good."

Timothy ignored Hawkins's sour comment. "The captain also spoke with Mistress Hardraw. She remembered the fight—"

Hawkins snorted. "It wasn't a fight. I didn't get a chance to land a blow."

"An ambush, then. She didn't know what caused it. She did say Marston was a troublemaker and she won't miss him. She pointed out several of the men who had been present, who also had nothing to contribute on the subject and one who did. He took Marston away afterward, thinking it best he not stay and mayhap continue the brawl, which he would have. George Grissom was willing to tell Easterday what Marston told him. Not much point in keeping the confidences of a dead man. Marston was mad as fire."

"He could be hasty."

"So I've heard. He spoke pretty free to Grissom while they drank punch."

"Did he say what made him attack me? That's what I can't understand. We'd parted on good terms after he accused me of slandering him."

"Marston claimed you'd told him to compromise the girl." Timothy's voice and face were empty of expression, giving Hawkins to understand he did not approve.

"Oh, hell."

"Did he lie, Hawk?"

"It wasn't quite like it sounds, Timothy. I meant it

221

as a joke." Seeing his friend's expression, he went on. "Not a joke, exactly, a—a what-do-ye-call-it? Not a serious suggestion. I didn't mean he should do it. Particularly given how well it worked for me." Feeling himself flushing, he scowled.

Timothy ignored his last statement as if it were not worth commenting upon, which it wasn't. "Did Marston understand what-do-ye-call-it? Irony?"

"I never thought about it before, but perhaps not." He'd regretted his remark to Marston almost as soon as he'd uttered it. Devil take his careless tongue: he'd meant it in jest, but Marston, damn him, had taken him at his word. It had not crossed his mind that Marston, who was not always particular about his methods, might consider it a reasonable suggestion.

"He told Grissom he managed to meet secretly with the young lady. Easterday didn't go into detail; either it was nothing Grissom cared to repeat, or he felt I did not need to hear it."

"Marston might have done better to marry her at the Fleet Prison without banns or license. All done in a matter of minutes with no fuss and little expense." Another ill-considered remark. He never spoke in business without thinking.

"After he'd forced her, Marston suggested it. She refused, stopped weeping, and became hysterical when he tried to insist."

"He wouldn't have enjoyed that."

"He took her home and told her to tell her papa he would call upon him the following day to renew his offer. Cole threw him out."

Hell! He himself had been guilty of trying to compromise Olivia Cantarell into marriage. He hadn't raped or even seduced her, not that the latter hadn't occurred to him, but he'd no business holding himself better than Marston. He might have gone deaf for all he heard of Timothy's next words.

"Hawk?" Timothy's voice trailed off.

"Sorry. I was woolgathering."

"I'm looking into Salem Cole. I've a spy in his household."

"I wouldn't waste much time on him. Cole's a poxy, puritanical sort."

"He may seem sober as a Scotch dominie, but he's a suspect, all the same. Easterday says the man visited the West Indies when he sailed on a slave ship, so he can't be too delicate of conscience. He had a reason to kill Marston, either in revenge for debauching his daughter so that Cole would agree to the marriage, or to keep him from spreading the word he'd done so to achieve the same end."

"Huh. That's…unexpected."

"If there's anything to be learned, my intelligencer at Cole's will discover it. I'll meet with her on Wednesday."

"A female?"

"The only witness at the Haymarket who noticed anything. The only one I could find, anyhow. She almost certainly saw the murderer in the crowd outside. She hasn't seen Cole yet. When she does, maybe I'll have good news for you. In the meantime, I'll talk to Solomon as well. He'll poke around. Aren't most murders for gain? Except the ones for lust or jealousy, that is. I can't see that fitting here, though I won't ignore anything. Any instructions before I go? Or anything you want?"

"I don't know what instructions I could give you. I don't have a chart for these waters." With forced good cheer, he added, "I have everything I need. I lived worse than this for years."

After Timothy left him, he stared at the letter he had been trying to write, but his memories made it impossible to concentrate. Always the worst memories, of occasions when he had behaved badly. While he was no parson, he had some standards, though he had not always lived up to them. His temper flared up or he seized a chance without strict regard for morality, though he had never taken unfair advantage of anyone who hadn't deserved it. Except Olivia Cantarell.

The realization struck him with the impact of a fist to the gut. He had wronged her. That he had not exactly meant to do it was no consolation because he would have been cheating her however he tried to justify his actions. That he had been willing to marry her made it no better. He had fallen into outright dishonesty the way men were said to fall into sin. First a little transgression, then a greater one, and ultimately the everlasting bonfire.

When Jonas Cantarell died leaving no heir but his daughter, it had seemed a reasonable and even decent thing to do, to buy the company before it failed. It wasn't as though a female could operate a shipping firm. Then Munns, Cantarell's clerk, informed him of Olivia's intention to keep the business and offered him information he could use to encourage her to sell. His price was high, but Cantarell Shipping was successful in a small way, with particularly good contacts in the eastern Mediterranean, from whence came so many desirable things. Dye stuffs, Turkey carpets, medicaments, coffee, currants, figs, raisins. Just as important, buying it would prevent its being bought by someone who might be able to give him some competition. Hawkins liked owning things. Saving a lady from the folly of losing everything when no one would do business with her had seemed like a good deed. He had paid Munns for the information that allowed him to divert one of her cargoes.

When he accepted Munns's offer, the traitorous dog hinted he had even more valuable knowledge about the company which he would impart for an additional fee. The information was worth every penny: Cantarell Shipping was only a tiny part of Jonas Cantarell's assets, and "that woman," according to Munns, did not know of the warehouses, rental properties, and money on deposit or safely invested.

What could be easier than to court and marry Olivia? By the time he had met her twice, he had decided that she possessed an odd, unconventional beauty, like the Chinese celadon porcelain he admired. She also knew a great deal about Chinese art and was the granddaughter of a baron. His own antecedents were gentry, and he was wealthy enough to move in the highest circles. Only his connections to trade, and the whispers of piracy, kept him out. It would benefit them both: she was a spinster with but little income from the shipping concern, and he was wealthy. Together they could ease their way into the best society.

The courtship had been going well. Not only did she have the right qualifications to be his wife, she showed signs of being passionate. He might have won her, if he had not been impatient. Abduction of a female violated his own standards. *Damn.*

He would have given her anything if she had married him, except the one thing she wanted: to keep control of her father's—her—shipping agency. Who could have guessed? Captain Marcus Easterday had understood, and so Olivia was Mistress Easterday rather than Mistress Hawkins. If he had been aware of her dedication to Cantarell Shipping, she might have married him. Or mayhap she was more perceptive than he, for he would have folded Cantarell Shipping into his business as a matter of right. He would not have been able to keep his hands off it, even if he had promised, a dismaying realization for a man who took pride in keeping his promises. When had his life gone wrong?

Chapter 29

Emily pummeled her pillow. Eight days remained until the quarter sessions began. She feared to inquire whether cases were heard in any particular order. Even if Ambrose Hawkins were the last prisoner to be tried, it would gain them little time: trials were quickly conducted. The most serious crime might take no more than an hour or two from commencement to sentence. She almost wished the uncertainty was over.

At first she had imagined her own circumstances as being no different from those of a wife nursing her husband in some serious illness. Yet there was a difference. If Hawkins had been ill, she would have conferred with the doctor, worried Cook with demands for beef tea, custard, and any other invalid dish she could think of. She would have written letters to all their family, to soften the coming shock, and made lists of what must be done if the worst came to pass. She would have sat by his bed, speaking or reading to him if he were conscious, or cooling his fever with damp cloths, or holding his hand. Trying to alleviate his pain and distress, however futile, would have kept her mind from dwelling on her own fears. Instead, she was helpless. She had always been helpless and dependent upon others.

When had she given up expecting his friends would prove his innocence? Captain Easterday's belief that they could find a likelier suspect had never truly reassured her. After two weeks went by with no results for all Easterday's efforts, her faint, wavering hope became the enemy. Resigning herself to widowhood was less painful. The captain's assertion that Guysbridge, Cousin Henry, and the Earl of Barlyon would join in petitioning the king for a pardon also failed to convince her. The granting of a pardon seemed no more likely than a miraculous deathbed recovery as the result of prayer. She expected to be the widow of a convicted murderer.

During the day her face sometimes felt stiff as if it were porcelain, from the effort of concealing her feelings. At night, she buried her face in the towel from her washstand, lest Putnam notice the pillowcase was wet with tears. Displays of anxiety or grief, like transports of joy, were for actresses and young girls too indulgently reared. But oh, how she missed Hawkins.

Emily stood abruptly and groped her way to the washstand to hang up the damp towel and to the armoire for a supply of handkerchiefs. Tears were welling from her eyes again. For the first time since childhood, she had felt safe, and now that safety was being torn away. She wanted to curse and rage against fate and God and Cousin Henry and Marston and Hawkins, too, and with only a little effort she could probably think of other targets for her fury.

But of course a lady could not make such a spectacle of herself, even in private, or someday she might do so in public. The most she could do was weep in her chamber and conceal all signs of it from others. She must accept what she could not change, and make plans for afterward. What would become of her?

The question she had asked of herself so many times before made her frown. Remembering her governess's dictum that scowling caused wrinkles, she forced her expression into blandness. She was not going to be cast into penury. If Hawkins really had left everything or even a sizable part of his wealth to her, she would be secure. She did not doubt Captain Easterday would protect her interests as no member of her own family ever had.

If she inherited enough to live comfortably, the chief disadvantage of her situation was eliminated. She would not be completely at ease until the will was read, but she had no reason to doubt the captain's word, and Hawkins was generous. The scandal of her husband's execution would still exist. However vexatious, she could weather the resulting talk. The daughter of a duke, particularly if she were not impoverished, would always have standing in society. In a year or two, she would marry again...perhaps. She could insist on a man with a title, as many noblemen sought wealthy brides. It would be necessary to winnow out the ones who needed a well-dowered wife because they were inveterate gamesters or spendthrifts, or else drunkards, bad-tempered, or libertines. Well, she would be guided by Easterday; he would warn her if an aspirant to her hand was unsuitable.

Still, some minor drawbacks came to mind. No matter how suitable a man might seem, would he be as indulgent as Hawkins, who permitted her to furnish the York Street house as she would, apart from his study? Would her second husband be as—? She colored up, remembering their wedding night and the nights after. She would miss his lovemaking. Not all women enjoyed That Activity. From married women's talk overheard before her marriage, she gathered not all men were as accomplished in That Activity as Ambrose. She would miss it a great deal. She would miss Ambrose. What would she do without him?

Chapter 30

A letter, hastily written in pencil, directed to Mr.
Timothy, Hawkins & Co., Cinnamon Street, Wapping,
with the word "Urgent" writ large, a duplicate letter
having been sent in care of Captain Easterday at
Easterday & Co., Leaden Hall Street, by East India
House.

Mr. Timothy,

*The master's nephew, Will Kimber, came to the
house today to leave a letter for Mr. Cole. Will Kimber
is the man I saw at the Haymarket Opera House the
night of the Ridotto.*

Margaret Ash

He had stopped at Leadenhall Street to report to
Easterday on his recent inquiries. The captain being out,
Timothy remained to write a note, consisting largely of
"nothing new." As he handed it to Easterday's head
clerk, the man said, "Stay a moment. There's something
just come for you," and passed him a folded square of
cheap paper sealed with a wafer.

Only Maggie knew he could be reached at this
address. He ripped it open, standing by the desk. His
first thought on reading it was of her danger if Kimber
perceived she had recognized him. His second thought
was that Kimber had no reason to think she had been
near the Opera House or would have taken any notice
of him if she had.

"Mr. Elliott, is it known where Captain Easterday is? This letter contains information he will want immediately."

"He has gone to see his banker. Martins Bank, Lombard Street, Sign of the Grasshopper."

Not far, then. He'd have walked. "Thanks. Please give him this letter on his return, in case I should miss him." Timothy bolted for the door.

The supercilious clerk behind the desk at Martins Bank refused in the politest way to interrupt Captain Easterday's appointment with his banker, while his expression suggested that no emergency of Timothy's was worth a Martins client's attention. Timothy suppressed an oath. He was wearing his poor-but-decent tradesman's suit, as he had errands for which he wanted to be inconspicuous. Even his best suit might not have impressed the clerk.

He could claim an accident had befallen the captain's wife. Two considerations prevented him. First, the clerk would not believe him: if Timothy had come for that reason, he would have said so at once. Second, he dared not risk Easterday's anger when he learned such a message had only been a ruse. In the same circumstances, Hawkins's response would have been immediate and physical. He'd have got over his fury soon enough and laughed about it. Timothy could not guess Captain Easterday's reaction. Hawk might flare up briefly; Easterday's wrath might be cold and long-lasting. Some tension already existed between the captain and Hawkins, having to do with Easterday's having married the woman Hawk wanted. Adding to it would be a mistake.

"Do you have any notion of how long the

appointment may last?"

The clerk said primly, "As long as it takes. Sir."

"I'll wait." He paced back and forth before the counter no more than two minutes when the clerk came out from behind his barricade and opened the door.

"I must request you to wait outside. And not before the window," he added. "Our gentlemen must not be inconvenienced by loiterers."

Stifling another oath, Timothy stalked out to take up a position by the mouth of Exchange Alley, letting his attention stray from the Martins Bank entrance only long enough to ensure he was not taken by surprise. Thus he became aware passersby were giving him a wide berth or crossing the street to avoid him. He forced a neutral expression; looking like bull beef made him conspicuous, a state he avoided. Why was he tense? Maggie had identified the murderer, which should save Hawkins. Kimber had delivered a letter to Cole's house, which implied he had left afterwards. Maggie would be in no immediate danger. It was only to pass on the information to Easterday to present to the magistrate.

Maggie would probably have to go before de Veil to support the accusation. He could collect Maggie, claiming her sister had taken a turn for the worse, and take her to Bow Street, to explain…but would her testimony be enough to warrant taking Kimber into custody immediately? She would have to explain how she had seen Kimber outside the Opera House and that she had been placed in Cole's home as a spy. The word of a ruined maidservant who had taken to the street in order to survive would carry little weight against the word of a wealthy merchant's family. No doubt de Veil would investigate—Easterday's reputation should be enough to assure the magistrate took the information seriously—but while he was doing so, Kimber would be warned and might kill her to eliminate a possible witness.

Nor would Salem Cole be pleased to have his nephew accused and to know Maggie had spied upon him. She would lose her place. No great loss; Timothy would find her another position. Hawkins would hire her, or Easterday or his wife would make sure she was taken care of. From what he had heard of Cole, he did not think the man would accuse her of theft in revenge for her testimony. Such things happened, but the grocer's servants thought him an honest man and a good master. One less contingency to plan for, at least.

Easterday emerged from the bank and turned to go east on Lombard Street, as if he meant to return to his office. He did not survey the street, all the proof Timothy needed that the curst clerk had not informed him he was wanted. Timothy loped after him.

Chapter 31

Emily sat at the little escritoire in the drawing room, attempting to compose a cheerful letter to Cousin Cecily. Cousin Henry might have written her already about Hawkins, except that he never wrote anything until he could no longer put it off and Cecily's recent letter gave no indication she knew. Emily did not like to mention it, for how could she explain? Nevertheless, Cecily was sure to hear of it sooner or later—certainly when Hawkins was executed—and then it would seem odd that Emily had not written of it. Emily could not delay replying, or she would have to write of Hawkins's death and explain the whole of it then. Emily wiped her pen and set aside the almost blank sheet, which had stuck at "I received your letter." What could she say to her cousin's lively account of the lambing on her husband's estate and the cook's attempt to make iced cream for a dinner party which had yielded a sort of chilled soup. "...Cook having failed to employ enough ice, or perhaps not having let the pots sit in the ice she did have for a sufficiently long period," as Cecily explained.

Olivia Easterday had left Queen's Square with one of her employees and Samuel, the brawny head footman, to deal with some problem at a warehouse, saying she might not return until evening. Sarah had retired to her room, ostensibly with a megrim. She was likely suffering from melancholy rather than an aching head and merely wished to avoid inflicting her despondency on anyone else. Emily had certainly done the same often enough in the past. She was older now and a married lady and owed it to herself, her husband, Sarah, and her host and hostess not to reveal her worry.

"Begging your pardon, your ladyship, ma'am," her own under-footman's deferential murmur interrupted this chain of thoughts.

"What is it, Thomas?"

"My lady, Mr. Givens being out for his half-day, Peter sent on an errand, and Samuel out with Mistress Easterday, I don't rightly know what to do with this letter as was delivered for the young lady."

"For Mistress Sarah? Put it on the hall table with any other mail that's come, I suppose."

"That's what I would do if it'd come in the usual way, my lady, if I'd anything to do with it, which I wouldn't, Mr. Givens or Samuel being in charge of the mail. This was delivered by hand by a fellow that looked like a tradesman, and he said 'twasn't to be given to Mistress Sarah till late this afternoon."

"Really. What did the fellow look like? His face, not merely his dress."

"He was thin. There was nothing remarkable about him. He might be four-and-twenty."

Thomas would have to learn to observe more carefully, if he wished to advance. "Did he have a long, thin nose, and a wide mouth with thin lips?"

"Why, yes, your ladyship. That's him to the life. Thin all over, he was."

Will Kimber. "I will give it to Mistress Sarah."

Emily held the sealed sheet for several minutes

after Thomas left her, having shifted the responsibility to the highest authority available. A young lady should not receive correspondence from a man, unless he was a close relative. Kimber was almost a foster brother, and she had seen how fond Sarah was of her cousin. The family connection made it permissible. Yet Sarah's pensive mood since his last visit worried her. When she had gone to Kimber, he had promised to call upon Sarah in two days' time. Today, in fact. Instead he had delivered a letter with instructions to delay giving it to the girl.

The easiest thing would be to turn it over to Olivia on her return. As Sarah's hostess, it should be her responsibility; the letter could then be delivered in accordance with Kimber's intention. The idea appealed strongly. Sarah was not in Emily's charge. She secreted the letter in her pocket.

But she had been spending a great deal of time with Sarah, and something about the letter made her exceedingly uneasy. She pulled it out of her pocket. If she had married a man from her own class, she would have had the running of a large house with many servants. Eventually, if she bore daughters, she would have made many of the decisions which would lead to their eminently suitable marriages. She would not have hesitated to do what was necessary. Something was wrong, both with Sarah and the letter, and in the absence of Olivia, she was Sarah's chaperon. Emily took a deep breath, raised her chin, and marched upstairs.

She took the indistinct response to her brisk tap as permission to enter and found the girl sitting on the edge of the bed, sniffling. This and the evidence of

Sarah's reddened eyes testified she had been indulging in a fit of weeping. Emily did not pretend to believe in the megrim or to ignore the signs of distress.

"Sarah, I know more is amiss than a headache."

The girl mumbled a greeting without meeting Emily's eyes. She could not deny her state. "My head does ache vilely, and I miss my papa so much that I could not help but weep, Emily."

"Yet I have not noticed this tendency to be a watering can until recently. When you first came to stay here, you were shy but not distraught, and I formed the opinion that you are usually of a cheerful temperament. I do not believe this is all because you learned of my husband's unfortunate predicament." Despite her concern for Sarah, she was tempted to smile. 'Pon rep! A decent restraint was all very well, but such a ridiculously understated description of Hawkins's danger was ridiculous.

Sarah made no reply beyond swallowing hard and mopping her eyes again with her damp handkerchief.

"You are desperately unhappy. Now your cousin has left a letter for you, saying it was to be withheld for several hours. The Easterdays are not here. As your friend, it falls to me to try to help. Tell me what this is about." She held out the letter.

Sarah stared at it much as Emily had done, before sinking onto the dressing table's stool. Emily took the armchair near the window and watched while she broke the wafer and unfolded the sheet. Her lips moved as she read.

It would be embarrassing if it were no more than a note excusing his failure to call upon Sarah today. Still, Sarah had been miserable for days, though she had tried to conceal it. Men might laugh at women's logic, but one need not always be able to spell out one's reasons to know something was true.

Abruptly, Sarah's lips stilled. A second later, she started up off the stool, shrieked, and collapsed to the floor, wailing. No girl as young as Sarah was noted for self-discipline, in Emily's experience, but even for one of the lower classes, this showed an appalling lack of restraint.

"Sarah, get up this instant! Whatever is wrong, a tantrum will not improve matters. Take a deep breath." The method her own mother had used with a maid in a fit of hysterics worked with Sarah, too.

The girl raised her head to gaze blindly at her and tried to stifle her sobs. Emily took her by the arm and pulled her up. It was a very good thing Sarah had recovered enough to struggle to her feet, as Emily was slight and Sarah was plump. Having pushed her onto her stool and offered her own handkerchief, Emily picked up the letter and returned to the window to read.

"You mustn't—what shall I do?" Sarah whimpered.

Having asked herself the same question on many occasions over the years, Emily was able to answer. "Dry your eyes and blow your nose. Let me see what all this fuss is about."

Sarey,

I told Lady Emily I'd visit you today, but I knew what I have to say is best done in writing. You were upset to hear Marston was dead, which I had to tell you as you still thought Uncle would make you marry him. I understand why you were upset to hear it, because you cried when Atkins's rabid dog was shot. I expected you would get over it in a few days. He hurt you and would have hurt you more if you married him, which you did not want to do anyway. Lady Emily came to see me because you were distressed. I could not think why at first, because you said you were not breeding, and Marston being dead meant he couldn't marry you even if Uncle had changed his mind. Recently I learned from Lady Emily that her husband is in Newgate Prison, charged with Marston's murder. I never thought anyone would be charged. It would not be fair for him to be punished for something he did not do. She told me the poison I used was known to be from the Spanish Main. Probably I should have read the newssheets after I saw the notice of his death. I thought it would be over and everything would be made right.

When I found out the poison was known and Mr. Hawkins was suspected because he had sailed in the West Indies, I realized Uncle might also be suspected. Do you recall his telling us about the natives shooting game and Spaniards with poisoned arrows? You may not remember, being younger than I was, and a girl, or he may not have talked of it in your hearing for the same reasons. In his cabinet, he had a tube of the stuff he had been given or maybe won at cards. The sort kept in cane tubes was the most powerful. I did not know if it was still strong enough to kill a man (if it ever had been), but he said he was told the natives who made the mixture did not touch it if they had any cut or broken skin on their hands. The other kinds were kept in gourds and in clay pots, but I don't think Uncle knew their relative strengths, and he hadn't any of those, so it did not matter.

The natives expelled the poisoned darts from reeds

with the force of their breath (which I think a very interesting idea which should be studied) or poisoned the tips of their arrows. Neither method seemed good to use on the street. In the same cabinet, there is an arrowhead and pieces of something like black glass, though I believe they are really a kind of stone. Years ago Uncle let me handle them. He warned me they were sharp, and he was correct. Blood was flowing from the palm of my hand before I realized one of the shards had cut me.

I took some of the poison paste and two of the shards, knowing that two out of fourteen pieces were not likely to be missed. I made a walking stick with a tip which could be retracted and fixed a shard loaded with the poison in the end. I followed Marston every time I could, until I saw my chance outside the Opera House.

I have written out my confession and will deliver it this afternoon, so all will be well. This is the important thing, Sarey: I will say I killed him because he was a bad man who was cruel to animals and kicked an old dog in my sight. You must not mention the other thing or take on about this, lest it damage your reputation, about which Uncle is very worried.

Your cousin,
Will Kimber

"Lud!"

Sarah had regained some control of herself while Emily read this startling account. "Lady Emily, where would he go? To Newgate? I must stop him."

What could Emily do to help her when a lady's proper sphere lay in dealing with servants, menus, social events, and the training of daughters to be accomplished and dutiful? Dutiful. She had a duty to

Sarah in the absence of Olivia or Captain Easterday.

As Kimber's letter had been received hours earlier than he intended, he might not yet have confessed his crime. Of course Sarah would want to save her foster brother from hanging: she loved him. If she succeeded, Hawkins would probably hang in his place, and oh, dear God, Sarah was depending on her. If they reached him before he did so, Will Kimber might yield to Sarah's entreaties not to reveal his guilt. Kimber clearly loved his cousin and did not like to see her unhappy. If he were dissuaded from a public confession, Hawkins would hang.

And what of her duty to Ambrose Hawkins? She now had proof Kimber had killed Marston. As a wife, her duty to Hawkins obliged her to present the evidence exonerating him. At the very least, she must stop Sarah from preventing Kimber's confession. She need only keep the girl from reaching her cousin before he announced his guilt.

"Get ready to go out while I try to think, Sarah." The silly chit stood staring until Emily added, "I'll go with you, but I must think how we can manage this. Mistress Easterday is a redoubtable lady, but she would not let me visit my husband in Newgate. She said even she would not go there. We must not fly into a panic."

As Sarah whisked into her dressing room, Emily slipped the letter into her pocket. Hawkins had been charged at Bow Street, and Captain Easterday had gone there to speak with the magistrate Thomas de Veil. Common sense told her that was where Kimber would go. Was it not where anyone who had proof exonerating a prisoner would present it?

If they went to Newgate, the trip would provide

some delay, given the distance and the crowded, maze-like streets. They would arrive, learn they had gone to the wrong place, and more time would be lost travelling to the Bow Street magistrate's court near Covent Garden and the Theater Royal.

If she agreed they should go to Newgate, she would be lying. She berated herself for giving Sarah the letter sooner than Kimber had intended she receive it. If she could but tarry a bit, Kimber might have the opportunity he needed, without Emily having to lie to Sarah. Ladies and gentlemen did lie: sometimes courtesy required it, for one really could not tell a lady her gown was ugly or a gentleman that he had trodden upon one's toes in the dance. Not that the lies were limited to such minor matters: she had pretended not to notice her father's lack of attention to financial matters and pretended to believe Cousin Claude's demonstrably false claim that raising the tenants' rents would solve all their problems. A social lie might be acceptable. What she was considering would have consequences beyond a well-meaning deceit to spare someone's feelings. She could not lie in this matter.

Yet one course of action would be a betrayal of her husband, the other of Sarah, to whom she also had an obligation. Strictly speaking, her duty as Sarah's chaperon would hardly permit her to take the chit to Newgate or to Bow Street. For two decent females to go to either place would be scandalous, unless they were accompanied by a gentleman. She could insist on sending for Captain Easterday. Objections to this reassuring notion immediately presented themselves. Easterday's office was farther away than Newgate, though a footman would make better speed than a coach. And what if he were not at his office? She and Sarah could go for Mr. Cole. His shop was closer.

No: he was said to be out of town. If he was in town, Cole might agree with his daughter that Kimber must be dissuaded. He had not wanted his daughter to marry Kimber, but all the same, he had shown a fondness for his nephew. And having a relative who was a confessed killer would reflect upon Cole and his daughter and perhaps damage Cole's business.

Yet she could not refuse to help Sarah. The girl was biddable, but Emily placed no reliance on her obeying a refusal to let her go in search of her cousin. Sarah would slip out on her own. She had not been reared to such exacting standards as Emily, and she surely had enough pin money to hire a hackney. The thought of the chit braving Newgate Prison on her own was not to be borne. There was no help for it: she would accompany her charge. But to which? Newgate or Bow Street?

In her own bedchamber's dressing room, she found Putnam mending a split seam in one of her gloves. "Leave that and have Thomas fetch a hackney. No, wait. There's a boy who does the boots and fetches and carries for the cook, isn't there? Send him for the coach and then he must take a message to Captain Easterday as fast as he can." She scribbled several lines, using the pencil and paper she kept in her dressing table for notes. There was no time to waste on writing it out in ink and fiddling with pounce. She folded the sheet and addressed it to Captain Marcus Easterday—Urgent and Confidential—Leadenhall Street. "Tell Thomas he must accompany us."

"What will you wish to wear, my lady?"

"I'll go as I am."

"But where?"

"I don't know yet. Either the Bow Street court or Newgate."

From Putnam's expression, Emily might have said, "Timbuktoo or Hell."

"My lady! You can't go there!"

"Do not tell me what I can do, Putnam. Now put this in the boy's hand and impress its urgency upon him. And tell Thomas to await us at the door."

"I will accompany you, Lady Emily. Thomas is useless for anything beyond opening doors."

"I do not think you would be much use on this errand, Putnam. It concerns Mistress Sarah and her cousin, and my husband's life."

Putnam dropped the glove in the mending basket and turned to the clothespress. Emily caught a few muttered words as she did so, which sounded like, "No great loss."

"Your plain, dark cape, I suppose, and—"

"If I must go into mourning, I will have no need for a dresser, Putnam. Go at once."

"But your ladyship's cape, hat, and gloves—"

"Go!"

Putnam caught her sense of urgency and hastened out the door. Emily scrabbled through the shelves of the clothes press until she found a plain short cape providentially left over from before her marriage. It would not look too odd with her simple jacket and petticoat and a straw hat. A drawer yielded gloves. She changed into stouter shoes and took all her pin money, a satisfactorily large amount, for Hawkins was generous in the matter of her allowance. They would need hackney fare, and who knew what other expenses might occur.

When she reached the hall, Sarah was already waiting, cloak over one arm, a broad-brimmed hat dangling by its ribbons, and gloves clutched in her other hand.

"Oh, please, Lady Emily, may we go?"

"The kitchen boy will fetch a hackney, and my footman will come with us, for the neighborhood will not be a good one. Put on your hat and cape. And your gloves." Emily pulled on her own gloves. She must decide what to do before the hackney arrived. If she told Sarah it would be better to go to Bow Street, they might arrive before Kimber. She wished Captain Easterday might arrive at Bow Street first. Impossible, even if he received her letter in time.

While her life in town had mostly been limited to Westminster, Cousin Henry had pointed out a few landmarks when they had come up from the country. After they crossed the bridge and turned to go west, Henry had jerked his thumb behind him, saying, "East India House is behind us, on Leadenhall Street. The Royal Exchange is ahead, on the right." He had a great deal to say about the Royal Exchange, though Emily's mind, East India House sounded more interesting, for its associations with exotic Eastern luxuries. London Bridge being farther to the east than Covent Garden, it was unlikely the captain would arrive at Bow Street soon after them. Nor had she told him their destination, not being sure of it herself. Instead she had limited her message to her possession of Kimber's confession, hoping he would take the appropriate action.

If only the captain were here! Or even Henry, or any gentleman. They would know what to do. Ambrose would be best of all. She could not imagine any predicament with which he would not deal expeditiously. But Ambrose Hawkins was in Newgate, unable to extricate himself from his own plight.

The more she pondered it, the less she could convince herself that going to Newgate would be the right choice.

"Sarah, I've thought on what to do. Your cousin very likely knows he must turn himself in to a magistrate. As it was at Bow Street my husband's arrest was ordered, that is Mr. Kimber's most likely destination." If Kimber had already confessed, all would be well. If she and Sarah intercepted him, Kimber might refuse to be dissuaded from confessing. And if he did yield to Sarah's entreaties, Emily had his letter in her pocket. She would decide then what to do with it.

Chapter 32

Sarah wrung her hands and expostulated. "Emily, is there not a shorter way to go? Can we not turn into some less busy street?"

Emily stroked the lump of her betrothal ring under her glove. Ambrose Hawkins had chosen a ring set with an emerald because he had noticed she was wearing her grandmother's emerald necklace and earrings the night he first saw her. After they married, he had examined them and said, "Spanish work, about a century old," and laughed. "A shame the stones were replaced." She had concealed her hurt that he could find it humorous. She had known they were paste, the real stones having been sold to meet expenses long ago, but she treasured the set as her mother had. A week or two later, he had taken her to a jeweler to see the emeralds already collected to replace the paste stones.

"It takes time to make a good match so the pieces will be worthy of you." She had been surprised and touched to the heart he would make the effort and spend the money. He had shrugged off her stammered thanks, saying only that he could afford it and the workmanship of the mountings was fine. She also cherished the memory of looking at houses with Ambrose. He had solicited her opinion. When had she ever been consulted on any question weightier than the dinner menu, or the style of a gown? In his company, she felt cared for.

"I'm sure the coachman knows the most direct route, Sarah. And you know any street we take is likely to be as busy."

She could not bear to lose Hawkins. Sarah, poor girl, could not bear to lose her cousin.

****

"I don't think this is a place for a lady, your ladyship," Thomas muttered as he handed Emily and Sarah down from the coach. The acrid scent of roasting coffee was in the air, signaling the presence of a coffee house nearby. Emily scarcely took note of the rest of the street. The building before which they stood seemed to have attracted the most custom, if custom it could be called. A number of disreputable-looking men lounged in front, almost blocking the door. Two others, watchmen or constables by their dress, stood talking in low voices.

"Make way for the ladies," Thomas croaked. The riffraff who heard turned to gaze at him in amusement or contempt and to ogle Emily and her companion. Sarah made a distressful sound in her throat. One of the constables took a step forward and raised his voice.

"Out o' the way, you men. Show some respect for the gentry-morts."

The rabble parted like the Red Sea before Moses, though not without some low-voiced comments. The constable who had spoken took the lead, with Thomas left to follow nervously at the tail of their group. Emily's heart raced. She had never set foot in such a place, on such an errand, and she prayed to God she would never have to do it again.

"The office is here, ma'am," their guide said. "A

mite noisier than usual, even. If you'll tell me what brings you here, I'll have a word with—"

The long, narrow room was thronged with people. Emily's first thought was of a humming beehive, though without the bustle of activity.

At one end of the chamber sat a middle-aged man in a long wig. A clerk sat at a desk, quill in hand, motionless. Every face in the room, including the clerk's, was turned toward the magistrate, as she guessed he was. And the magistrate's head was half turned toward the side, where two men were gripping the arms of a third. The constable let out a breath and murmured, "Strike me dead."

At Emily's shoulder, Sarah gasped. Her "Will!" came out as no more than a squeak.

The scene before Emily seemed colorless, the men all soberly dressed in dark colors, touched with the white of their neckcloths and wristbands. By contrast the blood flowing from Kimber's temple and right hand stood out shockingly.

Sarah tried to push forward. "He's hurt. They've hurt him."

Emily grabbed her by the arm, and the constable, a kindly man, stepped in front of her. "Now, young lady, you don't want to see. Ma'am, whatever your business with his worship, it'd be best to return tomorrow."

"This is our business." She nodded toward Kimber. The likelihood of removing Sarah without a scene equaled the chance of the sun rising in the west.

"Then keep the young lady here, and I'll go up and see what's toward, ma'am."

He approached the magistrate, who was still staring at Will Kimber, and waited to be recognized. Emily watched as de Veil glanced at their constable and spoke sharply. As the constable replied, Sarah pulled away and all but ran toward Will. No one tried to stop her; everyone in the room stood frozen in position, as if at some theatrical performance.

What could Emily do but follow? They were humiliating themselves before all of London. She heard Thomas's footfalls start after her. As she darted after Sarah, she saw the reason Sarah had broken away. Perhaps originally the constables bracketing him had laid hands on Will Kimber to restrain him. Now it was evident that they were steadying him. It was no longer enough. He was swaying between them. One put an arm around Kimber's shoulders; someone, de Veil, she thought, shouted for a chair to be brought. With commendable promptitude, the clerk dragged a straight chair over, and the constables lowered Kimber onto it.

Sarah pushed her way forward and grasped his left hand, falling to her knees. "Will, what have they done to you?"

He was having trouble holding up his head but mumbled thickly, "I did it. Proving how...Go..." His head lolled.

"Will, Will," Sarah sobbed.

As Emily reached them, she saw a crutch-handled walking stick with an unusually thick shaft lying on the table before the magistrate, together with a closely written sheet. She rested her hand on Sarah's shoulder, the only comfort she could offer at the moment.

De Veil glanced at her. "Madam, I would not have it thought anyone here injured this man. He presented a document purporting to explain how a certain murder was committed and said he would demonstrate. He slashed his temple with a bit of glass before anyone could stop him, saying, 'Be careful with the cane. There may yet be some of the poison on the shard concealed in the tip. This will prove what I have written in my confession.' Which I have not yet had time to read," he added acerbically. "Remove your friend, and tell her how it came about, when she is able to take it in."

Something dropped from the flaccid fingers of Will Kimber's bleeding right hand. One of the constables bent to retrieve it, only to freeze at the magistrate's bellow of "Leave it! If you cut yourself, you're like to be a dead man." More quietly he went on, "Don't touch it. Slide a sheet of paper under it and put it on the table. Hastings, fetch a surgeon."

"I misdoubt it's worthwhile, Your Worship," the constable propping Kimber in his chair volunteered. "I b'lieve the fellow's dead."

"All the same, we will have a professional opinion."

Still clutching Will's unbloodied hand, Sarah folded over it, weeping bitterly. Emily could be of no use to her at the moment. She did not need to look back to know Thomas, two or three paces behind her, was paralyzed with indecision. She had spent her entire life avoiding any public notoriety, being a perfect lady. She had always been shielded from any unpleasantness (except poverty and worry) by a man. Now, in spite of all, she was left standing on her own. Wishing ardently she were almost anywhere else, she took as deep a breath as her corset would allow. She was the daughter of a duke, trained to conduct herself accordingly and always to do her duty. This hour, Sarah was her duty, and Ambrose Hawkins, too, for as long as either one of them lived.

She stepped boldly toward the magistrate as someone deposited a blank sheet of paper holding a bit of black glass before him.

"Sir, I am Lady Emily Hawkins. Am I correct that Mr. William Kimber has confessed to murdering Captain Marston?"

He regarded her thoughtfully before replying, "You are."

"Then my husband, Ambrose Hawkins, is exonerated, and there is no need for him to be bound over for trial?"

He steepled his fingers. "As to that, there is some question in my mind as to why Kimber would commit not only the crime of murder but also of *felo-de-se*. The crime of taking his own life," he amended, for the benefit of a female ignorant of Latin. He cast a shrewd eye on Sarah, who had not moved from her place by Will. The constable still flanking his mortal remains kept a worried eye on her.

"In the letter he left for his foster sister"—Emily nodded toward Sarah—"he admitted he had killed Marston for mistreating animals, which I can believe, as she has often said how fond Mr. Kimber was of animals and how tenderly he treated them. She is beside herself with grief now, but I am sure she will swear out a statement about his concern for brute beings, with many examples. I think what prompted him to confess was discovering that my husband had been charged with the murder." She lowered her voice. "From what I observed of Mr. Kimber, and things my friend has mentioned, he has been somewhat strange since he was a child."

"I see."

Emily wondered if the magistrate did, indeed, understand. She hoped he would not ask if the letter was present. She did not think she dared lie to a magistrate.

Fortunately, just then the doctor came striding in. De Veil beckoned to him.

"I misdoubt you have a living patient, Doctor Brewster." De Veil's voice was pitched low. "I must warn you that he claimed the fragment of glass with which he wounded himself under his hair at his temple was smeared with poison. As his hand is also bleeding, I suppose it cut him there as well. You will wish to be careful."

The medical man's eyebrows lifted in surprise. "Thank you, sir. If the young lady could be persuaded to, er, remove herself?"

Emily and Thomas succeeded in pulling Sarah away from Will Kimber's limp form. Seeing she would cling to Emily, Thomas immediately released her, and took up his footman's stance a few steps away. The physician unceremoniously deposited his instrument case on the end of the magistrate's table and opened it.

Emily could not bear to look at Sarah. Kimber was past whatever pain he had suffered, while Sarah's anguish was only beginning. Instead, she focused on the doctor's case. It resembled the cases of the physicians who had attended her father and Cousin Claude in their final illnesses, having a top that lifted up and front panels that opened out and two or three shallow drawers. Inside were the usual bottles and medical paraphernalia, but in addition, the tray at the top held instruments she did not recall from the other medical chests.

Brewster removed a vial and wrenched out the stopper: hartshorn, its sharp scent sure to revive someone who had fainted. Receiving no reaction, he recorked it and replaced the flask in two swift, sure motions. He held the back of his left hand to Kimber's nose, frowning a little, while feeling in his case with the right. He gave over trying to feel breath and pricked the middle finger on Kimber's unwounded hand with a lancet. Emily had poked her own finger with a needle on more than one occasion, spotting her fabric. Even at a distance of six or eight feet, it was obvious that no drop of blood issued forth.

The medical man stood regarding the body before him for a moment before wiping the lancet on a piece of bandage and returning the instrument to its place. Then he raised the limp right hand to inspect the cut in his palm, protecting his fingers with the bandage. He released it to drop once again to Kimber's side, before taking out another instrument.

Emily hardly breathed as he shifted the hair at Will Kimber's temple with a probe, bending to examine the wound at some length. Emily drew her own conclusion.

"Your Worship, this man is dead."

"Are you certain, sir? He is not merely in a swoon?"

"Even one who has swooned yet breathes. He does not. Neither did he react nor bleed at a sharp jab from my lancet. The head wound is not now bleeding, and as we are aware, scalp wounds bleed a prodigious amount. He is dead."

"Then as he cannot benefit from your services, pray examine by sight the object on this paper and tell me what you see."

"It appears to be a piece of black glass, most extreme thin at the edge on one side, and smeared with dark matter. I observed traces of a similar substance at the injuries. I infer this caused the wounds, which are not deep enough to cause death in a healthy young man." His gaze shifted to the cane lying on the table, and he studied it a moment, paying particular attention to the lower end and then to the upper end, where Emily saw a little lever under the handle. The physician cocked an eyebrow at Thomas de Veil. "A sudden death involving a similar injury has been a subject of great interest in medical circles recently. I'm sure Your Worship is aware that there is a hollow in the bottom of this walking stick, with another glass shard within. I venture to suggest that if one manipulated this device"—he indicated the protruding peg under the crutch handle—"the lethal blade would descend past the bottom of the cane, making it a stabbing weapon."

"Pray stand back." De Veil picked up the cane carefully and turned it toward the wall behind him before fiddling with the little peg. He was not alone in jerking back when a shaft tipped with another piece of dark glass sprang from the walking stick's end. The magistrate contemplated it, then manipulated the lever until the central shaft retracted.

"I regret your testimony will not be needed at trial; the jury would be most impressed." Aside to Emily, de Veil said, "Dr. Brewster combines the practices of both physician and surgeon, having studied at Edinburgh, and has often been of assistance to this court."

"I studied at the University of Leiden, as well." Brewster closed his medical case and fastened its catches.

"You may safely assure that poor young lady that her friend or relative has been attended by one of the most skilled medical men in London, if not the richest or most fashionable." More quietly he continued, " 'Tis perhaps a mercy for his family and friends he did not survive, considering his confession. He will be tried before a higher judge than any at the quarter sessions."

Emily nodded. Kimber's death was a blessing, sparing his family the shame of his being tried and hanged.

"Now nothing remains to be done beyond some paperwork and the necessary arrangements…"

Sarah had paid no attention during the doctor's examination. She stood hunched, face buried in her handkerchief, with Emily's arm around her. Emily wondered what those arrangements might be, considering that a suicide could not be given a funeral.

"…which I think must include an inquest. While the cause of death seems obvious, any death of one held in prison would require an inquest. William Kimber was in custody in my court. Given the notoriety of the murder and circumstances of his own death, I shall refer the matter to the coroner. A public inquiry should go far toward laying to rest suspicion and scurrilous gossip. Doctor, I believe we need take no more of your time. Your surgery is at the sign of the Half Moon in this street, is it not?"

"It is, sir."

"Then no doubt you will receive your summons there."

The physician/surgeon gave a nod and sketched a bow.

"Good day, then. Morris! Write out an order to

release one Ambrose Hawkins from Newgate, as the charge has been dropped, the actual murderer having been found. And, er, someone find a pair of seats for these ladies so they may sit while they wait. Now, who's next?"

Sarah was silent except for an occasional sniff. Emily, sunk in her own thoughts, paid no attention to the procession of men and women accused of theft from shops, picking pockets, assault, and burglary. A younger clerk took down their names and the details relating to the charges, while the middle-aged Morris scratched away quietly at another desk. Emily, sunken in thought, was taken by surprise when one of the officers of the court approached to summon her to de Veil.

"Here is the order for your husband's release. You should send it by a male relative, as well as money. You may not be aware the prison will charge various fees before they turn a prisoner loose."

"I do not know who I could ask who would be able to come at once." Captain Easterday should have been here by now, considering how long they had been at Bow Street, unless he had been away from his office. Like Hawkins, the captain did sometimes visit warehouses and ships. He would have been a reassuring support. Cousin Henry, if he were available, was young and timid, a frail reed to rely upon. "I do not wish to leave Mr. Hawkins imprisoned even an hour longer than necessary. I have a footman with me." Though Thomas was also young and timid.

"Bates!"

The constable who had brought them into the court stepped forward.

"Escort this lady and her party to Newgate and assist her in securing the release of her husband. You have money with you, my lady?"

"Yes, thank you, sir."

She was aflame to set out, to be done with the whole sordid business, but few things wished for take place without delay. A hackney must be fetched; then the ride was interminable. Sarah sat in blank-faced misery. Between the shocking events at Bow Street and the embarrassment of occupying the coach with the ladies and a constable, Thomas sat stiffly, staring at his knees. Constable Bates was silent for the most part, matter-of-fact when he spoke.

As they waited for a dray blocking the street to move on, he said, "There's not many ladies would go to Newgate themselves. It's brave of your ladyship, if you don't mind me saying."

No one so far beneath her class had ever spoken to her unsolicited, except a servant or shopkeeper anxious to assist her. Certainly they would never address such a personal remark to her. The last month had certainly been full of new experiences.

"I could not let my husband remain in prison longer than necessary merely to spare myself a little unpleasantness, Constable."

"If you've a vial of scent with you, my lady, you might put a drop or two on your handkerchief and keep it over your nose when we get there. And the young lady, too."

"I will heed your advice. Thank you." The man was lower on the social scale than a domestic servant, though not as low as a ratcatcher. Absurdly, her mind began composing her letter to Cousin Cecily: "...On my way to Newgate to free my husband after the discovery of the real murderer, I received perhaps the most flattering compliment of my life, when the constable accompanying us praised me for courage..." If only he knew how frightened she had always been. Now, however, she feared being without Hawkins more than she feared visiting Newgate Prison.

Chapter 33

Newgate must be the anteroom to Hell. She had doused her handkerchief with the perfume she carried and had done the same with Sarah's, already sodden with her tears, though Sarah would remain in the coach. The air was thick with a stench composed of human waste, sweat, fear, dirty clothing, unwashed bodies, and misery, which penetrated even the scent of damask rose and musk.

Inside, the cacophony of shouting and cursing, interspersed by an occasional shriek of laughter or scream or wail, was a foretaste of Hell which assaulted the senses as much as the stench. If Constable Bates had not been at her side, she might have fled. Even the constable could not make Newgate loose its hold on a prisoner quickly. The keepers and prisoners alike gaped at her and made comments, a few of which were audible if not intelligible.

"The rum-doxy's here for some unthrift lover on the debtors' side, most like."

"She'd best leave him be and take another... Wouldn't mind applying a plaster o' hot guts to her..." Bates began a running monologue about the history of the prison, how Sir Christopher Wren rebuilt it a few years after the Great Fire of 1666, with an addition on the south side of Newgate Street. His calm voice steadied Emily as even reminding herself of her duty could not.

Yet more waiting. The warden must be sent for and then scrutinize the order. He questioned Bates, with much shaking of his head over the amazing events leading to its issuance. A keeper, glancing undecidedly between Bates and Emily, sidled up to Bates and muttered to him. The constable turned to Emily and relayed the sum necessary to release her husband. She passed the coins to him. Bates spoke sternly in the keeper's ear as he paid the fee.

At least the warden's presence as well as the constable's caused some of the onlookers to disperse or at least be silent. Finally, he gave instructions to fetch the prisoner out. Emily raised her chin and tightened her lips against their trembling.

Then it was over. It took a moment to recognize Hawkins approaching, a head taller than the keeper at his side. Her husband looked more like a hawk than ever, grim, hollow-eyed, and two or three days unshaven, though he was dressed neatly. A thin, pale man following in his wake clutched a valise which appeared to weigh little. A flicker of emotion lit her husband's eyes when he saw her, and his stride faltered. As he reached her, he inclined his head. But instead of greeting her, he gave the warden a curt nod and thanked him for his hospitality. At a nod from the warden, a keeper came forward to remove Hawkins's fetters in exchange for a coin. Her husband then gave a coin to the prisoner with the valise before taking the bag and turning to her.

****

When the keeper came to inform him he was to be released, the real murderer having been discovered, the details seemed unimportant. Hawkins continued to sit at the table, heart pounding. His meal, abandoned when he gave up trying to eat an hour or more previously sat cold and congealing. His guts roiled with nausea. The rats would find it appealing, no doubt. Ned, a skulking little fellow who had been acting as Hawkins's valet and fetched and carried for any prisoner who could pay him, had followed the keeper in.

"Will I pack your things, then, Mr. Hawkins?"

Hawkins answered through a fog of numbness. He had not expected to leave the prison but to be taken the short distance to the Sessions House for his trial. He had found it amusing to remember that several years ago the criminal court had received a new front faced with blocks of stone, enclosing the courtroom which had been open to the weather on one side, and adding fine, tall windows and a passageway directly from the prison to the court, eliminating the need to pass through the street. Sometime later, a cart would take him the longer distance to Tyburn to die.

"Pack the books and papers on the table. Keep the clothing. I'd only burn it when I'm home."

"Ay, sir, and thank you for a true gentleman."

The clothing Pirtle had sent, though plain and serviceable, was worth a fortune in Newgate, where everything was for sale.

"And your meal, sir?"

"Yours, too, if you want it."

Hawkins continued to sit while Ned tidily wrapped the meat pie in one of Hawkins's handkerchiefs before packing the books and papers into the smaller valise.

He was only dimly aware of his surroundings as he passed through the dank corridors and down the stairs, although he felt the stir of interest in his wake. A prisoner held for a capital crime being released without trial? Unheard of!

His wife stood straight-backed and calm in the mouth of Hell beside a burly constable. He imagined the scent of roses cutting through the prison reek. If news of his release had not already rendered him almost speechless, his shock at her presence would have silenced him. He did not know what to say to her, and so he made his farewells to the warden and his escort. How the devil had she come to be here?

She spoke before he could recover his wits. "Mr. Hawkins, this is Constable Bates, sent by the magistrate to help me secure your release."

"Bates, thank you."

"Pleased to be of service to your good lady, sir."

Hawkins found half a crown in his pocket and passed it to the constable.

"Thank you, sir. You'll be wanting to get home, and I'll be on my way."

Remembering his manners, Hawkins offered Emily his unencumbered arm. She twined hers around it, bringing to mind ivy girdling an oak. What was she doing here alone? Easterday could have come or sent an attorney or a clerk if he were too busy.

As they passed from Hell onto Newgate Street, Emily said, "Sarah is waiting in the hackney on Gilt Spur Street."

Sarah?

"Is that all you have with you? I thought your valet had packed a portmanteau as well."

"This is all I wish to keep. I want nothing else to remind me of this place."

Ahead, a gangling young footman—Thomas, Hawkins realized after a moment—sprang away from a coach's door and after an indecisive glance at the hackney, trotted forward to take the valise.

Later, only isolated images and words came to Hawkins. A girl of eighteen or nineteen years, eyes puffy, breaking the silence with a husky, "I am glad you are cleared, Mr. Hawkins," and trying to smile. He did not trouble himself to understand when Emily addressed the girl.

"Sarah, will you wish to return to Queen's Square and Mistress Easterday, or to your own home?"

"I want to go home." The last word ended on a sob.

"I understand. There is comfort in being in familiar surroundings when mourning. We will deliver you on our way, and I will have my maid pack and send your belongings."

Emily told the footman to stop the coach at the next hackney stand and gave him the fare to go to Queen's Square.

"And tell our coachman to go first to John Street, Golden Square."

It was wrong for his poor wife to have to take charge because he was not dealing with these matters. Somehow he could not bestir himself.

Who was the girl and why was she here? He had muttered, "Your servant," when the girl was introduced as Sarah Someone-or-other. He could not remember if Emily had explained her presence. None of them had anything more to say. Or if they had, he had not been listening; he could hardly have spoken to his wife the words he wanted to say and knew he should say, with a stranger present. Worse, the words were all a-jumble in his brain. He wanted to speak, but what could he say? He had been angry to find her in Newgate, almost the last place a decent woman should be, and at the same time, he was overwhelmed with gladness to see her, and not because she had somehow contrived his release. The coach ride must have lasted for many minutes, although he retained little memory of it.

He stared blankly out the window as the hackney stopped before a house Hawkins had never seen before. Emily spoke to the girl and patted her hand as a footman hurried out to open the hackney's door and lower the steps.

Sarah murmured something to Emily, and said in a more composed tone, "Thank you, William," as the footman assisted her to alight. The butler, standing in the doorway, cast aside butler-like behavior to demand, "Mistress Sarah? What's amiss?"

Hawkins did not hear her reply as the footman closed the coach's door and the rattling-cove signaled the horses to move. Then he was standing in the hall of their house in York Street in the center of a bustle of servants. Entwhistle forgot himself and exclaimed, "Thank God, sir!" before resuming his usual wooden demeanor. The man's pleasure at seeing him, and after such brief employment in the household, was oddly warming.

His wife issued orders.

"I know you will not have prepared for our arrival, so a light, simple meal will do, but there must be something hot. A hearty soup or a pie would do. Mr. Hawkins, is there some particular thing you would like?"

She meant to eat, of course, but he said, "A long,

hot bath." He made the effort to add, "The heating of water and the soaking will provide enough time for preparing supper."

He drank a glass of brandy in his chamber, and his valet shaved him while he waited for his bath. Hawkins could almost believe the Newgate smell was gone after he had scrubbed his hair and body thoroughly with soap scented to his specification with cypress and bergamot. Then he soaked until the water was nearly cool. Pirtle disposed of the clothing he had been wearing and helped him dress in clean linen warmed before the fire and his peacock blue suit. When he finally went downstairs to the drawing room, Emily was waiting.

Lady Emily told the butler, "We'll sup now." She added to Hawkins, "I don't know if you are aware Sarah Cole has been staying with the Easterdays, as have I."

"Easterday told me you were with them. I was relieved to hear it. I didn't know about the Cole girl." What did it matter, anyway?

In the dining room, two places were set, one at the head of the table, the other to its right rather than at the other end.

The food was served, the servants dismissed, and he still did not know what to say.

"I am afraid it's not an elegant supper, Ambrose. I hope you don't mind. Cook is good but as she's only been cooking for the staff, there wasn't much suitable for a celebration."

He groped for something to say. "It's excellent. I like the egg and onion dish. I see she has provided us with an apple pie, as well. I should raise her wages." But he was only able to pick at his food. Emily watched him force down a little of the pie and a bit of cheese. He should try to reassure her. The effort was beyond him. "You should have sent someone with the order for my release. You should never have seen that place."

"I would not let you stay there any longer."

"I'm grateful." He should ask how it had come about and how she had fared while he was gone. No, better to wait until tomorrow. His brain was too sluggish tonight to take in anything more than his unexpected freedom. His body felt boneless, a sensation he remembered from the aftermath of emergencies at sea when taut muscles relaxed. "Now that I've had a bath and a hot meal, my bed is all I want."

Since their wedding, there had not been many nights they had spent apart. He should want to make love to her all night. He thought he looked forward to doing so, just not now. He drank a warming mouthful of better wine than had been available in Newgate, brought in with his meals from a tavern. It had not been good wine, but it was preferable to gin, the common alcoholic drink in the prison. Why the devil was he thinking of that place when he was free and had his wife beside him? Her glance was troubled. Even longing? He owed her an explanation.

"I haven't slept well. No one does, in Newgate, unless they're dead drunk. And I want to rid myself of the last of the taint before…"

Her expression lightened. "I understand. I had no idea what it was like, though one hears stories."

"I wish you had not seen it."

"It was worth it, to have you home. I was not willing to wait until I could find Captain Easterday."

Part of the burden lifted from his heart. Not all of

it, but enough for the moment. His smile could not have been one of his better efforts, for her eyes were still troubled.

"Emily, tomorrow I will want to hear how you came to obtain my release."

She put down her fork, the color draining from her face.

"Emily? Are you—" He reached to touch her shoulder and stopped short, unwilling to soil her, unclean as he was.

She swallowed convulsively. "I forgot. In my relief, I forgot that Sarah has lost her foster brother, who was dear to her."

"She had been crying." He had not wondered why. Everything since leaving Newgate seemed insubstantial as a rainbow and as destined to fade away. "I'm sorry. Will you tell me tomorrow? Tonight, I'm…" He tossed off the last of his wine and stood.

"Of course." She rose abruptly, pushing back her chair in a markedly unfeminine manner. Two feet or less separated them. His wife was biting her lower lip and gazing up at him expectantly. He should kiss her. That was what she was waiting for. He could no more do it than he had been able to touch her shoulder.

Somehow she divined his thought. "Ambrose, should I send for a doctor? You do not seem well."

He could not explain. "I'm not ill. Merely tired. I'll be better after a night's sleep." His curt nod was the wrong gesture, but it was all he could manage.

"Very well. Time enough for a physician then if you are not restored in the morning."

"Thank you for understanding. May I see you up to your boudoir?" It was like being an actor in some tedious play. He had to escape to the solitude of his own bedchamber.

"I will not go up yet. Sleep well."

He bowed and fled.

Chapter 34

Ambrose must be exhausted by the strain of the last weeks. Emily would not have expected it of him: He was so vital, so vivid, that she could easily imagine him on a storm-tossed ship, battling the elements for days, doing...well, whatever it would be sailors did in such circumstances. Hauling on ropes or bailing water. Still, prolonged worry could take a toll on one's mind and body. She had seen it in Cousin Claude and then in Cousin Henry after he learned the true state of the duchy's affairs and felt it herself, and none of them had been facing the gallows.

Was it only anxiety and not the onset of some illness caught in prison? He was ordinarily a hearty eater though his muscular frame carried no padding of fat. His energy and constitution did not allow of it.

Her first sight of him had shocked her: he had lost weight, he moved without his customary briskness, he was pale. Tonight he had only picked at his food, then retired far too early. His attempt to put a good face on his condition might have deceived another. She had pretended to good spirits far too often not to recognize pretense.

Worse, almost, was that he had not wanted to bed her. He had not even embraced or kissed her. Did he suspect he was ill and fear to infect her? If he had been saved from the noose only to come home to die—That appalling thought brought the inevitable question, *Whatever will I do?* If Ambrose was no better in the morning, she would send for a physician. If her husband was ill, she would nurse him. She would fight for his life as she had failed to do when he was accused of murder. She would not soon recover from the shame of having been willing to give up and, worse, to believe he might be guilty.

After leaving the table, she wandered from room to room, making the servants nervous. Nothing had gone undone in her absence: every surface was dusted, and coal and kindling were laid ready in every fireplace that might require a fire. She detected no stale air, dampness, or mustiness in any room she inspected.

She was sitting in the small parlor with her embroidery frame before her, staring blankly at the design she had copied from one of Ambrose's Chinese bowls, when Entwhistle entered.

"My lady, Captain Easterday is here, accompanied by one of Mr. Hawkins's clerks. As Mr. Hawkins has retired, shall I tell him you are not receiving?"

"I will see him here. He must have come to inquire after my husband."

"Very good, my lady. I will wait nearby in the passage."

As a chaperon; heaven forbid Emily should entertain a man or two by herself, however exigent the circumstances.

"Lady Emily." Captain Easterday, who had seemed to her at previous meetings unlikely ever to be discomposed, was rumpled and dusty. Hawkins's man with the sharp eyes—what was he called?—stood a pace or two back. He made her a polite bow but said nothing. Timothy, that was his name. He looked even more frayed than the captain.

"Captain, may I offer you tea? Or would you prefer something stronger?"

"Brandy, please, Lady Emily."

She glanced at Timothy, who gave a faint smile and murmured, "Thank you, my lady. It would be welcome."

"Entwhistle, brandy for the gentlemen." The term was stretched in Timothy's case.

"And perhaps something to eat?" the butler inquired delicately.

"Whatever Cook can manage." They did look as if they needed food. She gestured them to chairs. Rather casual behavior on her part, but life was more than strict propriety. "You've heard Mr. Hawkins has been freed?"

"At Bow Street. By the time we arrived, the constable de Veil sent with you had returned and assured him Hawkins had been released."

"Yes, Constable Bates's presence made everything easy. You received my note, then."

"Note?"

"Before I set off for Bow Street with Sarah Cole, I wrote to you and sent it by your kitchen boy. Pshaw! I suppose he must have idled along or forgot where he was going."

Easterday said, "I left my office before midday and haven't been back since."

"Then how did you happen to go to Bow Street?"

"Timothy found someone who had seen Marston's likely slayer and insinuated that person into the Cole household. The...er, person recognized Will Kimber this morning as the same man."

From certain clues of expression and tone recognized by all sensible women, the captain must be omitting some details out of gentlemanly reticence.

"In other words," she said when he paused, "a woman of the town noticed the murderer, and Mr. Timothy somehow obtained work for her with Cole." She would not ordinarily let a gentleman know she saw through his evasion, but she was mortally tired of ignoring facts.

"Er...why do you assume the witness was a female, Lady Emily?"

"Had it been a man, you would have referred to him as a man rather than a 'person.' You did not specify what sort of position Timothy had found for him with Cole. It would be difficult to get some fellow loitering outside the Haymarket a post as a servant, because he would either be a gentleman, or already have some employment, or else would be unqualified to work in a gentleman's house except as a porter or boot boy. Possibly as a groom, but I would think a groom would be much less use as a spy."

Easterday smiled wryly. "I, of all men, should know better than to underestimate a lady's understanding."

Timothy's lips quirked.

"When he heard from the young woman that she had seen Kimber and recognized him, Timothy came to find me, although it took some time, as I was out of the office. We went to lay an information at the magistrate's court. I understand we missed a shocking sight, as you did not. Hawkins is not receiving visitors?"

"Not tonight." She would not reveal how affected her husband had been by his imprisonment. It would be disloyal.

Timothy spoke. "Newgate's not a restful place. He wasn't eating much. Hawk—Mr. Hawkins—likes a good deal of exercise, too, which he couldn't get. And I think he was worried about your ladyship."

In the past month, she had made a friend of a grocer's daughter and conversed with the grocer, a constable, and a clerk, persons of no consequence whatsoever. Yet Timothy's efforts might have saved Ambrose's life, if Kimber had not confessed. The world was a less stable and orderly place than she had imagined, growing up in a ducal household. She read understanding and sympathy in the clerk's expression.

"Lady Emily, how did you happen to go to Bow Street?" the captain asked.

She described the letter's effect upon Sarah and how she had decided they must go to the magistrate. Easterday complimented her on her fortitude in his temperate way. Did it count as courage when she had simply been afraid of losing Hawkins?

The brandy and a tray of bread, cheese, meat, and pickles having been finished, the men rose.

"Thank you, Lady Emily. I will call upon Hawkins tomorrow," Easterday said.

"I am sure he will be pleased to see you, Captain. And you, too, Timothy, if you are free to come."

"Thank you, your ladyship."

"Timothy?"

"My lady?"

"What of the woman? How is she situated? If Cole should hear she identified his nephew as Marston's slayer, he will surely discharge her. It is hard to keep anything secret."

"I am trying to find her another place, your ladyship."

Easterday cleared his throat. "Olivia is looking for suitable employment for her, Lady Emily."

"Oh, good." The memory of something de Veil had said, submerged by the visit to Newgate and worry for Hawkins afterward, floated to the surface. "Captain, are you aware there is to be an inquest on Kimber? At least, the magistrate meant to ask for one."

"So I heard. Better the public hear the facts to scotch any rumors about the death. And there are always rumors." Easterday stood.

Timothy said, "Your ladyship, did the magistrate mention who would be summoned to testify?"

"Why, yes. He told the surgeon to expect a summons."

Captain Easterday followed the clerk's thought. "I imagine you and Mistress Sarah will also be called to attend, ma'am."

What could Emily possibly be expected to testify about? Then she recalled her conversation with the magistrate. She had best make her preparations. Who could she trust? One's personal maid was a lady's usual confidant for most purposes. Putnam? No, Pirtle would be better.

Chapter 35

Having retired even earlier than she had grown accustomed to doing since marrying a man who went to his office at an hour when members of the beau monde might still be in their first, deepest sleep, Emily opened her eyes before her usual time. With Hawkins safe, she did not dread the day. Indeed, she felt full of energy and unwilling to wait for Putnam to bring her chocolate. Now that she thought of it, she no longer cared to lounge in bed, drinking chocolate of a morning. She had done so while staying with the Easterdays because she realized they enjoyed talking together over their breakfast, and she had lingered upstairs to allow them privacy.

She washed her face and hands and dressed—she could manage without a maid if she wore jumps rather than a corset—then tiptoed downstairs. By now the cook and her helpers would be preparing for the day. She would make sure that they made some of her husband's favorite dishes for dinner.

The kitchen maid curtsied, her eyes wide, at the unexpected sight of the mistress. The cook was less intimidated, but in response to her question as to what they had to serve Hawkins for breakfast, said apologetically, "The master has already gone out, my lady."

"Gone out? Without eating?"

"Ay, your ladyship. Near an hour ago. Betty was here alone, being the first in the kitchen of a morning to build up the fire and start heating water. Tell the mistress, girl."

Betty dropped another curtsy and squeaked, "Master come in and asked for a bite o' something, whatever was ready, which was no more than some mutton and cheese and yesterday's bread. He wouldn't wait for me to toast the bread, neither, but just ate it standing and told me to tell your ladyship he'd gone out to his business and would be back for supper."

"Betty told me, and I'd have informed Mr. Entwhistle as soon as he was available."

Surely Ambrose must be substantially recovered. She would have expected he would stay home for a day or two, given how weary he had been the previous evening.

"How did he seem, Betty?" She could not believe she was questioning the kitchen maid about Hawkins, but his leaving without eating his usual hearty breakfast or bidding her good day was unlike him.

"Not as cheerful or brisk as when he comes to the kitchen for a biscuit or gingerbread or such. He's always got a pleasant word or a jest then, your ladyship. I feared he was out o' sorts, and no wonder."

"It's very early for Mr. Hawkins to be going to his office, but perhaps he was anxious to make certain all was well." She had understood that between his head clerk and Easterday, little could have gone wrong at Hawkins & Company while he was confined, though it was understandable he would want to make sure. She wished her husband had shown as much interest in seeing her again.

"Master spoke of going to some coffee house," the girl said. "Said he could get coffee and something more to eat there."

Emily had not long been married to Hawkins, but she remembered both her husband and the Easterdays mentioning Lloyd's, the coffee house favored by those engaged in the shipping trade. It was where they went for news and gossip and to insure cargoes.

"Naturally he would want to see his acquaintances and hear the latest news." With a little spurt of amusement, she smiled and added, "In fact, he would be the latest news." With a nod, she left the kitchen. When Ambrose came home, everything would return to normal.

She dispatched a note to the Easterdays by one of the footmen, explaining that Hawkins had gone out and perhaps would meet the captain during the day, to spare him a bootless errand.

To her surprise, the footman returned with a reply from Olivia which read in part:

...Marcus will seek him out today, though very likely Hawkins is fully restored. From my own personal Experience, I can assure you that those who take a lively interest in their commercial Undertakings can scarce be Kept from them. To be sure, one would think a man parted an equal length of time from his Business and his Wife would first reassure her of his health and devotion. However, you must remember that Men are kittle cattle as the Scotch say. One must usually apply torture even to get a man to admit to love. It is most Annoying of them...

This was reassuring, as Olivia Easterday was better equipped than Emily to comprehend the mind of a man with commercial undertakings. If Ambrose was about his work, she would apply herself to repairing the damage to their reputation, by calling upon her closest friends and most influential acquaintances. And she would send a letter to Cousin Henry to apprise him of the glad news in case it did not appear in today's newssheets. He could be relied upon to spread the word among his friends, if she added some of the details which might not be published. Writing to him, and to two or three of her correspondents who lived at some distance, would occupy a little time until she could dress to pay her calls. She was like a child looking forward to a treat—or a cat on a griddle.

****

She had counted upon the Countess of Ashwell not refusing to receive her for fear of incurring the Duke of Normande's wrath. Even an impecunious duke was a social force if he cared to exert himself, and the countess had daughters to marry off. Emily found her entertaining several of her confidants, a stroke of luck. On her entrance, discussion of Lord Bray's pursuit of some well-dowered chit ("well-endowed in all ways," one of the ladies had been saying) ended. The countess's cool greeting indicated news of Hawkins's exoneration had not yet reached her.

"How nice to see you, Lady Emily. I think you know everyone here."

Four pairs of gimlet eyes speared her.

"Yes, indeed, Lady Ashwell, though it's been some time since we last met. I could not wait to share my news with you." She paused while four pairs of ears pricked like those of cats hearing mouse feet behind the wainscoting. "My dear husband has been cleared of the ridiculous charge against him. The real murderer confessed to the Bow Street magistrate yesterday and took his own life. It was a horrifying sight."

The predatory hags (even Lady Trutch's thick maquillage of lead powder failed to conceal the furrows from the sides of her nose to the corners of her mouth) gazed at her, for once bereft of speech. Finally, the Marchioness of Burwash quavered, "You cannot mean you saw it?"

"I did, my lady. The killer wrote a letter admitting his guilt, full of remorse that my husband was being blamed. I and a companion and footman hastened to Bow Street, and found William Kimber already there, expiring from a self-inflicted wound with a poisoned blade. The magistrate immediately ordered Ambrose's release."

"How shocking!" summed up the exchanges of the next few minutes, less conversation than exclamations of surprise and consternation. Emily took her leave to allow the little coven to chew over the tidings. They would then scatter to spread the word, precisely as Emily wished.

Until today, Emily would have sworn spreading tales served no good purpose. Her own family had suffered its share of idle speculation: whether her father had immured himself—or been immured—in the country because he was going mad, about the duchy's drained resources, and whether she herself would have to seek a position as a companion. A scandalmonger would claim she felt it her duty to warn others about this or that. Or the tattler would declare she mentioned a rumor only for its entertainment value or that she had every right to say what she thought. In theory, such talk would never reach the ears of the victim. In practice, one always had an acquaintance who would pass it on with a murmured, "I think you should know…"

Today, the beau monde's lust for rumor would be put to good use: who could resist the thrill of knowing details the papers would be unlikely to print? Why, it was as good as the most outrageous play! Emily proceeded to her next call.

Chapter 36

For once, the main topic of conversation at Lloyd's had nothing to do with shipping. When Hawkins strode into the coffee house, voices died away, and every head turned toward him. He nodded at the room in general, knowing most of the men, spoke briefly to some, and took a seat at a table with Easterday, one of Olivia Easterday's clerks, and two other men whose faces he knew, though he could not recall their names or businesses.

"You received my note," he remarked to Easterday as one of the servers bustled up to take his order.

"Yes." He looked as if he wanted to say more.

Easterday was not much for idle talk, but this seemed terse even for him. The others looked uncomfortable, though Olivia's fellow said, "We knew you'd be proven innocent," before he subsided into silence.

When no one spoke, Hawkins said, "I thought to meet my head clerk here."

"You'll be wanting to hear how things have gone on."

"Ay." Easterday had supplied him with brief reports during his visits to Newgate but without the detail he was accustomed to receive at his office.

He did not know what else to say. Mayhap the others suffered the same problem. He had not come to see Jenkins but to be welcomed back by his friends and others from the shipping community, and no one but Olivia Easterday's clerk had broached the subject. Had everyone already heard about his near-miraculous exoneration? Or did they think he would prefer it not be mentioned? He pondered the question while he drank his coffee. He had not had a bowl of coffee since his arrest. One could buy almost anything in Newgate, but coffee had been beyond the ability of even the greediest supplier of comforts, not only because it was always cold by the time it arrived but because much of the enjoyment of drinking coffee came from the atmosphere of the coffee house with its news, laughter, and sociability.

The men except for Easterday took their leave and drifted off to join other tables or go to their offices.

He and Easterday sat without speaking for several minutes.

"I don't know if Lady Emily mentioned that I called at your home last night. Your man Timothy, too."

"I retired early. I haven't had a chance to speak to Emily this morning." Numb and empty, Hawkins signaled for more coffee.

"Going to Newgate herself was courageous. If I'd been in your position, it wouldn't surprise me if Olivia came to free me. I would have expected Lady Emily, coming from a more sheltered background, to send for her cousin or me."

"So would I. I couldn't believe my eyes when I saw her. Thank God she'd brought a constable with her, though I wouldn't have had her see that place for all the riches of the Indies."

Easterday studied him. "Have you eaten, Hawkins?"

"I had some bread and meat."

"We might breakfast."

Hawkins meant to refuse. He had no appetite. Still, though he didn't feel hungry, he probably should eat something more than that bit of mutton and cheese on stale bread. "Very well."

They went to the Cross Keys on Gracechurch Street. Stretching his muscles felt good, and the captain's calm recounting of the most notable items of shipping news soothed him as his nurse's bedtime tales and songs had done when he was a child. Lord, he hadn't thought of Grimmy in years. Nurse Grimstone, who was nothing like her name. She had gone with his sister when Felicity married, on the theory that Felicity would soon need a nurse.

"…and no problem your head clerk couldn't deal with," Easterday was saying as they entered the coaching inn.

They must have arrived between coach arrivals and departures, as it was relatively quiet. The serving girl took their order and whisked away, leaving them in privacy at a table in the corner farthest from the door. Conversation lapsed while they waited for their ale. Not that they had been conversing, precisely. Hawkins's contribution had consisted of the occasional word or two: "Damme!" or "Lucky she didn't founder." In the absence of something to comment upon, he did not know what to say.

"You must be eager to return to your business after so long an absence, Hawkins."

"Ay."

"I would be, I know. And Olivia is only now learning to take her hand from the tiller for a day or two. Even she admits that, hmmm, in a few months she will have to leave Finley in charge for a while. Even so, she will be keeping a stable of messengers busy, I'm sure."

Hawkins laughed, for the first time in weeks. As well he had not succeeded in his suit to win Olivia Cantarell. Easterday accepted her desire to manage her father's shipping firm. Her own, now. The captain might own it according to law, but clearly he had left it in her hands, as Hawkins would not.

Before he could think of anything to say, Easterday remarked, "In your place, I'd miss Olivia more than my company. Is your lady recovered from your ordeal?"

There was a question that required more than a one word response, if ever he had heard one. "She seemed perfectly composed."

"She's been trained in a harsh school, I suspect. A strong sense of duty must be instilled in those reared in a noble household."

"I was astounded to see her in Newgate, like some fierce little angel."

Another silence, broken when the girl brought their food. Nothing elaborate, merely cold beef, bacon, and fresh bread and butter. Hawkins applied himself to a slab of beef, his appetite having made itself known at the first scent of the bread.

"This reminds me of the morning we turned the river pirates over to the Admiralty."

Hawkins looked up from his plate. "Ah, that was enjoyable. A good breakfast then, too." They'd come to know something of each other over that meal and become almost friends. His mood lightened infinitesimally. When they left the Cross Keys, they parted, Easterday to stroll to his office nearby and Hawkins to walk down Fish Street Hill to the Billingsgate Stairs. The river was the easiest way to his office in Wapping.

The location had made sense when he was starting out. He'd found a tiny, shabby space for rent and taken lodgings nearby. Eventually, he'd leased a building for his company. When he'd moved his residence west to fashionable rooms near St. James's, the length of his journey to or from Wapping hadn't mattered much; he'd spent long hours working and had few social engagements. If he stayed too late at Cinnamon Street, his house on Old Gravel Lane was not far, and it was convenient for assignations without the bother of travelling to a fashionable neighborhood in Westminster. Shame washed over him again, remembering his abduction of Olivia. Easterday was a better man than he, to be willing to help Hawkins in light of his behavior to the former Olivia Cantarell.

After his marriage, he had begun to resent the time it took to travel from York Street to Wapping and back. Before Marston's death, he had been thinking of moving his office. Leadenhall Street, where Easterday's office was, or near Lombard Street and Lloyd's Coffee House would be suitable locations. Or near Custom House Quay, west of the Tower. No, perhaps not there. Cantarell Shipping was close by, which brought Olivia to mind again. The thought was like probing a bad tooth.

He no longer regretted losing her. In Newgate, and again today, he had realized that he could not have contented her, nor would merely possessing her have satisfied him. He could not have seen her as a partner, as Easterday did. He had wanted a wife to make him acceptable to the beau monde, while Olivia had little patience with society. Easterday had been a far better choice for her, as Emily had been the perfect bride for him.

Before they married, he had planned to curtail his work day, to allow them time to take part in society's elegant pastimes. He had not yet begun the necessary arrangements when he had been taken into custody. They had still been on their honeymoon, after all, and coming to know each other. They had been busy with the York Street house, too.

Now he need not fear working shorter hours. His head clerk had done well while Hawkins was imprisoned. Jenkins could manage Hawkins & Company with little assistance. He had never had to consult Easterday about a problem, their interactions having been limited to the reports he had sent Easterday to relay to Hawkins. Olivia Easterday apparently managed her company from the Easterday home, only visiting the Thames Street office once or twice a week or when some problem occurred. He could limit his own involvement to half a day. He need not rise as early, and he could spend more time with his wife.

But mayhap now was too soon to make such a change, in the wake of his absence. Once he was back in control, he could begin the process of gradually reducing the hours he spent in the office and considering its relocation. As the wherry nosed in to the Frying-Pan Stairs at the foot of Cinnamon Street, he breathed in the riverside odors of pitch and tar, garbage and foul water, and the heady aroma of malted barley from the nearby brewhouse. Ay, a good decision, to postpone any changes for a while.

Hours later, he rose from his desk and stretched. His clerks would be cleaning their quills and tidying away their work before going home. Jenkins stood ready in case he should have any last-minute instructions or questions.

"That's enough for today. You did well in my absence." He would have expected some small problems or irregularities while he was gone. Instead, he'd found everything as serene as a shipping company could be. He must give some thought to how much to increase the man's wages; he was worth more than Hawkins had been paying him.

"Will you be leaving for the day, Mr. Hawkins?"

"Ay."

Timothy was yet in his little office on the lower floor. Their paths had not crossed earlier, Timothy having been out on some errand. Hawkins paused at its door.

"Thank you for your efforts on my behalf. You and Jenkins between you saved my life and my business." The words sounded formal, too stiff to address to a friend.

"I can't take credit for anything but finding Maggie Ash, who identified the killer. Even that wasn't what cleared you, Hawk. It was your lady did that."

"Emily? She came with the order to free me." He shrugged. "Kimber suffered an attack of conscience or some such thing and confessed."

Timothy was staring at him, furrows between his brows. "She befriended Cole's girl. Otherwise I don't think the chit would have shown her Kimber's letter confessing what he'd done. I'd not have thought a proper high-bred lady would take to a cit's daughter, but Lady Emily did."

His face blank—Hawkins knew he must look like an idiot—he gazed at Timothy. "How do you know this?"

"The captain and I went to see you yesterday evening. You'd gone to bed, so Easterday spoke with Lady Emily. We'd heard from de Veil how her ladyship came to Bow Street and took the order to the prison for your release but not why she'd gone to Bow Street. Lady Emily explained when we called upon her."

"Easterday didn't mention it when I saw him this morning."

"Didn't Lady Emily say anything?"

"Uh, no." Hawkins could not explain he had not spoken with his wife since reaching York Street the previous evening and had hardly spoken in the coach on the way. Well, he couldn't speak in front of the Cole girl, could he? He'd seen Emily at supper, but the dining room was no place to talk seriously, even if he'd been in the mood for talk. What was there to discuss, anyway? He'd been accused of murder and held for trial, then he was exonerated and freed. Not much to chew over there.

A niggling suspicion that most people would find a good deal to comment upon under the circumstances obtruded upon his brain. Still, he'd been unable to think about anything beyond the fact of deliverance.

"I guess you'd other things to talk about."

Best to let Timothy think what he liked. They parted at the entrance, where Jenkins joined them, after making sure everything was secure. Hawkins would share a wherry with his head clerk as far as St. Catherine's Stairs, near Jenkins's lodgings. Timothy had a room in Wapping, almost in sight of Cinnamon Street.

Hawkins intended to go home but changed his mind as the wherry approached the Old Swan Stairs. He would stop at the Fortunate Gentleman before going on to York Street. The coffee house had seen the beginning and deserved to hear the end.

****

When he entered the Fortunate Gentleman's Coffee House, Mistress Hardraw made for him like a bolt shot from a crossbow and bussed him heartily.

"Here's Mr. Hawkins, saved from the gallows," the proprietress announced, to the cheers and huzzahs of the room. "Say a few words, Mr. Hawkins."

He did as she bade, though he did not later recall what he had said. Something flirtatious about Mistress Hardraw, who was still a fine-looking woman with "a couple of outstanding talents," to guffaws and Mistress Hardraw's blush and "Go on with you, sir!" then something complimentary about the coffee house and the audience. Many came up to shake his hand or slap him on the back, with various jocular remarks he endured with more patience than he'd known he possessed. Five or ten years in the future, he might be able to laugh about Newgate.

At last he escaped up the stairs. Company was thin in the first floor room, which should not have surprised him. For the most part, those absent were the men with wives. They would be taking supper at home or preparing to escort their ladies to some evening entertainment.

The men who were present made enough noise for twice their number and many of the same jests. He rejected suggestions by several that they should go out in search of some lady-birds.

"Why rent a mount when I own one?"

"Variety?" someone called out.

"Ah, but Hawkins is a new married man whose honeymoon was interrupted," Durward crowed. This sally was met with hoots and jeers.

He did not linger long at the Lucky Bastards. He was not in the mood for raucous company. He was also not in the mood to spend time with his wife. What was wrong with him? He took a circuitous route as he walked home. He needed the exercise and the opportunity to think, with no one asking him questions or talking to him. If he were lucky, Emily would be asleep before he arrived. And if he were truly fortunate, some footpad would try to rob him.

****

Ambrose did not come home for the evening meal. Emily twice ordered the cook to set it back; her husband must have had a great deal of work awaiting him. Finally she gave up and ate by herself. In the morning, she would have to smooth things over with Cook.

Hawkins finally arrived in York Street shortly after ten of the clock. Emily was in the drawing room, sipping tea that had cooled while she sat lost in thought. Hawkins greeted her pleasantly and hoped she had contrived to amuse herself. He did not remain long enough to sit down.

"I have letters to write before tomorrow, if you will

excuse me." He turned to go.

"Ambrose, may we talk for a few minutes? I have scarce seen you, and there is something we must discuss."

"Is the house afire?" He asked it without a twinkle in his eyes.

"No."

"Then it must wait." He stalked from the room without another word.

Emily sighed.

****

Sometime after midnight, he sat in his study with a tumbler of brandy. He drained it and poured more. Getting drunk was not the answer. It would only take the edge off his regrets until he was sober again. A line from a play he'd seen before his marriage came to him. "What should such fellows as I do crawling between earth and heaven?" It had lodged in his memory, possibly because one of the Lucky Bastards who had attended the same performance had embroidered it wittily afterwards: begin by kissing the lady's feet and work your way up; creep to a chamber pot; hide under the bed if an outraged husband is at the door. Hawkins thought he now understood Hamlet's distress. Was there anything in his life of which he could be proud?

Chapter 37

Emily breakfasted in solitary state. Ambrose had been gone again before she came down, though she had risen early to catch him before he left. Now she had missed her chance to tell him she must go out in response to the summons she had received after returning from her round of visits.

Not that he needed to know where she was going. It was only that she had grown accustomed to seeing him at breakfast and supper. In a fashionable marriage, his absence would not be out of the ordinary. One or both spouses going out separately for an evening's entertainment would be unremarkable. One might go for a day or two with no sight of the other. It would be yet more common when the couple were not on good terms. She had not thought this was the case with her own marriage, nor was theirs the typical aristocratic union. She could not have mistaken Ambrose's feelings: her husband had been as fond of her as she was of him. They had been settling into a pleasant married life before Newgate.

Now her husband's valet stood before her, visibly ill at ease. "Whatever is wrong, Pirtle?" She set down the bit of wigg she had been nibbling. She must remember to tell Cook to add some cinnamon with the caraway seed, as her family's cook had done.

"I apologize for interrupting your ladyship at

breakfast, but I felt I must ask for direction."

Long experience of dealing with crises among the servants made it easy to interpret this breach of procedure. Either the matter was urgent or the valet wished to speak with her privately. Pirtle had previously seemed imperturbable, as any good servant should, except maids, who tended to hysterics.

"I am sure you would not have asked to speak with me if 'twere not important."

"Thank you, my lady. I do not know if you are aware the master did not bring his clothing back from That Place."

"I am aware of it, but you sent him only his older, plainer suits, so it is no great matter that he left them. I know he told you to discard what he was wearing on his return."

"Which I understood very well, your ladyship, as they carried a certain tang of That Place about them." He twitched like a horse troubled by a fly.

"He has any number of suits and waistcoats, I believe. The discarded garments can be replaced easily."

"The master does have many fine suits, Lady Emily. And the others could be replaced, but he won't."

"He won't?"

Pirtle all but wrung his hands. "I suggested ordering new plain ones for when he goes to his office, because he will visit the ships and warehouses, for which he needs good, dark cloth which will not suffer from rough wood or protruding nails, and if the garment encounters pitch or tar or paint, it does not matter much. When I suggested a visit to his tailor, the master waved me away."

"Well, Pirtle, if he ruins a few of his better suits swarming up the rigging, he will get around to seeing the tailor eventually."

"Ay, indeed, your ladyship. But the most pressing problem is shirts and drawers. I sent a goodly number of them to him so he might change them every day, and none returned but those he was wearing when he came home. Which are now disposed of."

"You do not need him to purchase those, surely?"

"I asked permission to buy more, but he did not reply."

"Did he not hear you, perhaps?"

"I believe he must have done, for he, ah, *grunted*. But a grunt is not really an answer."

"You may take it as agreement to the purchase, on my authority. He is likely concerned with his business, having been away from it." It sounded like a perfectly good reason for Hawkins's abstraction, if only she could believe in it.

"I understand, my lady, but I am not quite easy in my mind. I've served Mr. Hawkins six or seven years, and he's not himself. He's always been most particular about his wardrobe, and now he scarce has patience to let me dress him. Throws on his clothing as if it was a sailor's slops. He doesn't sleep sound, by the way the bedding is tossed around."

He would be welcome to disarray her bedclothes.

Pirtle pursed his lips. "I understand he's not eating well, either, which is not his usual way."

"No, he isn't," Emily admitted. "I think we must give him some time to recover from what must have been an extremely unpleasant experience."

"I don't mind that, your ladyship, or even the

master wishing the devil might carry me off, if I may replenish his shirts and drawers—and handkerchiefs and stockings, too, if I may?"

"Yes, yes, by all means."

"Then all that chafes me, apart from concern about the master, is, I can't put the valise away in the attic where the trunks and portmanteaux are stored, and there is really no place for it in the dressing room."

"Why can it not be sent up to the attic, Pirtle?"

"He won't let me unpack it, my lady. I did return the books to the bookroom, but when I asked where he would like me to put the papers, he told me to go to, ah, a very hot place."

"Dear me. Can you endure its presence a little longer? I will see what I can do."

"Certainly, my lady. Thank you."

****

Thomas, very nervous, and Putnam, starched up and thin-lipped at the idea of Lady Emily being summoned by the coroner, accompanied Emily. The inquest was to be held in the largest of a suite of assembly rooms, in recognition of the likelihood of a sizable audience being attracted by so shocking a death following hard upon an equally remarkable murder.

A table and chair for the coroner had been placed at the far end of the room, with another near it where a clerk was arranging paper, quills, and a bottle of ink. More chairs were lined up to one side for the coroner's jury. The rest of the chamber was filled with seats for spectators. Emily was directed to the first row of seats. Sarah and her father were already there. Emily led her entourage up to join the Coles, ignoring a buzz of whispers as they passed the idly curious who packed the remaining rows and also stood in the empty space at the back.

Emily sat beside Sarah and gave the girl's hand a reassuring pat. Her eyes were downcast but at least showed no signs of recent weeping. On Emily's arrival, Cole had risen, bowed, and muttered, "A terrible thing, ma'am. I thank you for the help you gave my daughter that day."

She hardly deserved thanks when she would never have lifted a finger for Sarah without having a selfish interest in the outcome. She was spared from having to reply when sixteen men filed in and took the chairs lined up to the right of the coroner's table, followed by the coroner, who gave the table a sharp blow with his gavel.

"Silence."

Miraculously, there was silence. Emily had never attended a play or opera with so quiet an audience.

"This is the inquest upon the death of one William Andrew Kimber, required because the said Kimber died while in custody." The coroner gave the date and location of the death and spoke of some few other matters to do with the coroner's jury, though Emily had ceased listening.

****

In his office at Cinnamon Street, Hawkins rested his head upon his hands. He had business to attend to if he could only settle to it. Oh, God. What was he doing? He wished he had not spoken so brusquely to his wife last night, but he could not talk to her.

A merchant came into the office at midmorning to arrange a shipment, which provided him a problem he could solve. Once the fellow's complicated needs had been satisfactorily arranged, they drank a glass of claret and enjoyed a discussion of the Crown's unreasonable tariffs.

At last, the merchant rose. "I'd best be on my way. You'll be going to the inquest, I have no doubt. I wish I might, but I have an engagement I cannot break. A terrible thing, that murder! And your being accused of it, too. Thank God he confessed."

"I do, most sincerely." Why would there be an inquest? No question could exist about Kimber's death, when he had committed suicide before dozens of witnesses in Thomas de Veil's magistrate's court.

"Good day to you, Hawkins. You'll let me know if there's to be any delay in the sailing? Not that it makes any difference. Boston will be glad of my silks, calicos, and chintz no matter when they arrive."

As soon as the fellow was gone, Hawkins went to Timothy, who was clearing off his desk and locking its drawers.

"Is there an inquest on Kimber today?"

"Ay. I thought I'd go, if you have no objection, Hawk."

"I will, as well. Why didn't you mention it?"

"I thought you knew."

"I didn't. You weren't going to tell me you meant to go?"

Timothy's voice was utterly without inflection. "It seemed to me you wanted to ignore it." He continued in his ordinary manner. "I arranged to rent a nag and ride. Faster than a coach. I expect they'll have one for you."

They were among the last to arrive at the inn off Holborn and squeezed in at the back. Sarah Cole's presence came as no surprise, but at the clerk's calling

Emily's name, Hawkins went rigid. Why was she present? How had he not known she'd been summoned to give testimony, or that an inquest had been set? *Because I've hardly spoken to my wife since she came to Newgate for me. This must be what she wanted to tell me last night.*

His attention was all on her as she spoke, her calm demeanor a striking contrast to the Cole chit's blubbering. Hearing Emily and the others describe the events conveyed the scene at Bow Street as Easterday's restrained secondhand account had not.

****

It worried Emily mightily that an inquest was necessary when Bow Street had been full of witnesses to Kimber's death. Knowing the hearing was only a legal requirement did not, however, relieve her nervousness about testifying. She would have asked Ambrose to accompany her, if she had been able to speak with him. His presence would have been reassuring. She need not be apprehensive yet, however: there must be others to give their testimony first. What had she to say, really? But it was too bad Sarah must be present.

The Bow Street clerk gave evidence of how Kimber had come to the magistrate's court and insisted upon speaking to Thomas de Veil. He had shown the magistrate certain items, to wit, a walking stick with a sharp stone blade concealed in the end, a similar shard, and a written document confessing he had slain Captain Joel Marston by means of the cane and poison on the blade. All these articles were displayed to the jury.

Constable Bates gave an admirably concise account of the astonishing happenings at de Veil's court.

Dr. Brewster, a physician as well as surgeon, described Kimber's wounds and gave his opinion that the symptoms exhibited by the deceased had likely been caused by the substance on the shard Kimber had held.

Salem Cole was called. He deposed that his nephew had been an odd, quiet boy since childhood. He was never any trouble, barring he was somewhat reserved and did not play with other children. Very fond of animals and clever with his hands. He was a skilled cabinetmaker. He never was bad-tempered or violent.

Cole was dismissed, and Sarah Cole was requested to come forward.

"Sir," Cole began to say.

"I have only a few questions for Mistress Sarah. She was present and knew William Kimber, having grown up with him, as I understand."

Trembling and pallid, Sarah went to take her place by the coroner's table.

"We understand you were present at the distressing scene. Please tell the jury why you were there." The coroner was a mild-looking man, and his tone was sympathetic.

It was to no avail. Sarah's chin trembled, and she burst into tears, managing only a few disjointed phrases, before giving herself up to unrestrained sobbing. "Poor Will!...oh, I can't..."

She was immediately dismissed, and her father assisted her to her seat.

"Lady Emily Hawkins."

She sensed Cole's reaction and ignored it; she could not afford the distraction. Taking a deep breath, she made her way to the front of the hall.

"You were present with Mistress Sarah Cole on the day in question?"

"I was."

"How did it come about that you and Mistress Sarah were at Bow Street?"

"Sarah received a letter from her cousin, Mr. Kimber. I believe he did not intend it to be delivered until later."

Emily had to explain that Sarah and she were staying with the Easterdays, which brought the question of why. Her own reason was easily understood by all. She explained Sarah's presence as an opportunity for the girl to be introduced into another level of society. The Easterdays were not much above Salem Cole, though both came of the gentry, but mentioning her own relationship to the young Duke of Normande, and their friends, the Duke and Duchess of Guysbridge, caused several of the jurors to nod, or exchange knowing glances.

"Did you see the letter delivered to William Kimber's cousin?"

"I did."

"Did you read it, or did Mistress Sarah read it to you?"

"Sarah was overcome. I read it."

She was asked to recount as much as she remembered of it.

"Mr. Kimber intended to confess having killed Captain Marston."

"Did he give a reason for doing so?"

"He had seen Marston mistreating a dog. I know from things Sarah had told me about her cousin that he was very fond of animals and could not abide unkindness to them." The girl had not actually told her as much, but from what she had said, Emily was sure it was true.

"It hardly seems a sufficient reason for slaying with malice aforethought."

She swallowed. "Sir, I met Mr. Kimber on two or three occasions. I would not have thought him a violent man, but I found him quite eccentric."

"In what way, Lady Emily?"

"While my acquaintance with him was slight, it seemed to me Mr. Kimber's interests lay almost exclusively in woodworking and animals. And perhaps natural philosophy," she added, thinking of the passage in the letter about the method used by the natives to launch their darts. "He was awkward in company."

Then came the question she had been dreading.

"Do you know what became of the letter, my lady?"

"The letter?"

"Kimber's letter to his cousin, Sarah Cole." The coroner would have been justified in showing impatience with her dithering; perhaps he was accustomed to having to pry information out of witnesses, or he might be treating her with deference because of her rank.

"Oh, of course. No, sir, I do not. After reading it, Sarah was distraught, and I admit I was discomposed and hardly knew what was to be done. Then, too, we were in such a hurry to reach Bow Street...I cannot say where it is now." Thank goodness she had put it in a locked case and told Pirtle to put it somewhere safe. She did not explain beyond saying it bore upon her husband's innocence, and Pirtle, blank-faced, did not inquire further. She did not know where he had put the box.

"Very understandable. It would have been useful to have it read into evidence, but I'm tolerably sure we have heard enough."

The jury put their heads together and whispered. From their animated gestures, they must not be in wholehearted agreement. The spectators murmured softly, but no one made any move to leave. The coroner and clerk conferred. After a few minutes more, the foreman rose and cleared his throat. The clerk scurried to his table.

"Has the jury reached a conclusion?"

"Ay, sir. We'd no trouble deciding William Kimber met his death at the Bow Street court about three o' the clock in the afternoon, on the nineteenth day of March."

"Yes, yes, that's well documented, but I thank you for stating it for the record. And how do you find he died?"

"We have now all agreed he was not in his right mind at the time and maybe not for his whole life, even if he wasn't a Bedlamite most of it, and while he was distracted and lunatic, took his own life with a poisoned blade, the same as he'd killed that Captain Marston."

Cole put his arm around his daughter and whispered something in her ear. Emily let out a breath. The inquest was closed, and those in attendance began to make their way out of the assembly room and down the stair.

"Best to wait until the crowd thins," Salem Cole told Emily. "You'll not want to be jostled by the riffraff."

When the hall was almost empty, they started down. Most of those who had come had dispersed either to their homes or to the inn's tap to discuss the entertainment over ale. Cole and Sarah having come by hackney coach, Emily took them up in her coach. There was not much conversation in the inquest's aftermath.

"I suppose Will's letter was lost or burned. I would have liked to keep it." Sarah was no longer sniffling, but she was still blotting her eyes with a handkerchief.

"I will see if I can find it, Sarah. I—" She stopped, having seen Cole shake his head and raise a finger to his lips. Perhaps he thought the letter would only distress Sarah more.

"I will call upon you in a day or two, if I may, Lady Emily."

"You are welcome to call, Mr. Cole. I will call on Sarah when she is more composed."

She owed Cole an explanation. She would discuss the letter with him, too, and return it to Sarah when she was less distressed unless her papa thought it unwise. She would also give the chit a few hints about maintaining her poise in all circumstances, if she was to be introduced into good society. Why not? Marston's murder and Kimber's death were past and would fade from everyone's memory in time. They could all move on, if only Ambrose could put it behind him.

****

"You'll want to speak with Lady Emily, I expect. Will I see you at Cinnamon Street or shall I return your mount?" Timothy asked as the proceeding ended.

"I don't care to make a spectacle of Lady Emily and myself. I'll not return to Cinnamon Street today."

Their late arrival and position at the back made it easy to be among the first to leave the room and escape his wife's notice.

He'd behaved badly ever since Newgate, and now he had failed Emily again. He should have been at her side, supporting her, for what gently bred lady would not find it an ordeal to give evidence before an audience of the vulgarly curious?

The hot tide of shame washed over him, followed by a flood of memories, the ones that seeped into his mind without warning: every time he had made a fool of himself and every slight he'd received, some of them decades old. Why should they still bother him? He was successful and possessed as much as any man needed. His wife was a duke's daughter. Why did he want to howl with fury over some old mistake? Not even a mistake, often merely a suspicion that his actions or words caused others to feel contempt for him, even if they did not show it. *Rot me, if they did laugh or think me a fool, they've forgotten it. Why can't I do the same?* But the thoughts always returned.

He contrived not to arrive home until he was sure Emily had gone to bed.

Hours later, he woke in darkness, sweating, his breath coming as fast as if he had been running from the Devil himself, as perhaps he had been. He swallowed hard, savoring the soft mattress, fine bed linen, and silence. Not still in Newgate, then.

Chapter 38

She heard footsteps pass her door very late in the night. Hawkins come home at last, of course, for the tread was firm. A servant prowling at night for whatever reason would have been going on tiptoes. He could not be drunk, for she knew the sound of a sot stumbling and staggering his way to bed.

A foolish woman would bolt from her bed to confront him. Such tactics would do no good; she had attempted something similar with her father, who had become almost a recluse in his library, seldom joining her for meals and going out only to wander the estate. It had accomplished nothing. Ambrose, at least, was not drinking to excess. Something must be done, but there was nothing she could do tonight.

By morning, she had determined her first step. She would deal with the purely practical matters first. Emily poured herself another cup of tea, made sure Hawkins had already gone out, and ordered the footman on duty in the front hall to tell Pirtle to meet her in the drawing room in half an hour.

In reply to her question when he presented himself, the valet admitted he had not spoken again to his master about ordering suits.

"I did not think he would receive the suggestion well," he confessed.

"Then order Hawkins a plain suit or two from his

tailor, who must already have his measurements." If they were a little loose now he had lost weight, it would not matter. He would not want them as close-fitting for shipboard visits as for his more formal attire. Before Pirtle could excuse himself, she asked, "And the valise in the dressing room?"

"I moved it to the far end under the window, as out of the way as possible. I have not dared to mention it again, your ladyship."

"I see. May I suggest you go to the tailor at once? The sooner he begins, the sooner he will be finished. I noticed when Mr. Hawkins came home the night before last that he was wearing one of his better suits."

"Thank you, Lady Emily. The green silk suffered cruelly that day. I'll go immediately." He bowed himself out as quickly as consistent with a valet's dignity. He would be off as soon as he could put on his greatcoat and clap on his hat.

Less than an hour later, having spoken with the cook about the next week's menus and with the housekeeper about smudges on the glass of one of the cabinets in the drawing room, Emily entered her husband's dressing room. She could understand Pirtle's frustration: it was not a large space, considering the number of suits, waistcoats, and other accoutrements her husband possessed. Outer garments hung on pegs, his shirts, neckcloths, stockings, and handkerchiefs would be in the press at one end of the narrow space. Boxes holding hats were stacked on shelves. The valise was wedged in between a straight chair and a cabinet that probably held small accessories like gloves, sets of linked buttons to fasten shirt cuffs, ribbons to tie back the hair, buckles, and who knew what else.

Once she would never have contemplated searching her husband's belongings, but that was years ago, before she'd met Hawkins. Before her father died, leaving drawers full of unpaid bills, many not even opened, which explained why the wine merchant did not care to continue to supply wines to a ducal household, and a dozen other embarrassments and inconveniences. She did not believe Hawkins had received bills at Newgate. Still, whatever documents reposed in his valise could not be ignored, with Ambrose acting so strangely.

She opened the leather case as cautiously as if it might contain some savage creature. Instead, as Pirtle had told her, only a sheaf of paper and letters met her eyes. She sat on the chair to look through the stack.

Some of the open sheets bore cryptic notes and some numbers or simple designs or sketches, the sort of thing one might do unthinkingly when sitting daydreaming with a pen and paper. Some of the paper was blank. Then there were the letters, folded and addressed but not sealed, one to Mr. Allan Hawkins, Whitchurch, Hampshire, the other to a Mistress Felicity Collet, Darlington, County Durham. She recalled Ambrose mentioning a brother and a sister; presumably Allan Hawkins was his brother. Was Felicity his sister or his mother?

It cost her a struggle with her conscience, although she was already violating her husband's privacy, to open the letter to his brother.

Allan,

I do not know if you thought me dead. I am sorry I never wrote, but I did not care to write if that scoundrel, our stepfather, might intercept the letter. I should have done when you came of age and inherited, but by then so much time had passed that I thought to leave well enough alone. In any case, I believe on the date of your twenty-first birthday, I was off the coast of Ceylon, on an East Indiaman.

I write now because I am like to hang for a murder I swear I did not commit. Please believe this, for although as you know I have always had a hot temper, I did not kill the fellow. However, the matter is one of some notoriety, and I have no way of proving myself innocent, although my friends are attempting to find the killer.

I would not write to you with this terrible news except that you will hear of it from my attorney when I am executed. Fortunately, our family name is a common one, and there is no reason to suppose our relationship will become widely known. In the twenty or more years since I ran away, I have enjoyed some worldly success. Knowing what a spendthrift Lewis was, it occurred to me that I could leave you a sum of money which might be of assistance. It will not be a great fortune but should serve to make needed improvements to the manor, or educate or dower your children (if any). I am also naming you trustee jointly with my attorney of a sum for the benefit of our mother. I enjoin you not to let the scoundrel know of it. 'Tis meant for her needs, rather than his greed. I am leaving a sum of money under the same conditions for our sister (or for her children, if she be dead, or if neither she nor her children live, 'twill revert to you, and if our mother is dead, the same). I cannot leave you my entire fortune, as I married not long since, and the rest goes to my wife.

I did not want your first knowledge of my continued existence to come from my lawyer on the occasion of my death.

Your brother,

Ambrose Hawkins

Tears stung in the corners of her eyes. She blinked them away and read the other. Felicity Collet was his sister; the letter did not mention his will, only explaining that he was facing death and wished to apologize for his neglect and hoped that she and her family were well. He added that he had written at greater length to Allan, who might share more details as he thought appropriate. Ambrose had probably intended to send the letters when he knew he would be executed.

She set them aside for the moment and riffled through the stack of paper to even the edges before she returned it to the valise. It was thus she discovered a closely written sheet at the bottom. It was addressed to her.

My dearest Emily,

I should have written sooner, but I'm no hand at correspondence. What was there to say? My trial approaches, and I realize I have something to tell you.

I have many regrets. I am sorry that I have lived my life so as to come to this end and bring you shame. I was pleased to think I had rescued you from your difficult situation and also that we seemed to suit each other well. I looked forward to our life together and hoped we would have several little copies in our respective images: two or three boisterous little boys and two sweet-natured little girls just like you. Easterday will tell you, if he has not done so already, that you are provided for. You will be a much-sought-

after widow for your fortune as well as for your own charms. The good captain will protect you from fortune hunters.

That evening I told you I had courted Olivia Cantarell, now Mistress Easterday, has been on my mind since I have been here. A man is foolish to praise another lady to his bride. I know you were hurt, as I would have been if you had spoken admiringly of some former suitor of yours. While I admire many of Mistress Easterday's qualities, I am more drawn to your quiet dignity and charm.

Thinking back, I also regret having mentioned my attempt to compromise Mistress Olivia and regret having done it, too. A pretty notion it must have given you of my character! My ethics in business have sometimes been questionable, but that action was indefensible. I would not wonder if you believed me guilty of Marston's death. I did not kill him, however.

You planted the idea that I should not have turned my back on my family. You were correct. I should have written to my mother, brother, and sister years ago. If you receive this letter, 'twill be because worse has come to worst, and I will also have sent letters to them. I do not wish them to know of my situation until it is resolved, one way or another. It is possible they will contact you.

Your influence might have made a better man of me in years to come. I regret the loss of those years.

Your devoted husband,

Ambrose Hawkins

Tears she could not hold back streamed down her face and dripped from the end of her nose before she could grope for her little handkerchief. How pitifully undignified. At least she had managed not to splatter the letter. When she had composed herself somewhat, she tucked it back under the other sheets.

The night before the inquest, Ambrose had claimed he had letters to write. Had he written to his family? She had no memory of seeing letters on the table in the hall. After she repaired to her chamber to wash her face, she would ask Givens if any letters to be sent out of town had been taken to the General Post Office.

She did not close the valise; Pirtle could not return soon, as he would choose the cloth and style of his master's new suits with painstaking care. Ambrose had complained, laughing, of Pirtle's finicky ways. Biting her lip, she took her husband's letters to his family with her. She had time enough to replace them before they were missed.

****

The next day Emily called upon Olivia Easterday, who raked her with a glance. Did she see the shadows under Emily's eyes, in spite of every attempt to conceal them? Olivia responded briefly to an inquiry about her health and spirits, and how Captain Easterday went on, before fixing her with a steely gaze.

"What is wrong, Emily?"

"Is it obvious?"

"Yes. It appears you have not been sleeping, and you are fidgety."

Emily stared out the informal drawing room's window at the garden, where the plantings stirred in a fitful breeze which threatened a storm. She blinked back tears.

"Mr. Hawkins—Ambrose—" she amended, because formality was ridiculous with Olivia, who did not give a straw for it, "I have hardly seen him since his release. He rises early and leaves the house and does not return until late. When he does appear, we do not converse."

"Not at all?"

Emily blew out a breath. How to explain? "We have scarcely exchanged a word since his return. He is gone in the morning, no matter how early I rise. He has not supped at home since that first night."

The maid brought in the tea tray. Olivia did not speak until she had gone. She made quick work of measuring out the tea leaves and sat, evidently perplexed, as they steeped. As Emily had grown accustomed to her friend's way of not speaking unless she had something to say, the silence did not bother her.

Olivia poured the tea, added the precise measure of cream Emily liked, and passed the cup to her. As she prepared her own cup, her cheeks flushed. Emily opened her mouth to ask if she were well. She knew little of the effects of gestation, apart from the recognized tendency of ladies in a certain condition to be queasy.

Olivia spoke, looking down at her tea. "Do you not converse in bed?"

No wonder Olivia had colored up. Emily's own face heated. "We used to talk." The humiliating truth came out in a rush. "He has not come to my bed since he came home from that horrible place."

A pause. "And you do not go to him?"

"I couldn't! Any man would be disgusted by such brazen behavior."

With a faint smile, Olivia said, "Some men might. Others would welcome it. I doubt Hawkins is a stickler for propriety."

"I suppose I could try." What if he rejected her? Their situation would be worse than it was now. "I only wish I understood what troubles him."

"One hears of the conditions in Newgate, but I cannot imagine what it is really like. He may need time to weather the experience, as one needs time to mourn after a death."

"So I tell myself, but is there aught I can do to help him, Olivia? I do not wish to tease him, and yet pretending all is well is not working."

"If Marcus reacted as you described, I would ask him what was wrong. But we are both rather alike in our attitudes. I think Hawkins is more complex than my husband, though I don't know how. Too, you and Hawkins are not much alike, though 'tis not unusual for man and wife to be very different in their natures. It must make it difficult for them to understand each other. All I have to suggest is, let him know you are there if he wishes to talk, and you might try visiting his bed."

****

After Emily heard his footfall in the passage, she allowed enough time for him to shed his clothing before she went through her dressing room to the door of her husband's dressing room. She hesitated with her hand on the latch. Was she bold enough to intrude upon him? She could think of no other way to show her support and affection. Men might discuss their problems with other men. In her own experience, they seldom confided in ladies, however much the issue might affect them. But when she tried to turn the handle, the door was locked.

Chapter 39

"I came to call as soon as I could, your ladyship," Salem Cole said. "I did not like to leave Sarah while she was still low in spirits, yet it seemed to me that a female friend might be able to comfort her better than I can. She tries to hide her tears from me."

Here was the awkwardness Emily had postponed thinking of when she was called to give testimony at the inquest. There had been no opportunity then to explain her use of her maiden name. Once, before her mother died and her father began to eschew all company, an elderly friend of her papa's had related something about honesty being the best policy. "Except in the beau monde," he had chuckled.

Cole was not part of that world. He probably disapproved of lying, an attitude with which Emily agreed as a rule. "I apologize for the deceit I practiced upon you, Mr. Cole. When we were introduced, I was using my family name and wearing mourning for the same reason I was staying with the Easterdays, to avoid the embarrassment of being recognized as the wife of a man charged with a shocking murder. But I needed to get out of the house, which felt like a prison to me, while at the same time not becoming an object of curiosity or scorn. I thought I could do so by disguising myself in mourning, and using my family name. My intent was to protect my privacy, not to deceive. I would not have done so, nor would Olivia have taken me with her to call upon you, had either of us known your family had any connection to, to…Please forgive me." She must be blushing. She could not let Cole know Olivia had set out to probe him for information, not even when her intent was to prove he had nothing to do with the murder.

After a pregnant pause, Cole said, "Under the circumstances, I cannot blame you. The debt is still on my side, as my offense against you was far worse."

"Your offense, Mr. Cole?"

"Mine. I lied both in speaking and in keeping silent." He sighed deeply, shoulders sagging. "I told you I wanted Sarah away from her cousin because I intended her to marry another. That was a minor falsehood. I thought she was less likely to hear loose talk about Marston and his death if she were away from our home, where one or two of the servants might have let something slip. Her old nurse is growing forgetful and knew of my daughter's indiscretion."

"Perfectly understandable, sir. Any careful parent would do the same."

"Ay, if only that was the worst. I was brought up to a strict standard, though I drifted away from it for a few years. Since then, I've prided myself on my little virtues. We've all heard how pride goes before a fall."

The man was working his way up to some disclosure. Emily could not imagine what it might be. She raised her eyebrows inquiringly, forbearing to prompt him.

"I can't tell you how I came to suspect Will Kimber had killed Marston, because I don't know. If you found two or three small pieces of broken china, you could still make a guess, at least, as to what sort of thing it had been. If the pieces were curved, it would have to be a bowl, cup, teapot, or vase."

Emily nodded her understanding.

"If the porcelain is thick, it's more likely the object was a teapot or large bowl. If it is decorated, you may be able to tell which set it came from." The corners of his mouth twitched upward in something which was not quite a smile. "We used to have a clumsy maid. She could never bring herself to admit she'd broken a cup or plate, so she would throw the pieces in the privy. Being fumble-fingered, she'd often drop a bit or two on the way."

"Oh, dear." Cole must have kept the girl on far longer than she herself would have done. Emily could imagine how Hawkins would react if one of his Chinese treasures were destroyed.

The humorous moment passed. "I knew Will. He was in my care from the age of three. He was always protective of Sarah. However, I didn't suspect him until the news came out about the poison. I had a sample of what I'd been told was arrow poison used by natives in South America. I won it in a game of hazard before I gave up drinking and gambling. I kept it and a few other curios in a cabinet in my study, safe enough, I'd have thought. I don't know if I ever told Will about it or spoke of it in his hearing, but it's possible."

"Children hear things they are not meant to," she agreed.

"Knowing I owned a substance that might have been the same as what killed Marston worried me, but how could I draw suspicion to Will, my own nephew, on so little evidence? It doesn't take much for the law to hang a man."

"I know."

"It troubled me to wonder if Will was a murderer, but it was only when Hawkins was arrested for it that I became truly concerned. But I convinced myself your husband might well be guilty. Your pardon, my lady: when I spoke with him, I was not impressed by his manner. I may have relied unfairly on what I had heard of his reputation. I do not know if you are aware of the rumors about his past."

"I am. I have heard no convincing evidence that he was a pirate more than briefly, and then only because he was forced."

"He had been in the West Indies, however, and he was a friend of Marston's."

"I understand how one might reasonably have suspected him, Mr. Cole."

"It's a lesson to me not to heed scandalous talk. I suppose we all sometimes take what we wish to be true for fact. I should have confronted Will."

"Would he have admitted to it?"

"Oh, ay. I never knew the lad to lie about anything, even if it meant a caning. I was a coward, my lady. I feared to ask him, feared even to see him, lest he mention it. He would have known it was a crime, but he would not consider it wrong if 'twere to protect Sarah. I sent her to stay with Mistress Easterday in case Will should speak of it to her, and I found business to take me out of town when I realized Sarah wanted to see me. If she had become suspicious, or he had told her outright what he'd done, I did not want to know."

"One has a duty to one's family, Mr. Cole. I understand."

"I had a duty to your husband and you, to the law, and to God. I was a coward and refused it as Peter denied his Lord. I hope you can forgive me."

"I accept your apology." Oddly, she found it easier to forgive him than to let go of her anger at her father for abandoning her in his grief. "Is there aught I can do for Sarah?"

"I am ashamed to ask anything of you, your ladyship, but for Sarah's sake, I must. Her old nanny cossets her, which is well enough when she has a cold or some other indisposition, but Sarah's no longer a child and needs more than soothing. I can see her trying to bear herself as she thinks you would. Last night she told me, 'Lady Emily would not give way to tears, no matter what.' She's lacked a mother's guidance. Not that you're old enough to be like a mother to Sarah, but you've been like an older sister to her, and I thank you for it."

Emily clasped her hands tightly, remembering how her father's spirits had failed. "If you think Sarah would be cheered to see me, I will call upon her."

"Sarah is fond of you, Lady Emily. I believe there is nothing she would like better."

"About the letter Kimber sent Sarah..."

"I suppose it was lost. 'Tis not surprising."

"I kept it. I took it with me to Bow Street, in case proof was required. It would have been a betrayal of Sarah, but I could not let my husband hang."

"Nor should you," Cole said stoutly.

"I will give it to Sarah. I think she will treasure it for the love it shows."

"He left me a letter as well, thanking me for taking him in as a child, and apologizing for taking some of that terrible stuff and a few pieces of volcanic glass. He spelled out how he killed the blackguard. I would give it to my girl, but there's not much comfort to be had from it."

"He wrote at some length to her. She did not read it all before she became too distraught to continue. If I received such a communication, I would cherish it." Her husband's letter lingered in her mind. Will Kimber's expressed less emotion than Ambrose's, but it was as heartfelt. Sarah had known her cousin all her life. Emily thought she would be able to read his affection for her between the lines. Emily wished she had been bold enough to remove Ambrose's letter to her from his valise. It would have been wrong, but it would have been heartening to read it again and again.

****

He heard Jenkins going around to check windows and make everything secure for the night on the ground floor. Measured footsteps on the stair prepared him for his head clerk's appearance at his door.

"Have you any final orders, sir? Everybody's gone bar Mr. Timothy, but I'll stay if there's anything you need."

"There's nothing. Go on. Tell Timothy to go unless he's working on something that won't wait."

Jenkins departed, and the sound of a murmur followed by the door opening and closing carried up to him. A few minutes later, Timothy's soft tread sounded on the steps. He entered Hawkins's office without invitation and dropped into a chair.

"Problem?" It must only have arisen, if Hawkins had not already been informed.

"No."

"The working day is done. You could have left with Jenkins."

"Jenkins has a family. I live in a boarding house. I sleep there. Sometimes I even eat there. Not much else to do at Mother Melton's."

"There's always the alehouse or coffee house for entertainment."

Timothy shrugged. "I visit alehouses to listen for useful gossip or for a pint if I'm dry. Spending every evening in one is poor entertainment. The conversation is better in the coffee houses, but coffee keeps me awake. Before you suggest it, Hawk, I don't care to spend every night in a brothel, either."

Hawkins glared at him without being quite sure why. Something Timothy had said raised his hackles. "Do I need to raise your wages so you can move to better lodgings?"

"I can't buy what I really want."

"If it's anything I can help you get, tell me. You stood by me when I was in Newgate."

"Thanks for the offer, but it's something I need to figure out for myself."

Hawkins bent to open the deep bottom drawer in the left pedestal of his desk and brought out a squat bottle and two tumblers. Timothy showed no sign of leaving and had as yet given no indication of why he had come into Hawkins's office in the first place. Something must be amiss; Hawkins trusted to brandy to shake it loose.

Timothy sniffed the contents of the silver cup appreciatively. "I hope you dole this out only to men who recognize its quality."

"Ha! Most of 'em get the cheap bingo in the other

drawer." He scowled at his own tumbler. It was dark with tarnish, as was Timothy's, and the several others in the drawer. "These need polishing up."

"Take them home, and your butler will see to it."

Home. He'd hardly been to York Street but to sleep. Hadn't seen Entwhistle in days: the man wasn't on duty when Hawkins had been leaving in the morning and was off duty or attending to matters in the butler's pantry or in the servants' hall when he came home. Whatever footman was about in the late evening could take care of it, of course.

"Or I could take them home for my wife to polish…"

Hawkins's head snapped up from his contemplation of the brandy.

"…if I had a wife."

"Huh." He himself had a wife and a home, yet here he was, drinking with Timothy. Still, drinking with a friend was better than drinking with strangers or alone. "Are you…?" In his experience, men talked about the females they were pursuing for sport or for marriage. Or maybe that was only among the poorer classes. Among the gentlemen and ladies of the beau monde, one's friends would observe the dance of courtship without a word spoken.

"I think I am, if you mean courting. Never thought I'd be ready again."

He knew Timothy had been married, or at least had kept a female. Sober, he had never once alluded to it after he and Hawkins met. Timothy had probably saved his life that night. No, definitely saved his miserable life. Hawkins could not have held his own against three hired blades. In a sea battle, with shipmates fighting all around, a man had a chance. Alone in a midnight-black alley with no one to call a warning or strike aside another cutlass, such odds were like to kill him. Timothy's dagger in one attacker's kidney had improved matters. Afterward, they'd both needed a surgeon, Timothy more than himself. From something his rescuer mumbled under the influence of several cogues of gin—cheaper than laudanum and useful for cleaning wounds as well, the medico claimed—Hawkins deduced he was a widower.

"I wish you happy, then."

"But if I wed her, I'll want to be home nights. Most nights, anyway."

Hawkins considered the matter. Timothy often was out at night on his business: picking up bits of gossip, asking questions, wandering past various wharves, watching. "Do I work you so hard you have to be out every night?" He poured them both more brandy.

Timothy stretched out his legs and crossed them at the ankle. "No. It took me one evening, and not all of that, to find Maggie Ash. But I don't like being idle, so…"

"So you prowl at night. Wouldn't you be idle at home with your wife?"

"Not the same way. We'd eat supper and talk, maybe I'd read to her while she sewed, or we'd take a walk on a fine summer evening. We might visit Vauxhall. We might have a child and tell him a story before tucking him in for the night, and then tucking ourselves in. Since you married, I've begun to wish for a woman to go home to."

Hawkins's brandy went down the wrong way.

"All right, Hawk?"

He could take it as referring to his coughing fit. "Uh…" Or he could be honest with Timothy, who was his closest friend. "No. I apprehend you know I've not been going home. Not until late."

Timothy shrugged apologetically.

"Lady Emily and I are not on bad terms. None of it is her fault."

"It started after Newgate."

"Ay. I failed my wife, Timothy. I exposed her to humiliation and uncertainty by being suspected and arrested, after her own family failed her by impoverishing her. I'm ashamed to face her."

"I failed my wife." All emotion leeched from Timothy's words. "I came home in time to kiss Molly's lips while she died in my arms from stab wounds, with our unborn child."

"Dear God. I didn't know. Still, you weren't responsible for her death."

"I was."

"Do you want to tell me?"

"It's time I told someone. Confession is good for the soul, they say." He leaned back in his chair. "You know I was an attorney's clerk and I investigated matters for the attorney, in addition to copying documents. Much as I do for you, in fact. I'd been looking into the doings of a baron who'd cheated, slandered, and reduced a client of ours almost to bankruptcy. I must not have been discreet enough."

"He had your wife murdered?"

"There was no proving it. I suppose he thought I'd be charged. His bravo or bravos should have made sure I had no alibi." His smile was cold. "No accusation was going to stand against the word of the Member of

Parliament and the viscount with whom I was meeting. Or perhaps he only thought Molly's loss would persuade me to stop tracing his activities."

"He must have been stupid," Hawkins remarked.

"He was. He's in hell now. One of his brothers-in-law heard rumors about the baron's preference for little girls and took a horsewhip to him. The satirical prints for sale finally did the trick. You know how brutal they can be, and they were all over London. His friends began to give him the cut. His wife took the children to her father's home. When the baron came to get them, the other brother-in-law called him out. The baron was too cowardly to accept the challenge. Then he killed himself, making it a moot point."

"I've known you for, what? Seven or eight years, and I'm hearing this for the first time?"

Timothy smiled lopsidedly. "Men talk about sport, women, and politics. About business, too, if they've commercial interests. We don't talk about emotions. Molly claimed it was why a man would never admit to love."

Hawkins flourished the bottle, raising his eyebrows interrogatively, while he mulled over that statement. Had he ever told Olivia he loved her? Or any woman?

"No more, thanks, Hawk." He turned the tumbler in his hand before setting it down. "I'd take these home to your lady. She'll have them polished."

Hawkins sat for a while after his friend departed, thinking.

Chapter 40

Emily set out for the Cole house with mixed feelings, trailed reluctantly by Putnam. She dreaded her imminent call upon Sarah Cole, whose mourning would be excruciating to see, when her own spirits had been rising.

Putnam muttered, "You should have ordered the coach, my lady."

"For a mere half mile or thereabouts in good weather?"

"It may be well enough for a cit's wife to go on foot, but a member of a duke's family should go by coach, especially when calling upon a cit."

"Nonsense, Putnam." Emily's anxiety over the visit was replaced by annoyance on Sarah's behalf as well as Ambrose's. Sarah was the daughter of a merchant but as ladylike as most young girls of the beau monde, and Hawkins came of landed gentry. She recalled something Hawkins's fellow, Timothy, had mentioned during his and Captain Easterday's visit after Ambrose's release. There was no time to weigh the idea now, virtually on Cole's threshold. She would consider it later, shocking as some might think it.

Sarah greeted her like a long-lost sister, despite her air of dejection. Or perhaps because of it; men were never much use in consoling the bereft, in Emily's experience.

"Papa said you might call. I am so glad you did." The girl was not wearing black, which would surely have been too much mourning for a cousin—particularly one who had died under such scandalous circumstances—but her plain grayish-brown mantua made its own statement. Dyed, Emily had no doubt, for no one would buy fabric of that color.

In the drawing room, once they had tea and Savoy biscuits, Emily could think of nothing to say beyond the standard condolences. She could not even say as she usually would have done, "I am sorry for your loss." If Kimber had not confessed his guilt, Hawkins would now be facing trial on a capital charge and would probably have been found guilty. Emily's mother had prided herself on always knowing the correct thing to say in any situation, but Emily suspected she would have been at a loss, too. Of course, the late duchess would never have found herself in a similar position. A regrettable amount of Emily's training was proving as worthless as studying the Turkish language or geometry.

"At...at the inquest you said you might be able to find Will's letter to me, my lady."

Now they came to it without Emily having to introduce the subject. "I did find it," she admitted. "I know you wanted to keep it." She drew it out of the pocket under her petticoat. "I am not sure you should read it again so soon, however. Perhaps you should put it away for a year or two, until your grief has abated somewhat."

Sarah took it. "I think I must read it now. My unhappiness cannot be greater than it already is. Would you mind if I did?"

"No." Better she read it with a friend present than in solitude.

Sarah unfolded the sheet and swallowed before lowering her gaze to the page. This time, thank goodness, she did not wail and collapse. As she read, her expression changed. Emily fixed her own attention on her tea cup.

"Oh, Emily."

Her eyes went to Sarah's face. To her surprise, she saw relief there, as well as a welling of tears.

"Emily, you can't know what a comfort it is to know Will did not die only to save my reputation."

She could not have missed Emily's complete incomprehension; Emily's mind had gone blank as a new sheet of paper.

"Did you not read his letter yourself? Oh, I beg your pardon. You would have been thinking of what to do, of course. Will knew I was terrified Papa would consent to my wedding Captain Marston if…well, you know. So he killed him to protect me. He was worried about my reputation, too, although he did not understand why it would have been damaged by what Marston did, but he did not sacrifice himself only for my reputation. My heart was breaking that he had done so. But Will's letter says that when he found out Mr. Hawkins was accused, he could not bear the thought someone else would be punished for his crime. Naturally he would confess to save your husband. I am more grateful than I can say that you saved the letter and brought it to me."

"I am glad if it has given you some comfort." Her training was useful for something: her first, unguarded response would have been, "Were you not surprised

Kimber murdered Marston for your sake?" Emily thought she herself would have been not only surprised but horrified if someone, her brother or father perhaps, had committed such a crime, though she could not imagine either of them doing so. They would more likely insist she marry the man. They would not have considered her fear a reason to protect her; their only concern would have been to avoid scandal. Mayhap it was not surprising Sarah could accept Will's guilt, when she saw it as proof of his care for her. She might feel the same. Ambrose Hawkins would have made sure Marston could not trouble her again, which would have led to his being hanged for murder. Or not: while she did not know Hawkins as well as she wished, she suspected he would manage the matter differently and escape any consequences. She preferred not to contemplate her lack of horror at the idea. Before she could think of anything more to say, Sarah spoke.

"When I heard from Will that Captain Marston was dead, I wondered if my father might have done it. He was very angry. I couldn't believe he would. It was only one of those thoughts that comes to you sometimes in the middle of the night. But I couldn't ask, for fear it might be true. And then what would I have done?"

"I understand, Sarah."

"Have you explained to Mr. Hawkins how it came about? Will not knowing anyone had been accused, I mean? He would have apologized"—Sarah's smile was small and twisted—"or at least explained to your husband, if he'd had the chance."

"I haven't had an opportunity to tell him. He's been busy, having been away from his company." She had copied out the letter, though she would not tell

Sarah. She would show it to Ambrose when she believed he was ready to see it.

Sarah sighed. "I know Will was peculiar, but I loved him like a brother. I'm thankful we could bury him decently. The funeral was private, both because of the talk and because poor Will had no friends to attend, except in our family."

"I think Mr. Kimber was more interested in his craft than in people."

"That is very true. It took him a long time to be comfortable with others. He liked Papa and me, and our cook and Papa's groom, and one or two others he'd known for years. I wish—but it's no use wishing. Papa has ordered a nice tombstone, and I mean to visit his grave often," she ended on a defiant note.

"As you should, having been as close as sister and brother. Closer than many. I mourned my brother's death, but we did not have much to do with each other. He would not have protected me from Marston. You were fortunate in your cousin. Sarah, I wish he might still be in his workshop, creating fine furniture." Though not at the cost of Hawkins's life.

Sarah sniffled, and then somehow they were both sitting on the settee, weeping in each other's arms, in sympathy rather than grief.

When they had no more tears and both their handkerchiefs were damp and useless, Sarah said, "We must wash our faces and have another cup of tea before we are fit to be seen."

Emily agreed. She did not want Putnam to see she had been crying. "Sarah, after we tidy ourselves, may I impose on you to let me write a brief message and send it to the penny post by whatever servant you can spare?" It was not a letter she wanted anyone in her own household to see.

****

His longing for Emily burned fiercely. He imagined the rift between them as prison bars and himself manacled to the stone wall. She tried to touch him, while he could not so much as stretch out his hand toward her. They lived in the same house, their beds no more than twenty feet apart, and still they could not bridge the divide. Or he could not; she kept trying, although he feared she was losing heart.

"Hawk?"

Timothy stood in the doorway, shifting from foot to foot. The everyday sounds from the ground floor had changed. Had a sudden stillness fallen over the clerks' area a few moments ago? The clerks normally worked in silence, apart from occasional hushed inquiries of Jenkins or of each other and the louder voices of men who came in to arrange for shipping. Something had happened while his mind wandered.

He closed the ledger and pushed it aside. Timothy seldom bothered him unless the matter was important. "What is it?"

"There's a gentleman to see you."

Hell. "I gave orders I wasn't to be disturbed. Who is he?"

"He wouldn't give his name—"

"Tell him he'll have to talk to Jenkins." Some fellow wanting him to invest in an Exchange Alley bubble: a gold mine in Scotland or a project to grow truffles in an oak grove in Wiltshire. Jenkins knew how to deal with flimflam. Timothy did, as well.

"He told Jenkins it was personal." There were twin

grooves between Timothy's brows.

"Was the junior clerk too timid to bring the message?" Timothy did not run errands for the head clerk unless he wanted to do it.

"Hawk, he looks like you." When Hawkins did not speak—his mind had gone blank again—Timothy continued. "He doesn't carry as much muscle as you, and he's a bit taller. Looks like a squire in his best town suit."

He regained his voice. "Have him come up." Was it possible his brother had seen some report of his arrest and had come all the way to London for the trial? Why would he? Timothy vanished into the passage. Only a subdued mutter carried up from below, then feet pounded up the stair. Timothy must have beckoned to the visitor.

"Brose, it is you." Allan halted in the doorway. "I couldn't believe it possible."

Hawkins near tipped over his chair in rising. "Allan. Come, close the door." He hurried forward to shake his elder brother's hand. When he released it, Allan threw his arms around him in a fraternal hug.

"I could not believe you were alive, when we heard nothing of you." He released Hawkins and stood scrutinizing him. "You're different."

"I grew up."

His brother's statements demanded an explanation, though not phrased as a question. Hawkins poured two tumblers of the good brandy and gestured his brother to a chair.

"At first it would have puzzled me to lay hands on pen, paper, and ink. If I'd had them, I would not have written, because why let that scoundrel Lewis know where I was?"

"That's what I told Mother for years." Allan sipped appreciatively. "I warrant you this paid no excise."

Hawkins grinned at him. The conversation might not be as bad as he feared.

"After the first half-dozen years, I suspected you were dead. She began to talk about how healthy children sometimes die before they are grown. Falls, fires, illness of all kinds, drowning, simple wounds that mortify."

Another lady he had failed. "I'm sorry."

"The notion reconciled her. She swore you'd have written if you hadn't been prevented." Allan set down his empty tumbler.

"I suppose I was ashamed to write when I was finally able to." Hawkins pushed the bottle toward his brother. Maybe their talk would not be as easy as he had begun to hope.

Allan shook his head. "No more for me. Later, maybe. I have no doubt Mother would have accompanied me had she not gone to visit Felicity, who is expecting an addition to the Collet family. Another one, the seventh, if I have not lost count. She scarce knows whether to be embarrassed or thrilled, considering her age. She wants another girl. I should mention that our mother will again be exposed to a certain old widower there. This time he may work up his courage to make her an offer."

Hawkins, who had anticipated Allan broaching a different subject, allowed himself to be deflected. In fact, he was glad, as it sounded like good news. "Is Lewis dead, then?"

"Ay. Ye gods, it's near sixteen years now. My

twentieth birthday was nigh, and old Foster, our
attorney, made sure Mother's guardianship was not
challenged. He took care of the financial work, of
course, but I'd already learned a great deal about estate
management by talking to our neighbors and observing
what Lewis failed to do."

Willing to postpone the less cheering conversation,
and curious as well, Hawkins asked, "How did he die?"

"He was crossing that cow pasture to the north of
us and didn't run fast enough when the bull charged
him." He smiled wryly. "If you wagered he was not on
his way to tryst with the farmer's wife, you'd lose."

"Rot me! Killed by a jealous bull." Hawkins shook
his head, still laughing. "Did Mother know?"

"That's the best of the joke, Brose. The buxom
little tart he meant to visit was stricken with guilt for
being the cause of his death and had strong hysterics at
the burial. She owned to all her adulteries at the top of
her voice and begged the Lord's forgiveness. 'Twas the
best entertainment ever seen in the parish. I didn't know
Mother was capable of rage. As God's my witness, I
thought she'd assault her with her prayer book.
Fortunately, she is a lady, and merely said to the
farmer, 'You should take your wife home as she is
somewhat overwrought.' By then, one of the women
had laid hold of the farmer's wife and was slapping her
face, another was having words with her own husband,
and a third was giving her man a most unloving look. I
treasure the memory, as it opened Mother's eyes as
regards Lewis. She had always believed his
protestations of devotion and his mawkish
endearments."

"It made me sick to hear him call her his 'dear

Mousie' in that cozening tone." Hawkins poured them both another tot of brandy. "I meant to write at the end. Then I was cleared, and I've been busy dealing with things that piled up while I was—"

His brother had frozen with his tumbler at his lips. Allan lowered it without drinking. "Cleared?"

"Wasn't that why you came? I suppose one of the London newssheets made its way to Whitchurch. The murder was a nine days' wonder. More than nine days," he allowed.

"Murder? What the devil have you been doing, Brose?"

"I haven't. I didn't do it. I was suspected because I knew the fellow and because of that business about being a pirate..." This was not the way to explain. He reached for his drink.

Allan grabbed his wrist. "Not another swallow until you tell me. Start at the beginning."

Hawkins frowned over the question of where the beginning was. "Perhaps if I wasn't known to have been a pirate, though it was only for a short time, and years ago, and not my fault, and if Marston hadn't been furious..." It took a long time to tell, requiring numerous explanations and some doubling back to fill in details. As he recounted it, Hawkins admitted to himself that possibly his reputation did not rest solely on his stretch as a buccaneer. He had been proud of being known as a hard, dangerous man, despite being as honest in business as most. It was not unethical in a strict sense to take advantage of a fool. Though, looking back, he wondered how some of his dealings had affected another man's dependents. Now he understood something of what Emily had suffered through no fault of her own, he wished he had taken some thought to the women and children.

"You were in Newgate, expecting to hang, and you didn't write? Why in hell's name didn't you scribble a note to let me know? I would have come, hired a barrister for you—"

"I did. I wrote to Felicity, too. I meant to have them sent if I was convicted and the appeal failed. Then Emily got me out, and I didn't need to send them."

"You didn't mean to let us know you were alive until after you were dead? What the hell do you mean, you 'didn't need to send them'? And your wife got you out? Brose, why do I find myself having to repeat things you say that don't make sense?"

Hawkins spread his hands. "I've been ashamed to write. Ay, Emily came to Newgate straight from Bow Street—wait, I didn't explain how the murderer was discovered, did I?"

"No. Listen, is there somewhere to get a meal? I haven't eaten since early this morning."

The midafternoon sun slanted in through the window.

"We'll get meat pies and eat them while you come home with me. I'll tell you everything"—or almost everything—"on the way. Then we'll eat a better meal at home."

"I would like to meet your wife. Little brother."

"Only by two years."

"And two inches."

"I outweigh you by two stone at least, all of it muscle."

Allan snorted. "Appropriate, considering the stone's the unit of weight used for cattle."

They might almost have been boys of twelve and fourteen again.

Chapter 41

By the time they were approaching St. James's Square, Hawkins had finished his tale, and Allan had done with both exclamations and questions. Something his brother had said earlier, or not said, teased him, like a word one cannot quite catch hold of.

"Allan. You were surprised to hear I'd been charged with murder. If you did not see my arrest or release mentioned in a newssheet, what brought you here?"

"The letter, of course."

"But I didn't send it."

"Lady Emily's letter."

The hackney coach rattled to a stop as Hawkins grappled with the idea of Emily writing to his brother. Why had she done it? How had she known where to send it?

By the time Emily reached the drawing room, his initial reaction, to demand answers to those questions, had faded. She appeared surprised by Allan's presence, suggesting she had not asked him to come. He would inquire later, when they were private, because he still wanted to know. He would thank her, too. He might never have written, once the shadow of the gallows no longer lay over him. Only his imminent death had overcome his shame at never having written when he could have done. "Emily, will you have a room prepared for Allan?"

"I gave the order at the same time I sent the message to the kitchen to move the meal up."

"I thank you, but I engaged a room at an inn before I sought out Brose."

"Why stay at an inn when you have family?" It would give them more time to talk.

"We can send a footman for your belongings. They will be here before we've finished supper," Emily said, then asked about Allan's family. Before he finished listing his children's names, ages, quirks, and talents, and praising his wife, the question of where he would stay in London had been settled without another word. Being at home with his wife was less difficult than Hawkins had anticipated. His avoidance of Emily since his release began to seem ridiculous as well as shameful.

Emily stood on little ceremony with his brother. Though the meal was plain, the cook not being able to hasten some of the dishes to completion, Hawkins could not regret it. At home, his family had been used to simple, hearty fare. He had not sat down to a family meal since his father died, nor a merry one since he'd been taken to Newgate.

****

Emily could not recall the like. Before her mother died, dinner and supper both had been formal occasions, even if no guests were present. Not that the family would be at table alone. Her brother's tutor, her mother's elderly spinster aunt, who served as the duchess's companion, and her father's secretary all took their meals with the family. Emily had eaten in the nursery until she was considered old enough to join the adults when no guests were present. No matter how small the party, however, the talk was confined to serious matters or commonplace remarks, and neither she nor Geoffrey, four years older, were expected to speak unless spoken to. Effectively, talk was limited to the duke and duchess, with the tutor and the secretary venturing comments as appropriate. Great-Aunt Eleanor, rather deaf, contributed little. Such conversation as there had been died with Emily's mother as her father descended into morose silence.

Tonight silence was in short supply. She hardly said a word, except to reply to Allan Hawkins's intermittent, courteous attempts to include her. Emily did not mind. Listening to the brothers' boisterous reminiscences was enough.

"Lord, do you remember the curate and the pig?"

Immoderate laughter and clinked wine glasses.

"Or the time when our papa found the kitchen cat's offering on—"

Ambrose, who had taken a hearty draft of wine, snorted and was reduced to a prolonged fit of coughing into his napkin, from which he emerged red-faced. "Sorry!" he gasped.

Emily took it as meant for her and smiled at him, as the sight of Ambrose choking with wine and laughter had left their guest in whoops. No, not a genteel occasion. Once Emily would have been appalled. But it was good to see her husband in spirits.

Emily stood. "I'll leave you to talk about the years you've missed and share a bottle or two of port. Good night." She was gone before they could rise from their chairs.

****

Filling their glasses, savoring the first taste and discussing the port's merits put off the need to say anything for a few minutes. They had touched on many things on their way from Hawkins's office to York Street without doing more than grazing the surface of the lost years.

Allan broke the silence first. "You had good reasons for running away. But maybe if I had done something to shield you from Lewis, you wouldn't have left."

"You couldn't have done anything. You were only two years older. We were both at his mercy."

"I should have tried. I did have some protection, and I should have used it for your benefit. He tried to stay on civil terms with me because as soon as I came of age, the estate would be mine and I could cut off the money. I would have, too. If he behaved himself, I'd let him continue to live there."

"He might have made sure you didn't live to inherit. I wouldn't trust him an inch."

His brother's grin was eerily reminiscent of his own, as it had been described to him by acquaintances: a wolf-like baring of teeth. "You didn't know about the provisions of our father's will. Before he died, he told me what he had done to make sure our mother wouldn't be taken advantage of by some blackguard."

"As she was anyway."

"Indeed. But he couldn't sell or mortgage the property. The most he could do was spend the profits, and killing us wouldn't do him any good, because in the event either of us died, his will specified that Uncle Nehemiah, the next heir, was to reside at Chalk Hill Farm to, how did he put it, 'lend support to my widow.' "

"Cousin Nem. I haven't thought of him in years. Was he making sure Nem was familiar with the property in case worse came to worst?"

Allan poured himself more port. "Father was cynical. You don't expect it of a man who's straight as a ruler in his dealings. He knew Mother would be easy prey for a bad man, and he was not inclined to optimism about men's motives. I wish I had seen Lewis's face when Father's attorney told him about the will. After Mother married the scoundrel, unfortunately, as Foster was away and did not have notice of the happy event beforehand."

"But to think a man she married might murder her children...why would Father suspect such a thing?"

"I keep forgetting you were only ten when he died. You missed hearing some of the family history. Or heard references and didn't understand them. Nem's parents died and left him and his brother to the guardianship of their mother's half brother. Nem always suspected the man had arranged the accident that killed his little brother while Nem was away at school. Luckily for him, lung fever carried off the half brother a few months later, and Nem was put in our grandparents' care. Father and Nem grew up close as brothers. Nem's suspicions about his brother's death influenced Father's thinking about orphans and guardians."

"Good God. I never knew." He shook his head, trying to clear it. "Is Nem still alive? I should write him, if he is."

"Oh, he knows you're back from the dead. When you ran away and were not found—no, let me be honest—when you ran away and Lewis scarcely raised a finger to find you, Attorney Foster concluded that if our steppapa did not bother looking for you, you must be dead, probably by his hand, as Foster's efforts failed to find you. Not enough evidence to try him but plenty to have him install Nehemiah in the house."

"When I was a child, I thought he was a giant."

"Close to one. Taller than me and more muscles than you. He worked with his farm laborers when he inherited his family home. Nem took charge of everything. He sent your description and name out to every place he could think of, but the trail was long cold by then. Mother and I missed you and prayed for you. But things were better afterwards. Lewis was a bully, but he never dared raise a hand to Mother or me with Nem there, looking like bull-beef."

"I was going to beg your pardon for having abandoned you, Allan. Instead, it sounds as if I did the right thing all unknowing. Better than doing the wrong thing with good intentions, I suppose." A portion of guilt evaporated.

"Brose." His brother's voice was tentative. "There has been so much to say that I have not congratulated you upon your marriage yet. I am happy for you…if you are happy."

He opened his mouth to say that of course he was happy. The words stuck in his throat. He had been happy, up to the day the constables arrested him. The realization diverted his thoughts from Allan's half question. He had been happy in his marriage. Before, he had been content with his life, which was not a minor blessing. Many men would welcome contentment.

Since Newgate, he had nothing. Hawkins

swallowed a mouthful of port before responding. "Emily is the perfect wife for me. She has social connections, intelligence, and beauty." True enough but not really what his brother had wanted to know.

"Good things, but is there nothing more?"

"Are those not enough?" Well, no. She was or had been, passionate as well, but he certainly couldn't mention that fact. "She has courage, too. She came herself to have me released."

"She must love you."

"She has a strong sense of duty."

"Brother, my own wife shows every sign of loving me. Nevertheless, I am sure she would not brave Newgate Prison to free me."

"Emily was accompanied by a constable from Bow Street and a footman."

"Even so, I don't believe Joan would do it. Go to the prison herself? No. Nor the magistrate's court, neither. Instead she would occupy our attorney's office like an invading army and would refuse to leave until he brought me back." Allan contemplated the ruby liquid in his glass. "I sensed some restraint between you and your lady. I hope 'tis only the result of some passing tiff."

What could he say to explain? He had already been through this conversation with Timothy, who knew him better than his own brother now did. He could have happily gone without talking to Timothy about it, but his friend had maneuvered the talk around to it gently as a knife slips into butter. Hawkins had pushed the matter to the back of his mind. But if his brother noticed something amiss between him and Emily during dinner, mayhap he needed to come to grips with it.

"I have not yet succeeded in putting Newgate behind me, Allan. Do you remember how we laughed over that bit in the Bible about Saul being struck blind, then the scales fell from his eyes?"

"Do you recall how Parson fair turned us to stone with his glare, like Medusa, for our snickering?"

Hawkins guffawed. "I'd forgotten. Still, our mother not letting us have any gingerbread because we'd made a spectacle of ourselves was worse." The amusement drained away. "Being imprisoned was like what happened to Saul. Not a religious conversion," he added hastily, meeting Allan's startled glance. It put him in mind of a horse shying.

"But you'd survived storms at sea and pirate attacks. How could Newgate be worse?"

"In emergencies like those, there's no time to think. All you can do is act. In Newgate, I had nothing to do but remember every mistake I'd ever made, realizing some of the things I'd done with a clear conscience were worse than merely errors, they were actually wrong. It is too late to make most of them right. Do you know, tonight is almost the first time I've sat down to dinner with Emily since I came home. I need to apologize to her, and I don't know how."

"Actions speak louder than words. Lewis was forever mouthing endearments to our mother as he let the property fall into ruin to pay for his gambling and indulgences and bedded other women. If you can't speak the words, show her that you love her."

"How?"

"It all depends upon the moment and upon what you are apologizing for. For a minor offense, I would bring my wife a gift. I don't know what I would do for a great offense, not having committed one against her yet." He frowned and added a qualifier. "As far as I am aware."

****

After changing into her best night rail, Emily dismissed Putnam, saying she would brush out her own hair. Putnam made a sour mouth as she turned away. A lady's maid always discouraged her mistress from raising a finger on her own behalf because God forbid she should realize she hardly needed a maid. A foolish fear, when one really could not put on any but the simplest clothing without help. If Putnam had any sense, she would understand why Emily wanted to be rid of her earlier than usual.

Dinner had been almost as it used to be, before Hawkins was sent to Newgate, apart from the presence of Allan Hawkins. But Ambrose's brother was what had brought her husband to the table and made conversation flow freely. Her husband was home tonight and he had talked and laughed.

Allan had reached London only this morning. Surely he would seek his bed early. His chamber was situated at the back of the house, where it would be quieter, some distance from her room. If he were tired from travel, he would fall asleep quickly. She hoped Ambrose would come upstairs at the same time as his brother. When the sound of movement in Hawkins's chamber stopped, she would allow him a few minutes to relax in bed or even drift into sleep. Yes, that would be better. Then she would enter by the passage door and creep in beside him.

She waited until she heard footsteps and the

murmur of voices in the passage, then the sound of her husband's door closing, followed soon after by a more distant door. It would not take long for her husband to undress and prepare for bed. He had his valet wait up for him only when they went out in the evening. On nights they stayed at home, Pirtle was released from duty after dinner. No doubt this freedom made up for the morning, when he found his master's clothing dropped or tossed at the nearest chair.

With heart beating as fast as a girl's on her introduction to society, she waited impatiently until Ambrose should be asleep. She hoped he was asleep. She longed to resume normal married life, but if he were awake, some awkwardness must result: embarrassment at being discovered creeping into his bedchamber like the veriest trollop, and the necessity for conversation. If she could slip unnoticed into bed beside him, she trusted he would do as he had when he woke in the night, before Newgate: embrace her, whispering endearments until she was also awake and ready to return his caresses. Then they might be able to move past their estrangement, if that was what it was, and go on with their marriage.

At length, she took up her candle, opened her door, and peered out. Only her fear of being caught in so brazen an act led her to expect to see someone. Pulling her door shut, she tiptoed to Hawkins's door and listened. Would her candle wake him? This was a possibility she had not considered. She dared not extinguish it. While she had been in his chamber before and was tolerably sure she could find the bed in the dark, she did not care to risk falling over his shoes or catching her foot in some discarded garment.

She could not stand outside his door all night. Was there not a line in *Macbeth* to the effect of, if 'twere done, 'twere best done quickly? Something of the sort. She glided in and took pains to close the door quietly. A soft groan from the bed alarmed her, but the mound did not move and the sound was not repeated. Emily picked her way around a coat, a waistcoat and neck cloth, then an archipelago of shirt, shoes, breeches, drawers, and stockings. Smiling, she set her candle next to his on the cabinet by the bed, extinguished it, and after brief reflection, dropped her dressing gown on the floor before sliding under the covers.

Ambrose was lying on his side, facing away from her. He did not wake, though now she lay beside him, she felt him twitch restlessly. He mumbled something and his body tensed. A moan, and his arm jumped as if to fend off some attack.

"Ambrose, it's all right." She put her arm around him, hoping he would not mistake her for whatever monster stalked through his nightmare. He tensed again, then let out a long breath like a sigh as his body relaxed.

He was warm. She had missed spending nights with her husband. Both at Petty Normande and in London, she had often been chilly in bed. She pressed against him and closed her eyes.

Contrary to her expectation, he did not awaken in the night. When she woke to faint gray light visible around the velvet draperies, Emily discovered she had turned to her other side. So, too, had Ambrose, judging by the presence of his arm around her. She wriggled, enjoying his solid, warm body at her back. Mayhap now he would wake up and—

Gray light. She had slept until dawn, and the servants would be about. She slipped out from under his arm and groped on the floor for her dressing gown. Oh, fiddlesticks! It was inside out. Heavens, Pirtle would be bringing hot water for Hawkins any moment now. Rather than fuss with her morning gown, she draped it over her arm, snatched up her candle, and scurried for the door. No sound reached her ear from the passage. She risked a glance and, finding all quiet, retreated to her own chamber.

****

Her husband's ebullient mood of the previous evening carried over to breakfast and a discussion with his brother of the attractions of London. Allan having never visited London before, such improving sights as the Tower, the monument commemorating the Great Fire, and London Bridge were proposed.

"Whatever else I see, I want to know how you spend your time, Brose. I can tell you've put it to good use by your elegant lady and your house."

Hawkins, visibly swelling with pride, suggested Allan accompany him to Wapping by way of the Custom House, which played so important a part in the seagoing trade. They might visit one of Hawkins's ships, too, currently riding at anchor.

"My head clerk can manage most things on his own for a few days, while I take you to all the most famous places."

"At least one evening you should see a play and on another, perhaps, an opera, for your wife will wish to hear about those, and the Mall, too. In those places, one may observe the fashions most efficiently."

"I fear you will have to advise me what details I am

to report to Joan, Lady Emily, for otherwise I shall only be able to tell her that the ladies dressed monstrous fine."

Ambrose glanced at Emily, as if struck by the recollection he had a wife.

"I do not wish to inflict my company upon you if you prefer to follow the play by the amusements preferred by gentlemen." Gambling, drinking, brothels, and the like. "Fashionable gentlemen seldom pass their evenings in company with their wives or female relatives."

"I am ignorant of fashionable pastimes and vow I am a staid country squire. I only wish Joan had been here to enjoy the metropolis." Thus it was agreed that they should all three see a play and visit Vauxhall Gardens, and that Allan Hawkins must bring his wife to London on his next visit.

Chapter 42

Hawkins bade his coachman set them down where Threadneedle Street, Cornhill, and Lombard Street met. "That's to be the Lord Mayor's Mansion House." Hawkins jerked his chin toward the extensive building site to their left. "By the time your boys are grown, it may be completed. The Bank is up Threadneedle. We'll look at the Royal Exchange. My first sight of it impressed me as much as anything I've seen before or since, including palaces. There used to be shops in the gallery, which sold all sorts of elegant trifles, but I believe they have somewhat fallen out of fashion and decreased in number."

"I would like to buy gifts for Joan and my boys before I go home. I cannot stay more than a week, but that should be enough time to find something."

His brother's remark sparked a memory. Had he not seen a letter a few days since?

"I have some business with a jeweler. We might go there after Lloyd's and East India House."

They cut through Exchange Alley to Lombard Street. "You look well today, Brose."

"I slept better last night than I have since I went into Newgate." He had dreamed of Emily, not even a lascivious dream, merely that she was there. When he woke feeling an urgent desire for his wife, they might have bridged the abyss between them, had she really been present. He missed her so profoundly he had imagined he could smell the scent of her soap lingering in the air.

The idea of going to her bed tonight was unbearably tempting. Yet he would not feel comfortable unless he apologized for his seeming coldness first. He knew what generally pleased women, though he had made mistakes in the past, notably with Olivia Cantarell. They liked compliments, particularly those they could believe. They liked to be told they were loved, and for some reason, they always believed it. Had he said those words even to Olivia, whom he had loved? Or thought he had loved, at least. He had not spoken them to Emily; theirs was not a love match.

Was it? Emily embodied (oh, ay, the body!) all the qualities he had described to Solomon de Toledo as necessary. In addition, they were well suited in bed. Those things alone were enough to make a comfortable marriage. They had seemed to be working toward something a little warmer, but he would never have expected her to come in person to Newgate to free him. Now he thought about it, Allan's notion began to make sense. If Emily did love him, it behooved him to find a way to make amends to her, and the sooner, the better.

"Today I'll show you the world of London's shipping trade, Allan, and make sure all is in order at my office. Tomorrow we might view more entertaining sights, like Salmon's Waxworks. 'Tis full of figures of the famous—or notorious—and portrays a scene in a Turkish harem. The mechanical figure of the prophetess Mother Shipton is thought remarkable."

Then they entered Lloyd's Coffee House, where Allan listened attentively to the discussions of cargo, insurance, and sailings as Hawkins turned his attention to a few items of business.

He was unable to banish the itch in his mind that was Emily as they strolled down to London Bridge, then east to the Custom House. The craving stayed with him as he pointed out the sights visible from the wherry on the trip downriver.

****

At breakfast, her husband had said they would be home for supper, making the choice of what gown to wear of paramount importance. Putnam was already laying out a pale blue watered-silk *robe à la française*.

"The diamond necklace will look well with the blue. It is not vulgar." She made the concession with reluctance, the necklace and ear-bobs having been a wedding gift from Hawkins.

"I will wear the rose mantua tonight."

"The rose would be best paired with the pearls. 'Tis a pity the ear-bobs do not match it."

Emily understood her lack of enthusiasm for the simple pearl necklet, her father's gift for her sixteenth birthday. Her brother had almost certainly reminded the duke her birthday required some sort of present. He must have chosen it, too, as her father would not have roused himself so far. It survived their financial woes only because it was hardly valuable enough to sell. Emily was glad of it, as she valued the necklace and the more-or-less matching ear-bobs, her brother's gift, for sentimental reasons.

"I think the pearls will do for a family meal."

"Very well, my lady."

As well the question was settled, as a scratching at the door proved to be the footman.

"Your ladyship, there are two persons at the servants' entrance asking to see you."

"Who is it?" She preferred not to reveal that she expected her callers.

"A common-looking fellow, your ladyship, who claims to work for Mr. Hawkins. He gave his name as Timothy. He is accompanied by a young female."

"Oh, Timothy. He does indeed work for my husband. I'll see them in the drawing room in a few minutes." This was something of a social dilemma. Maids were hired by the housekeeper. Emily was usurping the housekeeper's right by interviewing the woman. She should use the housekeeper's parlor or at best, the small reception room where unknown or unwelcome visitors were kept waiting. Maggie Ash's and Timothy's service to Ambrose deserved the drawing room, however. Well, Emily would speak with the young woman before summoning Mrs. Johnston. She must simply hope the woman was suitable for some position in the house. "Putnam, set out everything ready for me to dress."

Putnam's lips thinned. "This is an inappropriate time for a call. You cannot see these people alone."

"As Timothy is one of my husband's employees, I must see him. He was of great assistance in proving him innocent. Perhaps he is bringing a message."

Her maid's sour expression did not change. Putnam likely still held the opinion that Emily would be better off if Hawkins had been found guilty and executed.

"And who is the female he's brought with him, my lady? I do not think—"

"I do not greatly care what you think, Putnam, except regarding dress. But you may attend me."

The clerk, if that really was his position at Hawkins & Company, was standing when she entered, trailed by Putnam. A thin, painfully neat young woman waited nearby, hands clenched at her waist.

"Mr. Timothy, good day. Is this your friend?"

"It is, my lady. May I present Margaret Ash?"

The young woman curtsied, not without dignity.

"Margaret, I understand you wish to leave your current position."

"Yes, my lady."

"We have maids enough and too little work for them as it is, your ladyship," Putnam interjected. "Unless Mrs. Johnston means to get rid of that slack Bess? But she won't be happy if you take to hiring the lower servants yourself."

Timothy's eyes slid toward Putnam; Emily took his meaning.

Emily's mother's dresser had been just as free in airing her opinions. She had not cared to have a child underfoot while she arranged the duchess's hair or gowned her. As the duchess regarded the services of a superior dresser as more essential than the presence of her daughter, the woman had usually had her way. Emily turned upon her lady's maid the gaze of a duke's daughter on an insolent servant.

"Putnam, go tell Mrs. Johnston I will be sending Margaret Ash to her in fifteen or twenty minutes. You need not return."

"My lady, I—"

"Now, Putnam."

Putnam curtsied rather ironically, if such a thing was possible. She also made a slight "hmmpf!" before stalking out.

"Sit." Emily took one of the chairs by the fireplace, and the girl and Timothy seated themselves gingerly at opposite ends of the settee. Her mother's probable opinion of inviting persons of the lower classes to sit in the drawing room did not bear thinking of. She would never have agreed to see Timothy or anyone like him. He would never have got past the butler. Of course, Emily's papa had never been charged with murder and saved from trial by the efforts of a clerk and a ruined maidservant.

What did one ask an applicant for a maid's position? She would know if she were evaluating a lady's maid, but the duties of a housemaid or kitchen maid were largely unknown to her. "Tell me about your previous experience."

"I haven't been in Mr. Salem Cole's household long, my lady. I was hired as a temporary second housemaid while Mistress Sarah Cole was from home. Since her return, I've served as her maid, as I'd had a position as laundry maid in my last household."

Here Emily was on firmer footing. A laundry maid would know how to wash or otherwise clean delicate fabrics, how to press them, and how to goffer frills and ruffles. Emily determined she had been employed in that capacity for several years, and carefully did not ask how she came to leave. "Do you aspire to be a lady's maid?"

"Yes, your ladyship. I know it looks bad I want to leave Mr. Cole's house so s-s-s-soon..." She stammered to a halt.

"It would have been necessary if Maggie had had to testify about Will Kimber."

"I remember you mentioned as much, Mr.

Timothy. And now?"

At a glance from Timothy, Maggie replied, "They don't know the part I played, your ladyship, but I don't feel right about it. I'd never have talked about my master and mistress under other circumstances."

"No, I understand. It can't be a happy household at present, either."

"There is an additional complication, ma'am. When I sent Maggie to the house, I gave it to be understood I was her brother-in-law." Emily detected the faint reluctance in his admission only because she was familiar with the nuances of conversation and life in the beau monde.

Maggie blushed.

"I see. Very understandable." Honest of Timothy to admit he was interested in her, when many prospective employers would regard it as a reason not to hire her. And few households would hire her if they knew she had been dismissed from a situation without a reference. None would hire her if they knew of her history after her dismissal and before Timothy got her work at Salem Cole's home. However, Emily owed Margaret Ash nearly as much gratitude as she owed Timothy. Further, the maid impressed her as a capable and well-spoken young woman. "We need a laundry maid," Emily said. How fortunate Putnam had made it clear she felt those duties beneath her, though she certainly had time enough to carry them out. "I believe you will suit. Mr. Timothy, if you will call the footman in?"

Once Margaret Ash had been dispatched to the housekeeper with the instruction that she had been hired as a laundry maid at five pounds per annum and clothing, Timothy bowed.

"Thank you, my lady."

"Thank you, Mr. Timothy. Before you go, I would like to know if you have observed Mr. Hawkins in the last two days."

"I have." Timothy shifted uncomfortably.

"It seems to me that his brother's presence has lifted his spirits."

"Ay, it has."

"Until Mr. Allan Hawkins arrived, he had scarce been at home since his release." How humiliating to mention it! Yet it took no great perception to know Timothy was her husband's friend as well as being employed by him. "Something has been gnawing at him. What is your theory, Timothy? Your idea of what troubles him, I mean."

"It's more hypothesis than theory, my lady." He paused, evidently not sure how to continue. "If I were in Newgate on a capital charge, then was released…I think it would be like Lazarus being raised from the dead. You might suppose it would be cause for celebration. But it wouldn't be a thing you'd get over easy."

"He can't have regretted being freed?"

"No, my lady, of course not. But it wouldn't be the same as surviving a fight. There's the excitement and maybe the fear, then the relief. Sitting in prison, knowing you're more likely than not to hang, you'd think about things."

"You must have a wide range of experiences." Once she would never have thought to say it. The last few weeks had altered her outlook on many matters. Her curiosity about a lowly clerk who knew the meaning of the term hypothesis would not be gainsaid, however.

"I've turned my hand to whatever I had to, in order to prosper."

He sat there in his plain suit of coarse cloth and talked of prospering, a man who made his living as a clerk in a shipping company. How much did a clerk earn? She knew what servants were paid, but they received their food and lodging, and a suit of clothing every year, so she could draw no conclusion.

"I see." Emily was not at all certain she did understand.

He said, "I believe Hawk—Mr. Hawkins—will recover. Seeing his brother has helped. It might still take a while, as someone getting over a serious illness may be better one day and have a relapse the next." His personal revelations were at an end.

"Thank you. I am reassured."

"Thank you for giving Maggie a chance, my lady. I'll wait for her outside."

"By the way, I do not object to my female servants having respectable followers."

His smile rendered his face quite different from its usual watchfulness.

As soon as Emily reached her bedchamber, Putnam voiced the sentiments she had all too obviously been suppressing. " 'Tis 'The World Turned Upside Down,' indeed, Lady Emily, when a common fellow and maidservant are invited into the drawing room. And if that female came looking for work, why did he bring her? And remain with you without a chaperon after she was sent down to Mrs. Johnston!"

"You may not be aware of the role Mr. Timothy

and Margaret Ash played in freeing my husband. Indeed, how should you?" Unless she pried into her employer's affairs, as she must have done to know Timothy had stayed in the drawing room after Maggie Ash had departed. "Mr. Hawkins has thrown himself into his work since his return. I have feared for his health, working such long hours." If, indeed, he had been working and not disporting himself with some doxy. "I wished to ask Timothy if he thought Mr. Hawkins had now put Newgate behind him."

"As for that, your ladyship, there should never have been any need to speak. A gentleman does not give in to megrims." Implying Hawkins was not a gentleman.

"I fear my experience of gentlemen has been less encouraging than yours, Putnam. Now I must dress for dinner."

Putnam sniffed.

Chapter 43

Pirtle, clearing out his coat's pockets, said, "Sir, have you forgotten this?" He held out the flat kidskin case. Hawkins, washing his hands before changing for dinner, glanced up and saw it in the mirror. Emily would be pleased with it, but how to present it? Somehow he had imagined her greeting him at the door when he came home and he would bring it out with a flourish. She would open the case and be stricken speechless. He would fasten the necklace around her white neck, and it would all end in an embrace.

Even as the footman opened the door, Hawkins had recognized the problems with his fantasy. Emily was not waiting in the hall. Of course not; she would be doing whatever ladies did at home. If she had been, he could hardly make his gesture of apology and embrace her in front of his brother and the footman. No, it would best be done in private. Later tonight, when they retired to bed, so their reconciliation could be complete. He would go to her bedchamber as soon as he heard Putnam leave. He could give her the necklace, and things would develop from there.

Having resolved upon this sensible approach, which had the additional advantage of postponing serious conversation with his wife, he passed the evening in unaccustomed lightheartedness. Allan gave Emily an account of all they had seen and done—apart from their visit to the jeweler—with witty observations about London and its inhabitants.

Hawkins, listening, gazed at his wife rather often. When she glanced toward him and met his eyes, her own slid shyly away.

****

"Your best night rail again?"

"Yes, Putnam."

Her maid's thin eyebrows arched in critical comment.

"And I will have my hair down, not braided."

That annoying sniff. " 'Tisn't as if he's visited your bed any time recently."

Emily turned to stare at her. "You have a tendency to pry, which I do not appreciate."

"That I do not, my lady. It's easy enough to tell when a man's been in a bed and there's been intimate relations. Wears himself out with some strumpet, I suppose. Well enough if you were with child and didn't want to be bothered."

"You suppose too much." Inevitably, a personal maid knew everything about her mistress. It was not necessarily undesirable: a lady's maid might be her mistress's closest ally. But Putnam's attitude went beyond what Emily could tolerate. Maggie Ash was going to rise from laundry maid to lady's maid far sooner than expected.

She dismissed Putnam and took a deep breath to compose herself. She could not well slip into her husband's chamber hot with ire rather than...well, eagerness to see him. He had been almost like himself for two days now. Mayhap Timothy was correct and Ambrose had only needed time. If the worst was over, he might be glad to see her.

She did not quite understand how he could put it all behind him without talking about it. Women needed to unburden themselves of their fears and problems if they had a female friend to whom they could speak. Men did not care to listen to a mere female's concerns and would not talk of their own difficulties. There was no point in asking what troubled them, either. Gentlemen did not like to be questioned, nor was it proper for a wife to do so. A man could approach an important subject without going round about. A lady must resort to guile. If he would only take her into his arms, they could get past the awkwardness without having to talk about it. Emily waited for silence from her husband's chamber.

****

Standing by the door connecting his dressing room to Emily's, Hawkins took a deep breath. Marriage was unexpectedly complicated. Talking to a female was different from talking to a man. Apologizing…he didn't want to think about apologizing. He never apologized, unless it were an ironic "Sorry!" to a male friend for a trifling offense.

He regretted having spent much of his life doing things for which he needed to make reparation or at least acknowledge, because for many of them, no atonement was now possible. His treatment of Emily, however, was still fresh. She might forgive him. Mayhap he would not have to say much; actions speak louder than words, according to Allan. Though women did like to hear the words, didn't they?

Should he knock? He had been in the habit of knocking before Newgate. It was the courteous thing to do. But it seemed awkward now. He was her husband; he had every right to visit her in her bedchamber. And the element of surprise would be on his side.

****

Emily turned the door handle and pulled. For an appalling moment, it resisted. It must have been locked again after she had slipped in to unlock it in her husband's and Pirtle's absence. Then the door opened so suddenly she nearly overbalanced. Ambrose stood on the other side, one hand still stretched out, an arrested expression in his eyes.

"Were you going to come in, Ambrose?" Her voice trembled a little, infuriatingly.

Instead of replying, he closed the space between them and pulled her into an embrace. "Emily."

She melted into his solid warmth, inhaling his spicy and citrusy scent. She could feel the texture of his peacock blue banyan through her nightgown which was too thin for an early spring night but more than adequate if she shared a bed with her husband. His left hand caressed her back from nape to waist to—oh!—as they kissed. His right hand seemed strangely absent. It should be running down her back, too. Or doing something, she was not particular as to what. Where—?

He drew back and her heart plummeted.

"Emily…"

"Yes, Ambrose?"

"I'm sorry." He held out a flat case.

She took it.

"It's your emerald set. The jeweler finally completed it, and I picked it up today. They're not all the original emeralds. Porter couldn't trace them all, and I suppose many were re-cut. But the new ones are a good match."

She did not know her husband as well as she hoped to know him, but this was unlike him. Ambrose was nervous or he wouldn't be almost babbling. She opened the lid. In the soft light from the candle on her dressing table, her great-grandmother's necklet, earrings, and brooch glowed and glinted. Her husband had cared enough to restore her heirloom at considerable cost and effort, when he could easily have bought her a new set for less money. She ran a forefinger over the enameled setting holding the central stone of the necklet, and a tear fell onto the case's silk lining.

"Emily? I didn't want to make you cry."

"Oh, Ambrose, I'm crying because you're so dear to me. You can't know how much this means. They're beautiful. I'm glad our eldest daughter will have real emeralds rather than paste." This was not one of her more polished utterances. She sounded like a green girl.

A fraught silence ensued.

"Emily, are you—?"

"Oh! No, not yet."

"I would ask you to put them on so I could admire them on you as I did that night at the theater, but perhaps we have something more important to do. If we are ever to have a daughter, that is."

She set the case on the dressing table before pressing against him and breathing in the scent of spices, ships, and a hint of hot, foreign skies which was uniquely Hawkins. "Yes, we do. I've missed you."

He muttered something into her hair. As he swept her up and carried her to the bed, she wondered whether it had been a declaration of love, then decided it didn't matter.

"We are a good match, Ambrose," she said as he deposited her on the mattress, and those were the last words spoken for many minutes.

A word about the author…

Kathleen Buckley has loved writing ever since she learned to read. After a career which included light bookkeeping, working as a paralegal, and a stint as a security officer (fascinating!), she began to write as a second career rather than as a hobby. Her first historical romance was penned (well, word-processed) after re-reading Georgette Heyer's Georgian/Regency romances and realizing that Ms. Heyer would never be able to write another (having died some forty years earlier). She is now the author of four published Georgian romances: *An Unsuitable Duchess*, *Most Secret*, *Captain Easterday's Bargain*, and *A Masked Earl*.

Warning: No bodices are ripped in her romances, which might be described as "powder & patch & peril" rather than Jane Austen drawing room. They contain no explicit sex but do contain mild bad language, as the situations in which her characters find themselves sometimes call for an oath a little stronger than "Zounds!"

Thank you for purchasing
this publication of The Wild Rose Press, Inc.

For questions or more information
contact us at
info@thewildrosepress.com.

The Wild Rose Press, Inc.
www.thewildrosepress.com